SOMETHING TERRIBLY WRONG

"God knows how he survived the crash," Haldern was saying. "But thank God he did. Everything was on the plane, Luther. Everything relating to their research, that is. That's why we need you. We *must* save Townsend. Instead of saving hundreds or even thousands, the test for AirMore comes down to the survival of a single man."

"Why?" Moravec didn't know what to say.

"Because . . ." Haldern licked his lips. "Because something went terribly wrong." He leaned forward once more. "How old would you guess Townsend is in that picture?"

Moravec frowned and glanced at the photo. "Fifties, I'd say. Early fifties." A bead of perspiration caught the light on Haldern's temple as Moravec looked up.

"Stuart Townsend will be thirty-one on April fifteenth . . ."

PINNACLE BRINGS YOU THE FINEST IN FICTION

THE HAND OF LAZARUS   (17-100-2, $4.50)
by Warren Murphy & Molly Cochran
The IRA's most bloodthirsty and elusive murderer has chosen the
small Irish village of Ardath as the site for a supreme act of terror
destined to rock the world: the brutal assassination of the Pope!
From the bestselling authors of GRANDMASTER!

LAST JUDGMENT   (17-114-2, $4.50)
by Richard Hugo
Only former S.A.S. agent James Ross can prevent a centuries-old
vision of the Apocalypse from becoming reality . . . as the malevo-
lent instrument of Adolf Hitler's ultimate revenge falls into the
hands of the most fiendish assassin on Earth!
              "RIVETING...A VERY FINE BOOK"
                    —*NEW YORK TIMES*

TRUK LAGOON   (17-121-5, $3.95)
Mitchell Sam Rossi
Two bizarre destinies inseparably linked over forty years unleash a
savage storm of violence on a tropic island paradise—as the most
incredible covert operation in military history is about to be uncovered at the bottom of TRUK LAGOON!

THE LINZ TESTAMENT   (17-117-6, $4.50)
Lewis Perdue
An ex-cop's search for his missing wife traps him a terrifying secret
war, as the deadliest organizations on Earth battle for possession
of an ancient relic that could shatter the foundations of Western
religion: the Shroud of Veronica, irrefutable evidence of a second
Messiah!

*Available wherever paperbacks are sold, or order direct from the
Publisher. Send cover price plus 50¢ per copy for mailing and han-
dling to Pinnacle Books, Dept. 17-184, 475 Park Avenue South,
New York, N.Y. 10016. Residents of New York, New Jersey and
Pennsylvania must include sales tax. DO NOT SEND CASH.*

THE HAHNEMANN SEQUELA

HAROLD KING

PINNACLE BOOKS
WINDSOR PUBLISHING CORP.

PINNACLE BOOKS

are published by

Windsor Publishing Corp.
475 Park Avenue South
New York, NY 10016

Second Pinnacle Books printing: March, 1989

Printed in the United States of America

To Elaine,
Who Perseveres Most

AUTHOR'S NOTE

This book was inspired by a 1980 *U.S. News and World Report* article on genetic research and from browsing through my wifc's *Physicians Desk Reference (PDR)*. When I began the novel I knew almost nothing of the disease called progeria and very little about the intricacies of sophisticated computers. I am grateful to several people who gave their time to share with me their expertise in these specialized fields. The faculty and staff of the Department of Physiology and Biophysics and the Department of Medicine of the Louisiana State University School of Medicine in Shreveport were especially helpful and patient in rcsponding to my questions.

Particularly, Lee Bairnsfather, Ph.D., Director of Academic Computing and Biometry at LSUMS, did double duty as my informational source in answering medical and computer queries and otherwise putting me in touch with knowledgeable experts. Dr. Bairnsfather's help in proofreading the early draft of the manuscript and his suggestions and corrections proved an invaluable aid in establishing verisimilitude in the novel.

On blood and diseases related to it, Darryl Williams, M.D., Chief of the Hematology/Oncology Section of the Department of Medicine, and Allan Miller, M.D., were kind enough to endure several interviews.

On computers and what makes them work, I am indebted to the technical assistance and "brainstorming" sessions with Dalton Williams, president of Micro Business Systems, Inc., and David Humphry, a gifted teacher and freelance programmer. Also helpful were J. T. King and Mike Zabel, who market and service Vector Graphic computers, a magnificent machine and word processor through which the manuscript was written, revised and printed.

Where technical or medical detail and my imagination overlap—which abounds in this work—any errors that may result are purely mine.

Somewhere in every novelist's life, too often unsung and unattributed, is a reference librarian. Reference librarians are the most dedicated lovers of books I know and there is one I especially want to thank, Anne King. They don't come better than Mrs. King. Thanks, mom.

—Harold King
Shreveport, Louisiana, 1983

Sequela (se-kwe´ lah) [Lat.] *n*.: an abnormal condition following or caused by an attack of disease.

THE
HAHNEMANN
SEQUELA

THURSDAY
DECEMBER 30

ONE

MADRID

RIVULETS OF rain made crooked paths down the aircraft's passenger windows, marking Madrid's Barajas Airport as little more than a blur of scattered lights in the night. Dr. Stuart Townsend watched with sleepy interest as the ground crew in orange slickers refueled the aircraft, then waved an all-clear to the pilot.

The plane turned to take its place on the taxiway and light reflected from the window panned across the compartment, lightly touching Townsend's colleagues. It was precisely nine minutes after ten, Greenwich Mean Time.

Townsend settled back into the headrest as the sway of the jet and the patter of rain outside beckoned him to sleep. After nearly a year of nonstop madness—slides and micro-scopes and midnight conferences and the fear he might go blind before he succumbed to hysteria—he could finally sleep without fear. The race was over. The doctor's eyelids fluttered sleepily as he glanced through the window one more time.

The nose of the oncoming jet came out of the mist like a ship from a fog bank. It was suddenly there, filling his window, rushing toward him without sound. There wasn't time to scream.

The moment of impact destroyed his sense of time and space. The first explosion thrust him backward. He felt himself lifted, spinning, falling. He had only a vague recollection of isolated moments—a blast of wind, a deafening eruption in his head, bodies and debris exploding

3

past him, and a sudden, intense pain in his chest. There was so much heat he felt the melting buttons on his sleeves burn his wrists.

When he opened his eyes again he was on his back, a drizzling rain washing his face. One of his pants legs was burning. He tried to move but managed only to close his fingers and felt gritty mud in his palms. A burst of orange exploded in the darkness. A sheet of crumpled metal ejected from the firestorm, shot end over end above him. Intense fire boiled past him in waves.

He heard sirens but sound and sight began to fade with the onset of traumatic shock. It began in his fingers and toes, moving quickly until only a pinpoint of awareness survived. Before the darkness enveloped him, in the last instant of consciousness, he realized the race was not over. In some recess of his mind he heard, or sensed, a choking, pitiful scream.

It was precisely ten minutes after ten, G.M.T.

TWO

BOYDS CHAPEL, TEXAS

JUDD RANEY slammed the driver's door closed, sealing himself inside the station wagon with his wife and two children. His hair was matted down by rain and his fingers were blue with cold.

"Son of a bitch!"

Susan winced. She was trying to breast-feed the baby but Shelly only cried. Jimmy was awake in the makeshift bed of the back seat that, even with the seats down, was crowded with luggage and Christmas presents. The boy was already wet from the whipping wind and sleet that invaded the station wagon when his father opened the tailgate to get the spare tire.

"Well, that's it," Raney said. "We're stuck here." He glanced through the windshield as the wiper blades strained to keep the glass clear of frozen rain. Except for the beam of headlights there was only fog outside. "In the middle of an ice storm . . . in the middle of goddamn Texas nowhere!"

"Bad word, daddy," came a small voice from the back seat.

Susan turned Shelly in her arms and opened the flap of her blouse, offering the baby her other nipple. "Can't you fix the wheel?"

He turned to look at her. "There's nothing wrong with the wheel, Susan. It's the tire. It's flat."

"But the spare—"

"I'm *talking* about the spare!"

"Oh." Susan looked quickly down at the baby, adjusting

5

the infant to her breast. The only sounds were Shelly's sucking and the wiper blades.

"Didn't you ask Gary to check the spare? This is your car, goddammit, Susan. You *have* to have the station check everything. Now look where we are."

She didn't look at him. "We should have stayed on the interstate like I—"

He banged his palm against the wheel. "Don't say it, Susan! Not a goddamn word from you!"

"Daddy . . . somebody's coming."

Raney glanced into the rearview mirror and saw headlights approaching through the fog. "Thank Christ." He opened the door to the cold.

"Be careful," Susan said.

The truck pulled over and stopped about twenty feet past the station wagon. It was a large rig with an empty flatbed trailer. The driver was climbing down when Raney reached the cab.

"Boy am I glad to see you," Raney said. He held a newspaper over his head to keep the rain off his neck. "I haven't seen another car in twenty minutes. Nobody's driving in this weather."

The driver nodded. Rain dripped off his baseball cap. "What's the problem?" He was tall with a beard and wore a green plaid wool shirt. Raney figured he was in his mid-twenties.

"Flat tire. Right rear. Spare's flat too. It's my wife's car. She didn't—"

"Flat or deflated?"

"—check . . . What?"

"The spare. It might just need air. You have an air pump?"

Raney glanced back at the station wagon. "Pump? I . . . no . . ."

"I do." He took a key from his pocket and began

6

unlocking a compartment behind the cab. "Roll it over. Anybody in the wagon?"

"Yeah. My wife and kids."

He nodded again. "Turn off the engine and the headlights but leave the flashers on. I'll put out a couple of flares."

It was probably a slow leak, the trucker said after inflating the spare. He was changing the tire while Raney held the flashlight.

"I sure appreciate this," Raney was saying. His ears and fingers were freezing.

"No problem."

"We had Christmas with the grandparents in Sante Fe. I thought we could make it straight through to Shreveport. That's where we live, Shreveport. It's really not that far, you know. Course, I didn't figure on this weather."

"Should have stayed on the interstate."

Raney glanced at the rear window where Jimmy had his nose pressed against the glass. "Yeah . . . well . . ."

"You want to hold the light over here a little?"

"Oh, sorry." Raney noticed the trucker's back and shoulders were soaked through with melted sleet. The edges of his beard had crystals of ice caught in it. "So, where you headed?"

"Dallas."

"You live there?"

"Nope. Oke City."

Raney nodded to himself. He tried to keep the light from shivering off its target. He'd never been so goddamn cold. Truckers must have hides of leather. "I noticed you weren't carrying anything."

"Just delivered a mud pump to a rig in Lubbock."

"Oil field, eh? I—" Raney almost dropped the flashlight. He couldn't feel his fingers. "I'm an attorney . . . represent Ketner Oil out of Shreveport. You work for one of the companies in Oklahoma?"

7

"Nope. Independent. Hot shot driver." He tightened down the last lug. "There."

"Done?"

The trucker banged the hubcap on with his hand. "Done."

Raney switched off the light and stuffed his hands in his pockets. "Thank God."

They slid the flat into the back of the wagon with the tools—Raney didn't want to take the time placing it into the spare compartment—and closed the tailgate.

"You saved my life," Raney said. He had started the engine and turned on the headlights while the trucker doused the road flares. They were standing in front of the station wagon and Raney was digging in his pocket for his wallet. "I really appreciate this. We might have been stuck out here all night."

"No problem."

Raney pulled a wet twenty from his wallet. "Here. For your help."

"No thanks."

"C'mon. You deserve it."

"I don't want any money."

"You're soaking wet, for godsakes. Buy yourself a new shirt."

"I have a dry one in the cab. Don't worry about it."

"Well—" Raney shrugged, "I tried." He put the bill back in the wallet and took out a card. "Look, I know a Shreveport lawyer isn't much help in Oklahoma but . . ." He handed over the card. "Judd Raney. Okay?"

The truck driver took the card without looking at it. "Thanks."

"What's your name, anyway? We know some outfits up there. Be glad to mention your name."

"David Townsend."

"David Townsend. T-O-W-N . . . Townsend?"

The man nodded. "That's it."

8

THREE

MADRID

WHEN THE orderly came for him, Ian McPhearson was holding a sopping towel to his face over the sink, letting the water drip down his neck, wetting his surgical jersey. He'd been in Madrid only a few hours—nearly all of it confined to this floor, this corridor. His back ached and he desperately needed to breathe unfiltered air. He didn't know the time or even if it was daylight yet. There weren't any windows in the operating room.

"Doctor?" The orderly stood at the door to the lavatory, propping it open with his shoulder. He seemed barely awake himself. "Telephone. I think it's London calling."

"Bloody better be," McPhearson said. He glanced at himself in the mirror. The eyes were too red, the jowls too saggy. He should have been a plastic surgeon. There was no such thing as an emergency tummy tuck in plastic surgery. "Tell them I'm coming."

"Dr. McPhearson, this is MAGCOM operator." The satellite communicator's voice was distant but strong. "We have an intermittent positive satlok signal to London. Stand by, please."

The lines twanged and echoed beeps while he waited. McPhearson tried to imagine how it all worked, voices blasting into space and bouncing off a piece of tin then returning to some other spot on the globe. All that distance, what was the point? What was wrong with the regular telephone? He decided he really didn't care.

"This is MAGCOM. We have clear sync. Stand by. Nine

series on track. Oh three thirty-six Greenwich. Go, London. You have eleven minutes forty-two seconds to next stat track."

"Hello, Ian?" Haldern's voice seemed to come from the depths of space, wavy, fading. There seemed to be a teletype machine wildly calling for help somewhere on the line. McPhearson wondered what a stat track could possibly be. "Can you hear me all right?"

"I hear you. Not a very good line, is it?"

"It's the weather, your end," Haldern said. He made it sound like it was McPhearson's fault. He said something else but the noise drowned him out.

"You have to speak up." McPhearson pressed the receiver against his ear, covering the other with his hand. "It's a terrible connection."

"I said what have you to report? How is Stuart?"

"It's what I suspected from the angiogram." McPhearson raised his voice to help the satellite. He glanced at his feet. There was a spot of blood on his disposable shoe cover. "Myocardial infarction of the anterior ventrical epicardium. Descending coronary rupture. Massive hemorrhaging. A piece of metal is what it was, three centimeters by twelve."

"Thrombosis?" The word slipped through on faded static.

"No, no. Not that it matters. That section of the ventrical epicardium is degenerated beyond rejuvenation. Irreversible ischemia with subsequent necrosis."

"What's your prognosis?"

McPhearson imagined Haldern was at his desk, on the top floor of the Euromedic building. He wondered if he were perspiring. He should be. Stuart Townsend was the only survivor of the team. If he died—

"Ian, are you still there?" Haldern said.

"I don't see anything encouraging here. The infarction has lowered pressure to eighty over sixty. I expect gradual cardiomalacia, ventricular fibrillation . . . arrest."

"When?"

10

"I don't know. A week, probably less. If he were just younger . . . at least the myocardium is otherwise undamaged, but I just couldn't say positively. He might last that long. There are other complications that we needn't discuss now, of course. Hahnemann sequela, I'm speaking of." McPhearson added, "He isn't getting any younger, you know." It was cruel to say it, but he had a right. METHYD-9 was at stake.

"Yes, yes, I know. But a week, you think? He could live that long?"

"I don't have a crystal ball. *Perhaps* a week. *If* he remains stable. The chances of him surviving longer than that are, in my opinion, unrealistic. He may never regain consciousness as it is."

"What are his chances considering transplantation?"

McPhearson frowned. He hadn't even considered it. "I don't know."

"You're the heart specialist," Haldern said unkindly. "It's your field, your expertise. It's why we had you in. A transplant is a possibility that is not closed to us. But I have to know now."

McPhearson's back ached. He wished he could sit down. The thought of cardiac transplantation made him weak. "Of course it's possible," he said. "But there's too little time. Everything depends upon the donor. A hundred different things. Then you have to find one. The *right* one. It could take weeks. We have only days, probably only hours."

"We will do what we have to do," Haldern said from London. "Little Mary is on its way. I know it's too soon to discuss transporting him, but we want the option available."

"You're not considering moving him *now*?"

"We're relying on your best judgment there, doctor, but we don't want to leave him in Madrid. I realize the facilities there don't support a thorough trauma unit—"

"Facilities!" McPhearson glanced down the empty corridor. "There aren't any facilities. This isn't a hospital, it's a bloody cattle barn. I *am* the trauma unit."

"I understand, that's why we've alerted AirMore. It's fully staffed, of course . . . cardiac unit—"

A sudden clatter of twangs burst through the line, stinging McPhearson's ear.

"What was that?" He shouted into the phone against the ringing in his ear. "I can't hear. This bloody connection—"

"I said AirMore is fully prepared. We'll be able to move you and the patient anywhere in the world on a moment's notice."

It wasn't a thought that comforted McPhearson. He'd just got off a plane. "You've already moved me once. I was in Marseilles, did they tell you? Of course you knew. My annual holiday . . . in dead of winter, naturally, the only time I can get away. And what is waiting for me the moment I get off the train? A bloody red flag from Euro, that's what, from one of your people. Immediate priority, he tells me. He drove like a maniac to the airport, jabbering the whole time about Rennit. He's dead, he tells me. Charles Rennit is dead. Smashed to bits in Madrid. And he takes *me* to the airport."

"For an extraordinary emergency," Haldern said.

"I don't fly, Haldern. I don't *ever* fly. You know that. Rennit is dead in an air crash. An *air crash*! And you send *me* to the bloody place."

"You were nearest, Ian. You're one of the four best cardiac surgeons in the world. You know what's at stake and—" he emphasized the last word—"you've done scores of successful heart transplants. I'm sorry it had to be under these circumstances."

"You have no idea," McPhearson said. "A hundred people dead and more, smoldering hulks of twisted, wrecked plane parts strewn over the place like litter from a picnic. It's bedlam, absolute bedlam. It's the first bloody thing you see from the air when you come here. A Euromedic special transport—that's how I got here, Haldern—exactly like the one Rennit burned up in. Do you wonder why I have high blood pressure? Do you wonder at all? Those people shouldn't have been together at all. That was foolish, putting the entire team on the same plane."

"If you don't mind, we'll discuss accountability another time. The thing now is your patient—keeping him alive, I mean. He is the only one who can reconstruct." Haldern paused, but McPhearson remained silent. There wasn't anything to add. "Is there anything else?"

"Time," McPhearson said. "There isn't enough. A week is only a guess."

"And with transplant surgery?"

"Less. If you're really seriously considering it—"

"We are . . . very seriously."

"In that case I don't see that we have more than three days . . . seventy-two hours. Townsend must be strong enough to withstand the operation." McPhearson shook his head. "But I don't see it, I really don't. We can't find a donor that quickly."

"We have a candidate," Haldern said. "Actually, it is Perfect Case criteria."

There was only one circumstance for Perfect Case in any transplant surgery. Best Case was a donor from the immediate family. Perfect Case was an identical twin. "You said Perfect Case?"

"Stuart Townsend has a brother."

"A twin?"

"David Townsend. Lives in America . . . Oklahoma, actually."

"But . . ."

"A recovery team is already investigating. You do realize the importance of this case, Ian?"

"Of course, but . . . " McPhearson's mouth was suddenly dry. Cardiac transplantation usually involved a donor who was already deceased, or nearly. "You said the donor *lives* in Oklahoma."

"I did."

13

"He's a terminal patient then?"

Haldern's response came through clearly. "Not at the moment."

Oklahoma City, Oklahoma

The tall blonde in a dark blue parka stood at the door to apartment number six and knocked loudly. Melted snow collected in a puddle around her boots.

"He ain't in, sweetie, so you can stop banging on the door."

She turned to see a middle-aged woman staring out from behind a door across the hall. A cigarette was stuck in a heavy layer of lipstick. A roar of laughter bellowed from a television inside.

The girl glanced anxiously down the hall. "Do you know when he'll be back?" Her mascara was smeared as if she'd been crying. "It's very important."

"Yeah. Next year." The old woman smiled at the joke, exposing lipstick on her teeth. The cigarette stuck fast.

"Next year?"

"Sure, you know—tomorrow, maybe Sunday. January, get it? Next year?"

"Please, do you know where I can find him?" the girl asked in a cracked voice.

The end of the woman's cigarette turned red, smoke expelled from between her teeth. "What's the problem?"

"This *is* David Townsend's apartment?"

"Yeah, it is. You looking for a hot shot?"

The girl only stared at her.

"You know, quick delivery trucker." She nodded toward apartment six. "Like him."

"Oh, no, no. I don't need a trucker."

"Good thing. Three of the boys here run hot shot, but ain't none around on account no one wants to work on New Year's Eve. Tiny Smith and a couple boys was gonna go to Houston, raise hell."

14

The girl's eyes got round. "He's in Houston!"

The old woman studied the blonde girl before answering. Cigarette smoke curled into her hair. "You in trouble, sweetie?"

"No, I—I have to tell him something. It's . . . very bad news."

"Yeah?"

"Please, can you tell me where I can find him? It's terribly important."

The woman considered it, taking another long drag on the cigarette. "Somebody die or what?"

"*Please*—I have to find him!"

The old woman shrugged. "Well, like I said, honey, he ain't here. Sorry."

"Could any of his friends know?"

"He ain't got that many friends."

The blonde wiped her eyes. "If he comes back . . . " Then she shook her head. "No, never mind. It'd be too late. Thank you. You've been very kind." She started down the hall, toward the burned out exit light.

"Dallas," the woman said to her back. "He did say something about maybe going to the game."

The girl turned around with renewed hope. "Dallas? What game?"

"You just get in from China or what? The Cotton Bowl game, I'm talking. Oklahoma-Arkansas. National championship. Tomorrow's New Year's Day, y'know."

"Do you think I could reach him in Dallas?"

"Do I look like his mother?"

"I didn't mean—"

"Look, he's a driver, isn't he? You want to find a hot shot in Dallas you check Marty's."

"Marty's?"

"Trucker's motel. It's on Industrial Boulevard. Information'll have the number."

"Industrial Boulevard." She wrote it down on a small

15

pad. When she looked up again her eyes shone with gratitude. "Thank you. Thank you so much."

"So who died?" the old woman said. Her cigarette ash fell then, dribbling down the front of her robe. "Shit!" She brushed herself as if she were on fire. When she looked up again the hall was empty.

The blonde climbed into the passenger door of a gray van and peeled off her parka. The driver handed her the radio phone.

"He's in Dallas," she said into the receiver. "We'll need a clinic for phase two." She nodded then and glanced at the window. "No, no problems. We'll have him before noon." Her eyes were ice blue, and dry.

FOUR

LONDON

IT WAS 3 A.M. when word of the crash reached Luther Moravec.

As head of Euromedic's Disaster Care Division, Moravec would normally have been called first. As it happened, however, the initial communications between Madrid and London were routed through Euromedic's MAG satellite relay station in Gibraltar. The on-duty supervisor at Gibraltar then decided that "First Informed" should be Euromedic Central and diverted the call from DCD to Primary Office with a priority code flagged "Most Urgent." In the supervisor's judgment the Madrid message was less a medical emergency than an administrative one—a specially assigned Euromedic company jet had crashed. It had never happened before.

Consequently DCD was not immediately informed. When Dispatch Section finally called his residence on Prince of Wales Drive, Moravec was asleep and the accident was already several hours old. The dispatcher rushed through the details of it so quickly that Moravec asked him to repeat it again.

"They were all VIPs aboard," the anxious voice said after he'd outlined the situation. "That's why they contacted Central first. Doctor Rennit was one of them on the plane. They found his body . . . most of it, enough to identify." Then he added, "It must have been terrible."

Moravec imagined what the scene in Madrid must look like—a blackened, debris-strewn runway; a makeshift morgue in some cavernous hangar, the smell of burnt flesh and recent death. He knew it all too well.

"Thank God it wasn't an AirMore flight," the voice said, apparently without meaning to sound cruel. AirMore was Euromedic's fleet of emergency response aircraft, a section of DCD. They were all over the globe; Moravec was responsible for them too. "Actually, I didn't mean—"

"Yes, I understand," Moravec said.

"The director would like to meet with you as soon as possible, sir. Here at the center."

"Now?"

"Yes, sir. He's sent a car."

As he put down the phone he felt a tug on the bedcovers. Connie's touch was almost hot against his back.

"Luther?"

She always came awake that way in the middle of the night, as if she couldn't remember who slept next to her.

"Dispatch section," he said. The bed creaked as he reached for his trousers. "Crash-up at Barajas." He didn't know who Dr. Rennit was. He probably should have asked.

Her voice was small in the darkness. "Barajas?"

"Madrid."

The wood floor was icy. He felt in the dresser for socks and a shirt. He avoided turning on the light so Connie wouldn't feel obliged to get up.

"What happened?" She was coming around now, becoming alert. Except for her stirring the old place was quiet. At least, he thought, the phone hadn't wakened Christina. "Was it bad?" Her voice was slow, anxious. Moravec had long since passed feeling a personal loss for these things. Disasters weren't bad. There wasn't any evil or guilt or blame to be measured. People died. People always died. It was a matter of accounting, not mourning. The victims were no more and no less than people who'd been unlucky. The luckier ones you tried to do for. That's the way Moravec saw it. There wasn't any great plan to the universe—or any

18

great benevolent Planner. A hillside crash site strewn with mangled and decapitated corpses or the buried dead from a mudslide in Peru were proof enough.

"Luther?"

"A Dutch KLM plowed through a private jet on the runway," he said quietly. He didn't like to give her more information than necessary. It wasn't a subject they discussed at length, his work. Her ignorance of it was his wall of insulation against the reality. "There was some mixup in tower communications. Apparently it was raining." He found his shoes beside the bed.

"You're going then?"

"Yes. Haldern is to brief me himself."

He heard her move across the bed. She switched on the bedside lamp and squinted dully at the clock radio. The shaded light gave her hair a reddish tint and made transparent the thin nightgown where it stretched between the mounds of her breasts. She leaned back on her hands as if to counterbalance the size and weight of her belly. Pregnancy had taken nothing away from her quiet elegance. They'd met eleven years ago during a sailing competition at Dover. Her brother had fainted from the heat and he was the only physician in the crowd. He thought she was the most beautiful woman he'd ever meet, even in that silly hat she wore. She called him Sticky then, her private name for him from their first night together. After he'd started with Euromedic she used it less and less. After Christina she stopped altogether.

Connie's face was flushed pink, the sleepiness gone. "Shall I fix something? I don't mind."

He shook his head without looking at her. "I'm afraid there isn't time. They're sending a car." He found a tie on the closet door and sawed it back and forth on his neck until it slipped under the collar of his shirt. "You should get some sleep."

"Haldern, did you say?"

Moravec thought it odd too, not that the director would

19

be concerned, but that he'd be up. This was strictly a DCD mission unless they hadn't told him everything. Apparently Rennit made a difference. He stuffed change from the dresser into his pocket. "It was a company plane . . . a research group from the South African lab. They'd been sent special transport, I understand. God knows why."

"Was it terribly bad?" She asked it quietly, as if she didn't really want to know.

"I don't know all the details yet." It wasn't a complete lie. He knew enough to imagine what the site must look like. Both planes had been fully fueled. What didn't explode on impact would have burned intensely. Few would have survived. "Haldern will fill me in."

"I'm sorry, darling." She was always sorry and, Moravec felt sure, she always meant it. Compassion came easy to her. She had no idea of the other side.

He kissed her then, bending over the bed and holding his tie back. Her fingers were warm on his neck. "Sleep now," he whispered. "I'll ring you when I can."

He stopped at Christina's room and without touching her drew the bedcover over a bare shoulder, then waited in the dark in the foyer for the car. The grandfather clock in the den metered a quiet cadence as Moravec tried to place a face to the name Rennit. He didn't know anyone in South Africa outside Cape Town. Johannesburg was a research lab; cancer, he was sure. But Rennit was a blank. It was probably someone he should have known. Euromedic was too large to remember all the specialists. He still hadn't managed it by the time the car arrived. Moravec pulled up the collar of his overcoat and stepped into London's frigid air. Haldern will explain it, he thought. The clock from the den chimed the half hour as he locked the door. It was very cold.

FRIDAY
DECEMBER 31

FIVE

DALLAS

DAVID TOWNSEND slept on his back with his mouth open in room 219 in Marty's Motel and Restaurant. When the phone rang, he reached for it on the wrong side of the bed. He found it when he forced himself to open his eyes.

"Lo."

"David?"

He yawned and turned over on the pillow. "Uh-huh."

"Is this David Townsend?"

"Uh-huh." He glanced at his watch. He'd been asleep little more than an hour.

"Thank God I found you. Mr. Townsend, this is Becky Smith, Tiny's sister. Tiny needs help."

Townsend didn't know Tiny had a sister. He wondered if she looked anything like Tiny—he weighed at least three hundred pounds. If Tiny needed help it was either money or booze. Women wasn't one of his vices. "What's the problem?"

"Tiny was in an accident," the woman's voice said. "He's hurt bad."

Townsend sat up. "What? Tiny?"

"He was in a wreck. He needs blood. Lots of blood. God, I—" Her voice caught in her throat. "I've been up all night, trying to find his friends. They took him to Parkland emergency. He's really bad. He turned his truck over on the interstate. I've been calling and—"

"Slow down," Townsend said. "Tiny had a wreck?"

23

"Yes." She was sobbing now. "About five hours ago . . . Interstate 45 . . . six miles out of Mesquite . . ."

"I thought Tiny was in Houston."

"He was, but—God, please don't make me explain everything on the phone. Tiny needs blood. That's why I'm calling. I've been all over town trying to get every truck driver who knows Tiny to—wait—what's your blood type? God, you don't have some kind of rare blood, do you?"

"No, O-positive."

"Thank God. Will you help me, Mr. Townsend? *Please*. I don't know up from down anymore. I've been going since I left the hospital. I just don't know—"

"Where do you want me to go, Parkland?"

"No, they're taking blood at a clinic on Jasper. The PMC. You know it?"

"Jasper?" Townsend had to think. "Off Thornton Expressway?"

"Never mind, you probably wouldn't find it. I'll pick you up. I can be there in five minutes. Look for a gray van."

"Gray van." Townsend nodded. "I'm getting dressed now."

SIX

LONDON

A GUST of wind stirred the dead leaves in Russell Square, sending them skittering across the deserted park. Moravec moved against the wind, sucking in the frigid air, his short legs churning over the hard ground. It was not quite 4 A.M. and Southampton Street was empty of traffic.

Moravec had dozed in the car and come awake suddenly when the rocking motion of the ride had stopped. He was on the sidewalk before he realized that the driver had let him off at the wrong entrance. The Euromedic complex consisted of four buildings that surrounded a small park like a horseshoe. Three brownstones that had survived the war had been gutted and redefined as surgical infirmaries. St. Mary's Charity Hospital was a name that didn't fit the look of the place, Moravec thought. There was nothing that inspired a sense of charitability. The fourth building, a five-story structure of glass and concrete, across the square, was the Research Studies Center. If the research hospital was Euromedic's heart then the RSC was its soul. Stonehenge. But that was Euromedic, as much a paradox of architecture as of medicine. Old coexisted with new in a competition for attention that neither could win. Moravec trudged across the park unaware of the difference. Medicine wasn't a profession, it was a business. It didn't matter what one thought of socialized services.

He pushed through the first set of doors to BodyGuard's interlock and stomped the cold from his feet, waiting for the scanner to pass him through. BodyGuard was a passive first-stage security recognition system developed by Euromedic. Body-scan sensors checked the height, weight, bone structure and facial features of everyone attempting to enter RSC against a master list. When the computer found a match it unlocked the second set of glass doors. All others that the system did not recognize were interviewed through the two-way intercom and admitted by a security guard.

The doors opened with a buzz and Moravec stepped into the lobby. It was like stepping through the rabbit hole, leaving London's bleakness for a wonderland of shadowless light and the computer data banks of the Satellite Information Retrieval System, where the roof was crammed with dish-shaped receivers and transmitters that could instantly connect Euromedic to any of its thirty-odd medical stations around the globe. The RSC wasn't so much a place where he worked, but where he lived.

"Evening, Mr. Moravec." The uniformed security guard smiled from behind a half-round desk, his computer screen casting a pale green hue on the pages of an open book. "Rugged night, isn't it, sir?" No one called him doctor these days. He preferred that. He wasn't a healer anymore.

Moravec nodded and presented his laminated ID card. "Pass me through to Haldern, please. I'm expected."

The guard's fingers passed quickly over the keyboard. After a moment the plastic identity card ejected from a slot in the computer and the monitor screen blinked the message:

CARD VERIFICATION:
11-A-2929
MORAVEC, LUTHER (NMI)
CHIEF OF SECTION, AIRMORE
PASS: GREEN

"Number four, Mr. Moravec," the guard said. "Have a nice day." He took up his book as Moravec started for a row of open elevators.

26

Each floor in RSC was color-coded, corresponding to the security clearance of the personnel who worked on them. A white clearance allowed access to the first floor only; yellow to the first and second; orange to first through third; green to all five. The elevators were activated through the security guard's console when the magnetic tab on an identification card was inserted into the elevator's card panel. There were four elevators which moved only after a correctly matched card was inserted and then only to a predetermined floor. Moravec stepped into the elevator marked with a large Roman numeral four. He inserted his card in the slot and the LED display changed from white to green, printing his last name. The doors slid quietly together only after he typed his access identification code into the telephone-like keyboard. Euromedic demanded tight security when it came to mobility in RSC. All its secrets were here.

"Yes, I know all about the Swedes," Miles Haldern said into the phone. "They're still infatuated with thymic hormones." He was seated behind his large mahogany desk, MAG printouts spread out before him. He gestured for Moravec to take a seat on the sofa. "Never mind the Americans. Crane and Paddock are off on scavenger enzymes. See about Dr. Tatyana Borzov." He paused to give Moravec a frustrated look. "Yes, Leningrad. She's Russian, isn't she?" He nodded, turning to glance out the large window behind him. Moravec followed his gaze. London was black. The window reflected the office like a large mirror. Moravec wondered why the room seemed so dark, then realized that he'd never been here at night.

"Luther Moravec is just here," Haldern was saying. "We'll speak again after I've had a chat, this end." He nodded again. "Yes, of course." The director of Euromedic Industries set the phone down. He stared at it for a moment without expression. When his eyes met Moravec they communicated only weariness. "Luther, good of you to come so quickly. You've been informed about the incident,

27

of course." He gathered up several printouts as he spoke, coming around the desk.

Haldern had always been a meticulous man. He was the only person Moravec knew who would have used "incident" to describe what was surely a ghastly scene in Madrid. It was in keeping with Haldern's sense of neatness. Everything had its proper place, but organization was the ultimate priority. He was a small man and had a small man's passion for authority. He belonged to the Alias Club and played bridge on Thursdays. He'd been a widower since 1971, which explained, Moravec supposed, why he always wore the same dark suits.

"Dr. Charles Rennit," Moravec said, meaning to say Rennit's team. He suddenly realized that no one had mentioned survivors. "I'm afraid I don't know many of the details."

Haldern sat down in the leather high-back chair across from the sofa. "Rennit is dead," Haldern said. "Three of his four colleagues died with him in the crash. En route from South Africa. Did you know Rennit?"

Moravec shook his head.

"A brilliant biochemist, and slightly mad of course, but they all are, aren't they, the brilliant ones?" Moravec expected a smile but Haldern was deadly serious. He took a photograph from a folder in his lap and handed it over. "That's Rennit, there in the center . . . the balding one."

Moravec studied the black-and-white picture. Five middle-aged men squinted against the sun. Rennit wore an open lab coat over a suit and tie. The others were in their shirtsleeves. They were standing abreast on the wide step of a patio in front of a large jungle plant. The shadow of the photographer streaked across the lower right corner. The picture reminded Moravec of one of those severely posed shots of nineteenth-century outlaws from the American West. None of the principals was smiling.

"The research team from Johannesburg," Haldern said. "Crooks and Perry are on the left. Townsend and Graham on the right. Of course, this was Hahnemann's group before he died."

"Hahnemann?" Moravec recognized the name. Hahnemann had been a leader in genetic research. Died last year. Car crash in Kenya, if he remembered right.

"Julius Hahnemann and Charles Rennit collaborated in a special Euromedic program," Haldern said. "Afterwards, Rennit organized this team."

Moravec assumed by that he meant after Hahnemann's accident.

"The research project began, initially, studying premature aging—particularly the relationship of progeria to the pituitary process. Their research eventually led to combining altered DNA cells with a tissue culture, and creating a special enzyme-producing tumor that was surgically inserted near the gland in the brains of mice. The enzyme they developed was called METHYD-9."

Moravec nodded. He really wasn't up on enzyme research, but knew the pituitary was the pea-sized gland near the brain stem that controlled vital functions of organs which affected hormone secretion into the bloodstream. A surgical procedure involving the pituitary in humans wasn't usually life-threatening, Moravec knew, though it must be tricky in mice. Progeria was a form of infantilism; a rare and wicked premature aging disease that attacked children. He'd never seen an actual case of it except in photographs. The victims were grotesque, pitiful creatures. The case he remembered was an eleven-year-old girl—small stature, wrinkled skin, with sparse gray hair and the mannerisms of a very old woman. The disease was terminal. For a moment he was reminded of Christina, but he pushed it away.

"You see," Haldern continued, "what they'd been after was a process to right the chemical imbalance of progeria. Hahnemann was convinced that the key to solving the fundamental defect in the children's aging disease was hormonal. They concentrated on methylaminotetralin hydroxylase. And they were successful. What they discovered wasn't a cure, mind, the disease was still there, but they'd slowed the aging process to almost normal in laboratory animals." Haldern nodded for emphasis and said, "They were more successful than anyone realized." He looked at Moravec for a long moment. "This is all very confidential, Luther, what I'm about to tell you. Confidential to the highest degree. Very few people—" his eyes bore in on Moravec to make the point—"*very few* know about our work in South Africa. It is absolutely essential that we keep that knowledge confidential until we've dealt with this problem. You must understand that, Luther."

But Moravec didn't understand at all. What problem? What work? This was definitely not the briefing he'd expected. The research in Johannesburg had nothing to do with him. He knew all he wanted to know about irreversible children's diseases. He tried to escape Haldern's intensity. He glanced at the single ornament on the opposite wall, a faceless, glass-framed clock with its innards exposed, revealing a spinning flywheel and tiny rotating gears, silently measuring time. When he glanced back, Haldern was still there, waiting. Moravec stirred uneasily at the corner of the sofa. "I'm afraid you've lost me." He tried to smile but it didn't help. "I mean . . . I don't see what any of this has to do with me."

"Rennit is dead," Haldern said again. "Crooks, Graham, Perry and Rennit. All dead . . . except Townsend." He nodded at the photograph in Moravec's hands. "Second on the right, there. Stuart Townsend. Microbiologist. American. He's the only one left of the team and he's dying."

Moravec studied the figure next to Rennit. He was taller than the rest with light, longish hair. His exposed forearms were hairy and he wore a linked watchband with the crystal on the palm side of his wrist, the way fliers often do. His shirt was button-down with stripes and he was holding a pencil and eyeglasses in one hand. His face was drawn, tiny webs at the eye and creases at the edges of his mouth. He looked tired—they all looked tired—but there was something about him, the way he stood, perhaps, that Moravec put down as somehow rustic; as though he could mend a roof or fix a flat without minding the dirt—something manual, something innocent.

"God knows how he survived that crash," Haldern was saying. "But thank God he did." Moravec glanced up at him. "Everything was on the plane, Luther. Everything of consequence relating to their research . . . METHYD-9, that is. And now it's gone, all of it burned to a cinder. Stuart Townsend alone knows what they found." Haldern had been leaning slightly forward in his chair and now he sat up straight, with one eye cast in shadow. "That's why we need you, Luther. We *must* save Townsend. Instead of saving hundreds or even thousands, the test for AirMore comes down to the survival of a single man. What I'm saying, Luther, is that there is more at risk here than the life of one scientist. The survival of Euromedic itself is at stake."

"Why?" Moravec didn't know what else to say.

"Because . . ." Haldern licked his lips. "Because something went wrong. Something went terribly wrong. That's what you must understand." He leaned forward once more. "How old would you guess Townsend is in that picture?"

"I'm sorry?"

"Look at Townsend. How old does he look to you?"

Moravec frowned and glanced at the photo. "Fifties, I'd say. Early fifties." A bead of perspiration caught the light on Haldern's temple as Moravec looked up.

"Stuart Townsend will be thirty-one on April fifteenth . . . if he lives that long. The only way we can save him is by cardiac transplant. We need AirMore section to transport the donor heart. If Townsend dies then hundreds of others will die too . . . because he knows the secret. Only Townsend."

Moravec said nothing; he just stared.

"Let me explain it to you now, Luther. All of it." Haldern touched a handkerchief to his forehead, then brought his arm up to check his watch. "There's very little time."

SEVEN

DALLAS

THE GUY in the van obviously wasn't Becky Smith. His name was Grant, an intern from the clinic.

"We didn't think Miss Smith should be driving," he said. "The doctor gave her some medication. She's pretty upset about her brother."

Townsend nodded. "So how's Tiny?"

"He was on the table last I heard. Lost a lot of blood."

"Table?"

Grant looked over at him. "Operating."

An image of Tiny on an operating room table flashed through Townsend's mind. They'd have had to use a hydraulic lift.

"You ever give blood before?" the intern said.

"I had a blood test, I think. Pricked my finger."

"Needles don't bother you then?"

Townsend hadn't thought about a needle. It hadn't bothered him until now. "It doesn't hurt, does it?"

"Not a bit." The intern smiled. "You'll never miss a couple pints."

Townsend shook his head. "Course not." Until they reached the clinic all he could think about was an enormous needle siphoning his blood into a bucket.

The van stopped in front of a single-story building in the middle of a tree-shaded block. The adjacent parking lot contained only two cars. The sign was new.

2734 JASPER
PROFESSIONAL MEDICAL CORPORATION
WILLIAM SCOTT ACLIN, MD
MICHAEL FREDERICK TOOKE, MD
GENERAL MEDICAL CARE
A EUROMEDIC COOPERATIVE

"Just go ahead in," the driver said. "I have to park the van."

Townsend opened the door and got out. He was still thinking about the needle. "Do I ask for somebody?"

"Just go in. They're waiting for you."

The waiting room was empty. There were two vinyl couches, a magazine rack with copies of *People* magazine and *Popular Science*, a large potted plant and a coat rack. The voice of Rosemary Clooney singing "This Old House," came from a ceiling speaker. Townsend hung his jacket on a peg next to a blue parka.

"Mr. Townsend?"

The receptionist sat behind a cutout in the wall. She had to stand up to see over the counter.

"Yes, ma'am."

"We've been expecting you," she said. She was past thirty and not especially pretty, but businesslike. She pressed a button and Townsend heard a buzzer somewhere inside the building. "Right through there, please." She pointed through the opening of a pastel green door.

"I'm here to give blood for Tiny Smith," Townsend said.

"Yes, I know. Just step through there and someone will take care of you."

Townsend hated hospitals and hospital manners. He didn't need taking care of. A man in a white jacket was waiting on the other side of the door.

"Mr. Townsend?"

"Yeah."

"Follow me, please."

"Where's Becky Smith?"

33

"Who?"

"Tiny's sister. She's supposed to be here."

The man shrugged. "Ask the doctor."

He led Townsend to a small, windowless office that apparently doubled as an examination room—scales, examining table, a few stainless steel medical machines, plastic-wrapped wooden tongue depressors in a coffee mug. The desk was tidy with a brand new green blotter and a brass calendar that served as a paperweight. He sat in the chair and wondered where all the other truckers were.

When the doctor arrived Townsend was surprised to see it was a woman. She was in her mid-forties and wore a white jacket over a gray tweed suit. When she smiled her thin lips did not communicate pleasure.

"Good morning, Mr. Townsend," she said, and sat behind the desk without offering to shake his hand. Doctors were the biggest hypochondriacs, Townsend remembered reading somewhere. He wondered if she'd examined someone before him and if she'd just returned from washing her hands. "I'm Dr. Seagram." She spoke without looking at him. She hunted through a drawer as if she weren't familiar with the desk, pushing things back and forth, lifting papers. "We'll be as quick as we can. We know this must be an inconvenience for you and we appreciate your cooperation."

That was precisely what he disliked about doctors. *We* think . . . *we* hope . . . *we* are sure . . . It was an attitude they had in common with second-grade teachers and he suddenly remembered how much he hated it. Stuart did too.

"I'll need to take some information." She finally glanced up at him with a weak smile. "Background, medical history, that sort of thing. All right?"

"Sure, but . . . when Tiny's sister called me she said a bunch of other guys were giving blood too." He glanced around. "So where are they? I didn't see anybody in the waiting room."

34

"Nothing to wait for, Mr. Townsend. There are five or six other gentlemen here giving blood right now."

"Oh." Townsend felt better. "How's Tiny?"

"Still in the operating room." She took a form from the desk. "Now, if I can ask you a few questions. What's your full name?"

"David Michael Townsend."

"Age?"

"Thirty."

"Height and weight?"

"Six feet, one eighty."

"Eyes . . ." She glanced up. "Blue." She noted it on the form. "Hair, brown." She filled in the proper space with a ballpoint pen. "Do you know your blood type?"

"O-positive."

She nodded without looking up. "Allergies?"

"No."

"In the past five years, have you been hospitalized or undergone any type of surgery?"

"No."

"Any lab work in the last twelve months . . . X-rays?"

"No."

"Have you regularly used marijuana or any controlled substance except as prescribed by a physician?"

"This isn't going to the FBI or anything, is it?" Townsend said when she looked up. He gave her a weak smile.

She looked at him without expression. "The reason we ask these questions, Mr. Townsend, is to make sure that what you're donating is as healthy as possible. I'm sure you understand our concern."

"Oh, sure," Townsend said. He shook his head. "I don't take drugs. I don't use marijuana . . . regularly." He avoided her eyes.

She asked a dozen more questions from the form, then took his pulse and blood pressure, which she recorded on the form. When she'd finished she handed him a glass bottle.

"Fill this, please." She nodded at the door. "You'll find a lavatory behind the first door on your left."

"I thought I was going to give blood."

"Don't worry, we'll get to it."

He inspected the bottle. It was very large. "Fill it, you said?"

The bathroom was behind the second door on the left. While he stood there, aiming meticulously into the bottle, it came back to him why he really disliked doctors. They seemed always so damned superior, as if they knew something no one else knew. It was an attitude he despised. It wasn't just medical doctors; plumbers and electricians had the same disposition, but plumbers and electricians couldn't give you cancer. If Stuart could see him now he'd be laughing his head off.

Townsend returned to the office, carrying the warm glass carefully in front of him.

"Just set it there, please." Dr. Seagram indicated a metal table against the wall. She punched a rubber plug into the top of the bottle and taped a label across it: TOWNSEND, DAVID M (WKB-MAG IDEN). He wondered when she'd had time to type it.

"Now, if you'll roll up your right sleeve and lie down—" she gestured toward the examining table "—we'll take a little blood."

Townsend obeyed. He was thinking about the needle again. "You do this a lot—take blood?"

"Every day." She strapped a rubber tourniquet around his bicep and handed him a ball. "Squeeze this ball for me. We want to pump up the vein."

Townsend squeezed. "How long does this take?"

"No time at all. Ten minutes."

He saw the needle then. She held it to the side as she swabbed the crook in his elbow with antiseptic. It was bigger than he imagined.

"This might sting a bit. Keep your arm down at your side."

Townsend closed his eyes. He felt the pressure of her fingers. When he opened his eyes again she was fastening tape to a clear plastic tube on his arm. The fluid moving through it was bright red. "It's in already?"

The doctor smiled. "Just keep squeezing the ball. You're doing fine."

He laid his head back down. "Tiny better appreciate this."

"There are a few more questions, Mr. Townsend. Do you mind?" She had another form on a clipboard.

Townsend stared at the ceiling. "Go ahead." Anything to keep his mind off the blood draining out of him.

"What is your employer's name?"

"None," Townsend said. "I'm self-employed."

"I see. How long have you done that?"

"Two years . . . about."

She nodded. "Address?"

"Forty-one twelve North Side Drive. Oklahoma City."

"Previous employment?"

"I had a landscaping business for a while. Reaganomics killed it."

"In Oklahoma?"

"Is all this stuff necessary? I mean, I'm just giving blood, right?"

She didn't look at him. "We keep a complete record of our donors. Now, the landscaping business, it was in Oklahoma?"

"Yeah. Tulsa."

"You seem to move around a lot."

"I manage." A Boston Pops arrangement of "Yellow Submarine" drifted from the ceiling speaker. The framed diplomas on the wall behind the desk testified that Dr. W. Scott Aclin was a graduate of no less than four universities.

"Have you had an electrocardiogram exam recently?" She held the pen beside her cheek.

37

"Nope."

"Have you never had one?"

"Nope, never did."

She noted that too.

"Have you ever had syphilis, gonorrhea or any contagious venereal disease?" It was a different questionnaire, a green one, this time. She glanced at him, waiting.

"No," he said, speaking slowly and watching her check off the appropriate boxes. "How come your name's not on the sign?"

"Pardon?"

"Out front."

"I'm not from this clinic. Any history of diabetes?"

"No."

"Mental disorders?"

"Not yet. What clinic are you from?"

She looked up, a little surprised. "Dallas General."

"I thought Tiny was at Parkland."

"He is." She reached for a plastic cup on the stainless steel table. "Have some of this. It's orange juice. To replace some of the fluid."

Townsend sat up slightly. It wasn't real orange juice. It tasted like it came from a can. Metallic.

"All of it, please."

"Tang?" Townsend said as he handed back the empty cup. "Something with artificial flavoring, right?"

"Something like that. Just lie back down. Keep your arm straight."

"We're not finished?"

"Soon," she said. "Just a few more questions and you will be on your way."

"I'd like to see Becky."

"She's just down the hall. You can see her in a minute."

"I'm a little dizzy."

"That's normal. Just relax."

He had a headache too, but decided not to mention it. All he wanted was to get this over and get out. He wondered how the operation was going. He wondered what Becky looked like. He really was getting dizzy. It helped a little to concentrate on the gold ballpoint in the doctor's hand. He focused on it, watching as she filled in the boxes of the questionnaire. There were a lot of questions. After a few minutes he became fascinated by the movement of the pen in her hand. He stared at it, watched it make little jiggles as it moved, crossing *t*s, dotting *i*s, skipping to the next box. The more he watched it, the bigger the pen seemed to become.

"Marital status?"

"Single."

Jiggle, jiggle, dot the *i*.

"Next of kin? Parents?"

"Deceased."

Jiggle, jiggle, skip to the next space.

"Sisters?"

"None."

Nothing to dot or cross there, Townsend observed. He was light-headed, everything was distorted except the pen in her hand and her manicured fingernails.

"Brothers?"

"Yeah, one. Stuart P. Townsend. P for Phillip. He's a doctor too. Lives in Africa. Thinking about changing it to Schweitzer." He laughed. Everything seemed very suddenly funny.

The pen moved on.

"Girlfriends?"

It was an odd question to pop up, he thought distantly, but he didn't object. He was too fascinated by the pen. "Not lately," he said.

"Boyfriends?"

"You didn't write down that last."

"Just answer the questions now, David. Just relax. We've plenty of time."

There was something very soothing about her voice.

Townsend was faintly aware that he was drowsy. Every time he blinked it seemed harder to keep his eyes open.

"Is there anyone who might miss you?"

"Am I going somewhere?" He could not keep from smiling.

"Any close friends who we should call?"

"No. I don't—"

"Friends?"

"Ah . . . no . . ."

"No one at all?"

"No . . . maybe . . ."

"Who?"

The pen wasn't moving. The gentle flow of it stopped and he tried to understand why. He felt himself floating. It was getting darker.

"Who did you say, David?"

"Why is it . . . so dark . . . in here?"

"Who should we call?"

"Stuart . . ." Townsend said. "Did I tell you my brother was a doctor?"

"Look at me, David."

He glanced up from the pen. Dr. Seagram's face didn't seem to have any sharp lines. "Aren't you . . . going to . . . write anymore . . ."

"It shouldn't be long now. It's taking effect."

"What . . ."

"It's all right, David. How do you feel?"

He wished she hadn't asked him. Suddenly everything was fading. Something was rising in his stomach. He tried to blink back the darkness that was closing in around him. Something was constricting his vision to a narrow field. The dizziness was taking hold of him. When he looked up he could only see part of Dr. Seagram's face, as if he were seeing her through the wrong end of a telescope.

"I don't . . . feel . . . so good . . ."

"Good. Everything's fine." He saw her mouth move, but the words came later, like poor dubbing of an old film. She seemed to be looking over his head, talking to someone else.

He tried to sit up then. It wasn't such a good idea. He felt as though he was floating. His fingers were cold.

"What's . . . the matter . . . with me."

Dr. Seagram's mouth moved again but this time he didn't hear the words. She wasn't looking at him. He tried to speak, to make some sound, to register some complaint about the light, but nothing happened. If he made a noise he didn't hear it himself.

Then he saw other faces. A man's face. Then a woman's. Strangers. He heard someone say Becky, and he had the impression that they were trying to convince him that this face belonged to Becky and that everything was fine.

But everything wasn't fine. Something was wrong with him, he knew that, but something was wrong with Becky, too. He couldn't understand it. She had a beautiful face, this Becky. Blonde hair. Ice blue eyes. Pert little nose. Not at all like Tiny.

Then he was falling and he knew he was falling because falling doesn't feel like anything else. It was like a dream he'd had a million times . . . There was a well and it was dark and he was falling inside it and feeling sick as he watched the damp bricks whiz by. He was falling farther and farther away from the light. He opened his eyes wide but it didn't help. Before the darkness completely took him it came to him what was wrong. Tiny Smith was six-foot-four and wide as a mountain. He had curly hair and lousy teeth. A gentler guy you couldn't find. But that wasn't what bothered Townsend. Tiny Smith was also black. He was the biggest, blackest black man he'd ever known. It was very odd, Townsend thought, before he slipped away. What was Tiny Smith doing with a sister like Becky?

EIGHT

METHYD-9 RESEARCH started with rats in 1968.

Hahnemann's logarithmic tissue cultures of altered DNA cells were programmed to grow to an average weight of about 2.5 grams, after which it lost the ability to proliferate. Implanted along the anterior lobe of the pituitary gland through the nasal canal, this new heterotypic tumor produced an inhibitory extracellular enzyme which, reacting with methylaminotetralin hydroxylase, affected specific growth hormones, absorbing and neutralizing non-amino acid compounds. The result, in the case of congenital progeria, the fatal aging disease of children, was that the acceleration defect was arrested. It was not a clinical cure to the disease, buy what Hahnemann and Rennit had accomplished amounted nearly to the same thing.

What they'd also done was create a new organ.

The METHYD-9 tumor had two things going for it: One, it had been designed to be parasitic, sharing the blood supply that fed the gland's posterior lobe, which was a reservoir for hormones that were secondarily active. And two, it didn't act like a tumor—it didn't grow. It acted like an organ. It was an independent part of the body and had a specific function. And it worked.

In fourteen hundred sixty-eight implantations of laboratory animals from rats to small primates, only thirty-nine failed to meet the criteria objectives—a success rate of 97.343. Even then Hahnemann suspected the rate was low and put the fault to inferior test animals.

But as successful as the METHYD-9 trials had been, Hahnemann and Rennit found that the treatment produced an inexplicable though harmless side effect. All the subjects became hyperactive; they displayed more energy, more vitality and had a propensity to learn and retain what they'd learned far above their preoperative intelligence. For whatever reason, they were smarter and lived much longer than the control group. Hahnemann couldn't explain it. Rennit didn't understand it. It just happened, like most major scientific advances.

One theory was that since the pituitary was the governing endocrine gland of the body, METHYD-9 had some catalytic effect on one or several other hormones secreted from the anterior lobe. Their objective was to affect growth hormones but if they also affected hormones that regulated the proper functioning of the thyroid, gonads, adrenal cortex and other endocrine systems to do with growth, maturation and reproduction, and the relationship was not detrimental . . . then so what? If the effect was proved not to be negative, Hahnemann reasoned, then there was no effect. It didn't matter. Besides, in this case, the side effect was extremely positive.

The other theory was that since the pituitary gland was located at the base of the brain, in the sella turcica, that proximity to the midbrain (mesencephalon) of METHYD-9's chemical properties somehow affected electrical impulses to the primary cerebral hemispheres. Rennit likened METHYD-9 to an electrical power booster station; it energized mental and physical productivity.

But what Hahnemann and Rennit did know was that they were on the verge of cracking one of the most complicated mysteries of medical science—aging. Supported by Euromedic at the Johannesburg laboratory, the project labored another three years before they reached a milestone. They had perfected METHYD-9C, a super enzyme, slowing by half the aging process in diseased animals. Laboratory subjects implanted with the tumor lived twice as long as the control groups and were healthier, happier and smarter in their old age. The tumor had no effect, however, on subjects that didn't have congenital aging disease.

By this time the two researchers, who had not published a single word about their work, decided it was time to use their technique on a human subject. They found a terminal case in Kenya: a five-year-old boy in an advanced phase of progeria. He was taken to Johannesburg and underwent the implantation surgery.

It worked, just as Hahnemann and Rennit knew it would.

In two months the boy's degenerative aging symptoms began to disappear—his hair grew back, his breathing problems got better—and all the traces of the aging disease started fading. In eight months the boy was as healthy as any normal forty-year-old man, which was the chronological age he had attained physically due to the disease. Mentally and psychologically he was still a five-year-old. But the test didn't end there; they had to know if the higher productivity factor they had found in animals was present in human subjects as well. When the Johannesburg clinic received the boy he was, like his parents, illiterate. He couldn't read or write. Eleven months later, after special tutoring, he was not only writing Kikuyu and English, he had developed an aptitude for higher math and his appetite for reading was insatiable. Of course, the boy may have had a capacity for intelligence all along, but Hahnemann and Rennit were convinced that his accelerated learning capability was due to the tumor.

Successfully treating a rare disease like progeria is one thing, but with proof that they could inhibit the aging process *and* increase mental productivity—that was something else again. The problem was that their breakthrough only worked on subjects with the disease—not a bad accomplishment. But progeria occurs only once in eight million births. Less than one hundred instances of the disease have been reported since its discovery in 1886. But Hahnemann and Rennit now had a higher goal. They rationalized that if the enzyme would not work on an otherwise healthy patient, an experiment was necessary to induce the disease, then treat it with the tumor. If it worked then they truly had developed an age-inhibiting procedure that had universal applications. Why should just progerians benefit? Of course, there was also a profit motivation here that, though the two researchers weren't consumed with passion to follow, Euromedic Industries certainly didn't ignore.

Testing human patients meant finding volunteers—healthy subjects who meet certain criteria—who would subject themselves to a terminal disease that had no cure. The subjects would further have to agree to complete secrecy, which meant they could not seek medical treatment outside Euromedic, and to make themselves available for tests over a period of years. Such volunteers were difficult to find, even with a guaranteed financial arrangement, and the promise that they could expect to add twenty or forty or even sixty years to their life expectancy. It was a lot to ask, even if it would drive actuaries crazy.

Consequently Hahnemann took a dramatic step. In an effort to illustrate his absolute faith in METHYD-9C, he became the first test subject. On a warm April morning at the Johannesburg laboratory, Dr. Julius Frederich Hahnemann became the first man ever induced with diseased cells of hypophyseal infantilism's most terminal condition.

The disease took six weeks to manifest itself and another two weeks for severe aging symptoms to become established. The initial findings revealed that the degenerative effects of progeria in an adult were even more accelerated than in patients who'd been born with the disease—no one had ever studied a mature adult with progeria because victims almost never lived beyond the age of eighteen. Hahnemann was forty-three when he began the test. After ten weeks his heart functions, metabolism rate, kidney efficiency and insulin production were those of a fifty-five-year-old male of the same race. He'd aged twelve years in two and a half months—sixty times the normal rate.

Then the tumor was implanted. Within two weeks the signs of arthritis he had developed began to fade. His hair stopped falling out. Respiratory problems improved. After a month all negative traces of the disease disappeared. After six weeks he was healthier than when he'd started. In a relative sense, Julius Hahnemann stopped getting old.

Hahnemann's full recovery was the most important development in medical history, even though no one outside a tight circle of Euromedic scientists knew of it. The Hahnemann Trial, as the experiment was known, opened the door to intensified research. Over the next two years more than two hundred human subjects underwent the same procedure. In every case study the results were the same— the physiological aging process was significantly slowed while mental capabilities were substantially increased. And still, nobody knew why. But by then it wasn't a burning issue that anyone was looking to solve. Like a hundred other quirks in medicine, the miracle of METHYD-9C defied explanation. It wasn't faith and it wasn't magic and it wasn't divine intervention. It just worked.

It wasn't until later that it all went wrong.

NINE

LONDON

AN OVERCAST dawn cast an oppressive mood into the office where Moravec found himself staring at a swirl of snow outside the window. Fantasy and reality battled for priority in his consciousness. He was aware that Connie would be awake, that he should call her, remind her to turn up the furnace. He tried to connect Haldern's long view with the photograph in his lap; to comprehend the significance of the past hour; to visualize a young man, old before his time, who possessed the key to a great secret. Faces of children came to him; among them was Christina's. It was a patchwork puzzle of incongruous pieces that his mind attempted to analyze, searching for the one part that would give the rest structure. His public and private worlds were coming together, blurring the lines that kept them separate. For the first time since Connie's collapse he felt unsafe.

"Luther?"

Moravec turned his gaze away from the window to look at Haldern. He knew the story wasn't finished. His part was coming. "*What* went wrong?"

"I first want you to understand the long view here, Luther."

"I believe I understand the long view. The long view is Townsend."

Haldern wouldn't look directly in his eyes. "Well, yes, that's quite true. Still . . ." He took a sip of tea, watching Moravec over the rim of the cup. It had come half an hour ago while he was explaining how they'd found the boy from

Kenya. He had stopped his discourse while the serving tray was laid out on the table between them. There was coffee and tea and fresh toast. Haldern took cream and two lumps of sugar. Delicately, mixing it all precisely as if it were some elixir he had to get right.

"We have an enormous responsibility before us," Haldern said. "A crisis of priorities, really. There is a feeling in the world today that nothing can be done about anything. People don't believe that they have control of their lives. Technology is at the same time savior and beast, they think. They can't really say what's important anymore; they can't distinguish what's important from what's trivial. It's a result of the void in values today. Nothing is black and white anymore and it's caused an unrest, a distrust everywhere . . . look at America." Haldern nodded toward the clock on the wall. "Couples are suing their doctors because their babies *lived*." He shook his head.

Moravec waited. Haldern had a tendency to speak ahead of himself, to use a block of thought out of sequence from the well of data in his brain. The listener had to sort it out.

"The Hahnemann Trials are the most important research of our time," Haldern said. "You can appreciate that, surely. But there was a practical, indeed a moral consideration before us which we hadn't really dealt with. Part of it had to do with the technological advances that the Trials represented. In a prevailing atmosphere of values in turmoil, our development might very well have been misunderstood. We were, after all, advocating that otherwise healthy people subject themselves to an incurable disease to be treated and controlled all for the benefit of the side effect." Haldern's glance had wandered and now he brought it back to Moravec. "You can imagine the problems facing us there, yes? I mean, it isn't as if we're announcing a cure for halitosis."

Moravec interpreted it as a plea; Haldern, in spite of his position, needed reassurance, someone to agree with his point. Moravec nodded and felt guilty.

"But the more important dilemma had to do with distribution," Haldern said, letting his eyes wander again. "Perhaps I should say access. METHYD-9C will change medicine for all time. But not just medicine. We're talking about extending the longevity of humankind. It's a noble goal, you know, to strive to perfect our own species. But what would its effect be on a world already overpopulated? What was our obligation to a planet that at this moment can't feed all the people who inhabit it? If we double or possibly even triple man's life expectancy, does it also extend his sexual proclivities? Are we inviting families of ten and twenty members?" Haldern shrugged his shoulders. "We don't know the answer, of course. It will take years, perhaps centuries, before we understand. We may even have created a new order of life—the next rung up the evolutionary scale."

"Man-created man," Moravec said. He wasn't trying to be funny.

Haldern nodded. "Perhaps so." He looked at Moravec. "Which is why the overwhelming consensus focused on selective distribution. We decided METHYD-9C should be made available only on a limited scale." He let his breath out, a slow, defeated sound, which seemed to make him smaller. "Of course, that was *before* Dr. Hahnemann died."

Moravec suddenly knew that Hahnemann didn't die in any auto crash in Africa. He knew before the director looked into his eyes that they'd made some dreadful miscalculation with METHYD-9C. He *knew* it and his stomach tightened. *The survival of Euromedic itself is at stake.* He was about to become part of a colossal secret and he was frightened. Haldern had been leading up to it, feeling his way, testing the waters.

"What *really* happened to Hahnemann?" Moravec said.

Haldern placed his teacup back on the tray. He looked almost relieved. "Julius Hahnemann succumbed to emphysema eighteen months ago." He held his gaze steady with Moravec. "But it was progeria that killed him. The tumor failed."

"Good Christ!"

"It all happened very suddenly. The tumor stopped producing enzymes or the enzymes had lost their virility . . . no one knew precisely the cause, it happened so quickly. Somehow and without warning the arresting agent of METHYD-9C quit its neutralizing effect. And without the enzyme to check the disease—" Haldern shook his head "—Dr. Hahnemann became vulnerable to several aging maladies. He got sick and his body got older, physically older. The degeneration was extremely fast. From the onset of the failure until he died was only eleven days."

"The tumor failed?"

"Exactly so, but we didn't know that then. The autopsy revealed nothing extraordinary. The tumor was not diseased or damaged. It *looked* all right. We couldn't find anything to explain the failure. I mean, nothing absolute. We marked principal organs for further examination and kept the body . . . and announced that Dr. Hahnemann had died in a road accident in which his remains were destroyed by fire. That's all we *could* do. There was still the possibility that this wasn't sequela, that what had happened to Hahnemann was not inspired by the disease he carried. All we could do was wait."

"Wait?"

"The test group. The two hundred test subjects—they were all called back for immediate examinations."

"To Johannesburg?"

"No, no . . ." Haldern's eyes met Moravec's. "The test group was made up of different races, different ethnic backgrounds, different ages. Hahnemann wanted a microcosm to study. He chose subjects like the boy from Kenya—illiterates and poor."

"But healthy."

If it stung, Haldern didn't let on. "Of course. They were chosen from locations where Euromedic had a facility—to expedite monitoring—Europe, Africa, the Americas, Asia—"

"What happened?"

Haldern shook his head. "For a time, nothing. No reports of degenerative reactions of any kind. Then, six months after Hahnemann's death, it started." He stirred uncomfortably in his chair. The subjects began getting sick—very sick. The complaints ranged from hardening of the arteries to diabetes—heart diseases, arthritis, kidney malfunctions—"

"Diseases of old age."

"It was as if there was some sort of internal clock," Haldern said. "We had no way of knowing until the test group began to get sick. You see, the first of them hadn't been implanted with the tumor until six months after Hahnemann. That's why we didn't detect anything immediately. METHYD-9C failed, consistently, sixty months after implantation. It was like clockwork. The degenerative process started and . . . it was irreversible. There wasn't anything we could do about it."

"Why sixty months?"

"We think it was a mutation of the DNA function. Hahnemann had changed the growth rate of the original tumor by manipulating DNA cells. What he didn't realize was that he also caused a changed in enzyme interaction. METHYD-9C has a long-range causal effect on antioxidants, the immunity system's scavenger enzymes. Normally, with aging, antioxidant production declines. But METHYD-9C keeps them going and together they scan the body for free radicals. But after sixty months something happens. Instead of attacking free radicals, METHYD-9C goes after antioxidants. It's some sort of timed mutation. As a result, instead of inhibiting aging diseases . . ."

"It promotes them." Moravec felt his leg tremble.

"Hahnemann sequela, we're calling it."

"What?"

"We're calling it Hahnemann sequela," Haldern said. "An abnormal condition following or caused by an attack of disease." He gave the medical definition as if Moravec were a student.

"I *know* what it means."

"Oh, yes . . . sorry, Luther, I—"

"What has Townsend got to do with it?"

"Naturally, as soon as we identified the difficulty, Rennit's team began working to solve—"

"Townsend had it too." It just dawned on Moravec. The men in the photograph were middle-aged. "They *all* had it?"

"It was their own option," Haldern said lamely. "After the Hahnemann Trials they felt it was safe—"

"Safe!"

"Luther, please."

"That's why they were rushing back to London? They discovered a cure?"

"There isn't a cure per se, you understand. What they'd managed to do was restructure the original tumor. That's my understanding. METHYD-9C, actually."

"Why were they all on the same plane? All of them, and the data?" It was a question Haldern must have asked himself a hundred times since the accident, Moravec realized.

"It was a matter of security," Haldern said. "We were concerned about leaks. If they traveled separately, over several days, it only made the problem that much more difficult. Also, of course, was the matter of time. We wanted Rennit's team in London as soon as possible where they could begin training surgeons here in the technique."

"And now they are dead."

"Except Townsend," Haldern said.

"Who is the only one who knows what they've accomplished." Moravec felt an uncomfortable bunch at the small of his back where his shirt had come out of the waistband. He'd been sitting too long on the sofa. "And you want me to do what—deliver a donor heart? I don't quite see why you've brought me into this—" he had to search a moment for the right word "—confidence. There's nothing unique about that kind of transfer."

52

"As I said earlier, Luther, I want you to grasp the long view of the situation. Hundreds of lives are at stake. Not just Townsend. And not just the two hundred test cases. There are . . . others."

Moravec frowned. "Others?"

"You must understand, Luther. All the implantations had worked. Of the two hundred test cases there was not one failure. Hahnemann and Rennit were convinced—we were all convinced—that the procedure was safe."

Moravec blinked with astonishment. "You haven't treated more people?"

"I'm afraid we have."

"My God—"

Haldern went on, getting it out in a rush of words. "We approached men and women of science first. People we knew who would be discreet . . . many already in the Euromedic family. That was three years ago, two years after the original trials. We called them Hahnemanns, after Julius, being the first, you see. Then we went to other individuals prominent in their fields who we thought should be included in this program. To date there are slightly more than three hundred of these . . . ah, VIP Hahnemanns."

"But—why?"

"Cost," Haldern said. "This research was enormously expensive. After we'd proved that the procedure worked, we had very little difficulty finding people willing to pay for the opportunity to increase their life expectancy with a guarantee that they would also substantially benefit in terms of productivity." He paused looking sadly into Moravec's eyes. "I know. I was one of them. My sixty-month cycle comes due in less than two years."

Moravec rubbed his forehead.

"We'd intended to inform you of it," Haldern said. "Then there was that business with your wife and daughter and we thought perhaps . . . later."

"And what do the other VIPs think about this new development?" Moravec said. "They must be very uneasy, I would think."

Haldern gave him a surprised look. "They don't know, Luther. Of course, they don't know. How could we take a chance? It would cause panic. In eight or nine months the VIP Hahnemanns will reach the end of their sixty-month cycles. If we lose Townsend, we will lose them. It's that simple. We can't put *those* people away in a Euromedic facility as we did with the test group. A prominent scientist or head of state doesn't disappear without someone noticing. There are three other groups doing similar research—Swedes, Americans, Russians—but they aren't even close to METHYD-9C. That's why Townsend is so important. You do understand that?"

Moravec nodded. "Yes. I do now."

Haldern licked his lips. "I want you to oversee the transfer, now that you know what's at stake. Your field of expertise is exactly this sort of emergency. That's why I had you in. The rest is up to the surgeons."

"Where is the donor?" Moravec said. He wanted to leave, to get on with it.

"The United States. Texas, as a matter of fact. A special medical team is looking for him now."

Moravec frowned. "*Looking* for him?"

"The donor is Townsend's brother," Haldern said quickly. "They're identical twins, which means the surgery will be much less risky since there is no organ rejection factor."

"A cardiac transplantation?" Moravec was amazed. "Does his brother realize what he's agreed to do? Heart donors do not, as a rule, survive that particular surgery. Even Texans." The joke was meant to be ridiculous. It was a ridiculous notion.

"He did not agree," Haldern said quietly, "because we did not ask him."

TEN

DALLAS

"NEW YORK four-four-one-four. Can I help you?"

"Give me MAG Central."

"Verification code?"

"V for Victor, double five, double six."

"One moment. Thank you for waiting. Switching to Central, stand by."

"MAG Central."

"This is Turner. Recovery Team Six in Dallas. We have the transferee."

"Confirmed?"

"Confirmed."

"Stand by, Turner. Okay, Little Mary Four is already on her way. ETA Dallas/Forth Worth 1440 hours. That's one hour, twenty-two minutes."

"Got it."

"One drop from Brentwood, one pickup for Weeksbriar."

"We need an ICP unit. Our outgoing is chlorpromazine dependent."

"It's on board."

"The drop is a stiff, right?"

"On ice. You're prepped?"

"All we need is the surrogate."

"Right. One hour, twenty-one minutes."

"We'll be waiting."

ELEVEN

LITTLE MARY was like no other plane on earth.

Entirely white except for the green Euromedic caduceus on its tail, the aircraft was the glory of AirMore, Disaster Care Division's recognized ambassador of mercy. Part ambulance, part intensive care ward, part surgical operating theater, Little Mary was a mini-hospital with wings, an achievement that was a marriage between space-age technology and the most modern advances of biomedicine.

Originally designated MORE—Mobile Operating Room, Euromedic—the AirMore project had been the brainchild of Dr. Jahan Odtaa, a DCD arthrosteopedic surgeon from Stockholm. Odtaa had returned frustrated from the devastating 1974 earthquake in Pakistan in which five thousand people died. He had written an impassioned plea to London for a practical solution to the most troublesome problem facing his department—strategic medical care.

People were dying who could be saved. More often than not urgent medical needs were not immediately available at the scene. It was the unfortunate fact that most disasters occurred in remote areas where seriously injured victims died before help could reach them or before they could be moved to proper surgical facilities. His idea: develop mobile surgical units—a fleet of helicopters was his initial suggestion—equipped as mini ORs, which could be flown to disaster sites where more-than-first-care (thus the acronym) could be supplied to save lives. His experiences had convinced him that government and even private paramedic operations were uncoordinated and sloppily run affairs. Victims died in transit because first-care medics were not fully qualified or prepared, or because the trauma of the move itself was too great, or because doctors in fully equipped hospitals had to *wait* for their patients. In many instances the victims might have been saved except for that wait. There were hundreds of cases in which the injured were rushed to the wrong hospitals, even the wrong cities.

Odtaa's proposal was initially determined to be impractical and monstrously expensive. It meant organizing voluntary surgical teams that would be made up of surgeons and anesthesiologists and nurses who had probably never worked together. It meant fragile OR equipment would have to be purchased, maintained, adapted to battery generators and somehow transported quickly to the site of the disaster. There was serious doubt that a single helicopter could be successfully modified to accommodate the weight requirements of the equipment and personnel, and still be light and mobile enough to get into remote spots. But the most formidable task, if all the rest could be resolved, was one of logistics. Where would one locate this fleet of mini ORs?

Eventually it was decided that the idea should not be abandoned though the scope would obviously have to be limited. Two million pounds were set aside to fund the project over two years. The ultimate question was to find a cost-efficient method of providing the service. The difficulty was in assigning a workable cost-per-victim (CPV) formula from which expense-recovery projections could be computed.

Euromedic approached the European Economic Community with a plan called the Medical Emergency and Disaster Service (MEDS) which would offset routine and primary expenses with a yearly project-maintenance subsidy from each member nation; but Great Britain declined participation (the NHS could handle such emergencies) and the plan died for lack of multilateral support.

Even so, Euromedic went ahead. A single C-5A was

leased from the Royal Air Force and modified to Euromedic's specifications. The huge transport could accommodate three Chinook CH-47 helicopters which were in turn outfitted as mobile operating rooms. The plan called for the transport to fly to the landing site nearest the disaster; the helicopters, quickly refitted with rotors, would then proceed to the actual site. A small unit was assembled to staff this experimental enterprise, made up of three surgical teams from a pool of forty doctors of Euromedic's London research hospital, St. Mary's. The enormous plane came to be known as Little Mary in honor of its namesake. The sphere of responsibility for call to action was limited to Central Europe.

There were some minor calamities in the next eleven months; a railroad collision in Belgium, another in the Loire Valley in France, a chemical plant explosion in northern Germany, but nothing on the scale they had prepared for. Then, in May 1977, the unit was put to its first all-out test—an earthquake of 6.5 Richter magnitude struck northern Italy.

Little Mary was at the sites of worst devastation, set up and operating within five hours of the alert. There were problems, of course—one of the anesthesiologists missed the flight (he was later fired) and a generator burned out after only nine hours—but in spite of them the test was demonstrably successful.

All in all, three hundred eighty-six victims went through emergency surgical procedures for a multitude of life-threatening injuries. Fourteen patients ultimately died—a mortality rate of 3.62 percent, a seven point improvement over traditional disaster first-care statistics. The response was so overwhelming that it nearly overshadowed the impact of the disaster itself in which 946 people died.

Euromedic's effort was hailed around the world as a humanitarian and medical triumph. The Italian prime minister said Euromedic's AirMore units were "a godsend." The Pope called them "white angels in gray machines delivered from heaven." A Washington *Post* editorial stated, "Euromedic's disregard for staggering costs in this incredibly unselfish project to save human life is the finest example of philanthropy that our species can produce." The London *Times* called it "a magnificent gesture of goodwill."

The Italian campaign had been the proof of AirMore. Governments that had been hesitant to underwrite the MEDS plan now were eager to contribute. The Italian experience showed that an independently run organization, staffed and subject to immediate call, was "a moral obligation" to supplement national disaster agencies. It was a service that, fanned by public demand, created its own market.

AirMore quickly expanded into a full subsection of Euromedic's DCD. Within five years, twelve additional AirMore units had been located throughout the world. The operation was further streamlined to fit the nature of the emergency. Little Mary could be transformed (often in less than an hour) to accommodate helicopter ORs or be converted to a self-contained emergency room with sixteen modular operating theaters. The most recent innovation was the ICV, intensive care vehicle, an articulated bus fully equipped as a mobile intensive care ward for up to six patients, each individually monitored in an Intensive Care Pod (ICP), a self-contained capsule specially designed for critical patients.

In all, eighty-six countries joined the MEDS system, all of them underwriters, including four from Eastern Bloc nations. It was a sort of socialized medicine in its most capitalistic form. Victims still died, of course. But the promise of AirMore was like the promise of cancer insurance. If you needed it, it was there. Euromedic offered a service that people wanted and for which governments happily paid the premiums.

Moral obligations aside, it was also a service that came to be enormously profitable. When AirMore was not engaged in disaster relief it was free to respond to private emergencies. The premise that drew Euromedic's attention, and eventually its resources, was that rich people got sick too. They smoked too much and drank too much and found spots on their livers and lungs just like everyone else. They saw themselves as less than expendable when it came to medical treatment. If special medical transport was available, even if it was expensive, then naturally they wanted it. Therefore AirMore also filled, if not an urgent need, certainly a commercial demand. The arrangement satisfied almost everyone. Euromedic Industries was especially pleased.

So it happened that an AirMore mission was almost never questioned. When Little Mary Two glided to touchdown at DFW, the fading sun reflecting gold and pink hues from her glossy white skin, she was accorded all the courtesies befitting her station. A Delta flight from Atlanta had waived its landing priority over the mercy plane. Ground crews from American Airlines worked speedily to refuel her and help load the single passenger she had made this special trip to pick up. The chief tower communicator gave her his personal attention, sending her on her way after a seventeen-minute turnaround.

Little Mary was like no other plane on earth. She exacted respect wherever she went.

Townsend came awake slowly; his senses coming around without connection. He felt pain before he could see. His head throbbed. His mouth was dry, but the queasy sensation in his stomach told him to lie still. There was perspiration at the back of his neck and he smelled something sweet.

It took several seconds to make his eyes work. There was a dim light somewhere to his right, little more than a red glow in the thick haze of his consciousness. He rolled his head toward it and felt a wave of nausea rise inside him. It was difficult to keep his eyes open more than a few seconds at a time. He sensed movement, a slight sway as if he were in a car. There was the dulled hum like a faraway waterfall.

He couldn't move his head. Or his arms. His vision went in and out of focus and it was hard to push his senses past the throbbing in his brain, but he forced himself to look around. He was in a small room. The walls curved in above him. Everything was bathed in a rosy hue from the light. He stared at the ceiling and foggily understood that he was seeing it through a transparent enclosure—the arched lid of a glass coffin.

He closed his eyes against the throbbing in his head. It was a dream. He was having a nightmare. A whopper. He tried to wet his lips, but there was no sensation in his tongue. Then he realized something was in his mouth. Something big. He opened his eyes and saw the thing sitting on his chest. It looked like a pig with inflamed yellow eyes. No, a mole; a huge mole. No, it—he couldn't keep it in focus. It kept changing. Now it was a lizard. Now it was something else. Something he couldn't recognize. It moved closer. He felt its slimy feet on his chest. Its mouth telescoped toward him like the trunk of an elephant, touching him, leaving a wetness on his cheek. He tried to move his head away, but the thing followed. It was searching for something.

He tried to close his jaw, but the thing was quicker. He felt it push past his lips, past his tongue, filling his mouth. He closed his eyes and bit down hard. Cartilage snapped under his teeth. He felt it break and tear away; felt something ooze over his chin. When he opened his eyes he saw an enormous caterpillar. Half its head was gone.

Townsend screamed and the darkness that hovered at the edge of the mind rushed in to save him.

TWELVE

LONDON

MORAVEC OPENED the blind and stood at his window, waiting for Connie to come to the phone. His view of London wasn't so grand as Haldern's. Situated at an end of the RSC building, and a level below, Moravec's office faced the sooty corners of two brick apartment buildings that held the passageway to St. Mary's emergency entrance. Sunlight had not touched this stretch of cobblestone since before the last Great Fire. Rusted iron contraptions hung on the sides of the buildings in mute anticipation of the next.

"Luther?" Connie's voice was frail against the image before him, a plea from the darkness. "Estelle said you are leaving."

Estelle was the fiftyish housekeeper whom they had found through an ad in the *Times*. She was like one of the family now; always prompt, arriving every morning at seven, efficient and, after only three months, devoted to Christina. Moravec had paid her tuition to a nursing course. Connie's condition required that someone responsible be home always; she often forgot about Christina.

"I'm afraid so," Moravec said. "A few days, only."

"Oh."

"I told Estelle to expect to stay through the weekend."

"Yes, of course."

An ambulance, siren blaring, swerved into the lane between the buildings below. Moravec watched as it was quickly swallowed by the shadows.

"Will you be leaving soon? I could fix something, if

you've time. Breakfast then? I don't mind, you know. Really. We could sit on the balcony."

Connie hadn't cooked in more than two years and the balcony was frozen over with ice. She had forgotten. It had started—the misplaced time, the forgotten moments—in the hospital after her collapse. Sometimes she didn't remember the day, or the date. She still knew Christina then, but only as the little girl, the vision of herself.

Moravec turned back to his desk. "I'm sorry. I'm off straightaway."

"Not to worry," she said and Moravec felt like a criminal. "We'll all of us have cake when you're back. Is it far, this one? I mean, is it on the continent? How will you go?"

"New York," Moravec said, then added, "returning by way of Madrid. The director's putting me up in his own jet, actually."

"Guillam?"

"Haldern."

"Oh, yes, sorry. The little man always in the gray suits," she said quickly. "I remember him, Luther." It was a rare acknowledgment of her illness.

Moravec nodded. "I know."

Connie's breakdown had come six weeks after confirmation that Christina had suffered permanent brain damage. Christina was seven then. She had been recovering from a minor case of influenza while Moravec was at a conference in Copenhagen. On the phone Connie had said Christina was irritable and disobedient. Moravec had assumed it was the flu. When he returned, Christina was vomiting in her sleep.

Moravec remembered the ambulance ride to St. Mary's, Connie's crying, the turn down that dark corridor in the middle of the day. Christina was comatose with encephalopathy—Reye's Syndrome, it was finally diagnosed. Cerebral edema had already begun. A bifrontal decompressive craniectomy was performed to reduce swelling and pressure, but the damage had been done. Christina's electroencephalographic patterns proved abnormal, grade three. Clinically, she had suffered positive residual neurologic dysfunction. Part of Christina's brain was dead. The fact of it killed something inside Connie.

She bore up under the stress well enough at first, after the shock wore off. She seemed to believe Moravec that no one was to blame. Then in June, the day after Christina's birthday, Connie stuffed newspaper under the door of the garage, opened all the car windows, slid behind the wheel and started the engine. A passerby smelled the fumes and called the fire department. They found Connie unconscious, slumped against the door. Christina was in the rear seat.

"Your son kicked me this morning," Connie said.

"Ah, did he?" Boy or girl, it didn't matter to him. This child was for Connie. He was forty-four but he'd promised, when she was well again, that they'd have another. It seemed to help; she sometimes forgot about Christina, but she always remembered she was pregnant.

"Yes. He'll be just like you, Luther. I know he will."

There was a quick knock at his door and Moravec's assistant peeked round. He raised his forefinger as if for permission to enter. Moravec's eyes waved him in. To Connie he said, "Bill Mayford's here for me. I'd better be off."

"Who?"

"Tell Christina I love her."

"Bill—?"

"Love you too, Con. Bye now." Moravec hung up, hating himself, and managed a smile for Mayford.

"Central's on green line," his assistant said. "SCS wants your BriefPac."

"Mallerbe?"

"Something about a special file they want to load. He wouldn't explain. They never do, up there."

Moravec nodded. Mayford's specialty was toxicology—he had interned at London Hospital—and he raised hunting

64

dogs because he wasn't married. But he was ambitious and a little too bright for his own good. Brian Hagelin, AirMore's chief of surgery, thought he was an officious bastard. He probably was.

Moravec pressed the blinking button on his phone console. "Good morning, Toby."

"Just had a chat with Haldern," Mallerbe said abruptly. He didn't sound pleased. "Would you mind popping up? We've a little surgery to do on your machine."

"Right. Five minutes?"

"Your convenience, old boy." The line went dead.

Moravec hung up wondering how much Haldern had told him.

Mayford was leaning on his hands against the back of the visitor's chair. He had an impatient, officious look about him. "They say you're going to the States, straightaway." It was Mayford's way of making a question.

"Quite right. This morning."

"And what about that mess-up in Madrid? Are we supporting? Primary Office said we'd already sent Little Mary One." He paused to make the point. "Nobody told me."

"I've just been seeing to it. Here since three, you see." Moravec suddenly realized that he was terribly hungry. He thought of Connie and felt guilty. He *could* have seen her before he left. "We're treating it as routine. Little Mary will be transferring survivors."

"They say Charles Rennit was killed."

"So he was."

"Then . . ."

"Officially, we're not discussing it."

"Officially? With the press, you mean." Mayford's voice cracked.

"With anyone." Moravec took the BriefPac from his file drawer. He hated to look at the boy. Mayford would be crushed that he'd been left out of something. "You'll be on call status while I'm gone."

"I understand, but—"

Moravec glanced up. "Any problem?"

"No, I . . ." Mayford shook his head. "No." He looked as if he lost his best dog. It would have made Hagelin's day to see it.

Special Communications Section was a branch of MAG Central. They were located on the fifth floor and wore dark green identification badges. When Moravec arrived with his BriefPac, Toby Mallerbe was waiting at the security gate. Mallerbe was SCS chief of section. He gave the impression of a large man though he was scarcely taller than Moravec. He smoked a cherry bowl pipe and if he stood any straighter he'd have qualified as a sergeant major in the Royal Marines.

"I'm not quite sure I approve of all this, you know," Mallerbe said, holding the gate. He spoke around his pipe as if it were a perfectly normal appendage attached to his mouth.

"What's that then?" Moravec swung the briefcase to the counter top. "I feel like James Bond, lugging this thing about."

Mallerbe shook his head as if sizing up a recruit and finding him a hopeless case. He gestured to one of his specialists. "Robert, be a lad, take Mr. Moravec's BriefPac. They're waiting for it in Data-B." To Moravec he said, "They're not toys, you know, old man," and did a half turn to the right, moving with parade-ground precision along the corridor to his office. Moravec followed the trail of smoke.

BriefPac *was* a toy. Moravec had never thought of it as anything else. It looked like an attaché case but inside was a computer, a keyboard, a small monitoring screen, a hard disk drive and a device to allow what was known—inscrutably to Moravec—as telephone interfacing. There was even a small dot matrix printer. BriefPac's memory had the capacity to store the equivalent of two thousand pages of notes; it could be plugged into a telephone and communicate with another computer anywhere in the world. With it work became gamesplay; a medical report could be entered into a machine in Hong Kong, transmitted through the MAG relay network to Moravec's telephone modem in London, and be ready to read on the computer monitor in less time than it took Big Ben to announce the hour. BriefPac was advertised as the businessman's portable office, for the "executive on the go." It was all true too, but Moravec's machine was used most often to sharpen his chess strategies. It seemed a fitting exploitation for an organization of plastic and aluminum parts wired together from an assembly line in Tokyo.

"Haldern says you're to have certain restricted files pertinent to the Hahnemann program," Mallerbe said in his office. "Frankly, Luther, I was against it. Nothing to do with you, of course. I simply don't care for information like that leaving our control. You understand my position."

Moravec nodded. Mallerbe's office faced west, like Haldern's. In the last few hours the overcast had broken, allowing the light through. St. Paul's dome rose from the mist, its mantle of snow brilliantly white in the sun.

"As a measure of security we're adding a password routine to your machine. The file we're loading is called HAHNEMANN, obviously. Medical histories, profiles, a project summary, rundown on the recovery teams . . . what you'd asked for."

"I didn't realize you were that informed," Moravec said.

"SCS is the heart of the MAG network, Luther," Mallerbe said. "Everything comes here. We're the repository for Euromedic's critical data. We store it, code it, index it and cross reference everything. We pass it out according to access level. Most of it gets distributed to the network members by specialty, like pharmacochemical research to the drug boys. Project research is our meat, you might say, but the Hahnemann data is our highest-priority file."

"Secret, you mean."

Mallerbe took the pipe from his mouth to make the point. "More than secret, old boy. Vital, I think."

When Moravec's BriefPac arrived, one of Mallerbe's specialists instructed him on the security sequence. Admittance to the computer was routine but access to any information with a HAHNEMANN prefix code required no less than three password checks. It was a highly protected file, he was told with pride. Moravec hadn't the time for it.

"I'm supposed to remember that?" Moravec stared at the alphanumeric access number on the computer's monitor. The password was a series of twelve numbers and letters. "Without writing it down?"

"It's a computer-generated random alphanumeric figure," Mallerbe said with some annoyance. "Writing it down would defeat the purpose, wouldn't you think?"

"I just want to read the bloody file . . . I'm not launching submarine missiles here, Toby. I thought you people were so keen on simplicity."

"We have to protect—"

"Who do you think is going to use it besides me? If I run into any Russians I'll burn it or something. This is ridiculous."

"The nature of the information demands that we have safeguards," Mallerbe said. He was beginning to sound like Mayford.

"I'll only write it down, you know. I don't have time to memorize codes. I'm leaving in thirty-five minutes so don't—"

"Yes, yes, all right then." Mallerbe's lip was twitching. "Change it," he said to the specialist. "Something Mister Moravec can remember."

Moravec almost smiled. "Much appreciated, I'm sure."

"Yes, well, do take care of it, old boy. We don't want to lose it either."

The specialist typed REDEFINE LOGON at the keyboard and the computer monitor responded with ENTER CURRENT LOGON. The specialist typed the letters and numbers.

The screen went suddenly blank then displayed ENTER NEW LOGON . . .

"Go on then," Mallerbe said to Moravec. "One string of letters or numbers—not more than fifteen—no spaces or punctuation marks. Simple but not simple-minded."

Moravec leaned down to the keyboard. He typed CONSTANCE. It seemed fitting, under the circumstances.

THIRTEEN

DAVID OPENED his eyes when she touched him. She was dressed in a white, starched uniform, and her hair was pulled back in a bun. Her fingers were around his wrist and she jumped when he spoke.

"Where am I?" His mouth was dry. His tongue seemed to fill his entire mouth.

"You're awake?" She looked surprised.

"Where am I?" David tried to focus his eyes on her. He was groggy, a pain throbbed at the back of his head.

"Ah . . ." she released his wrist ". . . hospital." She took a step backward. "I'd better call the doctor."

"Hospital?" David pushed himself up on his elbow and was immediately sorry. The pain expanded inside his skull, almost squeezing the image of the nurse out of his vision. He lay back on the pillow. He tried to wet his lips. "Why . . ."

The nurse took another step back. "I'll get the doctor."

David wanted to agree but the pain in his head forced him to close his eyes.

When he opened his eyes again someone was standing over him.

"Well, well, you're awake." The doctor was a thin man with a mustache that failed to broaden the linear features of his face. He wore a white smock with an array of pens in the breast pocket. He had very straight teeth. "Feeling better?"

David tried not to move his head when he spoke.

"Head . . . hurts." There was less pain, he noticed, if he didn't try to move. His mouth was still very dry.

"Yes, of course," the doctor said. "That's normal, under the circumstances." He moved closer, took David's wrist and raised his arm to see his watch. He smiled. "Quite a little knock you took, eh?"

David blinked. "Knock?" He touched his head. It was wound in a bandage.

"Nothing to worry about," the doctor said with assurance. "Slight concussion is all." He studied his watch a few more seconds, then set David's hand back on the bed. "Good." He took one of the pens from his pocket and marked on a metal clipboard. "Very good."

"Where . . ." It was an effort to talk.

"Parkland Memorial Hospital," the doctor said. He leaned down and stared into David's face. "Any severe dizziness . . . nausea?"

David blinked. "A little . . . dizzy. Not as bad . . . as before."

"Before?"

"Where's Tiny . . ."

The doctor stood over him, staring into his face. "You were awake before?"

David nodded once and the dizziness returned. "In . . . the little room."

"Little room?" The doctor made a face. "Ambulance?"

"There were . . . things on me. Creatures."

"Hallucinations," the doctor said. He noted it on his chart. "Don't worry about it." He straightened up and took another pen from his collection and pointed it in David's eye. A light came on. "Any discomfort from the light?" He brought it closer, leaning over the bed and opening David's lid with his fingers. "Any pain?"

There was pain, behind his eye; a dull, nervous pain that caused his lid to twitch involuntarily. It wasn't the throbbing, crushing pain he'd felt when he woke up, but it

71

frightened him anyway. "Yes," he said. He tried to keep the fear out of his voice. "It's . . . very bright."

"And here?" The light moved to his other eye."

"Yes."

"Um-hum." The doctor switched off the light. He nodded to himself and wrote on the clipboard. His smile, David noticed, was not as full as before.

"What's the matter with me?"

The doctor continued writing.

"Hey?"

After a moment the doctor glanced at him. He put the clipboard under his arm and the smile returned. "You're going to be fine."

"What happened!" David shouldn't have raised his voice. An invisible vise took a quarter turn on his head.

"You don't remember?" The doctor's smile faded. He took out his clipboard again. "I see," he said, but he was busy writing. "You don't remember anything at all, is that right?"

"No, I . . ." His eyes watered, blurring the doctor's features momentarily. He held himself very still. "What happened to me?"

"There's nothing to worry about. You're going to be just fine. This type of reaction is common in an accident involving the head."

"Accident?" David looked at the nurse who stood silently at the foot of the bed. She held her face expressionless. He turned his glance slowly back to the doctor.

"You don't remember," the doctor said patiently, replacing the pen in the pocket, "which is perfectly normal." He looked at David with more interest. "Everything will come back to you. Don't worry. In twenty-four hours you'll be back to normal. You just need a little rest." He smiled. "You probably won't remember this little talk. The mind's a funny thing. Do you know who you are?"

"David Townsend."

The doctor's smile broadened. "Very good." He nodded

72

at the nurse. "You see, he's coming around already." The nurse smiled too. She looked at David but didn't speak.

"I'm Dr. Knopf, David," he said. "Do you remember when they brought you in? The emergency room? The ambulance ride? Anything before you woke up?"

David didn't answer. His mind was blank. The last memory he had was of the clinic, answering questions and squeezing a ball. He remembered Dr. Seagram's face before he remembered her name. She didn't wear a wedding ring. He remembered wondering if she was married or divorced or widowed. He remembered thinking he wouldn't want to be married to her. He remembered the tiny room with the curved walls and glass casket. He couldn't decide which were the hallucinations. "I don't remember any ambulance."

"You fell," Knopf said. "More than once, apparently. Do you remember the clinic? Giving blood?"

David nodded slowly. It didn't hurt to nod slowly.

"You just collapsed, they said. Right in the middle of the session. Good thing you were with a doctor at the time. Anaphylactic shock is nothing to fool around with."

David remembered trying to stand. He remembered nothing would hold him up. He remembered the well dream and falling. "What's Anna . . . fill—"

"Anaphylactic shock," Knopf said. "It's an allergic reaction to certain substances . . . bee stings, usually, sometimes penicillin. In your case it was orange juice. Either you forgot to mention that you were allergic to it or you've developed the reaction. Fortunately Dr. Seagram was quick enough to realize what had happened. She gave you an injection of adrenaline immediately. You fell down some stairs when they tried to move you. Apparently that's when you really banged yourself. They called an ambulance and brought you to Parkland." The doctor shrugged. "They're very worried over there—at the clinic, I mean—that you might sue."

David closed his eyes to think. The headache was coming

back. When he opened them again Dr. Knopf was a little blurry. "Orange juice?"

"Funny, isn't it?"

David shook his head. The pain made his eyes water. "I'm not allergic to orange juice."

"No?" Knopf sighed. "Well, perhaps you've developed the allergy. It happens, you know."

David remembered the taste. "It wasn't real orange juice. It tasted funny, metallic." He remembered the dizziness, the sudden nausea. "I think they put something in it."

"Something? Like what?"

"I don't know. Medicine, maybe. A drug. I don't know."

Knopf just stared at him. After a moment he slipped his pen back in his pocket. "Look, David, you're in Parkland Memorial Hospital because you've suffered a concussion. Whatever case you believe you may have against the clinic is irrelevant to me. I won't get involved in some frivolous malpractice suit, if that's what you're thinking."

"But it wasn't *real* orange juice. It was something else, like Tang with something added. I'm not allergic to orange juice. I'm not allergic to anything."

"You don't go into allergic shock from drinking Tang, David," the doctor said. "I don't care what else is in it." He was frowning. "Anyway, what you need is rest. I'm your doctor. Just do what I tell you and we won't have any problems." His smile returned. "Deal?"

"Yeah." David's face itched. He touched his cheek. His beard was gone. "What—"

"Oh, we shaved you," Knopf said offhandedly. "Sorry about that. You can grow it back."

David felt his jaw and chin nervously. "Is something—"

"Nothing at all wrong there," the doctor said. "We shave all our bearded patients admitted through the emergency room. That's Parkland Hospital policy."

David dropped his arm. He stared helplessly at the doctor. "How's Tiny?"

"Tiny?"

"Tiny Smith. The guy I was giving blood for. He's supposed to be here. Had an operation. Truck driver."

The doctor glanced at his nurse. "Tiny Smith?" She shrugged.

"Had a wreck in Mesquite," David said. "Big guy . . ."

"I don't know," Dr. Knopf said with a frown. "I'll look into it if you like. When was he admitted? Do you know?"

"This morning. Early."

The doctor nodded. "Ah, well, I came on at nine. He'd have passed through emergency before I came in."

"I want to know how he is," David said. "He was pretty bad."

"I'll check for you, but what I want you to do is rest. Okay?"

"How long will I have to be here?"

"Oh, overnight I expect," Dr. Knopf said easily. His smile was warming up again. "Just a precaution, you know, because of the concussion. A little rest is all you need. Tomorrow the headache will be gone. Believe me, when you go to sleep again you'll be out ten, twelve hours. We'll do a couple of tests in the morning but most likely you'll be out of here by noon."

"Who's paying for all this?"

"I wouldn't worry about that right now, David. The thing is to get you rested so you can leave. Which reminds me"— he looked at his watch—"you're due for some medication." He glanced at the nurse. "Meprobamate, two tablets, four hundred milligrams." When he looked at David he was smiling again; that same don't-worry-my-son smile. "Just something to help you sleep."

"Have I had any visitors?"

"Visitors?"

"I thought maybe Becky Smith. Tiny's sister."

Knopf chuckled. "You've only been here a few hours, David. Besides, I don't want you to have visitors. I want you to sleep. I don't want to aggravate that concussion.

Now, anything else? I have a couple dozen other patients I need to see.''

It was beginning to get on his nerves, the doctor calling him by his first name as though they were old poker buddies. He didn't have that many friends and nobody called him anything but Townsend.

"Just find out about Tiny. I'll go to sleep when I know how he is. He might be . . . Just find out, okay? I want to know.''

The doctor stared at him a moment, then a resigned smile passed across his face. "Okay." He raised his hands. "Okay. I'll check on your Mr. Smith. But then you'll sleep, right? It would look very bad for me if it got out that I had to make deals with my patients to get some rest.''

David nodded. "Then I'll sleep.''

David stared at the ceiling after Dr. Knopf and the nurse were gone, trying to piece together the vivid bits of memory he had left into some sort of order. He remembered everything from Becky's call to passing out. He vaguely recalled his well dream, and seeing a white, blue-eyed Becky Smith, and having some furry creature sit on his chest, but those were hallucinations. It was the little things that confused him. How could he have fallen downstairs? The clinic was a one-story building. Why would a one-story building have stairs? Where would they go? And why would a Dr. Seagram from Dallas General be at a clinic taking blood for Tiny Smith who was at Parkland? Why so many questions about his work? A lot of it didn't make sense.

He felt the bandage on his head. He proceeded slowly, carefully probing for some telltale sign. But he didn't discover anything—no large lump or painful spot or patch of crusted blood—nothing to confirm that he'd suffered a blow to the head. He wasn't an expert, but a concussion was produced by getting one's brain rattled, wasn't it? So where was the bruise? He was probably overreacting, he thought. After all, Parkland Memorial was a pretty good place to be if you had to be in a hospital in Dallas and whatever his personal prejudice against doctors, at least they were taking an interest in him. If Dr. Knopf said he had a concussion and that he'd feel better in the morning, then he probably would. His head *did* hurt. There wasn't anything imaginary about that. So, shut up and take your medicine, David told himself. The doctor knows what he's doing.

When the nurse arrived with a cup of water and a pair of yellow pills on a metal tray, David was ready for sleep. He hadn't really slept since the day before yesterday. At least here he wouldn't be bothered by a telephone.

The nurse set the tray down on the stand beside his bed. "I have your sedative, Mr. Townsend." It was a different nurse. This one was a chicken-necked woman in a white-starched uniform, but her smile was cheerful. "You also have a visitor."

David glanced up.

"Dr. Knopf said she could only say hello. Remember your promise?" The nurse turned to the door. "Miss Smith?"

Becky came in like a vision from heaven. She wore a white dress. White raincoat. White skin.

"Oh, David!" She rushed to the side of his bed. "I'm so sorry about your accident. The doctor said you bumped your head. I'm sorry. But I have good news." She smiled beautifully. Her teeth gleamed. "Tiny's fine. The operation was a success. He's in recovery, asking about you. He wanted me to thank you for what you've done."

"I owe it all to you."

Becky glanced at the nurse. "Isn't he a darling?"

David offered a weak smile. "I guess your mother is relieved, huh? I mean, Tiny talks about how she's always worrying about him driving a truck."

"Oh, you know it. Mom's with him now. It was pretty rough there for a while."

David nodded. "I'm sure it was." Tiny's mother had died in 1969.

Becky squeezed his hand. "Look, you just do what the doctors say. Get your rest. Tomorrow I'll drop by and we'll visit longer." She glanced at the nurse again. "I guess I better be off. I just wanted you to know that everything's fine."

"Thanks for coming," David said. "Seeing you was just what I needed." He gave her a farewell smile.

As Becky disappeared the nurse handed him the yellow pills. "Time for rest now."

"What are the chances of seeing Dr. Knopf before I nod off?"

"The doctor is making rounds. He'll see you when you wake up." She handed him the cup of water. "Swallow them, don't chew."

"I just noticed, there's no phone in here."

"You don't need a phone if you're going to sleep, do you?" She nodded at the button behind the bed. "Anything you need just buzz. A nurse will come."

"You think I could have some orange juice later?"

"You can have whatever you like," she said. Then more firmly, "*After* you rest."

David pushed his hand to his mouth then gulped down the water.

"Good boy," she said. She took the tray with the empty cup. "Have a good sleep."

David lay back on the pillow until she'd gone, then sat up. Whatever was going on here wasn't an hallucination— Becky Smith, or whoever she was, was no dream this time. She was real, but she was a lie. Everything was a lie. He wasn't allergic to orange juice and he didn't have anna-whatever shock and he didn't fall down any damn stairs and Tiny wasn't in any wreck. *So what the hell is going on?* David opened his hand and studied the yellow pills. Whatever it was he sure as hell wasn't going to sleep through it.

David pulled the bedsheet back and lowered himself to the floor. His headache wasn't gone but at least it wasn't ripping his head off. He moved to the closet and found only a pair of fit-all slippers. When he tried the door it was locked.

"Damn!"

He sat on the bed to steady himself; the headache was coming back. He stared at the white-and-green pattern of the tiles under his feet to control his nervous stomach. Then he noticed that the night table was bolted to the floor. So was the bed. The only things not bolted down in the room were the bedsheets and the drapes. If he hadn't had the headache he'd have thought of the window sooner.

He made his way slowly, fighting not to jar his head as he walked. Opening the drapes was like having another hallucination. The window was divided into eight panes of glass, each imbedded with wire. On the other side of the window were black iron bars. But the nightmare was outside.

Snow.

As far as he could see there was snow, whipped by a swirling wind. In the distance he saw the shadowy outline of mountains, dark and heavy on the horizon. David blinked at the white silence before him. He touched a cold pane of glass to prove it was real. David's throat was dry and his head was crushing in from all sides. Whatever he was looking at it wasn't from a room in Parkland Memorial Hospital. It meant he wasn't in Dallas. He wasn't even in Texas.

FOURTEEN

OVER THE NORTH ATLANTIC

THE PRIVATE jet's passenger compartment was dark except for the glow of BriefPac's six-inch screen. The portable computer hummed on the polished wooden lap desk, casting a soft green glow on Moravec's white shirt.

Moravec had been at it for nearly two hours, alone in the lavish executive cabin, studying the HAHNEMANN file's medical histories section. The Townsends were listed under separate headings: HAHNEMANN SEQUEL SUBJECT (Stuart) and HAHNEMANN DONOR SUBJECT (David). The brothers had such different life-styles that Moravec had difficulty remembering that they were identical twins. Born in Chicago, they had been raised in different households after their parents died in an auto accident. They were nine years old when separated and lived with the families of their father's brothers. Stuart became the oldest of three children in his adopted family; his uncle was an insurance executive. David became an only child; his adopted father ran a hardware store. Stuart was studious, well liked and political in school. He was valedictorian at Princeton and graduated second in his class at Johns Hopkins Medical School. He took a research position in microbiology at Columbia's School of Medicine, then was invited to join Euromedic's research staff under Rennit.

Where Stuart Townsend's ambition was scholastic and professional achievement, David Townsend was driven by competition. A spelling bee finalist in elementary school, a sprinter and discus thrower on school track teams. He played chess. He had built and flown an aircraft made from lawn mower parts. An architectural school graduate in Pennsylvania but, according to Moravec's file, he never took out a license. After graduation he'd had three different jobs—bulldozer operator in Michigan, tree trimmer in Illinois, logger in Oregon. His most steady work had been in Oklahoma where he operated a landscaping company for six years until it failed. For the past two years he drove a truck.

Moravec was fascinated by him. David Townsend wasn't a failure and he wasn't dumb. The common thread to his life was individual activities. Everything he'd ever done had been geared to a one-on-one relationship. It was a trait that stood in sharp contrast with his twin. Stuart Townsend was an outgoing, gregarious company man; David Townsend was an independent loner. Moravec wondered what had caused them to be so different. It was true that identical twins were physiologically the same person. It was an act of nature that split the egg in the mother's womb, creating two individuals of exactly the same cell structure. Case studies had proved that precisely because of their similarities twins had traditionally tried either consciously or unwittingly to overcome this challenge to their personalities by pursuing different goals. But Moravec had never seen a pair of twins so wildly different and suddenly wanted to know him, to understand him, talk to him. The meeting would be a unique situation for them both. Townsend wasn't really a victim, Moravec wasn't really an executioner. They were pawns in a larger game. Haldern had said that from behind his grand desk. The question really came down to this: Is one life a just sacrifice if it benefits the human cause? Haldern believed it was. What did Moravec believe?

Moravec wasn't a theologian or a legal theorist. He was a doctor charged with disaster care in which the primary issue was to save as many lives as possible. As far as DCD was concerned it was the only rule. What made it bearable was that no one had a name; not the victims, not the survivors. They were simply—and this wasn't cruel—statistics. It was mass market medicine for a mass market society. In that light he understood Haldern; he could agree. Medicine's obligation to save lives was a relative notion; what was good for the whole was good for its parts, whatever that might mean to the individual. If Townsend fell between the cracks in the pursuit of that goal, it wasn't bad; it was just acceptable. There were no villains. No blame. Medicine didn't work that way.

Moravec woke with a start when the crew member tapped his shoulder. He'd fallen asleep with the computer still running before him.

"Mr. Moravec," the attendant said. "Sir?"

Moravec's ears popped when he yawned. He glanced out the window at the Atlantic darkness. "Are we there?"

"No, sir. Not for another few hours, but there's a call, sir. MAG relay from Madrid."

Moravec rubbed his eyes. He noticed the monitor screen and turned it off. Mallerbe would have had a stroke if he'd seen it. He looked around the cabin. "Where?"

The telephone was white, built into the console of the conference table. Haldern's plane had everything.

"Hello?"

"Dr. Moravec?"

"Yes."

"Stand by, please. I have Dr. McPhearson in Madrid." There was sound a of distant clatter. "All right, go ahead, please."

"Luther? Hello? This bloody thing isn't working. Hello?"

"I'm here, Ian," Moravec said. "How are you?"

"Bloody exhausted, is how. Where are you? You sound like you're on Saturn."

"Haldern's plane. Middle of the Atlantic somewhere. How is your patient?"

"*Our* patient. Let me tell you about our patient, Luther.

Our patient is not terribly well. I assume you're aware of the specifics?"

"Yes, I've seen your D sheets."

"Have you?" McPhearson sounded surprised.

"MAG Central transmitted them."

"Oh, right. Then you know what we're up against."

Moravec knew exactly. "Time," he said.

"Precisely so. Frankly, I'm not optimistic but never mind that right now. There's something else. I've run a series of enzyme assays of spinal fluids. I thought it was mandatory under the circumstances. Townsend suffered the sequela, you know. He's supposed to be getting older."

"Yes, I know."

"I've run only three tests, mind, but I thought you should know what the results showed."

Moravec waited. "Yes?"

"The arresting factor, METHYD-9? The values aren't consistent. I was told the degenerative ratio was above one point six. Whoever came up with that figure was incompetent or a bloody fool. There isn't any degeneration. *My* tests show that enzyme production of the tumor is active, not degrading. The growth hormones are perfectly normal."

"Normal?"

"I want to know what the bloody hell is going on. I can't treat a patient who has a severely distressed heart condition, among other serious complaints, you understand, and at the same time depend upon data that is incorrect."

"You're confident in the assay results?"

"Your bloody aircraft arrived this morning. Your people did the tests. How confident are *you*?"

"Sorry."

"The arresting agent isn't supposed to be working, that's the point. Stuart Townsend is supposed to be getting older. But he isn't getting older. In spite of everything else that's wrong with him, he is *not* suffering from an aging disorder. What does that mean to you, Luther?"

"The tumor is working."

"Very good," McPhearson said dryly. "The question is—why?"

Moravec remembered the photograph Haldern had shown him of Rennit's team. Townsend and Graham stood to Rennit's left. They were smiling but what struck Moravec as odd was that they both had black eyes. He'd meant to ask Haldern about it, but now he knew. No wonder they were smiling.

"Townsend had the operation," Moravec said suddenly. "Of course. *That's* why he had a black eye. Both of them . . . Townsend and Graham."

"What operation? What are you talking about?"

"Haldern showed me a recent photo of Rennit's team. Townsend and Graham had black eyes."

"So?"

"Surgery involving the pituitary requires access through the nasal canal." Moravec's mind raced ahead. Crooks was the surgeon, he would have performed the operation. "In that respect it's similar to rhinoplasty. And what's one of the visible characteristics of a patient who's had a nose job?"

"A black eye," McPhearson said. He was silent for a moment. "I see."

"Time was running out for Rennit, for all of them," Moravec went on, sure of himself now. "They were in Johannesburg to solve the riddle of METHYD-9. When they thought they had it, Townsend and Graham volunteered to be the proof, they were the guinea pigs. Whatever they did, it worked. It's no wonder Townsend and Graham were smiling in the photograph. They weren't going to die."

"Well, Townsend isn't smiling today," McPhearson said. There was a long sigh from Madrid. "He *will* die, and soon, unless he has the proper surgery."

Moravec had forgotten about David Townsend. There wasn't any chance now that transplantation might be

84

avoided. David Townsend *had* to die. There wasn't any other way.

McPhearson's voice was almost gentle. "You realize this makes the donor patient even more important."

"Yes," Moravec said, "I understand that perfectly."

FIFTEEN

WEEKSBRIAR

THE COMPUTER flashed STAN9 BY FOR PROFILE DECLARATI%N in glowing green characters at the top of the monitor screen. Dr. Sara Mills tapped the screen with her finger. She glanced at Dalton Wilkie.

"There," she said. "It's doing it . . . substituting numbers for letters."

Wilkie crunched loudly into an apple. He was sitting at a console next to hers, his feet propped up on the edge of the table. The hematology lab was quiet and empty except for them. It was after midnight, the best time of day to get access to the multi-user computer system without worrying that a lab technician might bump them off-line to run hematocrits. It was also the best time to get the computer systems manager to respond personally to a problem. Dalton Wilkie worked at night, when things were quiet. He didn't like the hustle and bustle of the institute during the day. His two assistants split the day shift, which was all right, but they didn't know computers like Dalton.

"Occasional bit drops." Wilkie talked around a mouthful of apple.

"I *know* that, Dalton," she said. "I want you to fix it. I'm graded on performance in these profile evaluations. If the empirical data is wrong or unreadable—"

"You get a lousy test score," Wilkie said. He nodded as if he knew how important profile evaluations were to third-year residents. "Yeah, that program gets run more than anything else in the system. You residents are wearing it out." He sat up and dropped the apple core into a paper bag. Wilkie was in his late forties. He wore jeans and a heavy plaid shirt, his statement about who he was. Or, rather, who he wasn't. He didn't want to be mistaken for a doctor. He never wore a tie and coat, the unofficial uniform of the medical and research staff at the institute. The doctors were like robots, he told Sara, which was odd coming from a man who had devoted his life to understanding computers. It wasn't that Wilkie disliked doctors. His left arm had been amputated above the elbow when he was thirteen. It was a hunting accident. His shotgun had discharged while he was climbing a fence. Three fingers were blown off. Then there was some problem in the operation—infection, Dalton said—and the surgeon elected to amputate. Dalton hadn't completely trusted a doctor since, but he didn't dislike them. Residents were different. He seemed to tolerate the residents as if they weren't really doctors yet, as if they still had time to change their minds, and he tolerated Sara most of all. She liked to think it was because she took time to try and understand his work.

"Can you fix it?" Sara leaned back in her chair. Wilkie was staring at her legs. He sometimes seemed preoccupied with her sexiness. It was one of the few interests he shared with other staff members. "Dalton?"

He switched his glance to her face. "Hmm?"

"Can you do something about the computer?"

Wilkie's shoulders rose and fell. "Sure I can. Are you positive you want me to?"

"Dalton, why do you think I'm here?"

"You know, I've been wondering about that very thing. Has anyone told you that this is New Year's Eve?"

"It was in the paper, right?"

"A bright and desirable woman like you shouldn't be in a place like this on New Year's Eve." He stole a glance at Sara's legs again. "It's a crime against nature. You should be out with the rest of the residents—partying, drinking, dancing, breeding . . ."

"With qualifications in two weeks?" Sara shook her

head. "I could be in Hawaii this week, but I decided to stay here. I have too much work to do." She smoothed her smock down over her knee. Dalton's roving eyes were like fingers. "Now, the computer?"

Wilkie sighed. "Well, if you must." He sat up and rolled his chair beside hers. "Let me at the terminal, sunshine of my life. Let's take a look at this cantankerous old program of yours."

Wilkie's fingers flew over the keyboard. For a man with only one arm he typed faster then most people with two. Lines of data rippled across the computer screen.

```
CENTRAL COMPUTER
TIME SHARE
HEMATOLOGY FILE
SECTION 047
STATE ACCESS ID:
```

Wilkie glanced at her, his forehead wrinkled. "Let's see, you're VOLVO, right?"

"How do you know my access? That's supposed to be secret."

He smiled. "I'm the computer systems manager, remember? Hell, I know everything." He entered the name and waited for the acknowledgment, then typed RUN "PRO-FILE," MILLS, S. The screen responded immediately.

```
MILLS, S. (HEMA)
ANEMIA ETIOLOGY
SUB: ACUTE HAEMORRHAGE
CP 3061-LC705

%PROFILE—
OVERALL PROFILE SCORE: 896
RELATIVE STANDING: (AMER) 93.43 PERCENTILE
RELATIVE STANDING: (INTL) 97.39 PERCENTILE
END SCORE

ENTER "YES" IF YOU WISH NEXT CASE PROBLEM:
```

Wilkie typed YES and scooted his chair over to allow Sara room to get to the keyboard. "Okay, doctor, let's see you do your stuff."

Sara slid in front of the terminal as the screen cleared itself and began the run.

```
ANEM! A ET!OLOGY (EMPIRICAL DOCIMOL%GY)
SUB: CHRON!C HAEMORRHAGE
CLINICAL PROTOCOL NO. 2943-AB406
PROFILE—
FEMALE PATI%NT, AGE 5L, ADMITTED TO HO$PITAL
BECAUSE OF WEAKNE$S, PALLOR AND ABDOMINAL P¢IN.
INITIAL HAEMOGRAM AS FOLLOWS:
```

HAEMOGLOBIN	6.8 G%	WC COUNT	1L000 MM¹³
PCV	2&%	NEUTROPHILS	4&%
MCHC	28%	LYMPHOCYTES	45%
		MONOCYTES	5%
		EOSINOPHILS	2%
		BASOPHILS	$%

COMMENT, DR. MILLS?

"That's just what I'm talking about," Sara said. "It's throwing in odd characters. Now how am I supposed to interpret data that looks like that?"

Wilkie studied the screen. "Uh-huh." He rubbed his chin. "Ever get an error message from the system?"

"No."

"Hmm."

"Can you fix it?"

"It's an inconsistent drop."

"Dalton, it's a pain in the ass is what it is. I can't trust statistics that look like that. How am I supposed to know how old this woman is—five or fifty-something?"

"Fifty-one, probably," he said. "L's often get substituted for ones." He gestured toward the terminal. "Go ahead . . . let's see what else happens."

"I don't want to take a chance, Dalton. If I abort now I can skip this case. I don't want to get graded on a case with screwy data. Anyway, I'd rather wait until you get it fixed."

89

"Don't worry about it. If you get a lousy score because of bad data I'll erase the score."

"Can you do that?"

Wilkie gave her an I'm-the-systems-manager-look.

Sara sighed. "Okay, but if we get screwy data—"

"Try it, let's see what happens."

Sara called for an additional display of prothrombin time, sedimentation rate, reticulocyte count and blood smear result. The screen hesitated as it digested the request, then replied with:

```
PRO TIME  =  12        (NORMAL  =  1@)
SED RATE  =   2)       (NOR + AL  $ 9)
COUNTS RETIC  =  6%    (#ORM¢l  =  1 ± 0.50%
WRIGHT STAIN SMEAR:
INDICATE$ SEVER#L IMMÁTU6E ERYTHROCYTE FORMS

COMMENT, DR. MILL4?
```

"Not getting any better," Sara said.

"Yeah, but there's the challenge. Go ahead. Let's see how *you* work with a handicap." Wilkie flashed his exuberant grin. "What's wrong with this old woman, anyway?"

"A typical chronic hemorrhage case," Sara said, "except for the abdominal pain. The patient is gradually losing blood internally, which accounts for her anemia. Her red blood cells are hypochromic and microcytic; they show anisocytosis and poikilcytosis. There's a slight lymphocytosis, but the platelets are normal in number and appearance. The prothrombin time shows that her blood clots normally, the sedimentation rate is high, which means somewhere in her system tissues are dying. The smear confirms that—immature red cells in the blood indicated the body is struggling to replace lost blood and is sending young cells into circulation. The symptoms suggested a nutritional iron deficiency, but that doesn't explain the stomach pain."

The lines in Wilkie's face formed a frown. "It's my ex-wife I think."

Sara entered a request for the patient's medical history. It was sketchy, but there was no history of hemorrhage. She ordered a stool test for occult blood. The computer acknowledged the command and replied that the test was negative. It then waited for some diagnosis from Sara. She considered the data, then typed into the display, "Suggest gastrointestinal tract abnormality. What is result of radiology examination?"

The screen flashed quickly to:

```
RADIOLOGY XM RESULT = NO ABNORMALITY.
LABORATORY VALUES WITHIN NORMAL LIMITS
COMMENT, DR. MILLS?
```

"Normal, hell," Sara shot back. "Look at the lymphocytes!" She glanced at Wilkie. He shrugged. Sara drummed her fingers on the console. "A fifty-one-year-old woman is past her child-bearing years, so it isn't a menstruational problem and her anemia is not aggravated by iron deficiency." She let out a long breath. "Your computer's playing games with me, Dalton. I told you it was screwed up."

"It's easy to blame a machine."

"Dalton, I—" Sara stopped herself. Now she was angry. He was right. She pushed her chair nearer the terminal. All right, she thought, what's the matter with the woman? Forget about the data drops. Think. She reviewed the data again, but there wasn't a simple answer. Finally she decided on a laparotomy. Exploratory surgery was a last resort, but she didn't see any other choice. She typed "Suggest laparotomy," and prayed there was something there to justify it. The computer responded with:

```
LAPAROTOMY IS A SURGICAL PROCEDURE.
DO YOU WISH TO PROCEED? -Y/N-
```

Now I've done it, Sara thought. It was a trap. All of these profiles were meant to test clinical knowledge and judgment but they were also full of little things to trip you up. But she didn't know what she'd done wrong. It was the damned dropouts. She cursed herself, the computer, the program and Dalton. There wasn't anything else to do now. She typed YES at the terminal and held her breath. The screen went blank and after thirty seconds returned to life.

LAPAROTOMY RESULT = DISCOVERY OF ADVANCED CARCINOMA OF THE CAECUM. CONCLUSION: ANEMIA DUE TO CHRONIC HAEMORRHAGE OF FOREMENTIONED CONDITION. THE LAPAROTOMY JUDGMENT WAS CORRECT. THIS CASE ILLUSTRATES HOW LABORATORY TESTS CAN, ON SPECIFIC OCCASIONS, BE MISLEADING. THE ANEMIA IN THIS PATIENT WAS TREATED BY BLOOD TRANSFUSION BEFORE, DURING AND AFTER THE OPERATION. (NOTE: THE APPARENT DATA ANOMALIES IN THIS CASE WERE INTENTIONALLY PROGRAMMED TO EVALUATE YOUR HANDLING OF SUSPECT INFORMATION. RESIDENTS WHO DID NOT ABORT THIS CASE ARE TO BE CONGRATULATED FOR THEIR PERSEVERANCE.)
END PROFILE
STANDBY FOR SCORE

Sara let out an angry yelp. She looked blackly at Wilkie, who couldn't keep the grin off his face. "You knew! You knew there wasn't anything wrong with the program. Occasional drops . . . damn!"

"Well, maybe."

"Now I look like an idiot, calling you in."

"You look just fine to me, doc. Anyway, you did good, right? You went ahead."

"*You* told me to."

Wilkie nodded at the terminal. "Score's coming up."

It was going to be a good score, Sara realized. She'd done very well and she knew it. She didn't know the woman had cancer of the large intestine, but it wasn't her job to know that. What mattered was that she'd done the right thing. Surgery *was* the right procedure. When the score came up on the screen it was so good it shocked her.

SCORE: 998
RELATIVE STANDING: (AMER) 97.96 PERCENTILE
RELATIVE STANDING: (INTL) 99.92 PERCENTILE

At first she thought it might have been a mistake. She knew she'd done well, but a 998? When the score verification came back the numbers seemed to glow on the screen.

998.

No mistake. She'd never scored that high before. Sure, a couple of 990s, but this—

"You did good?" Wilkie was looking at the terminal.

"I did damned good," Sara said. "And you know it." She copied down the scores and typed in the sign-off code that told the computer she was finished. "I did so well I'm willing to show my gratitude. How about some coffee in the lounge before I head home? My treat."

"Is this my lucky night?" He raised his eyebrows. "How'd you like to show your gratitude down in CC, instead? A little Muzak, a little privacy, maybe a little snort of Jim Beam?"

"Locked inside Computer Control with you—the notorious One-Armed Groper?" Sara smiled her big warm smile. "I'm not that grateful . . . and you ain't that lucky."

SIXTEEN

WEEKSBRIAR

DAVID CAME awake, trying to focus his eyes in the darkness. He didn't know how long he'd been asleep. His pajama shirt was now dry, and the throbbing in his head was gone. He slid off the bed carefully.

He put on the slippers from the closet and tested the door. Still locked. He paced back and forth in the small room, occasionally stopping at the window to stare at the snow. He had no idea where he was. Once he'd accepted that—and that whoever put him here had gone to a lot of trouble—his fear became aimless. But *why* were they doing this to *him*? The more he paced the more his fear turned to anger.

When he pressed the nurse's call button David didn't know what to expect. Just play it as it comes, he thought, and make a break when it looks right. He knew it wasn't a brilliant plan, just simple. Anyway, this wasn't the Normandy invasion. All he had to go past was a scrawny old nurse.

David heard a jangle of keys before the door opened. A man in white looked in.

"You okay?" He pushed the door wider and took a step into the room. Light from the hall silhouetted his figure against the dark; his shadow fell across David's legs. "You ring for a nurse?"

David lay still on the bed.

"You awake?" The man looked back into the hall. "You sure it was eighteen? This one's asleep."

Come and check for yourself, David thought, but the man

stepped back and the door shut. In the darkness he heard the bolt click.

For several minutes David lay there. He hadn't figured on a male nurse. He wondered if he should ring again. What if the guy was too big to handle? What if nobody came? He had to try again. It didn't matter who came, as long as someone did. He wasn't getting out of here until the door was opened. David was reaching for the button when he heard the keys jangling outside his door again. The bed squeaked as he turned quickly onto his back.

Two silhouettes moved through the light from the hall. One of them was the male nurse. The other was a woman, carrying a hypodermic needle. David closed his eyes almost shut and the figures became shadowy enemies.

"He's awake," the man said. "I heard the bed."

The woman stepped closer. "I don't see how he could be. The sedative should have put him out for hours."

"He's moved." The man was beside the bed. "He's pulled back the sheet."

"Restless sleeper," the nurse said. She turned toward the light and held the syringe up. "This'll keep him quiet until they're ready to transfer him." A squirt of liquid arched out of the needle. David saw her face then, sideways in the light. It was Becky Smith.

David sprang. He propelled himself up on his elbows, swinging his legs around, bending his knees, kicking out with all his strength at the nearest shadow in the darkness.

He hit the attendant in the chest with both feet and felt the plastic name tag shatter under his heel. The impact slammed the man backward into the wall and David heard the loud crack as the attendant's head banged hard against it, then he slid to the floor. The nurse swung back around, still holding the syringe in the air, but David was on her before she could cry out, wrenching the needle out of her grasp, twisting her back against his chest. He clamped his hand over her mouth. Into her ear he whispered, "How's the family?"

Her eyes went wide when she saw his face. David slipped his forearm under her chin.

"David—I—what are you doing?"

"I'm not falling for any more of your Tiny's sister bull. Where am I?"

"Parkla—"

David tightened his arm around her neck. "I have an interesting view from my window here, only Dallas seems to be missing from it. When did they move Parkland Hospital into the mountains?" He relaxed his grip on her neck. "I'll give you one more try. Where am I?"

"Please . . . I'm . . . choking . . ."

"Answer me or—" He tightened his arm.

"Weeks . . . briar . . ." She could barely squeeze it out.

"What is it?"

"Private . . . hospit . . . al . . ."

The attendant groaned. David swiveled the nurse around to see him. The man was on his side, air wheezing in and out of his mouth. He made an O with his lips and passed out, rolling on his face. David held the syringe in front of the nurse's face.

"What is this stuff?"

"Thorazine," she said in a single breath.

"What's it for?"

She didn't answer.

David's arm tightened. "What's it for?"

"S-sleep . . ."

"You're sure that's all?"

She nodded.

"Good." He punched the needle into her shoulder, through the fabric of her uniform, and pushed the plunger all the way. She screamed into his hand. He withdrew the needle and tossed it on the bed. Becky Smith struggled, but after a few seconds her eyes rolled up and she sagged in David's arms. He laid her on the floor beside the attendant and patted her cheek.

"Hey?"

She didn't respond.

He slapped her a little harder. "Hey?"

David shook his head. "Fast stuff."

It took him a couple of minutes to get the attendant's jacket and pants off. It wasn't the best fit; the attendant was much bigger than he looked, but hospital whites were hospital whites. Nobody would notice another attendant in a hospital. He cinched the belt as tight as it would go. There were three keys on a ring in the right pocket of the jacket. David had to open the door to read the tags—RMS, UTIL and ICP.

He stepped into the hall. It took a moment for his eyes to adjust to the lights. His room was near the end of a long corridor that intersected with another. He locked it and moved to the corner. The sign on the wall had arrows pointing in opposite directions. PSYC 201–220 was to the left, PSYC 221–240 to the right. He moved again when he heard someone in the corridor behind him. An attendant and a nurse stepped out of a room a few doors away. The nurse was carrying a small tray with a syringe. Everybody was getting a little thorazine tonight. David walked quickly to another corridor and peered around the corner.

There were three nurses inside a glass-enclosed nurse's station, twenty feet away. Across from the nurse's station a uniformed security guard was leaning against a large gate, reading a magazine. The gate was barred, and closed.

David now knew what PSYC meant. Psyc for Psychiatric. He'd been locked in a psycho ward.

The door to the nurse's station opened and a nurse stepped out with a tray. She started walking in David's direction.

David moved. He had to find a place to hide until he could figure out what to do next. He walked fast, away from the nurse's footsteps, his fit-all hospital slippers whispering on the tile floor. He hurried into another corridor but the footsteps followed him. He passed a door marked ICP, remembered the key, and opened it. The nurse turned the corner just as he eased the door closed. He heard her footsteps pass him without pausing and recede down the corridor. He breathed again.

The room was completely dark. Somewhere near was the slow, steady rhythm of machines in harmony. David wondered if he'd stumbled into a hospital laundromat. He felt along the tile wall until he came upon a bank of knobs. Dimmer switches. He turned the first one until it clicked.

The curved surface of twenty bubble-topped capsules glowed at once. They were aligned in two rows of ten along opposite walls. Inside each capsule was a person.

David moved to the nearest capsule. It was about eight feet long and made of stainless steel. Below the bubble the frame was built to accommodate monitoring equipment in modular slots. The only machine David recognized was the EKG, but it didn't seem to be working. The whole contraption was on casters with a power cord leading to an outlet in the wall. David touched the bubble. It was cold. The man inside lay under a sheet with his arms at his sides. Wires were taped to either side of his neck and disappeared beneath the sheet. His wrinkled face was white. The only sound in the room was the pumping rhythm of the machines.

A card in a plastic sleeve identified the man inside the bubble.

ST. PE, Gregory Euromed #H-034093
DOB 04/02/51 Miami, FL (transient)
Arteriosclerotic kidney
Failed: Nov 18
Attending: J. Ellis

Failed? David squinted at the man's face. He noticed his chest. He wasn't breathing. David jerked his hand away from the bubble. Gregory St. Pe from Miami, Florida, was dead as hell.

Then David realized that he had been in one of these

things. It was exactly like the coffin in his nightmare. But this wasn't any hallucination. This was a real place and a real capsule and a real person inside it. And he was dead.

He moved to another capsule. And another. And inside all of them they were dead. They were from different places and they were old and they had died in the last two months. What kind of hospital stores dead people in glass coffins for two months? What in God's name was Weeksbriar?

He remembered what the nurse had said as she tested the hypodermic needle in his room. *"This'll keep him quiet until they're ready to transfer him."*

Transfer? Transfer where? David felt the hairs on his neck stand out. He moved quickly to the door. He'd been mostly angry for the past several hours. Now he was frightened. These doctors had brought him here for something.

He cracked the door, stopped, then let it close again. Something else was wrong here. He went back to Gregory St. Pe's capsule. He must have misread the card, he thought. He read it again.

DOB 04/02/51.

That couldn't be right. This guy was fifty-five, sixty. The card put him in his early thirties. He checked the other cards. All the dates of birth were mismatched. They had to be.

David switched off the dimmer knob and went to the door. I'm getting out of this damned place. It's full of live nuts and dead freaks.

He stepped into the bright hall and closed the door carefully. All he had to do was walk straight to the guard at the gate. He could say he had to go to the bathroom. He could say he felt sick. He could say anything, just as long as he got out. He wished he were playing poker. He was a great bluffer when he played—

"Checked two-thirty-eight yet?"

David swung around, startled. A nurse was standing behind him, frowning at a clipboard.

"Ah . . ." He glanced around. He didn't see anyone else. "Not yet."

"Better get going." She looked up. "You guys act like you get paid by the mile." Her eyes went back to the clipboard. "Hurry up."

David nodded. He started off toward the nearest corridor.

"Two-thirty-eight is this way," he heard her say.

When he turned around she was studying his face. "You new?"

"Yeah." He tried not to sweat.

"Where's your name tag?"

David shrugged. "I didn't get one yet."

She shook her head, sighing. "Try to get finished before break, will you? My feet are killing me."

David walked quickly away, jangling his keys, trying not to look nervous as he searched for room 238. Thank God she hadn't looked him over more carefully. He suddenly realized that he was wearing hospital slippers.

Number 238 was a corner room. The corridor next to it led to the security gate. David unlocked the door as a nurse passed behind him. He nodded at her without speaking, then slipped into the darkened room. It was as good a place to hide as any. He held the door open, watching the hall through a crack. When it was clear he'd make his move for the gate.

A light came on behind him. David wheeled around.

It was a room with four beds. One was empty. The occupant in the nearest bed had switched on his nightlight. He was an old man.

"Whassa matter?"

David shook his head. "Nothing." He glanced back through the opened door. The hall was empty.

"What're you doin'?"

"Just checking the room. Go back to sleep."

"The room's over here, young fella."

Another light came on.

David let the door close. When he turned around another old man was sitting up in bed.

The first old man had his glasses on now. "You doctor or attendant?"

"I'm . . . a doctor," David said. "Now turn off the lights and go back to sleep or I'll call a nurse and have her give you a shot."

Another light came on. Another old man sat up. He rubbed his eyes. "Breakfast?"

David took a few steps into the room. "No breakfast. Sleep time. Turn off your light. Go to sleep."

"I have to go to the bathroom."

"No . . ."

The old man with the glasses was squinting. "I know you."

"No you don't. You want me to call the nurse? I'll make you take a shot if you don't—"

"Townsend!" the old man with the glasses said. His eyes grew big. He motioned for the others to notice. "It's Townsend!"

"What?" The old man who had to go to the bathroom looked up. "Oh, my God!"

"It's Townsend!" someone shouted.

"Quiet down." David moved backwards toward the door. How did they know—

The old man with the glasses got out of bed. "You're the son of a bitch who put me here. Dr. Townsend." He looked at the others. "*Look* at him!"

They were fruitcakes, David thought. Three crazy old loons. But they recognized something. There was only one way they could have made that kind of mistake. It had happened to him all of his life. They were talking about Stuart.

"Look, you guys don't know—" David took another step back, reaching behind for the door handle.

"Get him!"

David turned with the key ready but for old men they

101

moved fast. They were on him, kicking, screaming, biting. David shoved the key into the lock. He got it open, but the momentum of bodies against the back slammed it shut again.

David backhanded one of them and knocked him down. "You crazy old bastards!" He punched another. "Get away from me!" He got the door open again, elbowing the old man with glasses in the chin.

He fell into the corridor, one man hanging onto his leg. David kicked him. "Get off me!" A nurse and an attendant appeared suddenly from around the corner. "Get them off me!" David yelled. Another old man staggered out of the room and attacked him with his fists. "Help me!"

Nurses and attendants came running from every direction. A claxon went off. The old men were screaming hysterically. Nurses shouted instructions to attendants. Somewhere a speaker was warning, "Inmates in the corridor. Inmates in the corridor."

David got shakily to his knees. Those old men hit hard. Someone helped him to his feet. It was a nurse, the same chicken-necked woman who'd told him to take his pills. She glanced at his face. David saw recognition cross her eyes. "You're not—" She spun toward one of the attendants. David didn't wait to hear what she had to say. He pushed his hand into her face, shoving her down. Then he ran.

He came around the corner like a train, running full out, and slammed into another nurse rushing toward the melee. They both went sprawling. He looked up to see the guard, thirty feet away. He was closing the gate.

"Wait!" David yelled. He got one leg under him, supporting himself against the wall. He saw the chicken-necked nurse come around the corner. She yelled above the claxon, the racket of voices. "Homer! That's a patient! Lock the gate!"

The guard was momentarily confused. He pushed open the gate to stand in the hall, cupping his hand to his ear. But

David was on his feet again, bolting for the gate. He'd lost his slippers and his bare feet slapped the tile floor as he raced toward the guard. The only way out was through that gate, David realized.

"Homer! Close the gate!" Now everyone was yelling. *"Close the gate!"*

Homer finally got the message. He started to swing the iron gate closed, groping for a key at the end of a leather leash attached to his belt.

David could hear them pounding after him. If he didn't get out now, then it was back into the crazy house.

"Hurry, Homer! Lock it. Don't let him out! *Hurry!*"

The gate closed.

Homer worked frantically to fit the key into the lock. His hat slipped off his head. He kept looking up at David, then back to the lock.

David hit the gate on a dead run, his arm crashing between the bars and connecting solidly with Homer's chin. The blow knocked the guard backward, arms windmilling, and sent him sprawling to the floor, his head falling against the tile.

David slammed the gate and twisted the key just as the first attendant arrived on the other side, reaching frantically through the bars. David backed away.

The attendant's face was red with exertion. "Open the gate!"

"What *is* this place?" David yelled above the claxon. "Where am I?"

"You're in big fucking trouble if you don't open this gate!"

David dropped the key into a laundry bin. "You gotta be nuts."

He found the stairway, but when he started down he heard excited voices and the trample of feet. Better not try to bluff any more guards. He turned around and went up.

The third floor corridor was emtpy. The doors were

marked with names of doctors and they were all locked. David ran to the next corridor and took a left. He didn't know where he was but it didn't matter. Just keep going. He found another corridor and followed it until he reached an unlocked office. He slipped inside and bolted the door behind him. When he had his breath back he switched on the light.

It wasn't a large office. There was a desk, a row of file cabinets, a couple of potted plants and a divan. David went to the window. It was still snowing. A lamp post about twenty yards away illuminated a walk. Beyond that, only trees; not a building or streets; just emptiness. If he could just get to a phone . . .

He opened the window and peered out. Below a snow drift piled against the building, but he couldn't tell how deep it was. He was *not* going to jump from a third-story window into a snowbank that could be only eight inches deep.

David closed the window and sat at the desk. The telephone had five buttons, marked with numbers 317 through 321. When he picked it up the 318 button glowed. David listened to the tone, then dialed. On the fourth digit the line broke.

"Switchboard."

David cursed to himself.

"Hello? This is the switchboard. Can I help you?"

"I, ah . . . I wanted an outside line."

"All outside calls are run through the switchboard. What number would you like, please?"

"Can't I make a call direct?"

"All outside calls are run through the switchboard," repeated the voice. "Do you want to make a call or not?"

"No . . . I . . ." David took a deep breath. "What hospital is this, operator?"

"What?"

It was a stupid thing to ask, but his head was aching again. "What's the name of this hospital?"

"Who is this, please?"

"Look, operator. It's very important that—"

"Which office are you calling from, please?"

David tried to remember the name on the door. "Whitehall," he said.

"Whitehurst?"

"That's it." He closed his eyes, rubbed at his temple.

"Visitors are not permitted on the third floor. Is Dr. Whitehurst there, please?"

"He's—Look, oh never mind."

"You're in Dr. Whitehurst's office?" The voice became alert. "Hello? Who is this, please?"

David slammed the phone back in its cradle. Now he'd done it. The operator would call the guards and the place would be swarming with them in half a minute. If he could find another office, another floor . . .

He searched the desk. There had to be a hospital directory, a fire escape plan, a diagram that would show him where he was. Nothing. When the telephone rang, David knew it was time to move. He'd have to find his own way. He started for the door when he heard running footsteps.

It was going to be the window after all. David raised the sash as the commotion stopped at his door. He stuck his feet out the opening and ducked his head into the cold. It looked a long way down.

When he heard the key in the lock he closed his eyes and pushed himself off. He seemed to fall forever, as in his dream. He felt the wind whip his face. He was afraid to open his eyes.

He hit the snow on his hands and knees, sinking into a large drift. He rolled on his side, staggered to his feet and started running even before he knew he hadn't broken anything. He made it to the trees before he had to stop to catch his breath. The cold air stung the tender skin of his face where the beard had been. He rested against a pine and looked back. Someone was at the window with a flashlight.

He moved clumsily through the snow, bumping into

branches in the dark, but keeping the hospital in sight. He should stay near the trees. They gave him cover and held the wind off him. He had to find out where he was. Somewhere he'd find a sign. The terrain of rolling hills and pine tree stands reminded him of the foothills of the Colorado Rockies. But it was too dark to make any valid judgment. Maybe he was in New Mexico, somewhere around the Sangre De Cristo range. Wherever he was, it was freezing. His bare feet were already numb, but he kept going, using his forearms like shields to keep the branches from slapping his face. Somehow he'd find a way out of this nightmare.

SEVENTEEN

WEEKSBRIAR

SARA'S BEEPER went off first. She and Wilkie were alone in the staff lounge, a tiled, windowless room with fluorescent lighting and plastic chairs and tables. An entire wall was filled with food and drink machines. The beeper went off with a tiny resonance. Sara glanced at her watch. It was nearly 1 A.M.

"That's strange." She frowned. "Who's around to call at this time of night?"

"It's the Euromedic board of governors," Wilkie said with a wry smile. He was eating a Twinkie and wiped a bit of filling from the corners of his mouth. "They want to congratulate you on your profile performance tonight. Nobody's ever finished that case before."

Sara rose and headed for the house phone. "Doesn't anybody think residents ever sleep?"

"Sleep?" Wilkie gave her a weary look. "Robots don't sleep."

She picked up the wall phone receiver and dialed the switchboard. "Hello, this is Dr. Mills. Do you have a message for me?" She turned when Wilkie's beeper sounded.

"Just a moment, Dr. Mills," said the operator. Then another voice. "Dr. Mills?"

"Yes?"

"This is Davis from security, doctor. We sent a man to your lab but no one was there. Are you in the institute?"

"Yes, I'm in the lounge. What's wrong?"

"We're checking on all staff members who haven't checked out of the institute. Are you all right?"

Sara glanced at Wilkie. "Am I all right? Of course I'm all right. What—"

"There's been an escape from the psychiatric ward, doctor. One of the patients. About twenty minutes ago. Are you alone?"

"No. Dalton Wilkie is here. What do you mean a patient escaped? How could a patient escape?"

Wilkie perked up. He finished the last of his Twinkie in one large bite and held his stare on Sara.

"He's somewhere on the grounds. We're contacting everyone who hasn't checked out of the institute. Are you planning to return to the hematology lab, doctor?"

Sara shook her head. "No, I'm going home in about five minutes."

One of the double doors to the lounge swung open behind her. Sara jumped. It was a security guard.

"Don't worry, Dr. Mills. My men are searching the entire facility. We'll find him. But just as a precaution I'll have a guard walk you to your car."

"One of your men just walked in," Sara said into the phone.

"Good. You'll advise Mr. Wilkie of the situation? We'd like him to return to the computer center at which time he should check back with us. It's SOP in an event of this nature."

Event? Security people talked as if everything were a military operation. "Yes," Sara said, "I'll advise him, forthwith."

"Very good."

"Is he dangerous?"

"Ma'am?"

"The patient you're looking for . . . is he violent or, you know—"

"He escaped from psychiatric," the security man said flatly. "He attacked an attendant, threatened a nurse and

108

beat up the ward guard. I'd say that qualifies him as definitely unfriendly."

Sara nodded. "Yes, thank you, Mr. Davis." She replaced the receiver and glanced at the guard. He seemed to be waiting for someone to tell him to do something. Talk about robots . . .

"So, one of the nuts got loose?" Wilkie said happily. "We're having all kinds of firsts tonight."

"They want you to go back to CC and call in," Sara said. "It's SOP, you know."

"Hell, I never have any fun." He cocked his head at her. "You know, it's safe inside CC . . . no crazy people running around. You want to go down with me?"

"You want to rephrase that, Dalton?"

"Hmm, oh—" He grinned. "Now that you mention it . . ."

Sara took her coat from the back of her chair. "I think I'll take my chances somewhere else." She nodded at the guard. "Anyway, this gentleman gets paid to watch over the staff. Isn't that right?"

The guard didn't even nod. "Yes, ma'am," he said. But he didn't smile.

David crouched in a stand of pine trees protected from the biting wind and watched the guard return to the lobby. Through the glass entryway he saw the guard take off his gloves and blow on his hands, then pull a cigarette from inside his jacket and light it. It was such an everyday occurrence that David wouldn't have given it a thought if he weren't freezing to death.

His feet were numb and probably turning blue. Any minute he expected his ears to fall off; at least he could try to save his fingers by huddling on his knees against a tree, his hands knotted and thrust under his armpits. He tried desperately not to think about the cold. But if he didn't do something very soon, he'd have to give up. Running away from a locked hospital room was one thing, but committing suicide was something else.

He had run as far as he could go, but he hadn't expected the fence. It was a ten-foot chain-link fence and it surrounded the hospital. David had followed it until it led to a gate manned by a pair of security guards who were obviously on the lookout for him. He wouldn't get past them as easily as he'd gotten past Homer. And he couldn't climb the fence. Not in this cold. And it was strung with barbed wire at the top. Even if he could get his numbed fingers to work he'd never get through the wires. This hospital was as fortified as an army base.

So he came back. He followed the road back to the hospital, to the parking lot. He had to find a car with keys in the ignition, steal it, crash through the gate and get to a phone where he could call for help. And a car would be warm . . .

The parking lot was lit up and nearly empty of cars. Anyone walking out there would be easy to spot, even in this snow. When he saw the guard he figured he was searching for him, checking cars. David had almost decided to take his chances on the fence when he saw the plume of a car exhaust.

It was a gray or white Volvo. Whoever was in it had been escorted by the guard and was letting the engine rev, probably with the heater on. David instinctively knew what he was going to do. He needed shelter and warmth now more than he needed to know where he was or why he was here or even who brought him. He needed to sit in a warm spot and unbend his fingers and try to make his toes wiggle. The rest he'd figure out later.

David stood up, supporting himself against the tree. One way or another, he was going to get into that car. He turned toward the road and felt a stinging wind in his face. The throbbing in his brain blurred his vision and he almost fell down. He took an unsteady step forward, trying to concentrate on the Volvo. Branches caught his clothes but he bulled past them, instinct powering him on. He plodded from drift to drift, dodging trees when he could see them. His eyes watered badly. His life was on the line. Survive. Get inside that car.

The wipers and defroster made slush of the hard-crusted snow that covered her windshield. She should have asked the guard to scrape off the windows, Sara thought, especially the back one, but after he made sure her engine started he nodded a good-bye and disappeared. She smoked a cigarette, waiting for the heater to warm up. Her mind drifted home. It was going to be cold in the house. She had set the thermostat at sixty when she left his morning. Not that it mattered. She was going straight to bed. It had been a long day and she was exhausted. Tomorrow she'd sleep until noon, read the paper in bed and loaf.

The wipers beat a rhythm that almost put her to sleep. She sat up straight behind the wheel and exercised her eyes. Go home, she told herself. Drive, then sleep.

The glaze of frozen sleet that coated the rear and side windows showed no sign of melting. The hell with it, she thought. She was not about to go out in that freezing wind to scrape windows. Anyway, she only had to see what was directly in front of her. There wouldn't be any traffic at this time of night and she didn't have far to drive. She yawned, switched on the headlights and put the Volvo into gear. Home, bed and sleep. Get the car into the garage, set the coffee pot timer, climb out of these clothes, head directly for the bedroom and just collapse into—

A man was standing in the middle of the road.

She was only half concentrating on driving when he appeared from nowhere, a motionless figure outlined against the swirling snow like a deer caught in the beam of headlights. He was staring at the approaching car, his arms hanging at his sides.

Sara spun the steering wheel to avoid him and the man

disappeared from her line of sight as the car slid sideways, fishtailing across the road and grinding to a stop in a bank of plowed snow. She cracked her head against the steering wheel and it took a few seconds to get her wits back. Snow whipped across the windshield as she had a sudden image of a man sprawled in the road with tire marks across his chest. Something bumped against the car, a figure moved outside and all at once she was angry. What the hell was someone doing out in the middle of the road?

A blurred face appeared at the passenger window. She couldn't make it out through the prism of ice and glass. The man's fingers slipped on the door handle, trying to get a grip. When the door swung open, Sara prepared to thank him for scaring her half to death. Then she remembered the alarm. The escaped psychiatric patient.

Sara scrambled for the door handle, fighting the restraint of the seat belt in her panic.

"Don't," said a heavy voice behind her. "Just . . . don't." She felt the weight of someone getting in beside her. The door slammed shut.

She turned slowly to face him. Snow clung to his eyebrows in clumps. His face was almost white. For several seconds he didn't move. He looked frozen.

"S-start . . . the car . . ."

"Please, I—"

"Start it!" His eyes were blue, alert. His lips barely moved when he spoke. "I'm too cold to drive . . . too angry to argue."

"Please, can't—"

"I'll hurt you if you don't."

Sara fumbled with the ignition key. The car moved back onto the road. She was too frightened to look him in the face. He wasn't wearing shoes, she noticed. She recognized his jacket by the faded Euromedic logo on the pocket. Hospital whites. She remembered Davis had said he'd attacked an attendant. The cotton jacket was actually frozen down the front. It looked stiff as cardboard.

112

"Wh—where do you want to go?"

He nodded at the road. The look in his eyes was deadly. "Out."

Sara put the car into gear.

EIGHTEEN

WEEKSBRIAR

THE VOLVO died twice before she got it to move. David was too cold to realize how frightened she was. The car jerked backward, slowly gaining purchase on the paved surface of the road, then spun its wheels wildly, suddenly accelerating, and died in the middle of the pavement. Desperately she turned the ignition key.

"Take it easy," David said.

"I'm sorry." She took a quick nervous breath, then blinked rapidly, as she continued to grind the ignition until the engine caught. She whipped the shift lever into low gear. She didn't look at him.

He put his hand over hers before she could straighten the wheels and she stiffened, closing her eyes. He was dizzy and in pain from the sudden change in temperature. He couldn't see the woman very clearly. He didn't even remember walking out of the trees to the road, only that he was there and the car slid off the side in front of him. His knees and elbows ached, and he felt a burning sensation in his fingers and toes. He knew that too sudden a thawing invited frostbite. But he was easily more composed than this frightened woman. Finding shelter, warmth, wouldn't do him much good if she smashed the car because she was scared to death.

"I said take it easy." David tried to take the hard edge off his voice. "I'm not going to hurt you. I just want to get out of here." He didn't smile because he knew his lips would crack.

She wet her lips. "You're the one who—"

"Yeah." He nodded at the dashboard. "Where's the heater knob?" He felt her fingers tighten on the wheel.

"Down there." She picked it out with her eyes.

David released her hand and turned it off. The sooner he could normalize his body temperature the sooner the pain would go away which meant gradually. When he could feel cold again he'd turn the heater back on.

"Why don't you take the car and let me go?" She was looking at him directly now, but her voice trembled.

David cupped his fingers together and blew into them. "No." He nodded at the road ahead. "Can you drive now without having a wreck?"

"Where do you want to go?"

"I'll tell you when to stop." He motioned for her to proceed. "Go."

The hospital exit was a chain-link gate across a two-lane road, electrically operated by a security guard from a building heated by a wood-burning stove. Smoke came from a galvanized metal chimney on the leeward side of the roof. Double-sash windows facing departing traffic were fogged over though a figure was visible inside. The gate was closed.

"Will a guard open the gate automatically?" David asked as they approached.

"I . . . I don't know." She cast a frightened glance at him. "It's always open when I leave. I've never seen—"

"Slow down."

She pushed on the brake and the car fishtailed slightly. "I'm sorry, I didn't mean . . ."

"Do you have to show them a pass or something?" David kept his eyes on the window of the security shack. The car was less than forty feet from the gate. He saw the guard wave. The headlights should keep the guard from seeing inside the car, David thought.

"No, no pass," she said. "Not to leave. Only to get in."

The door of the shack opened and a uniformed guard poked his head out. He was smiling and stepped out under a low porch. The guard raised his hand in a friendly gesture, apparently recognizing the car. At the same time the gate began to open.

David slid back in the corner of the seat against the door. The passenger window was frosted and opaque. Even if the guard saw him, he wouldn't recognize more than a blurred shape. He looked across the seat. "Don't stop."

She swallowed, crouched over the wheel, eyes intent on the road. "But what if—"

The car slipped past the gate and David watched through broken lines of glazed ice on the rear window as the guard waved after them. The gate closed. David let out a sigh and turned back. Cold drops of melted snow rolled down his neck.

"Where do you want to go?" She shifted into third gear but didn't look at him.

David realized that he didn't know. His only thought had been to get warm and get out. The rest he hadn't considered. He pulled a leg up on the seat and began massaging his toes. Ahead was an intersection and a blinking amber light. "Turn right."

She slowed to a stop. The headlights shone through the falling snow like beacons from a lighthouse. The Volvo was the only car on the road. She turned right.

"Where am I?" David said.

She cast a quick glance at him. "What?"

He nodded over his shoulder. "What hospital was that?" Feeling was returning to his toes in pinprick sensations. It was a good sign. They weren't frostbitten.

"Weeksbriar isn't a hospital."

He remembered the nurse had used that name. "I never heard of Weeksbriar."

"Weeksbriar Medical Research Institute." She licked her lips.

"*Where* is it?"

She took her eyes off the road long enough to glance at him again. "Don't you know where you are?"

"They tried to tell me I was in Parkland Memorial Hospital. They must think I'm nuts." He went to work on his other foot. "Concussion or not, I sure as hell know what Dallas looks like, and this sure as hell isn't."

"Dallas?" She looked at him. "Concussion?"

"Watch the road."

"You think you're in . . . Dallas?"

"No, I told you—"

"What happened to your head?"

"It was in the orange juice," David said. He blew into his hand and vigorously rubbed his toes. "She put something in the orange juice. Had to be her. Then I wake up in a hospital room and some doctor pokes a light in my face and tells me I took a bump on the head. Says I'll remember the accident tomorrow. Tells me not to worry, that all I need is a little—hey! Watch where you're going!"

The car had drifted off the road, tires crunched over the gravel shoulder, and she swerved back, fishtailing again. "Slow down!"

"I'm sorry. I . . ."

"Don't look at me—*watch* the road."

"I'm frightened . . ."

"Yeah, well, so am I." He pointed ahead to where the road widened beside a refuse container, a large barrel canted on a metal platform to receive litter from automobiles. "Pull over there."

He saw her blink nervously. She licked her lips. "What are you going to do?"

"Just do what I tell you."

"The car came to a slow stop about ten feet from the barrel, the car beams lighting its white lettering—NEW BROCKTON THANKS YOU FOR NOT LITTERING.

"New Brockton?" David studied the barrel. He looked at Sara. "Where the hell are we?"

"Ah . . ." Her chin trembled. "Lake Drive . . . the county road between—"

"What state?"

"State?" She nodded at the sign. "New York. This is New York state. Where did—"

"New York!"

She flinched against the door, away from him. "Please don't hurt me, I—"

"New York? New York *State*?"

She didn't respond. She clung to the steering wheel as if it were a lifeline.

"How did I get here?" David said it to the snow. He watched the wiper blades make several passes on the windshield before he looked at her again. "Where? Where in New York?"

"Up . . . upstate New York . . . near the lake."

"Lake?"

"Ontario," she said in a whisper. "About eighty miles north of Syracuse."

"Jesus . . ."

"Please, if you'll just let me go . . ."

"A psycho ward," David said suddenly. "That's what it was, wasn't it?" He glared at her with hard intensity. The look on her face was proof. Her eyes were round with fear, her mouth clamped shut. "You think I'm a nut, right?"

She didn't respond.

"Right!"

David's voice boomed inside the small car. He saw her eyes tear up.

"No," she said softly. "No, I . . ."

"What is that place?"

"Weeksbriar Medical Re—"

"Don't give me that. It's a sanitarium, isn't it?"

She blinded again. "We're primarily a medical research facility . . . but the institute also supports a—" she looked away from him "—a psychiatric studies clinic."

"Jesus!"

"Please, let me—"

"I'm *not* a crazy person," David said. He thought how

118

ridiculous that must sound. "Look . . . I drive a truck, okay? I'm from Oklahoma and all I do is drive a truck. This morning I was in Dallas. I woke up a few hours ago and I was here. I'm not supposed to be here." She was looking at him as if that's what all the nuts said. "Look, there's nothing wrong with me."

She stared at him without speaking.

"All right, all right. I know this looks funny, but I'm telling you the truth. My name is David Townsend. Somebody brought me here. I don't know why. Okay?"

She nodded.

"Say something!"

"I . . . yes . . . okay."

"You don't believe me." He shook his head. "Well, I can't blame you for that."

"I'm frightened. I've never . . . been kidnapped."

"Well, neither have I." The car was getting cold. He turned the heater on. "What's your name?"

"Mills. Dr. Sara Mills." Her voice quivered but she was getting a handle on herself.

"Doctor!"

"No, not that kind," she said. "I'm a hematologist. I don't have anything to do with the clinic."

"Hematologist?"

"Blood. I'm a blood specialist. I work on the research side. Weeksbriar is a medical research institute . . . where I work. We don't have anything to do with the psychiatric side." She sniffed. "Really."

A pair of headlights appeared in front of them. David shaded his eyes from the glare, suddenly calculating what he'd do if the driver stopped, but the car didn't stop, it didn't even slow down. When it was gone, he looked at Dr. Sara Mills. "We can't sit here all night."

Sara rubbed her eyes. "Why don't you let me go. You can take the car. I won't tell anyone.

"If I believed that I *would* be nuts."

"No, really—"

119

"Where's your billfold?"

"In my purse." She pushed it across the seat to him. "I don't have much money, maybe thirty dollars, but you can have it. Take it."

David pawed inside it. "I'm not a thief, either, doctor. I'm not going to rob you." He found the billfold and opened it to the driver's license.

"Nine seven oh three Windbrooke." He glanced up at her. "That's where you live?"

"Yes."

"What is it, an apartment or house?"

"House."

"You married?"

"What?"

"Are you married?"

"What difference—"

"Are you married?"

She shook her head.

"No roommates?" The question reminded him suddenly of the movement of Dr. Seagram's pen on her questionnaire. They were similar questions, back when he could remember all the answers.

"Why do you want to know?" Her expression was taking on that frightening look again.

"Does anybody live with you?"

"No."

He nodded. "It says here that you have a driving restriction for eyeglasses." He looked at her. "Why aren't you wearing them?"

"I *am* wearing them . . . contact lenses."

"So you can see all right then?"

"Yes, but—"

"Good." He stuffed the billfold back into the purse. "Let's go there."

"There?"

"To your place."

"Oh no, please . . ."

"I'd go somewhere else if I knew where to go, but I don't. Your house is the safest place I can think of right now."

"But—"

"Drive. I only want to use your telephone. I'll leave you alone after that."

"Who are you going to call?"

He thought about that. He wasn't sure. He had to contact someone real. "Someone who'll believe me. Maybe the Dallas police. I'll have to think about it first."

"I'll drive you to the New Brockton Police Department if you want to talk to the police. If this is a mistake, I'm sure—"

"It's a mistake, all right, you can bet your last nickel on it, but I'm not taking the chance that New York police won't just send me back to that place. I don't know how I got here and I don't have any ID. No cop's going to swallow a screwy story like that from a guy who escaped from a hospital. No, doctor, we'll just go to your place." David wrapped his arms across his chest. He nodded at the road. "Just drive to Windbrooke Street, number nine seven oh three, and everything will be fine. Otherwise I'll be very angry. You don't want an escaped psycho to get very angry."

"Look—"

"Go!"

She put the car into gear. "Drive," she said quietly. "It's Windbrooke Drive." She glanced at David helplessly. "I don't want to get clubbed to death over a technicality."

David smiled. It hurt but he did it anyway. "Hold that thought," he said.

NINETEEN

NEW BROCKTON

DR. JONATHAN ELLIS heard the telephone somewhere in the back of his mind as a chime and it grew louder until he recognized the tone. He rolled groggily on his shoulder. Margaret lay undisturbed on her back—arms at her sides, an ageless symmetrical face, small breasts—the Westport beauty queen of 1949 and God forbid if anyone remembered.

The phone rang again and Margaret stirred.

"Jonathan . . . *plee*-se . . ."

Ellis reached for the receiver on his night table, guided by the blinking extension. The digital clock radio changed to 3:06 A.M.

"Dr. Ellis?"

"Yes."

"This is Nurse Turner, doctor. I'm sorry to wake you."

"Turner?" The name didn't register quickly. Leader of Recovery Team 6, he then remembered. Ellis sat up and blinked at the dark. He and Margaret had been up late attending a benefit her father had sponsored on behalf of the Save the Seals Foundation. He still wasn't sure which goddamn seals they were toasting champagne to save. And Margaret had toasted more than seals. She'd taken a more than passing interest in one of the seal savers, an ecologist with flaming red hair and easily half her age. Ellis was awake now and angry. It hadn't been a good night. "What do you want? Has Moravec landed?"

"Dr. Moravec's plane is due in any time. It's not that. There's a problem here at Weeksbriar."

He waited for more, but the voice was silent. "Well?"

"Townsend's escaped."

Ellis tried to suppress a yawn. "Who?"

"Townsend," said the voice with impatience. "David Townsend. The special transfer case. The Hahnemann donor Moravec is coming to pick up."

Ellis sat up straight in bed, suddenly wide awake. The name finally took meaning. "Townsend?" He glanced at Margaret. Her position hadn't changed. Her nostrils flared slightly, exhaling sleep. "What do you mean he's escaped?" he whispered into the phone. "How—"

"I think you'd better come to the institute, doctor. Right away."

TWENTY

NEW BROCKTON

WINDBROOKE DRIVE was a cul-de-sac that at one time accommodated three handsome Victorian homes with wide, sweeping lawns. But that era had passed.

Two of the houses had been converted to apartment buildings and the wide front lawns were paved over to provide parking spaces. In the side lots between the estates, flat-roofed brick buildings squatted in the spaces like warts—duplexes and quadplexes with car-crowded drive-ways and plastic glass glued to the front steps.

Sara pulled into her driveway and switched off the engine. Her house was at the end of the street, the smallest of the three homes.

She held the steering wheel tightly in her hands. When she spoke she did not look at him directly. "Look, I . . . I've been thinking." Her voice trembled and she swallowed to get control of it again. "Why don't I just get out and you can have the car. I won't call anybody. You can just go . . . anywhere you want. They probably don't even know you're out of the institute." She licked her lips then glanced at him. "Okay?"

"Turn off the headlights," David said.

"Look you really don't—"

He leaned toward her. "Off."

She punched the toggle switch and they were suddenly in darkness.

David took the keys from the ignition. "Inside."

Sara didn't move. "Please, I don't want you to come into

124

my house." Her eyes filled with tears. "You can have the car. Take the money. There are credit cards in the billfold, just—"

"I'm not going to hurt you," David said. "You can believe that. I'm wet and I'm barefoot and I'm half-frozen to death. I need some dry clothes and some time to think." He looked at her a long moment. "I'm *not* going to hurt you."

"No—"

"And I'm not going to argue." He reached across her and unlatched the door. "Move."

She found a pair of jeans that fit him and an old denim shirt. She didn't volunteer whom they belonged to and David didn't care. They were dry and that was all that mattered. She made coffee after he'd had a look around.

The breakfast area looked out on a windowless 1965 Chevrolet supported on wood blocks in the yard. Most of the rooms were empty. Some were filled with makeshift bookcases fashioned from spray-painted boards on spray-painted cement blocks. There were medical books and journals everywhere. Professional magazines were stacked on the floor, on tables and chairs. *Abnormality of Hemoglobin Molecules in Hereditary Hemolytic Anemias: A Clinical Study*, a volume the size of the Oxford dictionary, served as a lamp stand on the breakfast table.

"Never mind, operator, I'll try later." They were in the den. Sara sat stiffly, deep in a chair, her hands around a coffee mug, her eyes on David as he put down the telephone.

"Nobody's home. They're all out drunk on their butts."

"It's New Year's Eve."

David glanced at the radio clock on the bookcase. The digital display showed 3:22. "It's New Year's Day." He toasted his mug to her. With a grim look he said, "Happy New Year, doctor."

Sara stared at her coffee. "What are you going to do now?"

"I don't know."

"You could leave."

"And go where? I don't even know where I am."

"You promised you'd leave," Sara said.

David got to his feet. His headache was coming back. "What did they pick *me* for? That's what I don't get. What does your hospital want with me?"

"It isn't a hospital," she said wearily. "I told you, Weeksbriar is a research institute. We're not a gang of terrorists. We don't kidnap people."

"*Somebody* kidnapped me."

"Why?" She looked at him evenly. "Why would anyone at Weeksbriar want to do that? The psychiatric side has all the patients it can handle. They don't have to run around the country kidnapping people and shipping them up here. Even people from Oklahoma."

"No? Then who are those people in the bubble machines?"

"What people?"

"Gregory St. Pe from Miami for one. He's in that nut ward with about two dozen other people. They're all in these machines . . . and they're all dead."

"I don't know what you're talking about." Sara shook her head. "Anyway, there aren't any dead—"

"I saw it!" David shouted. The outburst sent a bolt of pain through his head. He closed his eyes until the dizziness passed.

"What's the matter?"

"Nothing . . ." He shrugged. "Headache."

"You get headaches?"

"It isn't what you think. They put something in the orange juice." He sat down. "What do you do up there?"

"I told you. I'm a resident in the hematology lab."

"Blood, right?"

"Yes. I study anemic disorders. Hemolysis."

126

David nodded to himself. "Blood." He gave a little laugh. "That's what got me in trouble in the first place. I suppose you never heard of Tiny Smith?"

She just stared at him.

"What's he-mol-ye-sis."

"You wouldn't understand."

"Try me."

"It's really pointless to . . ." She drew a breath when she saw the look on his face. "Hemolysis is erythrocyte membrane damage. It could be fragmentation anemia, reticuloendothelial phagocytosis or intravascular. A dysfunction of the spleen can cause hypersplenism, which is an increased activity of the organ and hypersplenism in the presence of ineffective erythropoiesis leads to anemia." She looked at him challengingly. "More?"

David shook his head. "Maybe later. You know about concussions?"

"I know I don't want one if that's what you mean."

"They said I fell down some stairs at the clinic. Hit my head. Concussion. Only there weren't any stairs there. It was a one-story building, for godsakes!"

"Look, don't get excited."

"I'm not excited. I'm mad. I don't know what's going on. My name is David Townsend and I live in Oklahoma City. I am *not* a crazy person."

"And you want me to believe someone kidnapped you? Someone from the institute?"

"That's what happened."

"Who are *they*?"

"I don't know . . . the doctors. They fixed it up so I'd think I had an accident."

Sara twisted her hands nervously in her lap but said nothing.

David pulled a stool in front of her chair. "Just listen to me. I have to tell somebody. It might as well be you."

"Tell me what?"

"My story. The truth, doctor. Everything that's happened

to me that I remember from about nine o'clock yesterday morning until a few hours ago."

"Then what? Will you leave?"

"If you still absolutely don't believe me then, okay, I'll go. If you do believe me, then you'll try to help me." He looked into her eyes. "Deal?"

Sara settled back into the chair. "I'm not going to promise you anything . . . but I'll listen."

It took most of an hour and two trips to the coffee pot to explain. David told her about the pleading call from Becky Smith, about Tiny and the ride in the van, the sign in front of the clinic. He told her about Dr. Seagram and the orange juice and the glass coffin and waking up in a hospital bed. He told her about Dr. Knopf and the yellow pills and Gregory St. Pe and the old men who called him Townsend. The more he talked the crazier it sounded even to him. When he finished he got a drink of water and sat down in front of her again. She had to understand. There wasn't anybody else.

"There isn't any doctor named Knopf at the institute," Sara said.

David felt himself deflate.

"But the ICPs are real. Even so, it doesn't mean anyone was kidnapped."

"ICPs?"

"Intensive Care Pods. The bubble containers. They're primarily for transportation of critical patients on AirMore planes. The people you saw . . . I'm sure they weren't dead. The pods aren't coffins."

"*You* didn't see them. They were old people with young birthdays . . . and they *were* dead."

"You're making this very awkward for me. I don't know what you want me to do."

"I want you to believe me."

"Believe that Euromedic is kidnapping people and

bringing them to psychiatric wards?" She raised her eyebrows. "Euromedic?"

"What about those old guys? They thought I was Stuart."

"There isn't any Dr. Townsend at Weeksbriar either."

"He works at a research place in Africa. I don't know the name of it."

"You have a twin brother and you don't know where he works?"

"We haven't been that close," David said. "Does J. Ellis mean anything to you?"

"Jonathan Ellis?"

"J. Ellis is the name that was on the card with St. Pe and the rest of them. Attending, it said. Who is he?"

"He happens to be the chief-of-staff at Weeksbriar."

"Chief-of-staff? What's that mean?"

"Dr. Ellis runs Weeksbriar."

"Terrific." David cupped his hands over his head. The headache was starting up again. "I need some aspirin."

"If you've had a concussion—" he gave her a sharp look "—or whatever—what you need is sleep, not drugs."

David thought about it. Probably she was right. Mixing aspirin with whatever they'd given him might not be smart. He got up. "C'mon."

"What?"

"We're going to get some sleep."

"*We?*"

"C'mon."

"You promised you'd leave!"

David took her arm. "I lied."

The bedroom was at the end of the hall at the back of the house. It was large with flower-designed wallpaper and more books scattered everywhere. The double bed, David was not surprised to see, was unmade. He nodded to the door across the room. "Bathroom?"

"Yes."

"Do you want to change into a robe or something?"

"No, I don't." She wasn't as frightened as she was indignant. "I don't intend to sleep. Not with you in here." She sat on the bed while he looked in the bathroom, then checked the closet.

"What are you looking for?"

"You got any belts that aren't leather?"

"Belts?" Her eyes flickered.

David opened drawers in her dresser. "What about some pantyhose?"

"I'm fresh out," she said, watching him paw through the bottom drawers. "I don't think I'd have your size anyway. Will you please stop that? What are you *doing*?"

David stood up and leaned against the dresser. "You're sure?"

"Positive."

"Stand up."

"What for?"

He let out a sigh. "Those pantyhose you're wearing. Take them off."

Her mouth dropped open.

"I can't afford to trust you, doctor. I'm going to tie your wrists and ankles and then I'm going to sleep. I just need a couple of hours . . . until this headache goes away."

Sara got up slowly. "Now . . . wait a minute."

"Do you want me to do it?"

"Look, if I promise not to do any—"

"If you promise not to talk anymore, I won't gag you too." He held out his hand. "Give."

"No."

He pushed himself away from the dresser.

"All right—all right." Sara lifted the hem of her skirt to her knees. She shot him a fierce look and kicked off her shoes. Quickly she shed the nylon hose, then offered the undergarment to him. "Happy?"

David ripped the legs apart. "Sit on the bed and hold out your hands."

130

"This how you entertain your lady friends in Oklahoma?" She watched as he wound the nylon around her wrists.

"Legs."

She sat back on the bed and he made a knot in the hose around her ankles. "You expect me to sleep like this?"

He pushed her back on the pillow. "I expect you to be quiet. I'm the one who needs sleep." He walked to the closet. "Do you want a blanket?"

"I'm not sleeping!"

"Do you want a blanket or not?"

"No."

"It's cold."

"No . . ." She closed her eyes. "All right. Yes."

David covered her with a blanket, then flipped an edge of the bedspread over her and pulled the other side across so that she was wrapped inside it like a cocoon.

She wiggled against the pillow. "I can't move."

He lay down beside her and pulled another blanket over himself. "All you *have* to do is breathe. Just do it quietly."

She turned away from him and he switched out the light on the nightstand. In the darkness he heard the wind in the branches outside and felt the body aches from running and bumping into trees and slapping branches. His feet were sore. He tried to think about what he would do in the morning, whom he should call. He had to find someone he could trust.

The engergy drained out of him, and he felt himself drifting. He was too tired to think anymore. Just take it an hour at a time, he told himself. He was vaguely aware of Sara next to him. What was he going to do about her? But the answer didn't come before sleep.

TWENTY-ONE

NEW BROCKTON AIRPORT

MORAVEC STOOD at the window of the passenger VIP lounge, mesmerized by the snowfall and the flickering lights on the runway. He had been on the ground twenty minutes and still had the sensation that he was aboard the plane; his ears were plugged and his head was numbed from a muffled hum of engines. The appearance of the woman in the reflection of the window startled him.

"Dr. Moravec?" She was blonde with dazzling blue eyes. She wore a dark blue parka.

"Yes?"

"I'm Nurse Turner," she said. "Recovery Team Six. Sorry I'm late. Dr. Ellis sent me to pick you up."

"Hello." Moravec shook her hand. "I was just admiring the snow."

She glanced through the window and gave a tired nod. "Dr. Ellis said to hurry. He's at the institute." She motioned toward an exit sign. "The car's this way. Can I take that for you?"

Moravec held the BriefPac. "Thank you, no. I can manage it."

Their footsteps echoed as they walked through the empty terminal. "You know, I've never actually met Dr. Ellis. What's he like?"

She glanced at him. "You ever heard of George S. Patton?"

At the curb she held the car door for him. He paused to

watch a snowplow scrape past. It never snowed like this in London. Christina would be absolutely awed.

Inside the car Turner nodded to the driver. "Go ahead, Al." To Moravec she said grimly, "I'm afraid we have a crisis here, Dr. Moravec. Townsend is gone."

Moravec glanced at her in the receding light of the airport terminal. His ears were still playing tricks. "Gone, did you say?"

"Escaped."

"Townsend!"

"It wasn't our fault."

"How could he escape? He's only just been delivered!"

"Yes, I know—I *know*. He beat up an attendant and the ward guard. That was two hours ago. We've had people all over the grounds looking for him. He's not in the institute. We've checked every floor, every office. He isn't there. I don't know how he did it, but he's gone."

Moravec sat up in his seat. The man wasn't even supposed to be conscious. "I don't understand. How could he possibly know he should even try to escape? A man drugged on thorazine and tranquilizers is in no condition to stand up, much less take anyone hostage."

"He wasn't on thorazine."

"What?"

"Because the chloropromazine dosage wasn't enough to keep him sedated," Turner said. "We were specifically instructed not to allow the patient's blood pressure, pulse and respiration to drop below prescribed limits during the transfer. Within those requirements the medication was not effective in keeping him under. He woke up a couple of times."

"Do you know how important David Townsend is?" Moravec said incredulously.

"Of course I know. I brought him here."

"Was there any problem in the transfer?"

"No. We gave him four hundred milligrams of sodium secobarbital at his initial staging point. Transfer was made by private aircraft and he was at the clinic within five hours. Up to that point it was all routine . . . our usual procedure."

Moravec recognized the drug as a short-acting sedative and sleep inducer with a rapid effect. Four hundred milligrams was a bit much, he thought, but it wasn't dangerous. "Did Townsend require additional hypnotics during transit?"

"No."

"What was his medication after admittance?" Moravec was in control now. He made notes on a pad from the light over his seat. It was impossible to conceive that a patient could escape from the Weeksbriar facility, but that was behind him. Right now his job was to analyze the problem. Townsend was missing. Deal with that.

Turner said, "Because of the effect of the thorazine on his heart rate and respiration, we administered a non-barbituate, chloral hydrate, then phenobarbital at regular intervals. We realized the dosage was not enough to keep the patient sedated in the usual state. I knew he would return to semi- if not full consciousness eventually and, lacking further instructions, I proceeded on my own judgment."

Moravec nodded. "And?"

"We tried to persuade him that he was at Parkland in Dallas. He seemed convinced that he'd suffered a mild concussion. It was the best thing I could think of to insure his cooperation without prescribing more potent tranquilizers which would violate the sedative instructions we were given."

"I take it that didn't work."

"No, it didn't. He was confused, uncooperative. I didn't see any alternative except to put him on meprobamate and trifluorperazine . . . despite the instructions."

Moravec frowned. "I don't understand. If he were on meprobamate and tri—"

"He didn't take the medication. We found the pills in his room. Somehow he figured it was a setup. He rang for a

134

nurse. When the floor nurse came to give him a sedative, he injected her with it. Eventually he overpowered the ward guard and escaped from the psychiatric floor. He tried to make an outside phone call but couldn't get through the switchboard. Then he jumped out of a third-floor window into a snowbank. That's the last we've seen of him. We're sure, or relatively sure, that he didn't get past the security fence. It just isn't conceivable to me, if he's not *in* the institute somewhere, how he could have gotten off the grounds. It may be that he didn't and we just haven't found him yet."

"I suggest you do exactly that. There isn't a great deal of time, you understand. Dr. McPhearson is waiting for the donor in Madrid."

"Yes, I will, of course, but . . ."

"Something else?"

"Well . . ." Turner cleared her throat. "It's the weather here. As you can see, we've had a snowstorm. The temperature, considering the wind chill factor, is somewhere in the subzero range."

Moravec closed his eyes. What Turner was trying to say was that Townsend might by lying somewhere on Weeksbriar's grounds under a blanket of snow—frozen stiff. He had a sudden vision of a man slowly dying in Madrid with no way to save him.

"On the other hand," Turner said, "we can't dismiss the possibility that he did manage to get past the security fence and is wandering around out there."

Moravec stared out the window. Tree limbs bowed under the weight of snow. "How cold is it?"

"Ten, twelve degrees."

"He must be frightened out of his wits," Moravec said. His breath fogged the window. He turned back to the nurse. "He doesn't know where he is?"

"I don't think so."

"Find him quickly," Moravec said. "Anyone bright enough to escape from an institution as heavily guarded and secure as Weeksbriar—if that's what he's done—isn't going to let himself die of exposure." Moravec nodded to himself, not because it was a convincing theory but because he couldn't allow himself to believe Townsend was dead. He was too important to be dead.

"We'll find him," Turner said positively.

Moravec looked at her. "Yes, do that." He glanced outside again. "David Townsend is not an ordinary fellow. He's inventive and intelligent and is accustomed to doing things his own way. He's surely frightened and confused. If he's learned where he is, he certainly doesn't know why he's here . . . or whom to trust. If I know Townsend, that isn't an inviting situation for our side."

Turner frowned. "You *know* Townsend?"

"Not well enough." He leaned back in his seat and touched the BriefPac. "He's not a team player, like Stuart. He drives a truck, he likes one-to-one competitions and he plays chess."

"Chess? What difference does that make?"

"Probably none . . . except that David Townsend's life has been one contest after another."

"So?"

Moravec made a sad face. "I wonder if he's any good."

136

TWENTY-TWO

MADRID

A NURSE entered the dimly lighted room and checked the I.V. bottle that hung from a stand near the bed. The I.V. was nearly empty, the clear liquid down to the fifty milliliter mark. She charged a new plastic saline bottle with a syringe—five milliliters, epinephrine.

The patient was on his back, a respirator mask over his face. He was unconscious but breathing normally. The EKG oscilloscope screen and blood pressure monitor glowed bright green, soundlessly tracking the patient's vital signs.

Another nurse entered the hospital room. She moved to the patient's chart. "Changing?"

"Yes," answered the first nurse in a whisper. She pinched off the tube to keep air out and inserted it into the new bottle. "Lidocaine's done . . . two hundred milligrams."

"Good." The second nurse noted it on the chart, then unwrapped a receiver bag for the bladder drainage tube that hung below the bed. She made the change and deposited the full urine bag in a waste bin.

"Doesn't look good, does he?"

"No."

"You think he'll make it then?"

The second nurse shrugged. "I don't know." She bent over the patient. The bandage surrounding the drainage tube in his chest was gooey with viscous liquid. "Better change this one too."

"You think all this is going to make any difference?" the other nurse said, standing before the oscilloscope. The screen plotted a monotonous course of QRS deflections. She glanced at the man on the bed. The tubes and electrodes connected to his body made him seem more an experiment than a patient. The room was crowded with equipment. "I don't think he'll last another three or four days."

"The new one's coming. Little Mary is bringing him."

"Strong and healthy, is he?"

"Younger, anyway."

A nod. "I heard America."

The first nurse let out a long sigh. She stared at the patient. "They'd better hurry."

TWENTY-THREE

WEEKSBRIAR

DR. JONATHAN EUGENE ELLIS was a general and Weeksbriar was his command post.

It was an analogy that struck Moravec the moment he met Weeksbriar's chief of staff. Square-jawed and stocky, Dr. Ellis was much larger than Moravec and suggested physical strength rather than bulk. He was bald and wore teardrop eyeglasses. His hospital smock was starched and creased at the sleeves. He spoke with commanding authority.

"The man's escaped," Ellis was saying. "He's not in the institute and he's not anywhere on the grounds. He hasn't vanished so the only conclusion left is that he got past the gate. I don't like admitting it, but that's the way it is."

Ellis addressed the small gathering from behind his desk like a commander briefing his lieutenants. Only the office seemed out of place for such drama, Moravec thought. Every wall was painted a different bright color. High back, cockpitlike chairs were deep cushions and a glass-topped coffee table were placed strategically around a luxurious bone-white rug like set pieces. It was all very modern and reassuring, an antiseptic expression of Hippocratic purity. Distinctively American. Moravec studied the tense faces in the room. Turner and her team were present. Moravec hadn't been introduced to the others, though it was clear they would be involved in the search. He was here only as an observer. This was Ellis's show. He'd lost Townsend. It was up to him to find him.

Ellis clicked his ballpoint pen against a clipboard that

held his notes. It was the only nervous habit Moravec noticed in him. "Weeksbriar is not a state-supported institute. We're a private facility. Our patients come to us voluntarily, so there is no official police jurisdiction involved here. As a precaution, however, we have prepared a statement for the authorities. It simply says that one of our patients is missing. I don't *want* the police brought in, but if we don't have Townsend by morning then their cooperation may be unavoidable." Ellis leaned forward in his seat. "Each of you knows how important Townsend is to Euromedic. I don't have to impress upon you that time is critical. Just find him. Bring him back here." He looked around. "Questions?"

No one spoke.

Ellis acknowledged Moravec with a nod. "You've all heard of Luther Moravec, operations chief of DCD. He's on hand from the London office to supervise the transfer and see to the patient en route. Anything Dr. Moravec wants you may regard as a request from me."

Moravec nodded self-consciously at the faces that stared at him. It was plain that a request from the chief of staff was an order.

"Anything to add, doctor?"

Moravec cleared his throat. He was nervous addressing strangers. "Only that David Townsend is a confused young man at this moment, wherever he is. He will surely resist any effort to return him to the institute."

"Which means he's running scared," Ellis said. "But he isn't going to the police. Not with *his* story."

"Even so," Moravec said, "I most strongly urge that he be recovered without excessive force. He will be of no value in Madrid if he is harmed." He nearly said damaged.

Ellis glanced over lazily. "Agreed." He adjusted his glasses and rose from his chair. "So, unless someone has another comment . . ."

When only Moravec and Ellis remained in the office the chief of staff drew a cigar from his humidor. "Doctor?"

140

Moravec held up a hand. "Thank you, no." He looked at his watch, which hadn't been set since London. He tried to remember if the time difference was five hours or six. Either way, Connie would be up. He wanted to call her.

"Worried?" Ellis held the flame of his lighter beneath the cigar. The end glowed red as he inhaled.

"Bloody panicked," Moravec said.

Ellis waved the smoke away from his head. "It's a good staff. I expect we'll have him by morning."

Moravec wasn't sure if that was bravado or if he actually believed it. "I wish I had your strong sense of optimism. I still don't see how he got past the fence."

"If he did. We might still find him hiding in a dumpster."

Moravec frowned.

"Trash container," Ellis said. He made his mouth into an *O* and tried to form a smoke ring. He expelled a stream of puffs that disturbed a mobile above his desk. "Anyway, we're only dealing with a truck driver, right?"

"Only?" Moravec remembered a playground in Soho after the war when he was not yet seven. An older boy had kicked him in the stomach because his parents were refugees and he was "only a Pole." He'd always wondered what might have happened if the boy had known he was only a Czech. "Do you *know* anything about David Townsend?"

"I know he's from Oklahoma and he's keeping me up."

"He also graduated first in his class from Pennsylvania State University School of Architecture," Moravec said defensively.

"Did he?" Ellis rolled the cigar between his fingers, studying his last effort.

"Yes, he did." Moravec felt a moment of rage. "Also, I think we should be careful not to characterize Townsend's disappearance as an escape. I'd like to avoid the impression that Euromedic patients are criminals or that we are jailers."

Ellis's gaze moved to Moravec. Light reflected from a lens in his glasses. "Nobody's said anything like that."

141

"Townsend is more than a simple donor patient who's been misplaced," Moravec said. "He didn't volunteer for this, you know. *We* picked him. If nothing else he deserves at least some measure of our sympathy."

Ellis shifted impatiently in his chair. "Look, all I said was that the man shouldn't be too difficult to find. You don't have to take offense, doctor. I feel sorry for the guy, too."

Moravec nodded. "Yes, I'm sure." He got up. "I wonder, is there somewhere I might wash up? I've been at it since—" He glanced at his watch. "I don't even know what time it is here."

"Five to six," Ellis said. "I'll have a day room fixed up for you in one of the offices."

"And a MAG line."

"MAG?" Ellis frowned. "What for?"

"I'll need to be in touch with McPhearson in Madrid, of course. Also, Haldern will want to be kept informed of developments." Moravec picked up the BriefPac. "Right now I'd just like to call my wife."

Ellis rolled the end of the cigar lightly in a glass ashtray. "You're not going to give Haldern a bad report on us, are you?" When he looked up his eyes were cold. "I mean, about me."

"About you?" It took Moravec a moment to understand. "Look here, Ellis, I didn't fly across the Atlantic Ocean to evaluate your performance as Weeksbriar's chief administrator. My *only* interest here is David Townsend."

"I just don't want there to be any misunderstanding. What happened with him—" Ellis searched for a word "—just happened. That's all. It wasn't anyone's fault."

"I'm *not* blaming anyone," Moravec said. "It's not what I do." He walked to the door.

"We'll find your donor," Ellis said. "Don't let it bother you. He hasn't got any place to go."

Moravec turned back. "Except the police. That *does* bother me. David Townsend might seem like a fool to you but he isn't stupid." He pointed toward the door. "If he's out there and he convinces *anyone* that he's been kidnapped—"

"An escaped—excuse me—*missing* patient from a psychiatric facility?" Ellis smiled. He lifted the cigar to his mouth, holding it away from his lips. "Without identification or money? Dressed in hospital whites?" The chief of staff shook his head. "Would *you* believe a man like that if he told you he'd been abducted by doctors? The man's clearly paranoid. You'd call the police. Anyone would. Anyway . . ." Ellis chomped on the cigar. "It doesn't matter what he says or who he says it to. No one will believe him. Particularly the police. All his papers are in order."

"Papers?"

"If necessary we can prove to the authorities that he's one of our long-term confinees. As a matter of fact, doctor, I'd stop referring to our wayward patient as Townsend if I were you. If you noticed, you're the only one who has."

Moravec stared at him incredulously. "It's his bloody name, isn't it!"

Ellis shook his head. "You've never seen our recovery teams in action, have you? Well, believe me, they're very thorough. R-T-Six is probably the best. If you think your man is confused now, wait until *he* finds out." He inhaled a mouthful of smoke rings.

"Finds out what? What are you talking about?"

"David Townsend . . . does not . . . exist, is what I'm talking about. There is *no* such person anymore. Period." Then he blew a perfect ring, large and full, that sailed neatly between the elements of the mobile and finally obliterated itself against the ceiling. He looked brightly at Moravec. "Ah."

SATURDAY
JANUARY 1

TWENTY-FOUR

NEW BROCKTON

DAVID RAN up the stairs two at a time when he heard the crash.

Sara was on the floor, squirming inside the bedspread. Broken pieces from the ceramic lamp lay scattered on the floor. David knelt beside her.

"Take it easy."

Her hair was disheveled and covered her eyes. She was panting, her eyes blinking. He brushed a few strands back from her forehead. "You okay?"

"What happened?" Her eyes were wide, searching.

"You took a tumble. You okay?"

"Do I look okay?"

In the light of day, with her features more defined, David had to admit she did. She looked to be in her late twenties and the little makeup she used complemented her features. She wasn't pretty in the usual sense—the planes of her face were prominent, her nose sharp, her chin slightly jutted—but he found her extraordinarily attractive. Her green eyes showed a capacity for scorn and intellect and David thought she probably didn't laugh much.

"I thought you'd be gone. I thought you *were* gone. I woke up and you weren't . . . Obviously, you aren't gone. But you will be soon, isn't that right?" She didn't seem frightened anymore, only disappointed.

"Soon enough." David offered a bright smile.

"What in God's name was that crash? You didn't blow up

anything, did you? I know this place isn't much, but it's my—" Then she saw the broken lamp and the length of cord tied to the blanket. "Oh, Jesus."

"I wanted to be sure when you woke up that you didn't try—"

"Try! Try what, for godsakes? What did you think I was going to do tied up like this?"

"If I untie you, will you promise to behave?"

"How do you define behave?"

"No screaming. No running for a kitchen knife. Running for the door wouldn't be wise either."

"You'd solve both our problems if you'd just go."

"No screaming, no running," David said. "I don't have time to watch you every second. Make up your mind. I'm fixing breakfast."

"Okay, okay." She held out her bound wrists. "I promise."

David unraveled her from the tangle of bedding and untied the pantyhose from her wrists and feet.

"How long are we going to have to play this little game of yours?"

"I'll let you know."

"That's not exactly reassuring . . . ah . . ." She looked up at him. "I forgot your name."

"Townsend."

She nodded at the bathroom. "Do you mind if I wash up?"

"Go ahead, leave the door open."

"I just want to brush my teeth, for chrissake!"

"Then you better use the yellow one. I used the blue."

"You—!" She gave him an enraged look.

"Hurry up. I made coffee."

After a minute she returned to the door. She had washed her face, David noticed, and pulled her hair back.

"Look, I'd like to change and—" she glanced back into the bath"—and—"

"And what?"

"I want to use the john, okay? I want to close the door. Do you mind?"

"I don't mind, but the door stays open."

"What do you think I'll do, lock myself in and scream for help?"

David didn't reply.

"Well, I wouldn't. Anyway, who'd hear me? Besides, that window's been painted shut so many times it probably hasn't been opened for twenty years. Forty, probably. It's—what's so funny?"

"After I brushed my teeth," David said, "I opened the window to see what was next door." He smiled. "Nice try, though."

"Look, I—"

"You just do what you have to do. I can wait."

She moved slowly out of the bathroom. "Never mind."

"What about . . . ?"

"The urge passed." She walked by him. "For your information, the bathroom door lock is broken anyway."

David nodded. "I know."

He had cleaned the kitchen. She noticed that first because all the counters were clear. He had washed the dishes and stacked them in a rack in one well of the double sink. There was a skillet on the stove with bacon sizzling and two unbroken eggs in a cup between the burners. Coffee was brewing beside the sink. A radio on the refrigerator was turned to a classical FM station.

"When did you do all this?" Sara asked, amazed.

"While you were asleep." He motioned toward the kitchen table. "Sit down." He pushed a cup of coffee in front of her. "I did a little rummaging around this morning. I found some clothes in the attic. An army jacket, some socks, and fishing stuff." He glanced at his feet. His jeans were tucked inside hip waders that he'd cut down to boot size. "I had to trim a little off. Not a perfect fit, but they'll do."

"I've never even been in the attic. Keep them. They'll be my going away present to you."

David ignored her. He broke two eggs and beat them together in a cup with a fork.

"Look, Townsend, you're not helping yourself by holding me here like this. Sooner or later they're going to find out. You must know that. Why don't you let me call the institute."

"I've already made several calls this morning."

"And?"

"Nobody answers in Oklahoma."

"If you'd just let me call—"

"I don't need any advice right now, thanks."

Sara shrugged. "Course not. You know exactly what you're doing, right? I mean—"

David held up his hand. "Listen."

"All I know is—"

"Listen!" David turned up the volume on the radio.

". . . early this morning. Franklin, transferred to the Euromedic psychiatric facility yesterday only hours before his escape, is not a dangerous patient, according to Dr. Jonathan Ellis, Euromedic administrator. Dr. Ellis, while not giving specific details on the nature of Franklin's illness, said the patient is not violent. 'He is confused and disoriented,' the administrator said, 'and it's quite natural that he would display some rebellious tendencies especially so soon after his transfer to a new facility. But we're confident that once he's back in the institute we can put him on the road to recovery.' Franklin is thirty years old, approximately six feet tall with blue eyes and brown hair. He was last seen wearing a white hospital attendant's jacket and trousers without shoes. The New Brockton Police Department advises that anyone seeing a man of this description should contact them at . . ."

David switched off the radio. Sara sat rigidly at the kitchen table. "Who the hell is Franklin?"

She looked at him slowly. "Who are you trying to kid?"

"My name is Townsend! David *Townsend!* What are they talking about—transferred? Transferred from where?"

Her fingers trembled as she set down her coffee cup. "Look, I don't want any trouble, okay? I've had enough. I would just like you to leave."

"I wasn't *transferred* from any place! I was kidnapped!"

"Please don't shout."

"How many nut farms do you people run?"

"The Euromedic chain, it's . . . there're only two psychiatric facilities in the Euromedic group, Weeksbriar and Brentwood." She cleared her throat. "But Brentwood's not in Texas."

"Where is it?"

"Maybe you forgot. Maybe you just need to rest."

"Where is it!"

"California."

David went to the den and brought back the telephone, trailing the extension cord. He slammed it in front of her, bouncing the plates and spilling Sara's coffee. "Call them."

"Call? Who?"

"California. That other place."

"Brentwood?" She took a frightened breath. "Why?"

"I'm supposed to be Franklin, aren't I? I'm supposed to have been transferred from there. Let's see if it's true. Let's see if somebody named Franklin was ever in that place . . . and if he's come to this place." He handed her the receiver. "Call. Let's see if I really am crazy."

She got the Brentwood number from Los Angeles information and after several rings a switchboard operator answered.

"Brentwood Neuro-Psychiatric Hospital."

Sara suddenly realized that it was 9 A.M. in New York, but three hours earlier in California. "Hospital administrator's office, please."

"It's New Year's Day," said the California voice. "Nobody up there."

"What about admitting?"

"There either."

"Records?"

"It's New Year's *Day*," the voice said again. "There's only the main duty nurse here."

"May I speak to her then?"

"You can if you want. Just a minute, I'll ring her floor."

Sara looked at David. "Today is January first. There's nobody—"

"Duty station, Senior Nurse Lamonica speaking."

"Hello, Nurse Lamonica." Sara pointed at the receiver for David's benefit. "I'm calling about one of your patients."

"Yes?"

"A Mr. Franklin. I'm calling for a verification."

"We're not permitted to give patient-related information over the phone," the nurse said. "Who's calling, please?"

David moved closer to her to hear.

"This is the records clerk at Weeksbriar . . . in New York?"

"Yes?"

"We're running a computer verification check on all Euromedic psychiatric patients for Medicare financial statements and our printout entry shows Mr. Franklin listed on the last quarter as a Brentwood inmate, but it skipped his name for the present quarter. Can you tell me if he's been released? We should have been notified if he was, but we don't have any record—"

"You should be talking to the record department," said the duty nurse impatiently.

"Yes, I know, but there's nobody there. It's New Year's.

"You people don't have New Year's in New York?"

"We're a little behind schedule," Sara said. "If you could just check your in-patient log . . ."

"I know who all our patients are," the senior nurse said shortly.

"And Franklin?" Sara glanced at David.

"You'd better check your records more closely before you start making long-distance calls at six in the morning."

"I—"

"Franklin was discharged two days ago."

David closed his eyes.

"You're sure?" Sara said. "Richard Franklin?"

"Of course I'm sure."

Sara froze as David got up from his chair and moved to the sink. He stood there, staring through the window.

"Hello?"

Sara's eyes didn't leave David. "Sorry," she said into the phone. "The mistake must be here."

"Well, there isn't any mistake here. I'm looking at his D-T chart right now. Richard Kenneth Franklin. Forty-four. Five-nine, one fifty-five. Transferred to Weeksbriar by AirMore December twenty-nine. That's him, right? You'd better tell your computer."

"I will," Sara said weakly. "Thank you." She set the receiver back in its cradle. She was afraid to say a word. She watched the man at the sink. He didn't move.

"I guess I proved something," David said without turning around. He let out a long sigh. "Hell, maybe I am crazy."

"Franklin," she said, watching David, "was thirty. That's what the radio said. I mean . . ." Sara licked her lips. Her throat had suddenly gone dry. "I mean the description they gave fits you exactly."

"What did you expect?" He continued staring outside.

"The duty nurse at Brentwood said . . . I don't understand this, but the Franklin out there was forty-four years old, five-foot-nine and one hundred and fifty pounds."

"Forty-four years old?"

"Maybe she was looking at the wrong file or . . .
or . . ."

"Or maybe something very strange is going on?"

"I . . . I don't know." She tried not to look at him. "If
you're not Franklin . . . then who did they put on
an AirMore flight in California?"

"I don't care who he was, but he isn't me."

"Well, I care! Somebody left the Brentwood Neuro-
Psychiatric Hospital two days ago. If it wasn't you, who
was it? And if you're not Richard Franklin then where did
he go? People don't just disappear."

"I did."

Sara stared at the phone. It was a mistake, she told
herself. It had to be. Doctors don't kidnap patients. It was a
mistake. A simple explanation would unravel it. All she had
to do was call the institute. But if he were telling the truth—
no, it couldn't be. He was confusing her. He was *frightening*
and confusing her. Part of her wanted to believe him,
another part was afraid to. What did he escape from at
Weeksbriar? Paranoids could also be very clever, she knew
that too. So who was here? David Townsend? Richard
Franklin? Psychotic? Victim? She looked up at him.

"What now?"

"I think I'll go," David said.

Sara nodded. "I'm not saying I believe any of this. I
just . . ."

"Yeah." He poured the eggs into the sink. "I'll get my
jacket."

When the doorbell rang they both jumped.

David was up first. He grabbed Sara's arm and pulled her
into the den. He peeked into the living room. Through the
sheer curtains over the front window he saw a blue and
white sedan parked in the drive next to the Volvo. There
was a medical logo and a name painted on the door.
WEEKSBRIAR RESEARCH INSTITUTE.

"Who is that?" David asked in a whisper. He squeezed Sara's arm.

"I don't know."

The doorbell rang again.

"Shall I—"

David pushed her against the wall and covered her mouth. "No!"

They couldn't know he was here. If they knew, then the police would be here. They wouldn't have come like this. Right? The place would be swarming with police. It had to be someone she knew. He took his hand away from her mouth.

"It has to be somebody. Who is it?"

"I don't—"

The doorbell rang again. A long ring. "Dr. Mills?" It was a man's voice. Calm.

"It's probably someone to check on me," Sara said.

"Why didn't they call then?"

"Maybe they didn't. You said you used the phone this morning, didn't you?"

"Dr. Mills?"

"They know I'm here," Sara said. "My car's out—"

"All right, quiet down a minute."

"Hello? Anybody home?" A knock at the door. "Dr. Mills?"

David twisted her face to the wall, pinning her arm behind her. Sara let out a cry. He pushed her up on her toes. "Answer him. Tell him you're asleep." He turned her toward the door.

"Dr. Mills?"

He felt her take a deep breath. "Talk to him!"

She cleared her throat. "Yes? Who is it?"

"It's Fisher from security. The institute sent me out."

David pointed at her watch. Sara took another breath. "Do you know what time it is?"

"Yes, ma'am. I'm sorry. There was some trouble at the institute last night. A psychiatric patient escaped."

"Yes, I know."

"They wanted to make sure you were okay."

"I'm fine. I'm trying to sleep."

"They tried to call before . . . I mean, your phone's been busy and—"

"It's off the hook," Sara said quickly.

"Oh." For several seconds there was silence. "Would you mind if I came in, doctor? I mean, they want to be sure that you're okay."

David's grip tightened.

"I'm not dressed," Sara said.

"I can wait, ma'am."

"Look, I'm not going to get dressed for some stupid inspection. I'm fine. What do they think—that I brought an escaped psychiatric patient home with me?"

"No, ma'am . . . it's just that the guard at the gate thought he remembered someone was with you when you drove out last night."

Sara turned to David.

"Deny it," he whispered.

"There wasn't anybody," Sara called back. "A guard walked me to my car and I left . . . alone. The gate is mistaken." She closed her eyes. "Now, if you don't mind, I'd like to go back to bed."

There was a long wait, then, "Yes, ma'am. Sorry to get you up, doctor."

They stood together against the wall until David heard the car start. He watched it back out of the drive and leave, then released Sara's arm.

"Get your coat on." He went to the window and looked down the street.

"My coat?"

"We're getting out of here."

"*We?*"

David pushed her into the kitchen. He emptied the contents of her purse on the table, pocketing her wallet. He picked out the loose change. "Hurry up. They'll probably be back any time."

"*I'm* not going anywhere."

"You're going." He slid his arms into the army jacket and stuffed the car keys into a pocket. When he turned to face her, he was breathing heavily. "If they tracked me here then they know I talked to you . . . explained things. I don't think they want that."

"Don't hang any of your paranoid fantasies on me."

"Put your coat on."

"A hostage isn't going to help you."

"You're not a hostage."

"No? What the hell do you call—"

David sent a kitchen chair crashing across the room. "Quiet!"

Sara froze.

"Somebody's gone to a lot of trouble to get me up here," David said. "They invented a huge charade to make me out to be someone else. I don't know why, but one thing is sure—they didn't figure on me escaping. If they know where I am then they must figure I told you all about me. I know I'm in trouble. What I'm not sure of is if it's contagious. You're going because you *might* just be in danger too." He shoved her coat at her. "Now put this on and shut up!"

At the breezeway David held Sara's arm and scanned the neighborhood. His breath in the frigid morning air came in short bursts. He took the car keys from his pocket and clamped them into her hand. "You drive."

"Just tell me one thing," she said. "Why are you doing this to *me*?"

"You're in danger."

She gave a nervous laugh. "I already know that."

"Not from me. You know something you're not supposed to. C'mon." He pushed her toward the car, his grip on her arm tight above the elbow.

"I don't *know* anything."

David opened the driver's door.

"I want you to tell me what you're talking about, Townsend. What vital secret do I know?"

"What nobody else knows," David said. "That I'm not Richard Franklin."

TWENTY-FIVE

WEEKSBRIAR

"WE MISS you, darling. Happy New Year."

"Yes, and I you. Happy returns."

Moravec was in his assigned office, the telephone beside him on the sofa. The BriefPac was open on the coffee table, several pages of printout spread about. He had spoken to McPhearson and Mayford and briefly with Haldern's assistant, who told him the director was attending services at St. Ethelburga, Bishopsgate. He had been patient with all of them. McPhearson was in his usual state, complaining that while the surgical team had arrived from London one of the anesthetists was a substitute and what kind of bloody organization was that? Bill Mayford rattled off his efficiencies since being left in charge but, Moravec could tell from his voice, the boy pined for his hunting dogs in Sussex. When Moravec finally got through to Connie he was eager for the vision that her voice inspired. The telephone served to screen away time these last few years. He could force his mind's eye to remember her from before. The blessing was that her voice had never changed.

"We've built a fire," Connie said. "Estelle's made hot chocolate and we're all gathered together with the rain tapping at the windows. Is it terribly cold there?"

"Not so bone chilling, I think," Moravec said. He'd taken off his shoes. "It's been snowing for three days they tell me. Four inches since I arrived. A snowplow had to lead us out from the airport."

"Is it beautiful?"

"Yes, quite lovely." Moravec closed his eyes to see her. "How are you feeling? The little one is behaving?"

"He sleeps. He kicks. He turns on his elbows. He's cross because you're not here, I think."

"And Christina?"

"She's learned a rhyme," Connie said. "We were going to surprise you today."

"And I've spoiled it being away."

"You'll be home soon."

Moravec nodded. "Soon, yes. Another day or two."

"Estelle promises to bake one of her delicious breads. She wants to—"

The line clicked, followed by a hollow, spacey tone. "MAGCOM interrupt," a strong voice announced. Moravec opened his eyes. "Mr. Moravec, we have four minutes of clear sync until stat track readjust."

"Yes, thank you."

The line clicked again and they gave him back to Connie.

"—or banana nut. Which would you like?"

She hadn't noticed the interrupt. "Let me see," Moravec said. He waited a moment. "Well, banana nut, I think."

"Done," Connie said cheerfully.

Moravec sat up. He stared at the blank screen of the BriefPac. "I'm afraid I have to ring off now."

"All right, darling. Do bring us something from the States if you've a chance. Christina would like that. Will you be in New York City?"

"Sorry, no."

"Well . . . not to worry then. Christina would like to say good-bye if there's time."

"Of course." He glanced at his watch.

"Haa-oo . . . fa-fa-fahd . . . Abb-ee Nn-nn-nna Ye-yir."

Moravec closed his eyes. "And happy returns, my precious."

"L-L-Loph ye-yeu."

160

"I love you too," Moravec said quietly. He bowed his head. "Always."

"Be warm," Connie said. "We miss you . . . Happy New Year."

Moravec sat by the phone for several minutes. His hands felt warm on his face.

"Excuse me."

Moravec looked up, startled. Nurse Turner was standing in the doorway holding a walkie-talkie. "We found him."

"Where?" Ellis said. He was at his desk, sunlight bright across his broad shoulders. Moravec hurried after Turner to his office.

"New Brockton," the nurse said. "We've been checking every person who left the institute after the alarm last night."

Her walkie-talkie squawked loudly, static and a heavy voice. Moravec didn't understand what it said. She raised the transceiver and spoke into it. "Stand by." To Ellis she said, "We think he commandeered a doctor's car before she left the grounds last night. That's why we couldn't find him. He just drove out with her."

"Her?" Moravec said.

"Dr. Sara Louise Mills."

Moravec glanced at Ellis.

"Hematology research," Ellis said. "One of our brighter residents."

"What was she doing here at that hour?"

"Running profiles on Central C, according to the log." Ellis clicked his ballpoint pen against the clipboard. "It's not unusual for our staff members to work late in the institute."

"Didn't anyone check her automobile?" Moravec asked.

"She was escorted to her car in the parking lot by one of our security people. There wasn't—"

"I meant at the gate. Didn't anyone check it at the gate?"

"No." Nurse Turner had the walkie-talkie volume turned

down. Someone was talking on it. "No one searched her car. No one—just a minute." She turned the volume up on the transceiver.

Moravec tried to interpret the voice he heard against the static but it was no use. When Nurse Turner lowered the radio she looked pleased.

"Yes?" Ellis said.

"We attached a homing device to Dr. Mills's car this morning when our man was there," she said. "Just as a precaution." She nodded at the walkie-talkie. "That was Fisher. He's parked at the end of her block. They just passed him in her car. Dr. Mills is driving. The sequel is with her."

"The what?"

Turner looked at Moravec, surprised. "The Hahnemann Sequel. Your patient, doctor."

TWENTY-SIX

INTERSTATE 81

"WHERE ARE we going?"

"I'll let you know."

David studied the map he had found in the glove compartment. They had been driving on I-81 South for twenty minutes.

"I'm not driving you to Oklahoma, Townsend." She glanced over at him. "You hear me?"

"What do you think about Syracuse?" David said.

Sara stared at the road. "As a tourist or a hostage?"

"Looks like about fifty miles. It's a pretty good-sized place, isn't it?"

"You don't *really* want to go to Syracuse?"

"I don't know yet. I might love Syracuse." He fumbled with the map. It was worn out, the edges frayed and sections taped together. Texaco flags indicated stations on the highways. He unfolded it, turning it over to the insert of street maps of cities in upper New York state. A yellow Magic Marker line had been drawn over a route from New Brockton to Syracuse to a torn spot above Buffalo. "What's this for?" He held the map.

"That's how I find my sister's house. She and Ed moved to the Falls about two years ago."

"The Falls?"

"*Niagara* Falls."

"She a doctor, too?"

"Susan? No, Susan is cleverer than I am. She married

money. They're in Hawaii for the week." She let out a defeated sigh. "She even asked me to go with them." She glanced over at David. "Look, if we're going to be cooped up together until we get to Syracuse, please take off that jacket. It stinks."

David sniffed the collar. "What's—"

"Fish," Sara said. "*Dead* fish. I hate the smell of fish."

David pulled it off and tossed it in the back. "What was all that Medicare business about . . . on the phone?"

"Gibberish mostly. I had to say something. All I could think of what the nurse might accept as a patient verification request from WRCRDS."

David looked at her blankly.

"It's the Central Computer," she said. "The 'Primary CC,' we call it. That's a medical in joke—cc . . ."

"What's it do?"

"Almost everything. It's set up on time-share between the departments in the institute. Everyone has access to it during certain hours of the day, except when WRCRDS is doing its quarterly department auditing, then we get bumped off the system."

"Records?"

"W-R-C-R-D-S. It's an acronym—Weeksbriar Retrieval: Central Records and Document System. Records. It keeps all our files and research in memory storage. When we want something we just call it up on our department code. That's what I was doing last night before . . . before I bumped into you. Running profiles. It's the only time of day to get on-line when Records is doing its quarterly audit, which it *is* doing this week."

"What's a profile?"

"Etiology profiles on anemic case studies for analysis. Evaluation tests. I'm a second-year hematology resident. The profiles are individual case studies programmed into CC. I just call up a profile and make a diagnosis of the case. CC scores it automatically at the end of each run."

164

"You say you're a fellow? That means you're still a student or something?"

She sighed. "I graduated twelfth in my class from Boston University School of Medicine. I did my internship and residency at Massachusetts General. I came to Weeksbriar because they offered me a research grant and I took it because it is one of the finest sub-specialty institutes in the country. I am a *real* doctor."

David nodded. "What about this computer. What kind of files does it keep? Patients?"

"We don't have patients," she said wearily. "I keep telling you, it's a research institute. A privately funded research institute. Not a hospital. We don't treat patients."

"What about the other side?" David said. "The psychiatric clinic. Do they use the same computer?"

"Of course. It's plugged into the Euromedic system."

"Then the computer has files on those patients, right?"

"I'm sure it does."

"Then there'd be a file in it on me."

Sara avoided looking at him. "Probably on someone named Franklin, yes."

"Could you get a copy of it?"

"A copy? Of your medical file? Ha!"

"Would it be so hard? You're a doctor. You work there. You—"

"Look, Townsend, in the first place I'm not *at* the institute. In the second place, I don't have access to that computer information—everything is code-accessed. And in the third place it's a felony in this state to have unauthorized possession of a patient's history and diagnostic records—especially a mentally ill patient." She glanced in the rearview mirror, then back at the road. "Why don't you just concentrate on breaking one law at a time."

"I was just thinking out loud."

"You'd better think about Syracuse. Because that's going to be the end of the line for me."

"There's time to figure out something."

She glanced in the mirror again. "Well, maybe there is and maybe there isn't."

"What?"

"I don't want you to get into one of your screaming fits again, but" —she nodded at the mirror "—I think we're being followed."

David crushed the map between his body and the seat as he jerked around to look out the rear window. "Where?"

"The dark green one. It's way back there. I think I saw it in town before we left."

David squinted. He could see five cars and a truck behind them. The truck was passing the green car, an Oldsmobile. It was too far away to see the driver. David turned back in his seat. "How long's he been back there?"

"I just noticed a few minutes ago."

"Damn." David looked back again. He was staring at the car, trying to decide if there was more than one person in it. "Speed up a little."

"Why?"

"Just do what I tell you."

The car accelerated to fifty, fifty-five, sixty.

"That's enough," David said. "Slow down." He looked for the green Oldsmobile.

"Do you see it?"

The Olds hadn't changed position, hadn't speeded up. "He didn't move." He adjusted the rearview mirror.

"It might not be anything," Sara said. "Lots of cars are on their way to Syracuse."

David opened the map, smoothing out the wrinkles. "Where are we now?"

"Pulaski exit is coming up."

"Pulaski? That a big town?"

"It isn't Syracuse. Look, it might not be anything. I just wanted to get you off the subject—"

"There's an easy way to find out if we're being followed.

Take the next exit. If they're following, it's someone from the hospital. The police would already have stopped us."

Sara's tongue flicked across her lips. "Then what?"

"I don't know yet."

"I should have kept my mouth shut."

"Maybe."

Sara eased the Volvo into the exit lane. Halfway down the ramp, David swore.

"What is—"

"The Olds is getting off," he said. He swung back to see where they were going. "Pull into that Dairy Queen."

She crunched over a mound of plowed snow and drove around the deserted building until the Volvo was pointed back toward the street. As they came around the building, the Oldsmobile passed in front of them. There were two men in the front seat, dressed in parkas. Neither paid any attention as they drove by.

"You recognize them?"

"No."

David stared after the Oldsmobile. It had stopped at a traffic light. When the light changed it continued on. He let out his breath.

"What were you going to do if they were following us?"

"I don't know." Admitting it made him angry. "I'd have thought of something."

"Well, think about this." She nodded at the dashboard. "We need gas."

The gas gauge showed less than a quarter tank.

"And while you're chewing on that," she said. "I have to make a pit stop myself."

David looked at her with a blank expression.

"I have to go to the john," she said.

"Uh-huh."

"No, I really do."

He picked up the map and tried to find Pulaski. "How far is Syracuse?"

"Too far to wait." She opened a hand on the steering wheel, gesturing toward the traffic light. "There's a station at the corner. We could go there."

It was a Mobil station. A pickup was parked at one of the islands.

"How about it, Townsend? I'm not kidding. I have to go."

He looked at her but said nothing.

"I won't *do* anything. I just have to go to the john. I give you my word."

David stared at the gas station.

"Please?"

He folded up the map. "I'll drive."

The kid working the station was the only attendant. He was dressed in a fur-lined parka and wore a beard. David touched his face at the reminder.

"Yes, sir?" The kid was at least six-foot-four and he had to bend down to look into David's window. David kept the car running.

"Fill it," David said.

"Super?" The kid's expression was friendly. He was big, linebacker material.

"Yeah."

"Check the hood?"

Sara was looking at the rest-room signs. "No, just gas, thanks."

"You bet."

"Rest rooms locked?"

"Yes, sir." The kid pointed to the office. "Key's on a hook inside the door."

David rolled up the window. He turned to Sara. "All right, doctor. Let's do this slow and easy."

"I can go myself."

He turned off the engine. "We'll both go."

A portable television in the office was tuned to the Tournament of Roses parade. The ladies' room key was on a short length of chain with a red-painted nut at one end. The men's room key had a blue nut. David took both of them. They walked around to the side of the station.

"I can take it from here," Sara said. She held out her hand.

"I'll hold onto the key." He opened the door for her.

"Look, Townsend, I'm not—"

The station bell rang as another car pulled up to the self-serve pump on the other side of the island. David noticed Sara's eyes flicker. He turned to look. It was a police car.

He shoved her ahead of him into the rest room.

"Jesus, Townsend!"

"Quiet!"

David cracked the door and peered out. It was a patrol car with one cop. The name below the police emblem on the door said PULASKI. David waited for the cop to make some move, but he didn't do anything. The kid pumping gas into the Volvo waved at him. The cop nodded. He wasn't wearing a hat. Then he reached down for something, his head disappearing below the level of the window. David held his breath. When the cop reappeared he had a Thermos in one hand and a cup in the other. In his mouth was a doughnut.

"What's happening?" Her voice made an echo in the room. David felt her breath on his neck.

"Nothing. I don't think he's looking for us."

"Nobody's looking for us."

David eased the door closed and turned to her. "If you've got something to do then do it. I don't want to hang around here." He nodded at the stall. "You got one minute."

"Not with you in here!"

"You can shut the door."

"Goddammit, I—"

"Fifty seconds," David said.

She said something David didn't hear and went into the stall. The latch snapped closed with a clang. He heard a rustle of clothes as she hung her coat on the back of the door.

"Would you mind at least turning on the sink?"

"What?"

"The water faucet, turn it on."

"Why?"

"Townsend, just turn on the goddamn water."

A folded copy of the Pulaski *Democrat* was propped behind the faucet. David stuffed the newspaper into his army jacket and turned both sink handles on full. The room filled with the sound of water splashing in the basin.

"I didn't think doctors got embarrassed about things like that," David said. He glanced at the clean tile walls. "I've never been locked in a ladies' room before. I always wondered if you had graffiti on your side. It's kind of a disappointment."

The toilet flushed.

When Sara came out, coat over her arm, David said, "Okay now?"

She turned off the water faucet. "Let's just get out of here." She didn't look at him.

"Just like before," David said. He took her arm. "Slow and easy." He opened the door and stepped out.

The green Oldsmobile was parked behind the Volvo.

A man in a blue parka was looking under the hood with the attendant. The other man, the driver, was leaning against the car door, staring at David.

"Damn!"

Sara stiffened when she saw the Oldsmobile. "Oh, no—"

"C'mon." He helped her to the station office. He hung the keys back on the hook and pretended to watch the parade on TV. The cop was standing behind his car now, pumping gas with one hand and munching a doughnut with the other. He seemed unaware of the men in the parkas. "You still think I'm imagining things?"

She turned away from the window, taking deep breaths. "Look, Townsend, I don't understand what's happening, but this is scaring the shit out of me."

"That guy by the pump . . . I've seen him before."

"You saw him before . . . where?"

"The clinic."

"Dallas?"

"That's Grant, the guy who picked me up in the van."

"Jesus!"

David stared through the window. "Why don't they do something? If they want me so damned bad, why don't they yell or scream or something? They've got a cop right there." He watched as the attendant went to Sara's car and withdrew the nozzle from the tank.

The man watching David said something to his companion, who glanced sideways at the patrolman. They both put their hands in their parkas and, exhaling steamlike drafts, stared grimly at the engine.

"It's you," David said quickly. "They're afraid of you!"

"What?"

"They don't know how to handle this. They can explain anything I say to the police as the rantings of a nut, but they don't know what *you'll* say. If you back me up, they're sunk. Look at them. They don't want to have anything to do with that cop."

"I never said I believed you, Townsend."

"Then why don't you call me Franklin?"

"I—" She shook her head. "I don't know what to call you. I don't know who those men are and I don't understand any of this Franklin business, but . . . something is wrong." She looked at him. "That's all I know."

"That's all I need," David said. "You just tell the police that."

"You *want* me to talk to the police?"

"I want you to tell them what happened . . . that you talked to the nurse in California. That she said they

171

transferred Franklin here. I know it's a long trip, but even psychos can't age fifteen years and shrink four inches in two days. All I need is for the police to check it out." He took her arm. "C'mon."

"What are you doing?"

"Something that should make you very happy," David said. "Give myself up."

TWENTY-SEVEN

PULASKI

THE ATTENDANT snapped the Volvo's wiper blades down over the clean windshield as David and Sara walked up. The kid smiled at David. "All ready."

"How much?"

"Ah—" the kid glanced back at the pump "—eighteen seventy-five."

David handed him a twenty.

"Be right back," the kid said. He trotted off to the office.

David glanced at the two men standing by the Olds. They hadn't moved, but they were watching him. He handed Sara the car keys. "Just in case." He kept his voice down. "Don't get too far away from the car." Then he stepped across the island to where the cop was hanging the gas nozzle back on the pump.

"Officer?"

The patrolman turned. He had frosting on his lip. "Morning."

"My name's Townsend," David said. "David Townsend. I'm from Oklahoma."

The cop nodded. "Mr. Townsend."

"I've got a problem."

The cop looked at the Volvo. "Lost?"

"I want to report a kidnapping."

"Kidnapping?" He frowned. "Who got kidnapped?"

"Me. I was kidnapped from Dallas, Texas, yesterday morning and taken up the road to a place called Weeksbriar. Last night I got out. I was—"

"Wait . . . just a minute now." The cop turned serious. "What's your name again?"

"David Townsend."

"And somebody kidnapped *you?*"

The man standing beside the driver's door of the Olds was smiling.

"That's right," David said. "I want to report it."

"You got some identification, Townsend?"

"No."

"No? C'mon, you gotta have something." He nodded at the Volvo. "Let's see your driver's license."

"They took all my identification."

"Who did?"

"The people at Weeksbriar."

"Weeksbriar? You mean the place up in New Brockton?" Something sparked behind his eyes. "Wait a minute . . . we got a bulletin—"

"Yeah, I know," David said. "That was me. But it's a mistake. Look, my name is David Townsend. I want you to take me to the police station and we'll straighten all this out. They're doing some strange things at Weeksbriar. I think somebody better look into it."

"Uh-huh." The cop glanced at Sara. "Who's the lady?"

"A doctor. She can verify what I'm telling you."

"Well, somebody better. I don't think—"

"David!"

The men in the parkas were moving.

"Officer, my name is Norman Louis, Weeksbriar security," the taller one said. He had moved quickly toward David and the cop and held out an official looking identity card. His smile was as quick as his feet. "Hello, Mr. Franklin. Slipped away again, didn't you?"

"Sorry, pal, but you only get one chance," David said. He turned to the cop. "This is one of the guys who kidnapped me. There's a woman, too. She's—"

David felt his arm move. It was suddenly behind his back, twisting up, reaching between his shoulder blades.

"You're not going to make a scene, are you, Richard?" It was a calm, firm voice that came from over his shoulder. "Just relax. We'll get you home, don't worry. Nobody's chasing you anymore, Franklin."

"Hey!" David reached for the cop. "Hey, my name's Townsend! I'm not—"

David's arm jerked higher. He gasped and the cold air burned his throat. He was on his toes, mouth wide and inarticulate. His eyes watered and somehow the pain shut off his hearing. He saw the cop say something—a question by the expression on his face—then he nodded. It was the cop's nod that frightened David more than the pain. It was a nod acquiescing Weeksbriar's rights. The cop wasn't going to look into anything. He was going to get back into his car and have another doughnut and let the men in the blue parkas take care of the nut who had no driver's license.

All of David's senses returned in a rush when he heard Sara scream. The guard called Louis had half-turned David around, pointing him toward the Oldsmobile, and David saw the other man with his arm around Sara.

"Get your hands off me! I'm a doctor, for chrissake! Get your—Help me!"

The attendant had just stepped out of the station office with the change from David's twenty when he saw Sara flailing against a hammer lock and screaming. He saw a young woman in trouble and charged.

It was the best open-field tackle David had ever seen. The kid hit the man like a freight train, knocking Sara out of his grasp, and they bounced off the rear fender of the Volvo onto an oily patch of concrete between the islands.

"Burt!" The kid had him in a bear hug, rolling on the pavement. "Burt!" He was yelling for the cop.

"No!" Burt yelled back. The cop started for the fight, bumping through the opening between the gas pumps where

Norman Louis was holding David. For an instant the grinding pain in David's arm was relieved. It was enough to fight back.

David swung out with his good hand, reaching blindly for anything. His knuckles scraped across cold metal. He grabbed, felt the gasoline nozzle from the pump. His fingers slid down to the handle until he found the flow lever, and squeezed.

Mobil super unleaded sprayed everywhere.

The first stream hit Norman Louis in the back of the head until he turned his face into it. He screamed and his hands went to his eyes, releasing David's arm.

David dropped the gas nozzle and scrambled to his hands and knees. Sara was leaning against the open door of the Volvo, trying to get her breath.

"Get in the car!" David shouted.

The cop was yelling and wiping gasoline from his coat sleeve into his eyes. The kid sat on the ground, staring around dumbfounded.

"Go!" David's eyes were burning. He tried to get around the car, but crashed into the rear bumper. "Start the car!" He stumbled to the Volvo's passenger door. Sara twisted the ignition key. *"C'mon!"*

The Volvo roared to life as David got the door open.

"Hold it, Townsend!"

David swung around. Norman Louis was standing in front of the Oldsmobile, and he was holding something in his right hand. It looked like a large flashlight with a handle and trigger guard. The way he was holding it, David knew it wasn't any flashlight.

When the Volvo started moving, David lunged for the open door. So did Burt, the cop. David saw the muzzle of Norman Louis's flashlight jerk with a *thuumpt* as he dived into the front seat. Whatever came out of it hit Burt. The cop screamed, his arms splayed, and he crumpled to the ground.

David didn't see what happened next. Sara had the Volvo screeching on the pavement. The door slammed itself shut as she made a hard turn onto the street, jumping over the curb and nearly jolting David's teeth out.

"Where are we going?" she screamed. She shifted into third. The Volvo fishtailed on the slippery street, bouncing against the crusty peaks of plowed snow on both sides of the lane.

"Just go!" David yelled back.

Sara turned onto a two-lane state road, parallel to the interstate. They passed a gray farmhouse and a mailbox that stood out starkly against the bleak cover of snow. "Goddammit, Townsend! Goddammit!"

"Watch where you're going! Slow down! Watch—*slow down!*"

She wheeled around a truck, too wide, and spewed gravel from the shoulder, then overcorrected and swung back across the road. A Pulaski city limit sign whizzed by only inches from David's window.

She drove for five minutes, flat out, and David watched behind them. Nobody followed.

"Pull over," David said, but Sara didn't respond. She held the steering wheel like a weapon, her eyes staring straight ahead.

David grabbed the steering wheel. "Pull over. Sara—" He chopped a hand hard on her thigh. Her foot came off the accelerator. The Volvo slowed. David guided it to the shoulder of the road until it finally rolled to a stop. He snatched the keys from the ignition and got out of the car, moving quickly through ankle-deep snow to Sara's side. All he could smell was gasoline.

She didn't move when he opened the door. She just stared ahead. Tear stains streaked her cheeks.

"Move over." He pulled her hands off the wheel. A gust of wind blew icy crystals down the neck of his jacket.

"Damn it, *move!*" He shoved her over and got in, slamming the door.

"He told me not to make any trouble or . . . or I'd have more trouble than I'd know how to handle," Sara said. Her hair was askew, covering her face. "He told me to keep my mouth shut."

"Yeah, well, they're off my Christmas list too." David started the car, got it moving.

"He shot that cop. What—" She finally looked at him. "What was that . . . that thing?"

"I don't know." David took the map from the dashboard. He tried to unfold it and drive with one hand, diverting his glance from the road to the map every few seconds.

"They called you Townsend." She thought about that a minute, then she hit the dashboard with her fist. She looked at David with frustrated anger. "Christ, you really are in trouble!"

"You could sound a little more disappointed about it."

"What the hell have you got me into!"

"Listen—" David gave her a hard look. "These are *your* people running around shooting up Mobil stations. Remember that. Whoever they are and whatever they want from me, they're from the same place where *you* hang out."

She bowed her head. "I'm sorry. I . . . Jesus, I don't know what to think . . ."

"Don't cry."

"I don't cry, Townsend. And don't talk down to me like I was a simp without a goddamn brain!"

"You can knock that off, too. You don't have to talk like that. It doesn't suit you, swearing like a lumberjack."

"Doesn't suit me?" Sara rose up in her seat. "You simple bastard! Who the hell do you think you're talking to? I don't bake cookies for the goddamn P.T.A.! Get this straight, Townsend, I don't need your protection or permission for anything I do. I—for chrissakes—I drove *you* away from those maniacs!"

"All right, all right," David said. "I apologize." He clicked the turn signal on and glanced in the rearview mirror. He eased into the right lane, heading for the interstate entrance ramp.

"And I'll talk any way I—" Sara looked around. "Wait a minute. This is I-90 West." She looked at David. "Where are you going? Syracuse is *that* way."

"Not going to Syracuse."

"Not going? I know people in Syracuse. Friends who—"

"You want those guys visiting your friends? I think we'd better find a safe place that isn't so close to Weeksbriar. Someplace with a little privacy." He handed her the map with his finger on the yellow line. "Do you have a key to your sister's house?"

Sara stared at the map a moment. "No . . . but I know where the spare is. You don't think we should go to the police?"

"We did that."

"I mean some other place."

"You think it'll be different?"

Sara stared at the snow-covered country. When she turned back to David her voice was softer. "Just for the record, I believe you really are David Townsend from Oklahoma."

David nodded. "Thanks."

"I wish I knew what to do."

David rolled down his window a couple of inches. The gasoline fumes in his jacket were giving him a headache. "We'll figure out something. How about helping me out of this thing? The fumes'll put me to sleep."

Sara moved closer to get the jacket off. She didn't move away after she tossed it in the back. "I'm scared, David. I am really, truly frightened."

For a woman who didn't cry, she was about to break a rule. He put his arm around her and she moved against him. Her shoulders trembled.

"We'll be okay," David said. He squeezed her shoulder. Above the gasoline fumes her hair smelled of wintergreen. "Anyway . . . we got rid of the fish smell."

She laughed first, then she cried.

TWENTY-EIGHT

WEEKSBRIAR

"WE'LL HAVE David Townsend tonight, Dr. Ellis assures me," Moravec said into the phone. "By this time tomorrow I'll be in Madrid with him." He was sitting at Ellis's desk, using Ellis's notepad. Ellis sat impassively in one of the cockpit chairs. His eyes never left Moravec. Haldern was back from church. He had called from London as soon as he'd learned that Townsend wasn't on his way to Madrid.

"I see," the voice from London said. There was a pause as if he were reading something. "Who was it, did you say?"

"Again, please?"

"Who did Townsend kidnap?"

Moravec glanced at Ellis. "Junior staff. Dr. Sara Mills. She's a hematology fellow here at Weeksbriar."

"A woman?"

"Yes."

"How are you handling it?"

Moravec was surprised at the question. "My first concern is Townsend, of course. I really haven't given any thought to the situation otherwise." He avoided using the word problem.

"It may be a bit sticky, this kidnapping business. But let Ellis handle that end. He'll have to deal with her. Your only concern is the donor patient."

"Yes, I quite agree."

"Mills, you said. The name sounds familiar. She doesn't

know about the Hahnemann project, does she? I mean, she isn't one of our people?"

Our people? Moravec wondered how many people knew about it. "Dr. Mills is a twenty-six-year-old resident on the hematology research staff," he said. "All she knows is whatever Townsend has told her."

"Yes, well, never mind then. Just be careful, Luther. We don't want—we can't have this get out of hand. You'll contact the Center as soon as you've recovered Townsend, of course."

"Of course."

"I have the latest report from McPhearson in front of me now. It isn't good, Luther."

"Yes, I know. I'm getting reports as well."

"Are you? Oh, of course. Well, get this business over quickly, Luther. Get Townsend to Madrid as soon as possible. We haven't time to waste." He sounded like McPhearson.

"I will."

"We made contact with Borzov," Haldern added without enthusiasm. "I'm afraid the Russians are years behind. They're implanting hybridomas directly into the hypophysis. Hahnemann tried that, I believe, in 1975. Anyway . . ."

"I will keep you informed of developments here," Moravec said. He wanted to get off the phone.

"Good. Good. We'll all be waiting."

Moravec set the receiver back in its cradle as Nurse Turner entered the office.

"I just spoke to Greer," she said, addressing Ellis. Moravec might as well have been invisible. "They had Townsend . . . and lost him."

Ellis came out of his chair. "What?"

"They were at a service station about twenty miles south of the interstate. The recovery was complicated because a police patrolman was there too . . . gassing up his car.

182

Townsend recognized one of our people and made a run for it. They tried to use the stun pistol, but the cop got in the way."

"Pistol?" Moravec looked at Ellis with astonishment. "You're not letting them use a *weapon* on Townsend?"

"It's an electric stun device," Ellis said. "Shoots a pair of positive and negative contacts, high voltage at low amps. The electric shock immobilizes the target but doesn't hurt him."

"My God," Moravec said, "David Townsend is not a *target*."

"Look, nobody's trying to hurt him. Just let me take care of this." To Turner he said, "Where is he now?"

"We're not sure. They lost contact. The homing signal on the car is out of range of the tracking unit."

"It's supposed to have a five-mile range."

Turner shrugged. "The weather cuts that in half. But we'll find it again. There are ten cars in the area."

"Then do it. Get him back."

Nurse Turner nodded. "There's just one other thing."

"Yes?"

"Dr. Mills. When they left the station, she was driving."

"So?"

"Nobody forced her to go with Townsend," she said. "Dr. Mills didn't make any attempt to get away from him." Her glance touched Moravec before she delivered the rest of her observation. "I think we have to assume that Dr. Mills isn't a hostage."

Ellis brooded a moment. "She's confused, that's all. Frightened."

"Yes, sir. It just makes our job more complicated." Nurse Turner let out a sigh. "I don't know what Townsend told her, but—" she looked directly at her boss—"she's on his side now."

TWENTY-NINE

INTERSTATE 90

AT THE Waterloo turnpike exit they stopped at a Burger King and ordered hamburgers at the drive-in window. Townsend drove for another hour. The windshield wipers batted against a light snow. Sara fell asleep against the window. Traffic wasn't heavy and David kept a running tab on the cars behind him, pulling onto the shoulder every twenty minutes to stop and wait, but there wasn't any sign of the Oldsmobile. He felt safe as long as he kept moving.

Sara came awake suddenly when he opened the door and slid behind the wheel. A swirl of snow came with him. "What's the matter?" She looked outside. "Why are we stopped?"

"Nature call," David said. "About sixty miles to Niagara Falls?"

She exercised her eyes. "You want me to drive?"

"No, I'm all right."

"You could rest."

"Rather drive." He watched the mirror and pulled out as a double tandem rig passed. "That's what I do—" he nodded ahead at the truck "—when I'm not being hi-jacked."

Sara yawned. "Do you like it, driving a truck?"

"What's not to like?"

"I don't know. It seems a lonely way to spend your time."

"Some people like that."

"Do you?"

184

"Yeah . . . sometimes. What made you want to be a doctor? It's not the usual profession people go into, is it?"

"You mean women?"

"I mean anybody. What do people call you?"

"Dr. Mills."

Townsend glanced at her. "C'mon."

"*You* can call me Sara," she said finally. "I like to be on a first-name basis with the men I sleep with."

"You have many of those?"

"Those what?"

"First-name basis . . . friends?"

"This may come as a shock, David, but everything I do is not a subject for conversation."

"Sorry." He watched the passing countryside for a while then asked, "So, why *are* you a doctor? I mean, when you were a little girl and all your little friends played with dolls and made pancakes, what was it that turned you onto blood?"

"My grandfather was a surgeon."

"Ah."

"He lived in Chicago when I was a little girl. When we went to visit he used to take me on rounds with him at the hospital. From the time I started school I knew I would be an M.D."

"How'd you get hooked up with Weeksbriar?"

"Look, David, whatever you may think of the institute, it isn't something evil. I don't know who brought you there or why, but everyone I know is involved in bona fide medical research."

"So, who runs it? I don't mean who. I mean what—corporation, government—"

"The institute itself isn't supported by government funds though the staff can accept grants. Weeksbriar is a privately run facility. It's one of nine medical complexes in the United States, part of a larger network around the world."

"To study blood?"

"No. It's a medical conglomerate headquartered in

England. It supports research in every medical discipline. Weeksbriar is the base of the U.S. group. And not all of them are research-only institutes. We're supported by income-producing facilities within the parent corporation. My work at Weeksbriar, for example, is financed through a grant from Euromedic Industries. When I'm finished there I'll have a choice of working anywhere in the Euromedic system that supports a hematologic subspecialty."

"That's good, is it?"

"Very. Euromedic is a progressive medical phenomenon. There isn't another organization like it in the world. It's a rare privilege to be invited on staff. Applications for grants run over fifty to one."

"And you're one of the chosen few?"

"I'm good at what I do."

Townsend passed the truck. "So, Weeksbriar isn't the only one around then?"

"It's the only one around here."

"How many are there?"

"Altogether?" She shook her head. "I'm not sure. In the States there are nine Euromedic stations."

"Stations? Sound like a herd of FM channels."

"As a matter of fact, they are connected—through CC's big brother, MAG, Medical Assimulation Group, in London. Satellite communications."

"Big Brother?"

"I didn't mean it like that. MAG is a centralized communications network of independent systems. Weeksbriar is the headquarters for the American group. There's also a South American group . . . African, European, Middle East . . . Each group has a station master, like Weeksbriar in this group. It's like CBS with six affiliates. That's what makes Euromedic so unique. Every group shares its research information with every other through the MAG data clearinghouse operations set up in London. We're not competing like everyone else. Euromedic is humanitarian minded. We really do intend to heal the sick.

186

That's a simplistic overview of the Euromedic philosophy, but essentially that's our primary mission. We aren't preoccupied with medical corporations as tax shelters or seeing only patients who have their Blue Shield papers in order. We aren't in it for the bucks, if that makes sense to you. Our ultimate goal is to cure without discrimination, not to have an answering service and an expensive home in the suburbs."

"I noticed that," David said. "What about the psycho ward? How many of those are there?"

"Weeksbriar and Brentwood are the only two facilities that support a psychiatric unit in the American group. The rest are research orientated or R&D, like Carraway Biomedical Technologies in Houston."

"What do *they* do?"

"I don't know exactly. Develop biomedical monitoring instruments, I think. That's where the ICP came from."

"The bubble thing?"

"Yes. There's a toxicology and osteopathic medicine center in Atlanta and a cardiac and neurologic studies institute in Saint Augustine. A facility in North Carolina does pharmaceutical research. The one in New Mexico has something to do with cryosurgery. The only hospital in the entire Euromedic organization is Saint Mary's in London. A teaching hospital. But there is enough work to keep everyone busy without resorting to kidnapping likely patients."

"You don't think there's maybe a sudden shortage of patients over in England? Maybe they need people to experiment on. American truck drivers, say."

"Euromedic is not involved in a conspiracy to kidnap anyone, David," Sara said.

"I heard them say they wanted to transfer me."

"How? Where?" Sara shook her head. "It doesn't make sense. Why would someone at Weeksbriar take such an enormous risk? What makes you worth the trouble?"

David stared at the road. "I don't know, but it has

something to do with my brother. I've been thinking about it for the last hour and a half. Those old men locked up in the fruitcake ward, they recognized me. They thought I was Stuart. Stuart's involved in this somehow, I know it. My little brother was always getting into something that I had to help him out of."

"Little brother? I thought you were twins?"

"We are, but I'm older. Two minutes. It makes a difference." David nodded to himself. "As soon as we get to your sister's I'm going to find out exactly what the hell is going on."

"How?"

"I'll call him up on the phone."

THIRTY

WEEKSBRIAR

MORAVEC SAT alone in his office, sipping the wretched coffee
he'd bought from a coin machine in the staff lounge, and
studied Dr. Sara Mills's file. He wanted to know what sort of
woman Townsend was dragging around with him. He was
surprised to discover that Dr. Mills was a very bright
hematologist. She had interned at Massachusetts General
after graduation from Boston University and Yale. She had
published in several journals including a clinical review on
thrombocytopenia in the *Journal of Internal Medicine* that
he remembered reading. The file contained a single pass-
port-size color photo that, he was sure, didn't do her justice.
Moravec held the photograph and tried to imagine the
woman. He wondered how they were getting on, the young
doctor and the frustrated architect-truck driver.

The last page of her file was a yellow insert sheet. It said:

Mills, S.
ID 357938
See also "WNTGRN" ref, WRCRDS DIR 601 (CC)

Moravec sat up. WNTGRN was a special file that Toby
Mallerbe's SCS people had dreamed up. WNTGRN was
computerese for Wintergreen, the project name for what
Moravec had believed was simply one of SCS's computer
exercises.

Wintergreen was a computer analysis of information
relating to Euromedic employees. It was a simple process to
code certain data already stored in the computer's memory

from personnel records—age, sex, specialty, service, achievements—and analyze it to find likely candidates for the Hahnemann project. SCS programmed the analysis not because it was needed or even significant, but because they *could* do it. The personnel files of every employee at Euromedic/London were made available to the computer. Moravec saw some of the results. Of the original twelve hundred files that were analyzed and ranked, he was listed as number 189. Mallerbe himself was ranked 342. The computer ranking used weighted criteria in assimilating the data. For instance, the age group twenty-seven to thirty-two was given more points than any other age range. Women were preferred over men if they were over thirty-seven. Specialties in certain medical fields took precedence over technical expertise. The ideal candidate for consideration as a Hahnemann subject, according to the computer, was a man, aged twenty-eight, whose specialty was inventive genetic research. But the analysis was done, after all, by a computer that had only coded figures to work with, and some of the results were amusing. The number one ranked Euromedic employee was a young surgeon at St. Mary's who had been involved in dozens of liver transplants, which, considering his achievements, was a reasonable enough choice. But number four was a twenty-six-year-old woman employed as a cook in the Research Studies Center's kitchen. Her personnel file job description was listed as nutritionist. Ironically, no one of Rennit's team was ranked above 532. Townsend, Moravec remembered, was number 610. The entire exercise seemed to reinforce the notion that as fast and efficient as computers might be, they were still machines. They were tools, not decision makers.

None of it explained the yellow page Moravec held in his hand. He was sure it was a mistake. They weren't seriously considering *using* this ranking, he thought.

Moravec went to the couch with the insert page. The BriefPac took less than five seconds to boot up. WNTGRN was listed in the memory directory as the fifteenth of twenty-seven files. He called up the file and the screen displayed the coded banner and an index of where else the file could be found.

```
WNTGRN (WINTERGREEN)
BRIEFPAC #6 (MORAVEC, L)
NOT ADMITTABLE W/O PREDESIGNED ACCESS CODE
INDEX REGISTRY:
     MAG CENTRAL      (WNTGRN DIR 1132)      [COMPLETE]
     MAG CENTRAL      (WNTGRN DIR 4201)      [PARTIAL]
     WEEKSBRIAR       (WRCRDS DIR 601)       [PARTIAL]
     BRIEFPAC/6       (BRFPC DIR 15)         [23459 BLKS ONLY]
     SPECOMSEC        (SCS DIR 843)          [COMPLETE]
     SPECOMSEC        (SCS DIR 1057)         [COMPLETF]

THIS UNIT CONTAINS 23459 BLKS OF 839032 BLKS FROM THE SOURCE FILE.
FOR ACCESS TO THE COMPLETE FILE CONTACT SCS FOR CLEARANCE.

FILE NOTE: THIS FILE CONTAINS WINTERGREEN CANDIDATE LIST, RANKING AND
SHORT FORM INDIVIDUAL STATISTICS. FOR MORE INFORMATION SEE ABOVE.

TO REVIEW LIST TYPE "REVIEW." TO DISPLAY INDIVIDUAL TYPE "SEARCH:"
[SURNAME, CHRISTIAN] SOR [ID NO.]
```

On the keyboard Moravec typed Dr. Mills's ID number from the yellow insert page. He expected the machine to keep him waiting for several seconds as it searched the file twice for the number. It would make two passes because when it didn't locate the identity number on the first pass it would try again. Moravec was stunned when the screen blinked after only two seconds.

```
FOUND "357938"

MILLS, SARA    ID: 357938      DOB: 6/14/53
POB: S. HADLEY, MA    EMP: WEEKSBRIAR MRI
NAT: U.S.        WNTGRN RANK: 12
REL: (SIB) SUSAN (MRS. EDWARD) WOMACK/NIAGARA FALLS, NY
     (PAR) THOMAS R. MILLS/HOLYOKE, MA
     (PAR) LEAH R. MILLS/HOLYOKE, MA
```

Moravec stared at the screen. The Hahnemann project had gone much further than anyone had told him. They were actually ranking candidates and inserting addendums to personnel files. Wintergreen wasn't just a silly computer exercise. If Euromedic had gone this far then they were taking it very seriously.

When Moravec entered Ellis's office, it had all the appearance of a command center. Two computer terminals had been set up on the desk and an operator sat before them, typing inquiries into one, then the other. Ellis and Nurse Turner stood in front of a large map of upper New York State taped to the wall. A dark red line marked the map from New Brockton south. Near Syracuse the line turned sharply west.

"We've reestablished contact," Ellis said when he saw Moravec. He jabbed a finger at the end of the line. "They're here. Interstate Ninety. Moving west. Since we picked up the signal they've stopped several times. Townsend's checking to see if he's being followed."

"How do you know that?" Moravec said.

"Why else would he stop on an interstate highway? There's nothing wrong with the car."

"Could he be making calls?"

"We thought of that." Ellis made an impatient face. "No, he's just stopping along the road . . . two or three minutes. He's clever, but he doesn't know much about surveillance."

"No?"

"We're using different cars," Turner said. "Two cars are tracking him from adjacent roads. The only car on the interstate is ahead of him."

Moravec nodded. "I'm surprised you don't have a helicopter."

192

"We do," Turner said, "but the weather's too bad."

"Do you know where they're going?"

Turner shook her head.

"If we knew that, doctor, we wouldn't have to waste the manpower following him," Ellis said. He looked at the map. "I think he's afraid to call the police. That's why they haven't gone to the authorities. The incident at the service station scared him." Ellis glanced at Turner. "It scared both of them. I don't think *they* know where they're going. We've had people on the phone to Dr. Mills's friends and acquaintances. Discreetly, of course. I don't want anyone knowing she has been kidnapped."

"And?"

"No one's heard from her."

"Have you called Mrs. Womack?" Moravec took an address book from his jacket pocket.

"Who?"

"Mrs. Edward Womack," Moravec said, searching for the page. "Dr. Mills's sister."

"We haven't been able to find a phone listing for her sister," Nurse Turner said. "Anyway, her sister lives in Tennessee. Townsend and Dr. Mills are not headed in that direction."

Moravec handed her the address book open to the Ws. "I was just in Dr. Mills's office. I wanted to verify something I found in the MAG computer file. Her personnel file here identifies her next of kin as Mrs. Womack, address in Nashville, Tennessee. But the MAG file shows an address in New York." He pointed to the listing under her sister's name. The Nashville address had been lined out and another written in the margin. "She moved."

Ellis went to the book. "Let me see that."

"I called the number there," Moravec said, "but there wasn't any answer. Dr. Mills's desk calendar has two weeks blocked out. It says 'Susan and Ed in Hawaii.' Her sister's name is Susan."

"Niagara Falls? You think they're going to her sister's house?"

"I think it's a reasonable assumption," Moravec said. "It's a place Dr. Mills knows . . . and it's vacant. I didn't realize it until now but"—he pointed to the map "—Interstate Ninety goes straight to Niagara Falls."

Ellis snapped the book shut. "Right." To Turner he said, "How soon can you get your team there?"

"Break off the track?" She looked surprised. "We don't *know* that they're going to Niagara Falls."

"Moravec's right," Ellis said. "Where else are they going to go? How soon can you get me air transportation?"

"Within an hour, but—"

"Set it up. I want to be there when Townsend is recovered. Same routine as earlier, sodium secobarbital before departure, chlorpromazine as required."

Nurse Turner jotted notes on a pad. "The chlorpromazine won't be necessary. The flight from Niagara International should take less than an hour."

Ellis nodded. "I want two attendants from Weeksbriar, yourself and—"

"I'm going with you," Moravec said.

Ellis looked at him sharply. "No. There isn't room."

"Make room." Moravec was tired of Ellis's orders. Townsend was ultimately his responsibility. The only way he could be sure that Townsend was carefully treated was to be there when they picked him up. "I'm going with you."

"Are you *telling* me?" Ellis said.

"I'm making a very firm request."

"This is *my* operation, Moravec. My recovery."

"I won't interfere."

For a moment Ellis studied him. "Dr. Moravec is going with us," he finally said to Nurse Turner. He turned to Moravec. "Just don't get in the way. There's more at stake now than recovering a missing patient."

"More?"

"Dr. Mills. She's become a problem for us. Townsend

194

may be your primary concern, but Dr. Mills is from *my* staff. I will deal with her. Understood?"

Moravec nodded. "I'm sure she'll understand when you explain the situation to her."

"Yes, I'm sure too."

THIRTY-ONE

NIAGARA FALLS

DAVID REACHED Niagara Falls by midafternoon and stopped at a 7-11 to let Sara drive. He bought half a dozen Almond Joy candy bars and a newspaper. The attendant was watching television. The Rose Bowl had just started.

As Sara drove up a winding, wooded drive, David saw a frozen creek off to the left and a dozen skaters practicing their single-bladed skills on the scarred and rutted surface. They passed some residences in a park, large homes with roaring chimneys tucked behind bare-branched sycamores and towering pines. It was the country club professionals' domain, David realized; the territory of the local high rollers.

David studied the lines of a low-roofed ranch-style house with a stone patio as Sara negotiated a tight curve, shifting into second gear. "Your brother-in-law must do very well."

Sara guided the Volvo cautiously along the snow-covered road. "You could say that."

"What's he do?"

"Real estate," she said. "His father started the first national chain. For years their only competition was Century 21. I've never actually seen Ed sell or buy a piece of property, but he talks like he knows what he's doing. The telephone might as well be attached to his ear. He's got one in his car and in every room of the house. Different colors."

"You don't seem to care for him much."

"Ed's all right, if you don't mind an affair or two on the side. And Susan doesn't mind."

"She doesn't?"

"When he made a pass at me I introduced him to my knee. I told Susan. She thought I overreacted. That's Susan." Sara jammed the gear shift back into third. "We're almost there."

They topped a small hill and David saw the house. It seemed to rise out of the ground as if it were set on an elevator. The timbered bridge leading to it seemed to have grown there among sharp-faced rocks and boulders that bordered the steep-walled creek. Set across an eight-foot waterfall that fed the creek, the house was immediately familiar; its criss-crossing cantilevered decks protruded from the central structure like wooden elbows supported on a mountain of jagged rock. Its clean lines were broken only where they merged with the natural features of the terrain around it. Even with the bare trees that dotted the gray wintry landscape, the house was magnificent. "The quint-essence of artistry in environmental architecture," he remembered a professor had referred to it. David gaped as Sara maneuvered the Volvo toward the entrance. It was more beautiful than any picture he'd ever seen of it.

"*This* is your sister's house?"

Sara stopped the car on the incline of the gravel parking apron that allowed a view of the creek behind the house. "What's the matter with it?"

"Nothing's the matter." He studied the house, scanning from cantilever to cantilever. "This is the Gill Creek House," he said almost hoarsely. "Henry Gale Mara's Gill Creek House."

"So?"

"So! I studied this house. It's in every architectural textbook as the preeminent example—"

"*You* studied it?" She gave him a questioning look.

"Everybody studied it! There isn't a landscape design course in any architecture school in this country worth its salt that doesn't know this house. Henry Gale Mara built it in 1935. It's probably Mara's most famous work of environmental architecture, for one thing. It's—"

"It's drafty as hell, for another," Sara said. "Something about the support foundations being higher than normal in case the creek ever rose. Also, the stone walls sweat in the summers. C'mon, it'll take an hour to warm up the place."

Sara found the spare key in a crevice of the rock wall and opened the door. The redwood-paneled foyer was flanked by wide floor-to-ceiling windows designed to provide morning and afternoon sunlight. David pocketed the keys and stood at the railing where an open stairway led down to the first cantilevered level and the enormous room with a fireplace twenty-two feet wide. The waterfall was visible outside through a wall of plate glass that rose to the cantilevered balcony above. He had done a perspective drawing of this room from a photograph in an architectural design class ten years ago. But it didn't look as good as this.

"Well, here it is," Sara said. "It's not exactly the cozy cottage but it is a roof over our heads."

"It's incredible," David said, craning to look at the exposed support beams in the ceiling. "Really. A master-piece."

Sara blew at the hollow place between her cupped hands. "The trouble with living in a masterpiece is that nobody else knows where the warts are . . . or that there are any."

"Those are oak beams from the original Waterloo Bridge in London, did you know that?" David said. "Mara bought them for practically nothing when they rebuilt it in 1935."

"Actually, I did know that. Look, do you mind if we get on with it. The furnace will have to be lit which means it'll be hours before there's any hot water. Also I'm hungry. Later you can tour the shrine. Take notes if you want."

The furnace was in a small room behind the kitchen and took three matches to light. While Sara looked for something to cook, David made a quick tour of the house. There were five bedrooms, each on a different cantilever, all with a view of the creek behind the house. The master bedroom was on the highest level and from the walkout balcony one could see the entire mountain slope. It was like looking out from a magnificent castle keep.

Downstairs David found the study. The bookcase was filled with simulated leather-covered classics that were as stiff and unused as the day they were printed. The desk was neat and orderly and the telephone was a multi-line instrument with buttons and lights, an FM radio, an answering machine and an automatic dialer. Built into the wood panel in the wall across the desk was a color television. The wireless remote was beside the telephone. David wondered what Ed Womack did all day.

He switched on the television. A sports broadcaster was highlighting the bowl games. Arkansas had beaten Oklahoma in the Cotton Bowl, 27 to 21. Oregon State was whipping Michigan, 17 to 3, in the third quarter at the Rose Bowl. David watched with fascination. The rest of the world was rocking along as if nothing had happened.

"Hey, tough guy."

Sara was standing in the doorway, still wearing her coat. It was covered with flour.

"This may just be a romp in the country for you, sports fan, but the rest of us oar pullers are freezing our fannies off. You think you could tear yourself away long enough to build a fire?"

David found a covered log bin on the patio and made half a dozen trips to the fireplace loaded with split wood. He stuffed paper and splinters under the grate and worked at it for half an hour before he got a decent fire going. He hated leaving when Sara called him from the kitchen. The house was really cold.

"Pancakes." She was standing at the stove in her jacket, wielding a wide spatula in one hand while she brushed hair

199

back out of her face with the other. "This is one of the few gourmet meals I can handle. How many do you want?"

David inspected the pan she was working over. "A little thick, aren't they?"

"You want to do this?"

"No, no. They look delicious." The kitchen island was a mess. Bisquick was everywhere.

"There wasn't any milk so I used water."

"Fine. I think you can turn those—"

"Look, you want to be chef, I'll go sit by the warm fire."

She had set two places at the breakfast bar and made coffee. He sat down and poured himself a cup. "After dinner I'll start calling. I figure it's about seven or eight hours difference between here and Johannesburg. It'll be after midnight there."

"What are you going to tell him?"

"I'll tell him just what's happened."

"How's he going to help . . . if he's in Johannesburg?"

"I expect him to know what's going on, and why. First we'll get some questions answered. *Then* we'll figure out what to do about it."

"You seem pretty sure he'll know."

"If you'd seen those old men, you'd be sure too."

"I hope so. Anyway—" Sara flopped a pair of thick, dry pancakes on his plate "—dinner's served."

David stared at them. "You put eggs in these?"

"There weren't any real eggs. I used powdered egg mix." She plopped two on her plate. "You don't like it, don't eat it."

David poured syrup over them, cut off a piece. She watched him take a bite.

"How is it?"

David chewed, swallowed. He tried to smile. "Terrific," he said.

"Is it, really?"

"It's delicious," he said. "Really."

"I don't claim to be a homemaker, you know. I don't

spend a lot of time cooking." She took a bite of her own. David watched her. "Even so . . . this isn't bad."

David nodded and took a sip of coffee. He opened the Buffalo *Courier-Express* he'd bought at the 7-11. The headline said DEATH TOLL RISES IN MADRID CRASH. The picture under the headline showed a runway strewn with wreckage. The third paragraph identified one of the planes as a private jet, bound from Johannesburg to London.

"Oh, Jesus."

Sara glanced up.

The fifth paragraph identified the private jet as belonging to Euromedic, carrying a group of research scientists.

"Jesus."

"What is it?"

The story was continued on page six.

"David?"

David tore the front page and handed it to her. He turned quickly to page six. The story didn't list any names, victims or survivors. Only numbers. Statistics.

"A Euromedic jet?" Sara said. She looked frightened again. "From Johannesburg?"

"Stuart was on that plane," David said. "He must have been."

"You don't know that, David. Does it say that? Does the story give any names?"

David didn't answer. He was staring at the facing page. The photograph of the truck crash was on page seven next to an ad for diet pills. The accompanying story was brief.

FREAK EXPLOSION
KILLS OKLAHOMA MAN

DALLAS, Tex. (AP)—An Oklahoma City man died Friday when he lost control of the truck he was driving and collided with a stalled gasoline tanker truck parked beside an interstate overpass and exploded.

Texas State Highway Patrol officials said the freak

accident occurred on the I-635 interloop late Friday afternoon near the interchange with I-20. Miraculously, authorities said, no one else was hurt.

Witnesses at the scene said the truck collided with a Grand Oil refinery trailer rig loaded with 5000 gallons of high octane gasoline. The explosion collapsed the unfinished interstate overpass.

The driver of the gasoline rig, Charles White, 42, of Terrell, said he jumped from his cab and "ran like hell" when fire erupted from the gasoline truck's ruptured gas tank. The fuel exploded a few seconds later, collapsing the bridge structure and sending fifty tons of concrete and steel crashing across the highway.

The body of the dead man was not immediately identified.

David stared at the photograph in shock. Twisted sections of reinforcing rods with clumps of concrete still attached lay in rubble across the four-lane highway. The cab of the gas truck was turned on its side, crushed under the weight of a guard railing. There were smoldering truck parts all over the road. But David saw past all that. On the edge of the photo, almost cropped out, was the door of one of the trucks. It was lying sideways on the highway, the front crumpled and black, but part of the painted name was still visible. Part of a scorched T. An N. An S.

Townsend.

David knocked over his mug with his elbow. Coffee spilled on the floor.

Sara jumped. "What? What is it?"

David folded the paper and held it out to her. "Those murdering bastards." He stabbed a finger at the picture. "This."

"I don't under—"

He pointed out the door in the foreground. "That's my truck," David said. "That's *my* truck."

"But—" Sara still didn't understand. She looked at him with fear, searching his face for some clue.

"That isn't me in that truck," David said. "It's somebody, but it isn't me. You want to take a wild guess who I think it is?"

She shook her head. Her face was ashen. She swallowed before she spoke. "I don't—" Then she knew. She drew her hands to her lips. "Oh, my God!"

"Yeah," David said. "The guy who's *really* missing. The guy who's *supposed* to be in the psycho ward at your lousy hospital. The guy who *isn't* at the Brentwood Neuro-Psychiatric Hospital. Richard Kenneth Franklin." He gave her a bitter look. "What in God's name is going on?"

THIRTY-TWO

GILL CREEK POND

"OPERATOR TWO-THREE."

"Operator, I want to call Madrid, Spain."

David was speaking into Ed Womack's ultra executive telephone. The machine also had a phone speaker—another button on the console—and David pressed it so Sara could hear. She was sitting beside him with a pad and pencil to take notes.

"Madrid, Spain?"

"Yes."

"Do you know the country and city code and the local number there, sir?"

"No."

"Just a minute, please. The country code is thirty-four and the city code for Madrid is eighty-seven. Would you like me to connect you with directory assistance in Madrid?"

"I want the hospital where they've taken the people from the plane crash," David said. "The survivors."

"The operator in Madrid will help you. I'm trying now."

David waited, tapping his fingers on the green blotter.

"Sir, I'm sorry but all the lines to Madrid are busy. My supervisor said there is at least a ninety-minute wait. Shall I take your name and number and call you when we have a line?"

"Wait? To Spain?"

"Overseas traffic is always heaviest on Christmas and New Year's. It's especially bad to Madrid since the accident there. An American singing group was on one of those planes. Shall I take your name—"

"No. Can you get Johannesburg?"

"South Africa?"

"Yes."

"I can try, sir. Do you—"

"I don't know the codes. Just get me the information in Johannesburg, please."

"One moment, please."

David asked, "Do you have any idea what the name of Euromedic's lab is?"

Sara shook her head.

"Johannesburg information is ringing. For your information, sir, the time there is two-ten A.M."

"Information, please. May I help you?" It was a man's voice, deep and articulate, with a British accent.

"Yes, I'm calling from the United States. I'm trying to locate my brother, Stuart Phillip Townsend. Do you have a listing?"

"Spelling?"

"T-O-W-N-S-E-N-D. Stuart with a U. Middle initial P as in Paul."

"I'm sorry. I have no listing for a Stuart Townsend. No S's at all."

"Probably stays at the reasearch clinic," Sara whispered.

"Do you have a listing for a Euromedic research clinic in Johannesburg? He works there. It's probably not called that. I don't—"

"Could it be the Rhodes Institution for Biomedical Research?"

"That's it," Sara said. "Rhodes."

"Is everything you people use called an institution?" Into the phone David said, "Yes, that's it."

The operator gave him the number. "The Rhodes Institute will probably not answer at this hour, sir. I don't believe they have a twenty-four hour staff."

"That's all right," David said. "I'll try in a few hours."

"This is Sunday morning, sir. Most establishments are closed today. Also, it's a holiday weekend."

"Nuts!"

Sara wrote quickly on her pad and pushed it over to David.

American consulate . . . keeps addresses of Amer. citizens.

"Can you give me the number for the American consulate?" David said.

"Yes, sir. I can ring for you, if you like."

"Please do."

David waited again. The phone rang five times before someone answered it.

"United States Consulate, Corporal Leon Elmore speaking."

"Hello," David said. "This is David Townsend. I'm calling from New York and I'm trying to find my brother, Dr. Stuart Townsend. He's a medical doctor in Johannesburg. Who can I speak to who can give me an address or phone number for him?"

"I don't know, sir," Corporal Elmore said. "There's nobody here tonight."

"It's an emergency," David said.

"I can get you the night duty officer, sir, but he'll tell you the same thing. Consulate personnel in charge of American citizens are all gone until Tuesday morning. It's New Year's weekend."

"Yeah, right. Thanks anyway." He hung up. "Does the whole world close down on New Year's Day?"

"I could call Euromedic in London," Sara said. "At least they'd know if he was on the plane."

"No."

"But—"

"Let's not invite any more trouble than we've already got. If they traced the call back here through an overseas operator . . ."

"Okay," Sara said. "So what now?"

"I'll leave one of these numbers for the Madrid waiting line. Then I'll start calling home."

"Home?"

"I'm supposed to be dead, remember? If I can get someone who knows me I'll have some credibility with the police. I think the Dallas police will be interested to know that the guy who burned up in my truck wasn't me."

Sara nodded. "I'll make some more coffee. There's an extension phone in the kitchen. Make me a list of names. I might as well help." She smiled. "It's probably a lousy night for television anyway."

"Saunders residence."

"Hello, Mrs. Saunders?"

"Mrs. Saunders isn't home right now."

"Is Mr. Saunders there?"

"No. They went out to dinner. This is the babysitter."

"When will they be home?"

"Around eleven-thirty, they said. Who's calling, please?"

"I did some work for Glenn Saunders last summer. They . . . eleven-thirty, you said?"

"Yes, sir. About then. You want to leave a number so they can—"

"No, that's all right. I'll call back later."

"I'm supposed to get everybody's name and num—"

"Hello?"

"Hello, is this the McNally residence?"

"Yes."

"Judge McNally?"

"Speaking."

"Judge McNally, I need some help. I—"

"My office hours are nine to four-thirty, Monday through Friday."

"No, no. I don't mean that. I did some work for you about three years ago. The bathhouse and lattice walk for the pool?"

"Yes?"

"I designed it."

"For my wife, yes. What about it?"

"Well, I . . . do you remember me?"

"What's your name?"

"Townsend. David Townsend."

"We paid you, didn't we?"

"Yes, sir. This is going to sound very strange, Judge McNally, but—"

"Tall young fella. Blond hair."

"Light brown, yes, sir. I—"

"Landscaped the Thomas place, didn't you?"

"Yes, sir. Judge McNally, I'm in some trouble. I'm in New York—"

"New York?"

"—and need someone who can recognize me. My voice, anyway. You see—"

"Hold on. Townsend, you said?"

"Yes, sir. I—"

"The architect?"

"Yes. If you'll just give me—"

"Who is this? Townsend was killed in a car crash. I just read it this morning."

"No, no. That's not true. *I'm* David Townsend. That wreck was . . . hello? Judge McNally? Hello? . . . Hell—oh . . . *damn*!"

"Hello?"

"Bud Castor?"

"In the flesh."

"Castor, this is Townsend."

"Hey, sport."

"You recognize my voice?"

"Why, you change it?"

"Castor, I need some help."

"Yeah?"

"I'm in—can you turn the television down a little?"

208

"Television? Just a second. Stereo. I gotta little party going. C'mon over."

"I'm in Niagara Falls."

"No shit?"

"I need some—"

"You get married or something?"

"I need some help."

"Yeah?"

"I want you to call the Dallas police."

"Do what?"

"Just listen."

"Who is this again?"

"It's Townsend. Are you drunk?"

"Stoned on my ass. C'mon over. You're not really in Niagara Falls, are you?"

"Did you read the paper this morning?"

"Newspaper? Hell, man, I watched three football games today. You see Oklahoma get their asses whipped?"

"There was a crash on the interstate. A big one."

"Oh, yeah. It was on TV last night. Helluva mess."

"That was supposed to be me."

"You? C'mon."

"In the tandem. Didn't you recognize it?"

"What was left to recognize? Hey, where are you *really*?"

"I want you to call the police, tell them you talked to me and—"

"Hey, man, I ain't that drunk."

"Castor . . ."

"Dallas Police Department."

"Hello, I'd like to speak to the detective division."

"Just a moment, please."

"Investigations, Lieutenant Moore."

"Lieutenant, I want to report a murder."

"In Dallas?"

"On the interstate."

"Yeah? Who got killed?"

"That crash Friday, it wasn't what it looked like. The man who died wasn't the man you think it was."

"Uh-huh. Just a minute."

There was a shuffling of phones. Then: "This is Sergeant Kelly. What's the problem?"

David went through it again.

"The guy in the truck wasn't David Townsend," the cop said. "Okay, so who was it?"

"I'm pretty sure it was a man named Franklin. Richard Franklin. From California."

"How do you know?"

"Because *I'm* David Townsend. That was my truck, but it wasn't me in it."

"Lieutenant Moore said something about murder?"

"That accident was set up to make it look like I was killed. Franklin was put there in my place."

"I see. Why don't you come down to the office, Mr. Townsend? We'll talk about it."

"I can't. I'm not in Dallas."

"Where are you?"

"New York."

"City?"

"No, no—I'm . . . somewhere else. I'd rather not say where I am right now."

"Why not?"

"It's pretty complicated, sergeant. I was kidnapped and someone put Franklin in my truck and rigged that accident so it'd look like I died."

"You were kidnapped?"

"Yes, by some doctors from a place called Weeksbriar Research Institute in New York. Look, I know this probably sounds bizarre, but I promise you I'm dead serious. I am David Townsend . . . I'm not dead."

"It's bizarre all right."

"Look—"

"Who's Franklin?"

"Three days ago he was a patient in a . . . a hospital in Los Angeles. Brentwood Neuro-Psychiatric Hospital. You can check it."

"Psychiatric Hospital? Is that what it sounds like it is?"

"They moved him to Dallas and put him in my truck—"

"Some doctors brought this guy Franklin from California, put him in your truck, had him drive into a gasoline tanker truck and blow himself and half the interstate into little pieces. That it?"

"Look, sergeant—"

"Then these doctors took you to some unidentified place in New York state and now you're calling me to report it. That right, too?"

"I escaped. Dammit, I'm telling you the truth! I need help. I need—"

"I'll go along with that. These doctors—the ones who kidnapped you—they psychiatric doctors?"

"You don't understand."

"I think I got the picture. Tell you what you do, Mr. Townsend. You call the nearest police department up there. Tell them what you told me. If you're not in Dallas, there's nothing I can do for you. I don't have much pull in New York."

"You're not going to *do* anything, right?"

"Yeah, I'm gonna finish watching the Orange Bowl game which you interrupted. Then I'm gonna go home and give my wife a big treat on account I haven't seen her for two days because I'm on night shift which means I get all the weirdo calls. So, unless you want to come down here we got nothing else to talk about."

Sara jumped when David slammed the phone down. He put his head in his hands. The room was dark except for the flickering light from the fireplace in the next room. David looked exhausted. He reached for his cup, found it empty and held it out to her. "More."

211

"Why don't you quit for a while?" Sara said. "You've been at it for hours. You could use a break."

David stretched his neck. "Just get me some coffee."

"Look, you need to get away from this telephone for a few minutes."

"That your professional advice?"

She touched his hand. "You need a break."

"What I need is time. Just get me some coffee. I'll be all right."

Sara started to say something then decided against it. She wanted to reassure him, but there wasn't anything to offer. He was frightened too, as frightened as she was. From the doorway she looked back at him. She wanted to tell him she was sorry, but David had the receiver to his ear. He was dialing again.

THIRTY-THREE

GILL CREEK HOUSE

THE ASSAULT came three minutes after midnight.

David had placed another log on the fire, moving carefully so as not to wake Sara. She had fallen asleep on a sofa an hour ago. He hadn't wanted to waken her, send her to a refrigerated bedroom. The house was still not warm, and the only comfortable room was this one with the fireplace. He had covered her with an afghan and switched off her reading light. Let her sleep here. Besides, he wasn't prepared to admit to her that Henry Gale Mara's Gill Creek House was an underwhelming piece of work when your toes were numb with cold.

He had stoked the fire since he quit making calls. Four hours on the phone had produced nothing. It was a revelation how few people he really knew. Or who knew him. And he had a new appreciation of the power of the press. When the Dallas *News* announces your death in banner headlines, you *are* dead.

For half an hour David tried to sleep but it wouldn't come. He lay beside Sara's sofa with a blanket around his legs. He closed his eyes and listened to the rhythm of the waterfall. He had lasted another day. Sooner or later they would give up looking for him. If he were lucky . . .

His eyes flicked open when he heard the car. The sound seemed to come out of the waterfall, becoming louder, closer. David was on his feet. The floor to ceiling windows allowed a good view of the road leading to the house, and the car was moving slowly toward the bridge.

David stood in the shadow of a tall potted plant beside the window. Whoever was driving wasn't going to get high marks for stealth. The car moved to the mouth of the bridge, stopped, backed up, then started forward again in a clumsy turn that nearly got itself trapped in a snowbank. David could hear the tires slipping in the ice. The driver almost stalled the engine as the car bumped over an outcrop of rock and then rested on an incline, pointed in the direction from which it had come.

"What's the matter?" Sara was sitting up. She rubbed her eyes. "What're you looking at?"

"A car."

"A car?" Sara threw off the blanket. "Here?"

"Down by the bridge." David watched as the headlights went out. "Somebody's down there."

"Where?" She crept beside him.

"Down there. A Chevy, I think." He pointed. "See it?"

"Kids," Sara said.

"Kids?"

"They come up here a lot. It's a good spot, you know. Isolated."

David squinted into the darkness. Without the headlights on, he could barely see the outline of the car. "Any binoculars in the house?"

"There are some field glasses in Ed's study."

"Get them."

"David, I don't think we have anything to fear from a couple of teenagers. A little primal groping never hurt anyone."

"I'm feeling an urgent primal instinct for survival. Okay? Just get them."

Sara gave him an exaggerated sigh, then went to get the field glasses. She handed him the case.

They were powerful binoculars, wide angle lenses, and he had to search the darkness before he located a landmark he recognized. Then he found the bridge and the car. It *was* a 1975 Malibu. The engine was running; he could see the exhaust vapor.

"Well?"

"I can't see them. They must be below the window."

"They didn't come out here to shake hands, David."

David kept the glasses trained on the front seat. "I don't see any—wait. There's . . ." A head popped up. She had long blonde hair and wore a heavy sweater. It might have been a jacket—it wasn't easy to see in that light—but he figured it must be a sweater when she pulled it over her head. Her bare skin was unmistakable. The blurred movement was confusing, but he recognized the vigorous activity. He was sure he saw a heaving breast.

"Kids, right?"

He shook his head. "You'd think it would be too cold for that kind of exercise."

Sara grabbed the binoculars. "Let me see."

She was trying to adjust the lenses, as though studying a blood culture.

"Sara?"

"The windows are fogging up."

"Your breath or theirs?"

Something caught her eye and she concentrated through the glasses. "Wait a minute . . . There's somebody out there."

"We've already established—"

"Somebody *else*."

David was beside her, peering over her shoulder. "Where?"

"I *thought* I saw something—" she squinted through the binoculars—"it's so dark . . . maybe it's just a branch of a tree blowing in the wind."

"Let me see." David focused on the car. The windows were fogged; there was movement inside, shadow outlines. Then the engine gunned, the headlights came on and the car came suddenly to life, spewing snow and rocks in its wake as it shot up the narrow road, slewing back and forth until the spinning tires found purchase on firm ground and disappeared over the crest. A man was briefly outlined in the red flow of the taillights. David saw him for an instant, one arm held protectively against the spray of gravel; then he was gone in the darkness. But it was a man, not a tree, and he held something in his hand, and it sure as hell wasn't a tree branch.

"Did you see—" Sara started.

David scanned the area of the bridge with broad sweeps of the binoculars. Without the car as reference point, he had lost his place.

"What?"

"Get your coat! Somebody's out there and he isn't thinking about erections." He shoved her toward the kitchen and made one more pass with the binoculars.

David had one arm in his jacket as he pushed Sara ahead of him up the stairway toward the bedrooms. The binocular case was still strapped around his neck, banging his chest as he moved. "Move."

"Is it them?"

"I don't know, but whoever it is sent those kids running." He pulled Sara to her knees when they reached the top of the stairway. He made another sweep with the binoculars. It wasn't a good angle. A large pine blocked his view of the bridge. He couldn't see anything else because the light of the fireplace was reflected in the window. There wasn't anything to hear but the roar of the waterfall. When David turned to her she was staring anxiously at the darkness beyond the windows. "Where are the car keys?"

"In my pocket. David, I don't see anything. Are you sure?"

"I'm sure. We're going out on the balcony. Stay close beside me—"

The wail of the burglar alarm cut him off. He heard a crash of glass below. The front door seemed to explode as two men in parkas broke through it.

He grabbed Sara by the arm. "Let's go!"

218

"David, my shoes! I left them—"

David clamped his hand over her mouth and shoved her to the floor. There were other voices now, loud, frantic, shouting instructions. The two men downstairs were joined by a third. They were scurrying in the dark. He heard furniture being overturned. Outside he saw a figure rushing toward the house from the bridge.

"Keep close to me," David said. He had to yell above the alarm. "Do exactly what I do." He took her hand and dragged her into the master bedroom. Automatically he locked the door. Footsteps pounded up the stairs. Someone yelled for lights.

"The balcony," David said. "We've gonna have to jump."

Sara tripped in the dark and he had to pull her toward the sliding glass doors that opened onto the cantilevered patio. A burglar alarm was mounted outside the patio and when he slid open the door the noise was deafening.

"Come *on*!" He held her up with one arm and pushed her out. Because the house was built into the side of a rocky hill, no level was more than five to eight feet above the slope. It wouldn't be dangerous to jump over the side. If they could get down the slope to the frozen creek, at least they'd be on familiar territory.

David pulled Sara to the railing of the balcony, threatening her, screaming above the noise, keeping one eye on the bedroom door where they'd be crashing through at any moment, when two figures stepped out of the shadows.

"David, please don't be frightened. We don't want to hurt you."

They weren't more than fifteen feet away. The speaker was wearing a long herringbone overcoat with a felt collar and a sporty hat. The other was in a parka. David pushed Sara away when he saw the silent one raise the flashlight.

"Watch out!" At the same moment David heard the *phoomp* as the flashlight fired and something struck his arm.

It went through the sleeve of his jacket and stung him, knocking him off balance against the railing.

David's arms windmilled, grabbing for support. He yelled for Sara as he fell over the railing.

He hit the ground flat on his back, the binocular case crashing into his chin. When he gasped for air his throat was seared by the icy cold. His eyes teared and for a moment everything blurred. Then he saw Sara at the railing, held by the man who had shot him. The man in the herringbone coat stood beside her.

"Run," Sara screamed. *"Run!"*

Then he saw the men in blue parkas. They were everywhere, surrounding Sara, bending over the balcony, searching the darkness.

David took another breath. He rose to his knees.

"There he is!"

Then he ran.

The slope was awkward to walk on and running made it even more dangerous. He bumped against rocky outcroppings and fell down on slippery pine needles, banged blindly into tree branches and pine saplings. He hit his shins and knees, over and over, and numbness replaced pain. But he didn't stop. He kept moving, half-crawling, sliding down frozen embankments and stomping through pockets of ice puddles. His trousers turned to ice that tinkled as he ran. At some point he was aware that the alarm had ceased, but he didn't turn around or even slow down. They were sure to follow him, and he wasn't going to make it an easy chase. Just run and keep running.

David ran on. Survival and escape pushed him blindly over fallen trees, through brush that tore at his clothes, and something built inside him with every stride. They had Sara. The men in blue parkas with their funny black flashlights . . . they had her. He was beyond anger and frustration. Now it was rage and hatred, and he ran with the heart of an animal in panic. When he reached the top of the slope, and found the frozen pond, he ran faster. Even as he ran fear and rage and thoughts of Sara left behind fought for dominance within him.

He was quickly approaching his limit of fear. His territory had been taken from him, his property assaulted. He was the most dangerous kind of animal. Cornered now, he could kill.

THIRTY-FOUR

GILL CREEK HOUSE

"MY NAME is Luther Moravec," he said. "I'm from London. I'm sorry about the ordeal you've been put through."

He had removed his herringbone coat and carried it over his arm. She was still in the master bedroom, which the men in blue parkas hadn't allowed her to leave since David escaped. There had been several minutes of people scrambling around with black pistols that looked like toys and hand-held radios. In the first minutes of confusion, when they were bumping around in the dark, someone had tumbled off an outcropping of rock near the creek and had broken his arm. She had been left with a blue-eyed woman named Turner who kept pumping her about Townsend. Had he called anyone? Was he injured at all? What did he talk about? And to every question Sara said nothing. She saw Dr. Ellis briefly, when Turner opened the door to ask for a cigarette. Sara called to him for help, pleading, but he looked at her with his hard eyes and closed the door.

So she was alone. The man with the herringbone coat entered and brought her coffee in a cup and saucer. He wasn't like the rest of them. He didn't have a radio or a gun, only the coat over his arm and a briefcase which he carried like a tray with the coffee on top. It was Susan's favorite china.

He set the coffee down on the table beside Sara's loveseat. There were two cups. The briefcase seemed heavy.

"I thought perhaps we could talk," he said.

"You can think whatever you like." She watched him step back, looking for a seat. He finally sat on the edge of the bed, laying the coat beside him. He wasn't a big man. There was nothing formidable about him, but there was a sense of dignified authority in his voice, his manner, the way he moved. She didn't have to ask to know that he was someone important in London.

"Dr. Mills, please believe me when I say that I don't mean for any harm to come to you. I know this all must seem blatantly criminal. I can't offer any excuse for it. But David Townsend is extraordinarily important to Euromedic. We want to recover him safely, without any violence. I don't want him harmed in any way."

"That's why you shoot him with those things?"

"They aren't actually weapons."

"What the hell do you want?"

Moravec inhaled, sighed. His shoulders moved. "What I'd like most is to go home." He looked at Sara. "Of course you deserve an explanation, doctor. But there are certain things that, at the moment, I cannot tell you. But I will not lie to you. I promise you that."

"You kidnapped him, didn't you?" Sara lifted her head to wait for his answer. "In Texas."

"Yes, I'm ultimately responsible for that."

"And all this has something to do with his brother? David thinks he was on that plane that crashed in Spain. He's right, isn't he?"

Moravec nodded at the coffee. "Do you mind if we drink that before it turns cold. This is not a warm house."

"Answer my question."

"Stuart Townsend was on one of the jets, that's true. He wasn't killed."

"Then—"

"I won't discuss Stuart Townsend any further," Moravec said. "He is alive. That's all that I may tell you."

"Which cup is drugged?" Sara said.

"I pray neither. Hand me one, if you don't mind."

Sara did. Moravec drank half of it down.

"Is David all right?" He held the cup and saucer on his knee. "I mean, he isn't hurt, is he? Exposure, anything like that?"

"He was fine until your goon blew him off the balcony."

"He doesn't understand any of this, does he?"

"Goddamn, Moravec, of course he doesn't understand! I don't understand! What I want to know—"

Sara stopped when the door opened. Dr. Ellis came in. Behind him was the woman with the ice blue eyes. She had a large handbag on a strap over her shoulder. Ellis was carrying a walkie-talkie. He turned it off and pulled the parka hood down from his bald head as he pushed the door shut.

"I told you I didn't want anyone talking to her except Turner," Ellis said. He was standing over Moravec, his back to Sara. Sara could see the veins standing out in his neck.

Moravec set his coffee on the nightstand. He said nothing.

"Dr. Ellis, what is going on?" Sara said. He was the only person here she knew. She couldn't accept that he was involved in kidnapping and possibly murder. Dr. Ellis was her boss. He ran Weeksbriar. She'd been to a thousand staff meetings with him, had drunk coffee with him in the lounge. He was a taskmaster but he wasn't a criminal.

Ellis turned to face her. "I'll ask the questions here," he said. His eyes were angry black holes. "You're in a great deal of trouble, Dr. Mills. Aiding an escaped psychiatric patient may cost you your job. Perhaps even your medical license."

She was stunned that he'd try to threaten her. "Townsend isn't a patient," she said. "I *know* who he is."

"You don't know anything."

Sara glanced at the woman with the bag. She was leaning against the wall, doing something to her fingernails.

"I know about Richard Franklin," Sara said to Ellis. "I know he isn't at Weeksbriar. I think what's left of him is on a slab at the Dallas morgue with David Townsend's name on it."

Moravec looked up quickly. "What?"

"David and I called Brentwood. Franklin doesn't even remotely resemble Townsend. That's why you burned him, isn't it?"

Ellis's eyes narrowed. "That's quite enough, Dr. Mills." He looked at the woman with the handbag, nodded. She pushed herself off the wall with an elbow and opened the clasp of the bag.

"I don't know how you figure to get away with this," Sara said, "but you're dead wrong if you think I'm going to play along with it. You can just—" Sara lost her voice when she saw the woman extract a clear liquid vial and a hypodermic syringe from the bag.

"The one who's dead wrong isn't me," Ellis said.

Sara made up her mind to run even before she knew where to go. She lunged out of the loveseat and was nearly to the sliding glass doors when she heard the *phoomp* and felt the stabbing pinpricks in her side. There was only time for the sensation to register before the shock knocked her off her feet. It wasn't that she heard anything, but her whole consciousness was suddenly paralyzed by a violent explosion that propelled her forward.

She hit the hardwood floor on her breasts, her back and neck arched, her legs and arms spreadeagled out from her body. The pain of the fall was nothing compared to the electric jolt that overwhelmed her senses. It lasted only a second, but its aftereffect left her gasping and nearly senseless; she could see but not speak, hear but not move. Her motor reflexes had been short circuited; it was as if she were swimming in a pool of molasses. Movement was absurdly exaggerated to a kind of slow motion melodrama played through a fish-eyed lens where faces distended comically, like carnival mirror distortions. Only nothing was funny. That was the one thing she was sure of as she blinked her eyes to ward off the darkness that was rushing in.

These maniacs wanted to kill her.

"I forbid you to harm that woman!"

Moravec's breath was visible in the night air. He was outside with Ellis, away from the others, on the pavement of the drive. Ellis was smoking a cigar. He had his foot on the bumper of the Volvo.

"No one said anything about hurting her," Ellis said. "And *don't* raise your voice to me, Moravec. I told you that she was my responsibility. I'll take care of it."

"Dr. Mills is not to be harmed," Moravec said again. "You may take that as a direction from the highest authority in Euromedic. Do you understand that clearly?"

"I know my job."

"I promise you, doctor, if anything happens to Dr. Mills, your job will be the least of your worries."

"Don't threaten me," Ellis shot back. "You don't know . . ." He glanced around, searching for anyone within earshot, then threw his cigar into a bank of snow and opened the rear door of the Volvo. "Get in. I want to tell you something."

Moravec slid across the seat. He put the BriefPac in the foot well. Ellis got in and shut the door. "You don't know everything you think you know," he said. "We're up to our necks with Hahnemann sequels at Weeksbriar. I don't know why Haldern didn't tell you that. Ever since Hahnemann died we've been collecting sequels . . . people suffering from the sequela or those who died from the first group of experiments. As they die we put them into controlled environmental ICPs and change out their blood with perfluorocarbon and keep the circulation system operating. They come to us from all over the world—one or two a month. We'd keep them until we got a shipping order, then send bodies to Rennit and his bunch in Johannesburg in lots of three. The remains were perfectly preserved so that they could explore the effects of the disease. Weeksbriar is the largest psychiatric facility in the Euromedic chain, Moravec. It's the ideal staging area for storing sequels. We have AirMore flights in and out of here every day and up to now nobody's ever questioned an AirMore mission. I don't want to risk losing that.''

Ellis nodded at the rear window of the car, toward the house. "Dr. Mills could do a lot of damage to us if we just let her go. I think we could discredit any story she might come up with, but it would cause us a lot of time and trouble. And I don't want any trouble. I have other problems to worry about . . . like the sequels. They keep coming. That plane crash in Madrid effectively put an end to any more shipments from Weeksbriar—at least until Dr. Townsend is well enough to pick up where Rennit left off. In the meantime they're stacking up. I have Hahnemann sequels up to here. So don't threaten me, Moravec. I'll do whatever I have to do to protect the institute. Anyway—" he paused to find another cigar in his jacket pocket "—we're doing the same thing, you and I. Essentially. Right?''

Moravec didn't answer.

"Think about it," Ellis said. He lit his cigar, then opened the door. "Leave Dr. Sara Mills to me," he said before he climbed out. "You just worry about Townsend.''

Moravec sat alone in the Volvo for a long time. When he went to the house, he walked back empty-handed.

THIRTY-FIVE

GILL CREEK HOUSE

THEY WERE clumsy nitwits, whoever they were.

From his hiding place overlooking the bank of the frozen creek, David had been watching them stumble around in the dark with their flashlights—real ones—and hand radios. They might have been good kidnappers in controlled environments, like doctors' offices or sanatoriums, but as trackers over wooded terrain they were about as subtle as a herd of hippos.

He had run until he thought his lungs would burst, a mile, maybe more, along the edge of the creek, past the widest section where the skaters had been earlier in the day. He rested on a bench in a three-sided wooden shack that had been built as a shelter for skaters. Its open side afforded a view of the creek and, thanks to the binoculars still strapped around his neck, his pursuers. A pot-bellied stove on a concrete slab in the shelter had been warm to the touch from the last embers of a fire. He propped himself against the stove for warmth and supported his elbows on top, and trained the field glasses on the flashes of light beams in the treeline across the creek. They had paired off and were methodically making their way out from the Mara House. They were noisy—their radios carried across the ice like a shot—and they were snapping every twig and branch they came across. And they were slow. Their methodical ways might be useful in daylight, in a city, anywhere that confined the prey to streets and sidewalks, and where time wasn't a factor, David thought, but not out here, where they gave up surprise and speed. At the rate they were moving they'd never find him. For a change the advantage was on his side.

But only for the moment, he realized. There was still a logistical issue to solve. He didn't have transportation, he didn't know precisely where he was, which made escape a problem of direction, and he hadn't any money or identification. Some advantage. How long was he going to last hanging around a kids' skating hole or tramping around in the woods?

David swept the binoculars across the uneven horizon. If there were other houses on the creek he couldn't see them. He remembered passing a park and a golf course when they drove in. If he just started off, keeping the Mara House directly behind him, he was bound to run into a road. But then what? If there were six of them after him with flashlights, how many others were there? And *where* were they—patroling the roads? Maybe that was the idea; the guys with flashlights were bush beaters, driving him toward the real hunters.

But what bothered him most couldn't be put off anymore. Sara Mills was still back there. She was with *them*. He had to do something about that. He took a long, deep breath. He warmed his fingers briefly on the side of the stove, then he stepped out of the shelter, into the cold. If he was going back after her, he'd better get started.

The thing he had going for him—the only thing—was that nobody would expect him to come back. The trick was to get back without being spotted, scout the place, find Sara and get her out fast. That's all. If he had any advantage it was that he knew the house and grounds better than the hunters. It wasn't the most commanding edge he had, the odds were still against him, but at least it was something.

David crept out to the small pier that jutted over the ice. It had started snowing again—not a good sign. The men with flashlights were looking for tracks in the snow beneath the pines, and David had had the sense to keep to rocks and patches of brush. It had been noisy, until he made it to the creek and ran below the bank where a hundred kids had scuffed through the powdery snow on the ice; but what noise he'd made was cancelled by the fact that he'd been running for his life, and his pursuers were disoriented and disorganized in the first minutes. It had been enough then, but now he hadn't the luxury of recklessness. Going back meant the tactics, if not the roles, of hunters and hunted would be reversed. He couldn't risk prowling through the woods and snapping twigs with every step. Let them make the noise. That way at least he'd know where they were. And, he realized, keeping to the bank wouldn't work either; it was too near where they were searching, and the new snow would expose his tracks.

He knelt beside the pier and scanned downstream with the binoculars. They were on both sides of the creek now, four or five hundred yards away; but he counted only four beams, two on each side. That wasn't good either. It left two unaccounted for. Maybe they went back. Maybe they got too cold. Maybe they gave up. David rested the binoculars on a plank. Sure they did.

The only way to go back, he decided, was straight down the middle of the creek. It wasn't such a crazy idea. The creek here was at least a hundred yards wide, narrowing down to about twenty yards where it cut into the treeline. They wouldn't be looking for him on the ice, not out in the middle. Besides, a flashlight wasn't that effective over twenty-five or thirty yards. If he kept low and moved slowly, he might just slip past them.

Or slide. As he sat on his haunches to insert the binoculars in the case, David saw the sleds. There were five of them stored under the pier, tied together in a follow-the-leader fashion. He untied the lead sled, the largest and heaviest, from the pack and pulled it out. It was new, probably a Christmas gift, and the runners were coated with a thin film of oil and grooved, giving the low-slung sled the speed advantage it would need to pull others. "Red Rocket" was painted in streamlined letters trailing a fiery plume on the varnished wood. It was nearly six feet long with an extra, foot-steering tiller bar. David imagined the sled loaded with screaming kids slashing across the ice as he dragged it out to the middle of the creek. With a running start he should glide a good eighty or ninety feet before having to push off again. He lay down on it to check it for size and steering. The binoculars were the only problem; he had to slide the bulky case from his chest to his back, and as he did he cut a finger on the dart.

It had been there the whole time, embedded in the leather; the tiny wire had been ripped away when he fell over the railing. David shuddered when he realized what the flashlight gun really was—some kind of electric incapacitator. He'd seen something like it on a newscast demonstrating self-defense paraphernalia. The cop who'd volunteered as the guinea pig was easily over two hundred pounds. He went down like a sack of wet spuds when the darts struck him. But David didn't because the binocular case had blocked one of the darts. *Both* darts had to penetrate the skin for the contacts to deliver the job.

David gripped the sled with both hands and stood up. They were using some high-powered gadgets, armed with darts, guns. If they'd use something like that on him, what would they do to Sara?

He started off at a quick walk. He'd wasted too much time as it was. He had to get back to Sara. It *wasn't* her fault, what had happened, it was his. Gaining speed and momentum on the slick surface, he aimed the child's sled for the faint light on the horizon, then, on a dead run, with the raw cold biting his face and ears, he thrust the sled to the ice and hurled himself aboard in a single fluid motion. He ducked his head, pressed his chin over the sled's leading edge and, with his elbows tucked in, held tightly to the tiller bar, keeping the sled pointed straight downstream. God help him, he thought, he was committed now.

Red Rocket flew. It shot across the ice like a missile, slicing over ruts and pits without a tremor. Flakes of snow whipped his face from the aerodynamic force the sled created on the ice. The effect of the light layer of snow over the ice was like a coat of some anti-friction material. Whatever the reason—momentum, weight, oil on the runners, the streamlined angle of attack—he was covering ground faster, much faster, than he'd intended.

Too fast. The wind stung his ears. Snow caked his eyebrows and collected in the hollow of his eyes—impossible to see either bank. He must have sped over fifty yards but the sled showed no sign of slowing; it seemed to be moving faster. His fingers were already numb with the cold. God, how fast *was* he moving? The vibration of speed was a sound as much as a feeling that his body absorbed. He thought he'd have stopped long before now. He counted on it. He wanted time to lie and wait, listen and watch for the men on the banks. Be cautious. He didn't want to fly past them like a bullet; the idea was to be silent and smooth. And quiet. David's ears were full of snow but the muffled roar of the runners singing against the ice rang in his brain.

He shook his head, dislodging some of the snow, and had a blurred view of the area ahead to the left. Either he'd badly misjudged distances or this sled truly was a missile. He'd covered a hundred yards in seconds and he saw the flashes of light just ahead—twenty, thirty yards. He was almost on them. The sled had taken its own course, despite what pressure his frozen hands exerted on the steering bar, and it had drifted to the left. He was much too close to the left bank of the creek. If someone was standing there . . .

Someone was. There were two beams of light, one flickering among the trees about twenty feet into the stand of pines, the other, nearer, on the creek bank, which flashed across the ice. David guessed he was thirty yards from the man on the bank, nearly abreast of him, rocketing along at fifteen, twenty miles an hour. He could see the man's outline behind the light. He was wearing a heavy parka and holding a hand radio in front of his face. His flashlight beam was diffused by distance and the falling snow, but still it cast an illuminating sheen across the sled's path. So much for his theory on the effective range of standard flashlights—these guys didn't carry ordinary equipment. He'd tried, David thought. He'd given it his best shot, but they had him now. He wondered, if they shot him again with a dart gun would he feel it; he was so cold now he didn't care. At least the running would be over soon. Still, they had to catch the goddamn sled.

Red Rocket shot through the narrow pool of light like a blur. It was a flicker of time that lasted an eternity. David *knew* he'd been spotted. The light in his face nearly blinded him. They *must* have seen him. But no one shouted. The man on the bank didn't budge. His light didn't move. Nobody shot at David. Nothing happened.

He was past them.

It was because they were so prepared for the cold, and the hunt, David realized, that they didn't see him. Or hear him. He'd been too preoccupied with the sound of the sled in his ears to understand that they were making so much racket themselves, crushing through the brush with their radios crackling, that they probably wouldn't hear him even if they weren't wearing heavy parka hoods. The man on the bank didn't see David on the ice because he wasn't looking for him there. The knowledge that he'd beaten them at their game, at least so far, flushed David with a sense of triumph. He was staring back at his pursuers and gloating, his cheek on the center of the steering bar, when he turned his head forward, into the spray of snow, and saw the rock.

It was mostly below the ice, but enough of it protruded above the plane to make David gasp. The sled had been drifting off course and now it was in the shallows of the creek bed near the bank, slowing in the gritty ice. He had to try to make a hard turn with the steering bar. It wasn't possible to miss the rock, just turn and hope it was a glancing blow. David saw it coming straight at him and realized it wasn't protruding too far out of the ice. For an instant he thought it might slip between the runners without . . .

The rock struck the sliding bolt that held the steering undercarriage between the traverse rods, deflecting the sled's momentum, then caught the rear portion of the left runner, sending it into a slow spin. The impact jarred David's chin savagely against the center slat. His eyes watered from the jolt and he saw the fallen tree trunk cemented in the ice an instant before he hit it.

The ride was over in a breath-stopping collision. Red Rocket hit the tree sideways, wrenching David off the sled, propelling him into the trunk, then bouncing over it. He hit the ice on his right shoulder, rolled and slid feet first into the frozen bank.

His head cleared before he realized he was on his back. He was staring at a snow-laden branch of a pine tree thirty feet above him. His first thought was that he was alive. His head was ringing. He'd battered his face rolling across the ice and there was a lump over his left eye. His nose was bleeding. But nothing hurt as much as the pain in his shoulder. If it were broken, he was finished. He rolled to his stomach and looked back upstream. The lights were a good fifty yards away, none of them pointed in his direction. They hadn't heard the crash. Lucky me, he thought, until he tried to move.

The shoulder wasn't broken. It hurt like hell, but it wasn't broken. Both his knees were sore and the big toe of his left foot throbbed, but he decided he'd live. He limped up the bank and into the cover of the woods. It was too dark to see anything clearly, but he heard the waterfall. The waterfall at the house. He headed for the sound. It was a cold trek through the trees; his fingers were numb and he tried to warm them by blowing into his cupped hands when he stopped to get his bearings, leaning against a tree to take the pressure off his brutalized toe; but all the exercise accomplished was to smear sticky blood over his face. Then he found the sloped, rocky bank of the narrow creek bed and followed it to the house.

Henry Gale Mara had designed a cantilevered deck that ran the entire length of the house, affording a view of the creek. David was under the deck, crouched between concrete support columns. The sound of the waterfall was much louder—he was only twenty or thirty feet away from it—but he heard voices now from the house. His only plan when he started was to get to the house, somehow get Sara out and make a run for it to the woods. But how? He hadn't given himself much chance of making it this far. But getting her out now wasn't as simple as it had seemed back at the shed. He just couldn't burst in on them. Not with his aches and pains and a big toe that forced him to limp like a hunchback. And especially not when they were armed with electric zap guns. If he was going to outsmart them he had to get a head count—see exactly who he was up against— and that meant getting to a window.

The deck was sixty-two feet long. The stairways at each end were like wooden wings that folded down to a landing and turned back toward one another at the bottom. David went up the nearest stairs on his hands and knees. The kitchen, den and one of the bedrooms overlooked the deck. If they were in the living room, he'd see them through the kitchen window. If anyone was watching the creek from the windows they'd see him coming. Well, he'd come this far, he thought. He just needed to be lucky a little longer.

David froze when he smelled the cigarette smoke. He was halfway across the deck when he stopped still. Someone else was on the deck. David knelt, expecting a light to shine in his face or darts to suddenly sting his chest. He scanned the deck. There were five tables along the railing. The man in the parka was sitting at the table near the stairway, opposite the one David had climbed. He was more of a shape in the dark than a figure with recognizable features. His back was to David, but he was watching the progress of the men out in the woods with a pair of binoculars. David saw the glow of the cigarette as the man flicked ash behind him.

It was instinct rather than a deliberately conscious decision that made David act when the man turned and saw him. The man must have sensed someone was there in the darkness too. He turned, flipping his cigarette across the deck, and reacted with a startled bob of his head when he saw David kneeling twenty feet away. Then he nodded. It was not the response David had expected. The man didn't yell or reach for a weapon or scramble into a commando attack stance; he just nodded. And shrugged. David's heart was in his throat. He nodded back. It was like some absurd cartoon scene. The man looked back toward the creek and half-raised the binoculars before he stopped. It was as if David could read the man's second thought. The man hesitated then made a slow turn toward David. And David moved.

He didn't have a weapon and he didn't have the first clue to hand-to-hand tactics, but he was scared. He rushed the man in a fit of defensive frenzy. The man was having trouble getting up from his chair, groping at his jacket when David hit him. He used his fist, aiming for the man's face, but missing slightly and catching him solidly on the side of the head. It was over before David had time to get his breath. The man reeled backward, one arm windmilling for balance, then fell on his back without a sound. David just stood over him, not knowing exactly what to do next. If the man opened his eyes, should he hit him again? But he didn't move and David was satisfied that he'd knocked him cold; a good thing, because his fist throbbed as though he'd broken it.

He bent over the man. It was Grant, the guy in the van in Dallas, alias Norman Louis, from the Mobil station. David went quickly through his pockets. He found a flashlight, a wallet and a walkie-talkie. Evidently, he'd been monitoring the hand radio; a wire led to a plug in his ear. He also found the electric gun the man had been reaching for. The odd thing was that his right arm was held in a makeshift sling under his parka. Had he broken it tonight? David unzipped the fur-lined jacket.

He pulled the jacket on, drawing the furry hood over his frozen ears, and pocketing the wallet. He had a flashlight gun now too.

The radio squawked when David disconnected the earplug wire and he lowered the volume control with his thumb. He scanned the creek with the man's binoculars. The flashlight beams were specks in the distance.

"Looks like he stopped here." The voice from the walkie-talkie startled him.

"Where are you?" Another voice.

"West side. A shack. A man's tracks come in, go out."

David focused the binoculars where he thought the skater's shelter was. He couldn't see it, but he found the lights.

"The tracks head down to the ice. Hold on."

David held his breath. He prayed that the light snow had covered the sled's tracks. If they realized he had headed back to the house . . .

"He was here, all right. Looks like he's got a sled. He may be trying to get over to your side."

"A sled?"

"Kid's sled, yeah."

There was a long pause as the radio seemed to go dead, then: "Great. If he's going upstream he'll be miles away. Shit."

"Shall I follow the tracks?"

"What do you think?"

"Listen, this is a creek, you know. Is that ice thick enough to support a man? I don't know how to swim."

Obviously, David thought, he didn't know much about

the dynamics of ice formation in a shallow, slow-moving stream; the ice in this creek would support a tank.

"If you find sled tracks leading to a big hole in the ice," a third voice cut in, "then we can all go home."

It took David five minutes to make his way to a side porch of one of the bedrooms. From here he had a view of the lighted drive where he heard voices. He couldn't go into the house through this bedroom; he would be trapped inside the house. It was better to stay outside, where he had some freedom of movement. Besides, time was the enemy now; he couldn't waste it bumping around dark rooms. The moment they realized he was coming back to the house was the moment he was in big trouble. David took out the electric gun, pointing the yellow arrow away from himself. The trigger was a button on the top. I hope to God this thing's loaded, he thought.

The drive was lit by a floodlight high on the balcony cantilever. There were three men, one in a parka, the other two in overcoats. The one in the herringbone, the one who'd fired and missed on the balcony, had his back to David. He was the one he'd go for, if he had to go for any of them. They were at the car, studying what appeared to be a map stretched across the trunk. Not terrific odds, David calculated, three against one; still, it was better than facing all of them at once. Then he saw Sara. A woman was holding her up at the door and a man in a parka walked quickly to give her a hand. She didn't look too well. Her head lolled and she made no effort to walk, so that they had to half drag her to the car, but at least she was alive. They dumped her in the front seat, and as the woman turned back to the house David recognized her. It was Dr. Seagram, the doctor from the clinic in Dallas.

He was reckoning distances, trying to decide whether it was better to rush three of them at the car or wait until one or two of them wandered off, when his radio squawked again. The men on the creek had discovered that he'd doubled back on them.

"Dr. Ellis? Are you there? He's headed back toward the house. Townsend's coming toward you. Dr. Ellis?"

Run. They knew where he was. He wasn't going to surprise anybody now. They'd have their little dart guns out and ready for him.

He flattened himself against the wall, searching for a dark place. He glanced back at the three men at the car; they were still hovered over the map. Then David saw the radio. It was propped against the rear window, and it wasn't on.

"Earl?" The radio in his hand wouldn't be still. "Goddammit, Earl, answer me!"

"The sonofabitch is asleep," said another, panting voice. He must have been running.

"Earl? Get Dr. Ellis. Goddammit, Earl, I'll break your other arm if you don't answer me!"

Earl's asleep, David thought. He wouldn't be getting anybody for—

The woman he knew as Dr. Seagram stepped out of the doorway behind him and nearly hit him with the storm door. She spilled half the coffee from the cup she was carrying.

"What are you doing here?" she said, holding out the cup to him. "You're supposed to be—" Her mouth fell open, sucking in a lungful of air, and she dropped the cup when she recognized him. She screamed.

David hit her. He didn't hesitate and he didn't ease the blow. He hit her exactly where he'd meant to hit Earl and she catapulted back through the doorway. He should have hit her in the head, because she wasn't knocked unconscious and she didn't stop screaming.

He hopped over the low retaining wall and started running toward the car. He didn't know what else to do.

"Townsend's here!" David screamed as loud as he could. He pointed back over his shoulder. "He hit me! He's on the back deck! C'mon!"

The three men at the car scrambled past him. They accepted him for what he appeared to be, broken-armed Earl—he was wearing a parka and in the harsh light and falling snow no one was taking any second looks or checking his driver's license. David kept running for the car. Dr. Seagram was wailing somewhere in the house and everyone else was running. To hell with them. What was important now was Sara's car, getting to it and getting away from here. Then he remembered the keys. God, he thought, please let the keys be in her pocket.

THIRTY-SIX

GILL CREEK HOUSE

"PICK HER up . . . into car . . ."

" . . . over ravine . . . neutral . . ."

" . . . haven't time . . . lose . . ."

"Townsend must be . . . Weeksbriar . . ."

The voices came to her in bursts of consciousness. Someone had her on her feet, but she was too weak to support herself. Ellis's face loomed between flashes of darkness. Then the nurse. She felt uncomfortable from the cold that accompanied the prickly sensation over her body. She was vaguely aware that she wasn't inside; she smelled pine, but she couldn't see clearly to know for sure. She felt frightened, but fear wasn't the important thing right now. Staying awake was.

Sara averted her eyes from the beam of a flashlight. She was sitting in a car which she didn't remember getting into, and she was leaning against the window, her forehead pressed against the glass. The voices were coming faster now, but unintelligible. She was staring over the hood of the car at a patch of wood illuminated by the headlights. She saw faces again, unfamiliar faces; curiously humorless faces within a ring of fur. Faces drawn with the tightness that cold produces. Faces inside parkas, it dawned on her. It reminded her that she wasn't wearing a parka and that somehow she should be. She was freezing. Then there was the nurse's face and she was conscious that her face was a warning, but she couldn't remember of what. The woman wore such little makeup as to defeat the purpose of her wearing false eyelashes. She was also holding a small suitcase.

When Sara opened her eyes again she saw David's face and knew something was wrong with it. It didn't fit; it was like one of those aptitude tests where you search out the block or shape or word that doesn't go with the others in the sequence. David's face didn't fit with the rest of these faces, even if she couldn't explain why. He opened the car door and he was angry, and he was shouting unintelligibly and banging on things. That part wasn't odd, she thought. He was always angry and shouting and banging on things as long as she'd known him. What was odd was that he was wearing a parka . . . and his face was covered with blood.

David banged his head ducking into the car and the pain seemed to last an eternity as all the aches and pains returned to him; his blazing shoulder, his tender, scraped knees, his throbbing big toe, all the other bruises he'd endured up to now; inexplicably, he was most aware of his nose. He realized the absurdity of it somewhere in the back of his mind. The miracle was that he could walk, much less run or punch two people with a fist numb with the pain that shot down from his shoulder. But his nose took sudden precedence because the hurt was something he could see; it seemed to have tripled in size.

He sat behind the wheel in a head-ringing stupor. He was gasping for breath, taking in large gulps of frigid air; his pulse beat in his ears like an incessant drummer. The hand radio on the seat beside him shouted static-garbled, desperate commands. Somewhere a woman was screaming. He saw the car keys dangling from the ignition, saw Sara Mills leaning against the passenger door, her befuddled gaze focused somewhere in his direction. Then, like a punch-weary prizefighter coming off the ropes, he remembered his predicament. His mind told him to start the car, but the tormented muscles in his agonized arm wouldn't respond. It was as if he'd made it to the car but his body demanded a time out. He needed a recess, a rest, time to recuperate. Just a minute would do; half, even. David felt his eyes closing. His body was taking charge, overriding the circuitry of his brain.

"What the hell are you doing in there?"

It was the man in the parka whose startling voice stirred David to action. The man beside the car door, reaching in, when David opened his eyes. Where did *he* come from? He was one of the men who'd dashed by David just a few seconds ago. How did he get back here so fast?

"Hey, you're not—"

It wasn't that the man had suddenly frightened him— David was already at the limit of fear. It wasn't even that the man recognized him or shone a light in his face that forced a reaction. It was that the man was reaching through the open window—a gloved, outstretched hand on which he saw the leather seams along the bulky fingers—moving slowly, almost cautiously, straight to David's nose. The thought of that hand touching him, making contact with his swollen nose caused David's eyes to water. It also caused him to slam the car door into the man's body, knocking his flashlight away.

The man fell backwards, rolling in the snow, hugging his knees and screaming.

Now it was time to go. Now, before someone else showed up with more than a grim smile. He pulled the door closed with a violent jerk and reached for the ignition key. Voices were coming from the house. He didn't have to look back to see who they were.

David turned the starter.

The Volvo's engine coughed and died.

"Oh, Jesus—c'mon, *c'mon*!"

Flashlight beams from the rear window reflected from the mirror into his eyes. He could hear them on the run, stomping down the snow-covered driveway. He turned the key again.

"Please, dammit, *please* . . ."

The engine roared to life.

David didn't give it a chance to idle or warm up. With the engine racing, he released the hand brake and popped the clutch.

The car shot backwards up the drive in reverse.

In the second it took him to realize that he was in the wrong gear, he hit something; there was a bump and a scream and through the mirror he saw something crash against the rear window then disappear. Then suddenly everyone who was behind the car was now abreast of it, leaping and diving out of the way. David saw a hat roll across the white lawn as its owner bounced headlong into a drift, his herringbone coat all but disappearing in the eruption of snow. It was a fleeting instant of triumph to see *them* all running for their lives for a change. But only an instant, because the Volvo was speeding backwards, wheels spinning on the ice, forcing the car to swerve wildly up the embankment. He had lifted his right foot off the accelerator to jam it back over the clutch, put his weight into a hard stomp on the brake pedal, his right hand grinding through the gears in search of forward, when the car crashed into the oak door frame of Henry Gale Mara's masterful entryway.

The first miracle was that the car wasn't immediately crushed under the weight of the concrete slab supported by two pillars in the entryway, one of which David had managed to knock off its foundation. The second miracle was that the collision and abrupt stop hadn't killed the engine. He thought of that now because the people who'd scattered like bits of paper only moments ago, who had looked silly running away from him, were now moving slowly, cautiously, toward him, caught in the headlights of the car, and they didn't look silly or scared anymore.

"What are you doing . . . ?" Sara was slumped backwards in the passenger well, her head against the dash, looking out the rear window. She was blinking rapidly, suddenly jarred out of her stupor.

"Keep your head down!" David yelled. He found neutral but everywhere he pushed the floor shift the car shuddered with the grinding of the gears. He kept his eyes on the men coming up the drive. One of them started running.

Sara pulled herself back on the seat, a hand against her head. She placed the other on the shift lever and guided it into the correct slot. "It sticks sometimes," she said groggily.

David stomped the accelerator. The Volvo jumped as he let out the clutch, the engine screaming rpms, and Sara fell back with a cry. The car shot away from the splintered entryway in a spray of snow and gravel. The man who'd been running toward them dived aside at the last moment. There were two of them left, between David and the bridge; the one nearest was limping, favoring his right foot, and yelling into his radio. The other figure was about twenty yards behind him and didn't have a radio or a flashlight gun; he was standing to the side of the driveway, shocked by the scene before him.

David crowded the left side of the drive, the tires bumping over the gravel shoulder, forcing the man to jump back. He didn't want to hit him, only scare him away; besides, he wasn't going to take a chance getting hit with a zap gun. David saw him slip and lose his balance as he danced back between ice puddles. The man fell on his back when David passed him.

That leaves only one. David concentrated on the man ahead illuminated in the headlights. An electric zap gun wouldn't do him any good, David thought. They might work on people but not on Volvos. David pressed the accelerator. But the man didn't move; he stood stuck to the spot, glaring into the lights, one hand thrust casually into the outer pocket of his coat. When he withdrew his hand it wasn't a flashlight he held. It was a gun. A real one.

"David . . . ?"

"Get down!"

David saw him raise the weapon. He held it steady with both hands.

"Christ!"

David slammed on the brakes and the car skidded nearly off the drive. Sara braced herself for the sudden stop, holding the dash with outstretched hands. "Watch out!" she kept yelling. "You're going to hit him! Watch out!"

The car didn't hit him; it slid across the drive away from him and stopped diagonally in the road and died. The guy had to have nerves of steel, David thought. He never even flinched. Now he was walking toward the car, the gun down at his side. It was the guy from the patio. The one whose dart missed its mark the first time they met. He was about ten feet away when he smiled.

"I knew you didn't have the guts, Townsend. You don't have the instincts for it."

David's pulse was racing. He was sweating inside the parka. They were too close to end it here. He grabbed Earl's flashlight gun from the seat, laid the barrel on the open window ledge and pressed the yellow button.

The man with the gun had just enough time to recognize the sound before both darts struck him in the chest. The jolt knocked him backwards off his feet. He screamed and the gun fell into the snow.

"Wrong," David said. He tossed the contraption out the window and started the car.

"David! They're coming!"

He saw them in the rearview mirror. Four of them, pounding down the driveway.

"Hurry!"

In the next second the car was moving, spewing snowy debris in the faces of the men chasing them. The Volvo was over the bridge and halfway up the hill before David shifted into second gear.

They passed the Chevy Malibu about a mile later; it was off to the side of the road parked beside a dilapidated billboard advertising the 1976 Gill Creek VFW's Bicentennial Fish Fry. David saw two faces appear at one of the steamed windows as he raced past. He thought about stopping, shaking their hands, thanking them for being out on this night, but there wasn't really time for that. Besides, he had his own fish to fry.

THIRTY-SEVEN

NIAGARA FALLS

SARA WAS fighting to stay lucid but whatever they'd injected her with was beginning to take effect. She tried to keep awake, to give directions, but she became more and more groggy, inarticulate, and finally drifted to sleep against the window.

David parked in an alley shared by a closed Texaco station and an all-night McDonald's. He checked Sara for wounds but except for a bruise she seemed unhurt. He opened his door and lay Sara across the front seat, and she slid into a posture of fetal unconsciousness. David went around the Volvo inspecting it for damages. The tires seemed to be okay but all the sliding in the driveway had put the front end out of alignment and the crash into the house had broken a taillight, creased the trunk lid and dented the bumper. With the flashlight he looked under the engine to check for leaking oil. When he crouched down to check the differential, he found the homing device.

It was a black metal box the size of two cigarette packs with an eight-inch antenna. The case was magnetized so that it would attach to the bumper. A red light glowed at one end.

When did they put it on the car? Everybody at Weeksbriar can't have a bug attached to his car. Then he remembered the security man who came to Sara's house. David cursed. They'd been following them the whole time. He took a dime from his pocket, unscrewed the lid and removed the battery. The light went out.

David locked the Volvo and limped to McDonald's.

He scarcely recognized himself. In the rest-room mirror he saw what everyone had been chasing since midnight. His face was a mess; a double streak of dried blood trailed from his swollen nose, caked in splotches across his chin and cheeks. There was a lump over his right eye and a skin-scraped bruise on his forehead that stung when he touched it. He shed the parka and shirt to inspect his shoulder. It wasn't a hurt that showed except for the purplish bruise, but it was going to be stiff and awkward for days. His toe was the most serious injury all in all; he'd jammed it in the collision with the frozen bank and it was badly sprained. He'd be able to hobble around if he didn't have to run and there weren't any gashes or stitchable wounds. It was something to be thankful for.

He washed away the blood and dabbed his face dry with paper towels, then sat in a toilet stall to take inventory.

He went through Earl's wallet. Earl Stanley Hammond, according to his driver's license, was from Hackensack, New Jersey. He was thirty-four, single. There were an American Express card, two gasoline credit cards, an expired Bergen County voter's registration, a social security card, fifty-seven dollars and a Dallas car rental receipt. The van. David also found a plastic laminated card identifying Earl as employee number 22-4952-AG of Euromedic Group II, MAG Central, New York. An area code and phone number were written on the back of the card.

David stuffed the wallet back into his parka. He took out the homing device and leaned back on the commode to study it. The label identified it as The Trail Maker, a product of the Surveillance Associates Company of Rochester, New York. DO NOT IMMERSE IN WATER was printed in larger type than FOR OFFICIAL USE ONLY. What did official use mean?

Before he left he wiped his face again with a wet paper towel. When he glanced at himself in the mirror it was a different David Townsend who looked back—bruised, battered and sore, but determined. He'd beaten them again. It was a victory, a small one. The only problem was that he didn't know how to quit the game.

David propped her head up with one arm and put the McDonald's styrofoam coffee cup to her lips. "Here, drink this."

Sara's eye fluttered as the steam from the cup wafted before her. She took a sip then opened her eyes.

"How do you feel?" David said.

She put both hands around the cup and sipped again. "My head . . . hurts. Mouth tastes . . . awful."

"Can you hold the cup by yourself? I bought some aspirins."

Sara nodded and David put two tablets in her hand which she gulped down with a swallow of coffee. She made a face and closed her eyes, then took another sip. When she looked at him her eyes were more alert. "I didn't think I'd see you again. What happened?"

"I got tired of running."

"But you came back." She sounded startled.

"Yeah. And I told *you* to jump. Why didn't you jump?"

She took another sip of coffee. "I didn't have my shoes."

"That's why you didn't jump?"

"How long do you think I'd last running around in freezing weather without shoes?" She looked at him more closely. She touched his face. "My God, David, what happened to you?"

"Don't touch my nose. You want some more coffee?"

"No. This is fine. The coffee is wonderful."

"The night manager sold me one of these little aspirin tins. They're Bayers. That okay?"

250

"I think so."

She looked a little better, David thought. "I got black coffee. I didn't know if it was bad to have sugar with whatever drug they—"

"There might be a reaction to the acetylsalicylic acid," she said, then added, "the aspirin. I don't know what it was they gave me at the house, but it should be all right. The worst would be I'd throw up." Sara gave him a brave smile. "Thanks. I think I'll be fine as soon as this head goes down."

"You're not hungry or anything?"

"God, no."

"Is there anything I can get?"

"No, really."

"You'll be all right then?"

"Yes." She gave him an embarrassed smile. "Thank you for coming back." She moved closer and kissed him.

"I really came back for the car," David said.

"Bullshit."

David smiled back. "Finish your coffee. You need to be awake and alert. We have to figure out what to do now." It hurt to raise his eyebrows. "They won't find us as easily as they did the last time." He told her about the bug.

"Goddamn them!"

"Yeah, I wasn't too pleased either. But it might be something we can use against them."

"I don't want to follow *them*, David."

"We don't have a tracking unit."

"Good. I—That thing isn't on, is it?"

"No. Not yet. You ready to travel?"

"To where?"

"Had a nice chat with the McDonald's manager." David started the car. "How'd you like to go to Canada?"

"Canada?"

"Ontario. Across Rainbow Bridge. It's where all the

newlyweds go. We'll register as Mr. and Mrs. Earl Stanley Hammond of Hackensaw, New Jersey."

"That's your idea of a safe place? Five miles from here? Who's Earl whatshisname? And it's Hacken*sack*, New Jersey."

"Hammond's is the only identification I've got. The picture on his driver's license isn't a terrific likeness but what is? Anyway, that's all you need to get into Canada—a driver's license. That's what the McDonald's manager told me. I don't think they'll look for us over there."

"You seem pretty sure of yourself."

"You want to go or not?"

Sara started to answer but her face changed instead. She leaned forward, breathing through her mouth. What was left of the coffee went on the floorboard.

David grabbed her by the shoulders. "Sara? What's the matter?"

"I think—" She gasped for breath.

"What!"

"—I'm going to be sick."

"No."

"Yes . . . Open the door."

David reached across her and tugged the handle. She braced against the open door and threw up in the snow. When she pulled herself back inside she was panting, her eyes closed, her head back on the seat.

"Are you all right?" David smoothed strands of hair back from her face. "Sara?"

"It was the aspirin," she said between deep breaths. "I'll be okay."

David slid back behind the wheel. "I'm taking you to a hospital."

"No, it's all right. I feel much better."

"The hell you do. Where *is* a hospital?"

"Look, *I'm* the doctor." She opened her eyes. Her

breathing was less labored. "I'm okay. Really. It was just the aspirin." She looked at David. "Let's go to Canada."

"Promise me you're okay."

"Jesus Christ, David, I'm okay. Just go."

David put the car into gear. "All right. We have one stop to make first."

"Where?"

"Bus station."

"Bus station? Busses don't go to Canada from here."

David grinned. "Yeah, I know."

He bought a candy bar in the Trailways terminal and finished it in the waiting area, sitting across from a large black woman carrying a paper sack filled with coffee. David was surprised at the number of people waiting for a bus at this hour. He counted fifty people, most of them barely awake. Two transients were passed out on one of the benches. When the voice announced the next departing bus, he moved into the passenger loading area. The driver was taking bags with one of the handlers, throwing them into the baggage compartment.

David walked around the bus. He put the battery back into the Trail Maker, screwed down the lid and checked to be sure the light was on before he stuck it inside the rear bumper.

"What took you so long?" Sara asked when he got back into the car.

"We don't want just any old bus," David said. He pulled out of the parking space and stopped at a red light at the corner of the Trailways building.

"Did you attach it?"

"Yeah, I did."

"Which one?" Sara looked through the rear window as a bus rolled out of the terminal. It was heading in the opposite direction.

"That one."

"Where is it going?"

David smiled. "Denver." When the light changed he found first gear without any trouble and drove to Rainbow Bridge.

THIRTY-EIGHT

MADRID

AN ANGRY Ian McPhearson took the phone on the first ring. His communiqués to Moravec had stopped being acknowledged. He wanted to know why.

"McPhearson."

"Dr. McPhearson, MAG relay here. We have London."

"Yes, yes, get on with it."

"Go ahead, London."

"Hello, Ian. Miles Haldern here. I—"

"What's happening, Haldern?" McPhearson interrupted. "I've just received an SCS signal telling me that the donor patient is *not* in transit. It says—I'm looking at it right now—it says 'patient transfer delayed.' What do they mean? And where the devil is Luther Moravec? He hasn't acknowledged any of my updates. Not that I'm so concerned about that—he should be *here*. The donor should have been delivered already. Is this message correct? Is there a delay? If so, how long? I mean, my God, there *is* something rather urgently important about this case. Don't they know that?"

"I'm sorry, old boy, but there is a delay. And Luther's had something of an equipment malfunction. You won't be getting acknowledgments directly, I'm afraid."

"Good God, man—"

"Have you received the MAG medical data on the Townsend donor?"

"Yes, I have it here. I have everything here. What I don't have is the donor himself."

"How is your patient?"

"Well, he is *not* recovering," McPhearson said sarcastically. "I have a very critical heart patient here with myocardial complications, not a bloody case of tonsillectomy! If I can't operate in twenty-four hours, I won't be responsible. I must have time to examine the donor in person. I must *see* him. Sending me blood pressure readings and urology analyses and electrocardiogram printouts are not effective substitutes. I cannot put paper into this man's chest, Haldern."

"Yes, I'm well aware of that. What about the tumor?"

"Unchanged . . . that is to say it's operating normally. But I'm not worried about his aging processes, you know. He's beginning to slip. We're showing occasional runs of PVCs on his EKG tracings. I've increased the lidocaine drip but not the epinephrine dosage. He's putting out good water but his electrolyte values are not consistent; the potassium levels are low. He's taking one fourth normal saline with twenty-five milliequivalents of potassium at one hundred and twenty-five cc an hour. We're pumping everything into him just to stay even, doctor, but it can't go on indefinitely. BP is eighty over sixty. If it drops in the next twelve hours I expect premature ventricular contractions will follow. That's what we're fighting, you know. The moment he begins ventricular tachycardia is the moment we can begin to seriously doubt his chances of—"

"I'm sending the London AirMore," Haldern cut in.

"What!"

"That's why I called. I'm afraid you're not in a position to appreciate the present situation, doctor. I spoke to Luther not forty minutes ago. I've just left a meeting of the board. The decision is that Dr. Townsend should be transferred. Our AirMed transport with the mobile unit left London within the last quarter hour. It should be in Madrid in less than two hours."

"Townsend can't be moved!"

"It's no longer a question of marginal risks."

256

"Marginal—!"

"We can't guarantee delivery of the donor patient within the time left to us," Haldern went on. "Dr. Townsend is going to die unless we take bolder action. *That* is the primary factor, doctor. The decision was to transport him immediately. The mobile unit is equipped with every medical and mechanical need he might require. Dr. Ashley Graves and a surgical team are aboard to assist you should you need them. I want you to send your operating team ahead on the AirMore aircraft you have standing by there. The major concern here is not that your patient will be disturbed in the logistics of transfer—he will be as safe in the unit as he might be in any intensive care ward. The major concern is time, which you have acknowledged. We must get Dr. Townsend and his donor together as soon as possible. Since it is no longer feasible to transfer the donor in the short time remaining, other arrangements had to be made."

McPhearson wasn't convinced. "Can you guarantee that the donor will be there when and if Townsend survives the trip back to London? Have you alerted St. Mary's? Is Dr. Graves fully aware of our patient's critical condition?"

"But you're not coming to St. Mary's," Haldern said. "You're not returning to London."

"No?" The heart surgeon paused a second. "Then where the bloody hell *are* we going?"

"To the United States," Haldern replied as if it were perfectly obvious. "Where the donor is. Where he will be by the time you arrive there—Weeksbriar."

THIRTY-NINE

MADRID

THE AMERICAN built Galaxy C-5A was easily recognized as she glided to touchdown on the same Madrid runway that four days earlier had been the scene of a holocaust. The runway was still scorched and blackened from the fire.

Dr. McPhearson watched the plane taxi to the special hangar where he'd been waiting the past hour. He'd left the hospital forty minutes after talking to Moravec. He wasn't nervous, he told himself, just anxious. He had never worked with an AirMore Staff before. Of course he knew several of the specialists in the AirMore service—they all practiced at St. Mary's—but knowing them wasn't the same as working with them, especially not on a case as important as this one. It would be odd, the working conditions *inside* Little Mary—he'd never been inside the giant transport jet. He wasn't thrilled at the prospect. They were all top people, the surgical teams aboard the planes. They were specially chosen and in addition to their fields of expertise they were also trained for special emergencies. Like crash landings and aircraft evacuations in case of fire and other death-threatening contingencies. But AirMore, he reminded himself, was a bloody miracle. At least, that's what everyone said.

McPhearson had never ever *seen* the plane before today. That's what troubled him most as he watched the ground crew signal stop to the pilot. It troubled him more than an unfamiliar surgical team, or the sudden necessity to move his most important patient, or the possibility that even with

258

the transfer there might not be a donor waiting when they touched down in the United States. What troubled him was the plane itself, the idea of riding in it, the idea that there might be some emergency during the long flight. *That* made him nervous.

McPhearson didn't like planes. He always traveled by train. He didn't like the feeling when an airplane was no longer attached to the ground. And as much as he didn't like taking off, he enjoyed landings even less. He didn't like it when he looked out a window and saw nothing but clouds or, worse, the splotchy terrain of the earth thousands of feet below him. Which is why he insisted on an aisle seat on the infrequent occasions he was required to fly. His attitude was not bolstered when he thought of the circumstances that brought Stuart Townsend to be his patient in the first place. The idea that he would soon be leaving the same airport, the same runway, traveling over the same charred ground as Townsend had only a few days ago made his skin crawl. All the wonders of Little Mary didn't help. A plane—even this one—was still a plane.

"Dr. McPhearson?" It was a plump, rosy-cheeked man in a tweed coat who had got off the plane and approached McPhearson now. He extended a hand.

McPhearson shook it. "Dr. Graves, is it?"

The round little man nodded. "Yes, AirMore One COS." He smiled. "So, we have quite a challenge, I take it, eh?"

"Challenge?" McPhearson was distracted by the plane. It was much larger than he'd expected. He'd never stood on the ground next to one; always he'd seen them from a lounge through a glass partition level with the passenger cabin. Here, on the ground, looking up at the enormous engine pods and the great belly, it was more beast than bird. He felt an uneasy sensation coming—a weight in the pit of his stomach, a moist feeling at the back of his neck. "What challenge?"

"The patient, of course," Graves said. "Townsend.

Getting him to—I say, old man, are you feeling all right? You look deathly pale."

"No, no, I'm fine." McPhearson said quickly. "I haven't got my ration of sleep these past days, that's all. We should get to the hospital. I don't like leaving him." He glanced at the plane again. "When will it be ready to leave?"

"The moment we've returned with the patient," Graves said with an enthusiasm that made McPhearson uncomfortable. "We'll be ready to go as soon as the unit is unloaded."

There was a loud hydraulic hiss that startled McPhearson. His eyes flashed to the plane. The nose was opening. The clamshell doors cracked open slowly, exposing the cavernous interior.

"There we are," Graves said with a nod. "Won't be a moment." He turned back to McPhearson. "Ever seen our Mary up close, doctor?"

McPhearson shook his head. He couldn't take his eyes off the monstrous aircraft. The front landing gear was being lowered, which allowed the nose of the plane to hunker down. As the giant doors opened wider, McPhearson saw the MORE unit. It was a vehicle longer than a bus and nearly ten feet wide. He'd seen one parked in the receiving bay at St. Mary's. It was sixty feet long with a bellows-type section approximately forty feet from the front. An articulated mainframe, it was called. The thing was too long to maneuver around corners, particularly in European cities, so the articulation was engineered to allow an extra set of wheels at the pivot point. The unit was painted white to match the plane and it was windowless, except for the driver's compartment. It was almost as formidable looking as the plane.

"A beauty, isn't she, doctor? Our Little Mary."

"Yes, a bloody wonder," McPhearson said dryly. "Where is the staff? I would really like to return to the hospital as quickly as possible. I'll want to give my people a complete rundown on the patient's ICU history as soon—"

"All taken care of." Graves smiled again. "We've been supplied with all of Townsend's medical updates through MAG. The staff is quite ready for the transfer, doctor. They're onboard the unit now, as a matter of fact." He glanced at the AirMore vehicle when he heard the diesel engine roar to life. It crept out of the gaping mouth of the plane like a caterpillar.

"Here we are then." Graves reached for the handle of the entry port as the vehicle stopped beside them. A metal step-up glided down from the port as the door swung open. Graves gestured for McPhearson to enter with a wide sweep of his arm. "After you, doctor."

The inside was compact but not crowded. Everything was white, even the floor. The first compartment was called the cockpit, logically because it was the driver's compartment and there was headroom enough to stand. It was divided by a central aisle with three rows of seats on either side behind the driver and large tinted windows. McPhearson was introduced to the surgical/ICU team in the cockpit—an anesthesiologist, two scrub nurses, a circulatory nurse and an orderly who was also the driver.

Little Mary was actually a large German-manufactured articulated bus with a stainless steel frame modified to accommodate Euromedic's special purposes, Graves explained. It was made up of a power module—the forward section—and a trailer which were connected by a swiveling axle at the junction of the articulation. The power module was subdivided into two compartments: the cockpit and the Intensive Care Unit. The trailer housed the OR and was accessible via a single entry port through a lock between it and the ICU. The operating room was sealed to maintain its sterile integrity.

"We are entirely a self-sufficient mini hospital here," Graves said proudly. "Once the patient is aboard, of course."

"And exactly how is that accomplished?" McPhearson asked sharply. "I mean, this is a very special patient we're

261

transferring, you know. We can't just run him out of the hospital strapped to a gurney cart and stuff him into this thing."

Graves looked hurt. "Why, no, of course not. We'll place him in a capsule first. That's always been the drill. I thought you were familiar with AirMore procedure, Dr. McPhearson. Haven't you *ever* seen a unit?"

"As a matter of fact I haven't," McPhearson snapped. "I'm not a part of the AirMore program. I don't know enough about it to, to . . . and what the bloody hell is a capsule?"

Graves glanced at the other members of the team, then looked at McPhearson. "Well, sir, let me show you."

The ICU was approximately twenty feet long and brightly lit. The first ten feet along the left bulkhead held stainless steel cabinets above a counter with stenciled labels— PHARMACEUTICALS, PHISOHEX/SOAPS, ANES-THESIA, SYRINGE/IV PACKETS, WHOLE BLOOD, PLASMA. There was also a double scrub sink, a frosted-glass X-ray viewer, an electroencephalograph, an EKG, digital blood pressure and pulse readouts and a variety of other machines he didn't immediately recognize. Across the aisle were three bubbleglass-topped metal carts, seven feet long by three feet wide, aligned head to foot. They looked like incubators grown five times.

Graves leaned on one, tapping his fingertips on the glass. "These are our patient capsules," he said grandly. "They're temperature controlled and can be made pressure controlled to a factor of plus four. Each unit is equipped to handle the equivalent of six standard two-hundred-cc D5/W IVs to a limit of three hundred cc per hour normal saline, plasma or whole blood. They have their own bladder drainage systems and, due to the unit's pressurized capabilities, may be charged as respirators—any mixture, of course. The units are sterile and comfortable provided the patient is no taller than six foot nine.

"The procedure is that we will roll the capsule to the

patient's room, make the necessary intravenous transfers and move the patient into the capsule whereupon the transparent shield will be closed and he will be removed to AirMore. Incidentally, doctor, the shield is ultraviolet-sensitive and will immediately darken to protect the patient from the sun's rays should he be exposed. That's one of the reasons there are no windows here or in the OR. Anyway, once inside the intensive care compartment and locked into place, the capsule is maintained in level ballast which allows the patient to be unaffected by swaying of the vehicle or the aircraft. Believe me, doctor, with you aboard and with this staff and this equipment, Townsend couldn't be in better hands."

McPhearson nodded. He was anxious to get back to the cockpit, where he could see outside. The closed compartment was beginning to make him perspire. "Let's hope and pray you're right," he said.

"Oh, I'm right," Graves beamed. "Everyone knows you're the best."

McPhearson sat silently next to a window for the rest of the ride. He stared outside but didn't see anything. He was thinking of the nine hours ahead. He was imagining what it would be like, closed inside a compartment that was, itself, inside the belly of a windowless airplane. He knew he wasn't going to like it. He knew it because his stomach was knotting up and the back of his neck was warm and moist. He wasn't going to like it at all. He was getting that feeling again and he couldn't help it.

Planes made him sick.

FORTY

NIAGARA FALLS, ONTARIO

DAVID HAD stopped running.

The roar of Niagara Falls was like thunder that never stopped when he checked into cabin five of Jay Cotton's Resort Motel. It was a one-room cabin with one light fixture. And one bed.

Sara took her bath first. The overhead light was out when David made his way to the bed. She accepted him without debate and they made love without questions. Safe in each other's arms, they slept to the crash of the distant falls.

The sound of the bump woke David.

He was on his back and lifted his head, alert, listening. For a time there was nothing. It might have been a dream, he thought. The dinette table top glistened with sunlight from the window on the east side of the cabin. The bed squeaked as he shifted his weight to his elbows.

The noise came again. He felt as much as heard it this time. It wasn't a dream. It was coming from the wall behind the bathroom. He sat up and Sara's arm slid from his chest.

He whispered into her hair. "Sara?"

Sara's eyes opened sleepily. After a moment she smiled. "I'd love to." She was on her side, facing him. Their legs were intertwined. She blinked at him and her expression changed suddenly to fear when the wall behind them vibrated with another bump. "David . . . ?"

"Shhh."

264

He slipped out from under the quilt and swung his feet to the floor.

"They couldn't have," Sara whispered. "They *couldn't* have found us."

"Don't move." Nude, he crept to the bathroom door and pushed it open. A thud rattled the shower spigot. He heard muffled voices. A shadow floated over the window above the mirror. The spigot rattled again. David set a foot on the lid of the toilet seat and hoisted himself to the window.

The ball seemed to come from nowhere. The shadow passed over David's face as the basketball's shallow arc missed the rim and bounced against the wall. Two kids, dressed in mittens and red parkas, chased after the ball as it dribbled away into the snow. He let out his breath.

"David?" Sara was on her knees beside the bed when he returned. She held a shoe in each hand.

"Kids and a basketball," he said. He limped back to the bed.

"Kids!"

"Don't worry, they're not armed." He sat on the bed and massaged his swollen toe.

"God . . ." She slid back under the covers. "It's freezing in this room."

"Do you know what a broken toe looks like?"

She peered down at his foot, the quilt up to her chin. "Probably something like that."

"Terrific."

"I don't think it's broken, David." She lay back on the pillow. "I don't think you'd have been able to . . ."

David looked at her. "No?"

"Aren't you cold out there?"

He got into bed next to her.

"God, you're freezing!"

David kissed her and she melted against him. "You're a beautiful woman, Dr. Sara Mills. I don't remember if I told you that last night."

Sara pushed a strand of his hair back from his forehead. "I remember."

He kissed her again, pressing her head into the pillow, then pushed down the bedcovers, exposing her pink breasts. He drew circles around them with his finger.

"Magnificent."

"We'll freeze," Sara said.

"No we won't."

He caressed her breasts, gently kneading them, then moved his head to work them with his mouth and tongue. His hand stroked her thighs and she opened to him, lifting herself to the touch of his fingers. Sara moaned deep in her throat as he found the moistness inside her, raising her bottom to the rhythm of his hand. Her fingers held his hair as he moved his lips from one breast to the other, holding her, taking her into his mouth, arousing her nipples with his tongue. Sara's grip tightened in his hair as his fingers slipped deeper inside her. She pushed against the pressure, urging him further, her hips rotating, her heels dug into the bed. . . . She came before she wanted to, before she could stop.

Sara reached for him then. His fingers slid away as he rolled on his back. David shut his eyes when he felt her hands grip him. She stroked gently, moving her tongue and fingers, then closed her lips over him and began to take him slowly, bobbing her head, easing him in and out of her mouth.

When he pulled her back to him, Sara was out of breath. "Oh, yes," she said. She still held him, her fingers sliding urgently over him. "I want you . . ."

Sara opened her legs, guiding him to her. David went in deeply and Sara cried out, gasping, arching her back. The bed creaked and groaned with desperate rhythm. David was perspiring despite the cold. The quilt was thrown off and Sara lay under him, eyes closed, breasts heaving, her breath catching with his every stroke. He was coming to the end and he thrust himself harder, deeper, faster, rushing toward the finish. Sara's frenzy matched his own. Her bottom rose off the bed to meet him. "Oh, David . . . ah . . . ah . . . ahhhh!" Her legs opened wider, extended over his back, then wrapped around him when she came, squeezing him in, riding him, holding him tight until he came too. At the finish they collapsed, gasping and spent.

"I'm starving," David said.

Sara had pulled the quilt over them. She was nuzzled under his arm. The frayed edge of the quilt covered her lower lip so that when she exhaled the frays stirred.

"I figured that was next. How is your toe?"

"I guess it isn't broken. You want to go eat?"

"After I take a bath." She kissed his chest. "Why don't you see if you can find a thermostat. If not, let's burn the sofa."

When she came out of the bathroom, wrapped in a towel, the cabin was warm and she felt wonderful. David had found the thermostat. He was sitting at the dinette table with his back to her.

"I meant to ask before," she said cheerfully. "Do all truck drivers make love like you?"

"I don't know. I haven't slept with all of them." David turned to her. He wasn't smiling. "You better come and have a look at this."

Spread out on the table were Earl Stanley Hammond's pieces of identification. David took a small suitcase from the seat and put it on the table.

"I went out to check the car again. I found this in the back seat."

Sara watched him unsnap the clasps. It wasn't a suitcase. It was a briefcase. The man in the herringbone coat had carried coffee on it.

David opened it.

Inside was a computer console. The monitor screen

popped into place when the lid was fully extended. There was a keyboard, printer and, Sara thought, a modem.

"What do you make of this?" David asked.

The kids missed another shot at the hoop before Sara answered.

"It's a computer," she said. "Moravec was carrying it. What was it doing in the car?"

David shook his head. "I don't know. What *is* it?"

Sara folded her towel under her and sat down. She found a laminated card stuck in with printout sheets from a pouch in the lid.

"It's a telecommunicator," she said, reading the card. "BriefPac." She pointed to the components. "Memory, keyboard, display, acoustical coupler . . ."

"Speak English."

"A telephone receiver fits into those slots," Sara said, touching the suction cups. "To sign on to a data base." She turned the laminated card over, reading it. "It also has hard memory. God, there must be a million bytes of storage there."

"Bites?"

"Bytes." She spelled it for him. "Computer memory." She took another card from the pouch and studied it, then another. "Good grief."

"What?"

"Station codes, primary computer access numbers, alternates, MAG ID, update summaries, satellite lock numbers . . . This thing's loaded."

"What are you talking about?"

"This computer . . . it has everything. We can call up any computer in the network. Even MAG."

"I haven't been real lucky with a telephone lately."

"David, you don't understand. We can get *information* with this. Unless I'm a complete idiot, I can get into *any* Euromedic computer that's on the system." She held up the laminated cards. "All the codes are here. Look at this . . ." She placed one of the cards in front of him and pointed out the first listing:

Action Group Central (NY Mag)-----212 + 555—4412-----"SBS013"

"That's a computer number and that's an ID code access. If we can get into the system we might just find something."

David looked at the card. Nothing on it made any sense to him. "Like what?"

"Like why Euromedic wants you so badly. If we can get into CC at Weeksbriar we could request your file."

"Are you sure?"

Sara shook her head. "No, but we could try."

David stared at the machine. He picked up the power cord coiled in a compartment beside the suction cups. "What do we need to get this thing working?"

"A telephone," she said. "Just a telephone."

FORTY-ONE

LITTLE MARY

A TRAY of blood smear slides rattled in a magnetic holder on the stainless steel counter as the ICU compartment leaned in a turn. The sensation of movement was almost defeated except when the AirMore bus negotiated a turn. It wasn't a sensation McPhearson enjoyed.

The surgeon gripped the handhold at the side of the ICP unit's plastic shield. Fascinated but frightened, he watched the patient while the pitch of the bed inside the Intensive Care Pod changed, then returned to level as the bus came out of its turn. Actually, the bed never changed at all; it was maintained in a constant level attitude relative to the ground by the ICP's independent gyrometric system. It was McPhearson and everything else aboard the AirMore bus that did the leaning. But watching his patient and experiencing the sensation of a shift in his equilibrium caused McPhearson's stomach to rise.

The transfer of the patient to the mobile unit had gone as smoothly as Graves said it would. The patient was, by all signs, comfortable. The digital BP reader showed him 101/74 and steady. Pulse was unchanged. He was taking one-fourth normal saline with twenty-five milliequivalents of potassium at 125 cc/hr through the ICP's IV system. Everything looked good.

Everything *was* all right, McPhearson told himself. There wasn't anything to worry about. Townsend's status was stable. In a little over nine hours they'd be safely at Weeksbriar. He checked his watch and saw one of the nurses looking at him. She smiled. He nodded. Mustn't appear nervous, he told himself. He was the captain of this miracle ship now. He mustn't let his crew suspect he was on the edge of panic.

"Dr. McPhearson, we're on the runway apron. Would you like to come up front while we load?" It was Dr. Graves's voice. It came from a speaker in the ceiling.

McPhearson looked around for a button to push. "Nurse? Ah, how do I answer that?"

"I can hear you, doctor," Graves replied. The ICU reverberated with his chuckle. "The intercom is a hands-off system."

Naturally.

"We are cleared for takeoff as soon as we're secure," Graves added.

"Yes, ah . . ." McPhearson spoke to the ceiling. "How soon is that?"

"Five minutes."

"Right. I'm coming now."

They approached the plane from the front, driving directly toward the ramp that spilled out from the mouth like a huge silver tongue. McPhearson watched as the bus drove onto the ramp and into the dark superstructure.

He leaned nearer the window to watch the ground crew below him. He heard the clamp of metal, but could not see what was going on.

"Fascinating, isn't it?" Graves said, sitting beside him.

McPhearson didn't look up. "What on earth are they doing down there? We haven't slipped off the bloody thing, have we?"

"No, no," Graves laughed. "Nothing so dramatic as that, old man. They're just pinning the bus into place."

"Pinning?" McPhearson twisted round to see the plump little man. "Pinning!"

"Of course. A safety precaution only. The ramp is part of the aircraft. They're just pinning . . . well, bolting I suspect is the proper term. In any case, the vehicle is

271

fastened to the ramp and an electrical umbilical cord from the plane connected to our system on the bus. Oh, it's quite safe, I assure you. We don't want the vehicle moving about, once the nose doors are closed and locked into place. It's all quite safe." Graves chuckled to himself. "It would be too much an embarrassment, wouldn't it—if we slipped off the ramp?"

"What's that?" McPhearson said with a sharp look.

"You know—" the little man pointed his index finger at the ceiling"—at thirty thousand feet." He laughed again.

McPhearson didn't smile. "You mean there are just those bolts holding us inside the aircraft?"

Graves slapped his pudgy hands together and let out a sigh of admiration. "Amazing, isn't it?"

McPhearson held tight to the armrest as the aircraft's large clam doors began to close, shutting off the light outside. The entire team was in the cockpit now except for one nurse who sat in a special seat in the ICU compartment. She would remain there through takeoff, Graves had said. Someone would be with the patient at all times. That was AirMore procedure once a patient was aboard.

But McPhearson wasn't concerned with procedure right now. His total concentration was on the sound of the hydraulic motor that closed the doors, sealing him in. He sensed the sound of the hydraulic pump coursing through the plane. There was a slight vibration in his seat. Was the ramp straining under the weight of the bus? What would happen if the bloody thing started to move, snapping loose of its bolts? The ramp ran the entire length of the aircraft. There were doors at the rear end of the plane, Graves had pointed out, so that the vehicle could be loaded from either end. What if the bus broke loose and slid against those doors? He pictured in his mind a large airplane over the sea. *This* airplane; its pure white exterior marred by an ugly, black hole at its ass end where the bus had broken through and was falling thirty thousand feet to the gray ocean below.

There was a bump as the nose doors clamped shut. The

hydraulic whine stopped. A red light came out somewhere below McPhearson's window and he saw the curved, holed frame members of the interior superstructure. It wasn't a comforting sight. He'd never seen the actual metal skeleton of an airplane and looking at it now was less then consoling. It seemed so . . . fragile. Then the light went out and it was totally dark outside McPhearson's window, and now all he could see was his own reflection in the glass. It was a final reminder that they were now completely sealed inside the plane. When he heard the engines start he put his head back on the rest and closed his eyes. His palms were perspiring.

"Doctor?"

Graves was leaning against the seat in front of him. "Yes?"

"You might be more comfortable in the staff quarters," Graves said. "They aren't quite the luxury of an airliner, but they are private and you could rest."

"Staff quarters?"

"Oh, didn't I mention it?" He shrugged. "I keep forgetting. Yes, we have three compartments aboard the aircraft. They're frightfully small I'm afraid, but they're available for the staff. On these long flights they come in handy."

"You mean we're not sealed up in here for the duration?"

"Oh my, no." Graves chuckled. "That *would* make it tedious."

"I don't think I should be away from the patient."

"I understand, doctor, but—" Graves pulled at his ear "—it isn't as though you'd be *far* away. The aircraft is only two hundred feet long." Graves raised an eyebrow. "Would you like to see it then?"

McPhearson considered it. He should remain as near Townsend as possible. Still, a private compartment . . .

"Good afternoon, ladies and gentlemen," said a voice suddenly from the overhead speaker. "This is Captain Collins, first officer of AirMore One. Unless otherwise instructed we will begin taxiing in three minutes. We are cleared for a priority takeoff in eleven minutes. Please secure loose items and fasten your safety belts. Thank you."

McPhearson felt his mouth go dry. He nodded at Graves. "Yes, I think I would like that very much." He stood up. "Where do we go?"

An inflated rubber air lock connected the bus's entry port to a narrow padded corridor along the bulkhead. It served, Graves explained (he was a bloody tour guide, McPhearson thought), as a redundant pressurized feature of the aircraft. In case the cargo hull pressurization failed, he said.

Dr. Graves was also a sadist.

The compartment wasn't as small as Graves had described it. It was about six feet by four and featured two large, comfortable seats that could be reclined to nearly prone positions with the added convenience of counterbalancing footrests. A plastic writing table that folded down from the bulkhead in front of the seats allowed plentiful room for a briefcase. There was also a small window, but the shade was closed.

"This will do nicely," McPhearson said. He sat down.

"Jolly good." Graves pointed out a panel beside the writing desk. "This is the intercom. Just push this button if you want anyone of the staff. We can ring you as well. This button connects you with the flight deck." He nodded toward the front of the plane. "We have a galley aboard with tea and coffee and sandwiches. Not the usual commercial fare, I'm afraid, but we struggle on."

McPhearson nodded. "Fine. I'll just sleep a bit then. But I want to see the patient when he begins his second bag. You'll call me?"

"I'll see to it."

"Run electrolyte values every hour."

"Don't worry, doctor," the little man said with a smile, "your patient is in the best of care." Graves left with a wave and McPhearson settled back in the seat.

He heard the engines begin their scream and felt the plane move. He looked at his watch. Four twenty-two. In nine hours it would be half-past one in the morning. He wondered what the time conversion was—what time would it be in the United States when they arrived? He'd forgotten to ask anyone. It didn't matter, really. Townsend didn't have any conception of time. The thing was to try and get some sleep. Townsend would be all right. Just try to rest and not think about where he was.

The panel speaker startled him as it crackled to life. "This is Captain Collins. We are prepared for takeoff. Are you secure, Dr. Graves?"

"Yes, all secure."

"Touchdown in nine hours and eleven minutes," the pilot said. "Off we go." The speaker clicked and was silent.

McPhearson cinched his seat belt tighter. He sat straight up in his seat, hands gripping each armrest. He felt the vibration of the engines as they revved into high pitch. He held his breath when the plane started forward. The rumbling filled the enclosed cabin and suddenly it seemed a tiny place. There wasn't a fellow traveler to chat away the nervousness that welled in his stomach. There wasn't a flight steward to point out the emergency exits or a plastic card to examine from a pouch in the seat ahead. There was nothing to do but wait and listen for that moment, that *particular* moment when the plane was at its most critical point of flight, when the passenger cabin suddenly tilted, when the sound and feel of tires on the pavement was replaced by a whir of retracting gears and closing doors. That dreadful moment.

McPhearson waited. He strained to hear it, to feel it, he felt the moistness at his neck, but the moment didn't come. The plane was still rolling. He wiped at his eyes. How long had it been? Ten seconds? Fifteen? Why was it taking so long? Was the aircraft too heavy? He remembered that they'd taken on extra cardiac monitoring equipment. There was an additional circulatory nurse aboard too. He'd insisted on that.

His mouth was dry and he hadn't enough saliva to properly wet his lips. God, he thought, what had he done? What if the plane *was* overloaded? What if there'd been some miscalculation? He glanced at his watch. How long had it been now? *Why didn't the plane get off the bloody ground!*

McPhearson touched a sleeve to his face. He leaned forward in his seat, against the force of acceleration and reached for the plastic shade that covered the cabin's only window. He broke his own most steadfast rule. He looked outside.

He squinted in the bright sun as the runway markers flashed past in a blur. The leading edge of the starboard wing swung back from the fuselage in direct alignment with his window and he had an unobstructed view of the two huge engines. The aircraft was still on the runway despite the combined deafening roar. When he glanced forward, his breath caught in his throat. The runway and infield turned black as the plane passed the spot of the wreck. The ground was littered with bits of metal, none larger than the spread of a hand. Wooden stakes with tiny orange streamers had been driven into the earth. He saw a seat cushion, or part of one, half-buried in a trench of mud, its frayed, blackened fibers fluttering in the breeze. He couldn't take his eyes off it. Someone had been sitting on that very cushion when . . .

The plane tilted up suddenly and left the runway in a smooth but steep angle of attack. The runway disappeared almost instantly as the plane banked to the west. AirMore One was safely airborne but it was too much for him. McPhearson couldn't keep the image of a sea of broken and burned bodies out of his mind. He yanked the window shade shut and lay back and closed his eyes. The weight in his stomach was increasing. Sweat rolled into his eyes. He tried to swallow and breathed through his mouth.

276

The speaker crackled again. "This is Captain Collins speaking. I want to welcome you aboard, doctor. We'll do everything to make this a pleasant flight for you and your patient. If there is anything I can do, please don't hesitate to buzz."

McPhearson kept his eyes tightly closed. "Yes . . . yes, thank you."

"Only nine hours ten minutes to go," said the pilot. "Next stop, New Brockton." The speaker crackled then went silent.

McPhearson pushed himself forward, reaching desperately for the bin marked DISCOMFORT CLOSET. He found a green airsick bag just in time.

Nine hours and nine minutes.

FORTY-TWO

JAY COTTON'S RESORT MOTEL

SARA DRESSED while David went to see Jay Cotton about a phone. When he returned he had a yellow desk phone and a cord to plug into the wall jack.

"I had to *rent* a telephone," David said sourly. He plugged it in. "Can you believe that? *Rent* a crummy phone? This cost fifteen bucks."

"Stop complaining. If it works it'll be worth every penny."

Sara sat in front of the machine and David watched as she typed commands on the keyboard. The first display on the screen was a banner identification:

```
EUROMED COMPUPAC
BRIEFSET #6
MORAVEC, LUTHER
DIR MAG 4 LONDON
```

"Luther?" David said. "Now that's a cheerful name. What's that other gibberish mean?"

"It means this belongs to Moravec. The guy in the herringbone coat." She typed another command. The screen went blank, then printed a file directory of data in the computer's memory. There were thirteen listings in the directory, unrecognizable acronyms and abbreviations, ranked alphabetically with a brief description of each file, the date it was entered into the computer, the last time the file was updated and the size of each file measured in bytes.

TITLE	COMMENT	ENTERED	UPDATED	SIZE
BIOENG1	BIOENGINEERING:PHARMACEUTICS	APR	DEC	230293
BIOENG2	BIOENGINEERING:ENZYMES	MAR	JAN	203493
BIOENG3	BIOENGINEERING:CURRENT R/D	JUL	NOV	239223
BIOSYN	BIOSYNTHESIS:CURRENT R/D	AUG	SEP	190342
BIOTECHS	BIOTECHNOLOGY:CURRENT UPD	DEC	JAN	238232
GENSPLIC	GENE SPLICING: INDUSTRY ANAL	FEB	OCT	304321
HAHNEMANN1	HAHNEMANN FILE: (CLOSED)	—RESTRICTED—		PROTEC
HAHNEMANN2	HAHNEMANN REF: TOWNSEND, D.M.	—RESTRICTED—		PROTEC
INTERFER	INTERFERON RESEARCH CURRENT	OCT	NOV	293293
MET-HGH	METHIONYL HG HORMONE: CURRENT	JUN	SEP	259532
MONOCLO	MONOCLONAL ANTIBODY PROTEIN R/D	MAY	DEC	320133
PRO-10K	SEC PROSPECTUS: 10-K REPORTS	JUN	DEC	210339
WNTRGRN	WINTERGREEN FILE: (CLOSED)	—RESTRICTED—		PROTEC

David pointed to the eighth item on the screen. "Look at this. That's me." He squinted at the screen.

"What does Hahnemann mean?"

"I don't know."

"What about RESTRICTED?"

"It means it's a protected file." She looked through the cards. "Access restricted. It's a personal double-lock code. There isn't any reference to it in these cards."

"Meaning?"

"I can't get into them without an access code."

"Not any of them?"

Sara shook her head. "No, just those three. These are read-only files, which means we can read them, you know, call them up on the screen. But those particular files have been protected. We'd have to know what Moravec's personal entry code was to get at them."

"I hate this already."

"We can still read these other files, David."

"I only want to see *my* file," David said. "I don't care what—" he looked at the screen " –bioengineering of enzymes is doing this month. I don't even know what it means. Do you?"

"Not precisely, no, but I'm going to find out," Sara said. She entered another command into the computer. "Why don't you sit down and be quiet a minute and we'll take a look."

David sat. "I hate pushy women, too."

The files were organized into specific fields of ongoing developments in biotechnologic research, mostly genetic and enzymic engineering. The information in each file was mostly cryptic notations on private and public companies with medical research facilities. The data was on companies engaged in such research as biosynthetic insulin for the treatment of diabetes, laboratory-made methionyl human growth hormones for the treatment of dwarfism in children, anti-viral protein studies, enzyme research—a hundred different enterprises, who was doing what where. In each case was an analyst's report of brokerage and banking firms' investments in the companies, as well as a Security and Exchange Commission prospectus and current annual and quarterly reports. Did the company have sufficient capital or assets to get a proposed product to market? Did a company have a licensing or patent arrangement with other companies concerning a particular product? Most companies' annual reports showed that they hadn't earned a dime; those that did had got them from interest collected on unspent venture capital rather than sales—none of them as yet had a product to market.

Established firms with capital to fund research were listed with double asterisks. DuPont, Eli Lilly, Pfizer, Upjohn, Corning Glass, SmithKline, Beckman had their own gene-splicing programs. Novo Industri A/S, a Danish company, was the world's leading producer of industrial enzymes. Large investors in the genetic research included Standard Oil of California, Koppers, Monsanto and Emerson Electric. They were all in the files, nearly five hundred companies that were researching or investing. And at the end of each entry were cross-references to files in MAG's Special Communications Section. Several of them referred to Hahnemann.

"This is incredible," Sara said. She looked at David. "There is current information here on biogenetic and enzymic medical research projects *outside* Euromedic."

"Is that bad or good?"

"It's *supposed* to be secret. No one outside the research teams is supposed to know what they're doing. At least, not to this detail. This kind of research is jealously guarded. I know, I work in a research lab. But—Jesus, look at this stuff. How'd they get all this?"

"Industrial—medical—espionage?"

"There are *doctors*, David."

"That makes them different all of a sudden? They're people, aren't they? Doctors can spy on each other just as well as industries. Anyway, who cares? I thought everyone was in there working together, trying to cure cancer and rabies and the rest."

"David, do you *know* how competitive medical research is? Careers can be won or lost in it. It's a high stakes game because of the costs involved. But it can be very profitable. Not to mention prestigious, which in some circles is more valuable than money. Nobody remembers the also-rans for best actor. It's the same for research. If you had a shot at the Nobel Prize in medicine, would you tell anyone what you were doing? You can bet your family jewels you wouldn't."

David glanced at one of the entries on the screen. "To develop animal vaccines from a raccoon's liver?" He shook his head. "I don't see much money in that."

"Ever heard of penicillin? That's just a green mold. David, there are a hundred different projects here and Euromedic's got classified medical information on all of them. Don't you see what that means? Euromedic supports its own research and development division. That's expensive, *ungodly* expensive. What they've done is somehow tapped into all these other research projects. And it looks like they're taking the information and feeding it to their own research labs. It's a race, David. Especially now that big-time investors are involved. Did you ever hear of the Chakrabarty decision? U.S. Supreme Court?"

"Sorry, my subscription to Law Review Quarterly lapsed last spring."

"A couple of years ago a General Electric scientist developed a new life form in the laboratory. A microorganism—a completely new living thing. It's an oil-degrading organism that can clean up oil spills. The Supreme Court ruled that it could be patented just like another invention. Do you have any idea how profitable that can be? That decision opened the door to investors. Don't you see? Oil companies, insurance companies, brokerage firms—they're all investing in biotechnologic research. I'm not just talking about oil microorganisms. I'm talking about genetic engineering, gene-splicing—" she waved a hand at the computer screen—"hormones, enzymes . . . all of this. The company that develops something marketable stands to make billions. The only problem is funding the company that will eventually make a breakthrough. And Euromedic's keeping ahead of everyone because they know what they're doing. With information like this . . ."

"They know what works and what doesn't." David stood up to straighten his back. "In spite of the fact that this is all relentlessly interesting, it doesn't have anything to do with me. I'm not a microorganism and I don't know any medical secrets."

"Of course you don't." Sara stared at the screen. "But maybe your brother does."

"Stuart?"

"Moravec confirmed that your brother was in that Madrid plane crash. When I pressed him he told me in effect that it was none of my business. He said that your brother wasn't killed. His exact words. And that he was alive. He didn't say he was okay or fine or he's broken four ribs, he said he was *alive*. What does that mean to you?"

David shrugged. "What does it mean to *you*?"

"I think your brother is seriously hurt. I think that's what he meant. Your brother was in a plane crash, after all. He might be in critical condition."

"Sara, we keep coming back to the same thing. What's it got to do with *me*?"

"I don't know. You don't have some kind of rare blood or something, do you?"

"O-positive?"

"No, of course not. But it has something to do with your being twins. I mean, identical twins are the best possible organ donors because there isn't any rejection factor."

"I know all about being a twin, thank you. And I don't think they'd kidnap me and go to such a risk just for a lousy kidney or something. Stuart and I may not be the closest brothers in the world, but if he needed something like that, I'd give it to him. Anyway, you don't *have* to be a twin to have a transplant. It's just more convenient. Right?"

"Right. Unless time is a critical factor."

"Time?"

"If you couldn't find a donor right away, you could be in trouble. I mean, if the situation was life-threatening."

"Then you put him on a machine until one turns up. There's an artificial means for everything, isn't there? I mean, kidneys, hearts, livers, lungs . . . all that stuff. Right?"

Sara sighed. "That's right. Some if it is considered experimental, but there is something. I don't know, David. I can't think of any other connection between you and your brother."

"Look, we can't get to my file in this gizmo. All right, we can't. But you said you could call Weeksbriar's computer." He pushed the telephone toward her. "So let's call it. That's why we paid fifteen dollars for a phone. You can do that, right?"

"It shouldn't be any problem. We have all the entry access codes."

"Then let's do it." David sat down again. "I can't wait to find out how this story ends."

Sara tried, but nothing worked. She entered every number on the card listing and used all the access identity codes. The result was the same every time.

David stared at the words on the tiny screen. He broke the connection and dialed another number at the keyboard. He had watched Sara initiate the procedure so many times, he knew the routine.

"It's no use, David," Sara said wearily. She was seated beside him, elbows on the table, her head propped in her hands. "We're locked out."

He continued anyway, driven on by hope. He typed the computer access number and waited ten seconds for the identification code prompt, then typed it, glancing at the laminated card and pecking out the correct sequence of letters and numbers. Then he sat back and waited.

"I'm telling you, David, we're locked out."

David concentrated on the computer screen. It had to work. There wasn't anything else. He watched the blinking cursor. It didn't move. Minutes seemed to pass and it didn't move. When it finally did, it was like two streaks across the screen, leaving the same unfamiliar message in its wake:

UNAUTHORIZED USER TERMINAL
SYSTEM DISCONNECT

David slammed his fist against the table top, popping the telephone receiver out of the mounting on the computer.

Sara hung up the telephone and switched off the computer. The screen died in a pinprick of light. "We'll just have to think of something else."

"I don't get it," David said. "If we have all these damn code numbers—"

"They've locked out the terminal, not the code entry. It's a feature of the remote system. I mean, calling through telephone lines. When we connect with the network, the portable unit sends a signal that identifies itself to the host computer so it'll know how fast to transmit. They've just programmed the host computers to refuse remote access. This one, anyway."

"So what we have here is a computer that might as well be a carrot. Right? None of these codes do us any good. Right?"

"Not as a remote, that's right."

"Terrific." David picked up Hammond's identification card from the table and turned it. "We're running out of options."

"At least we're safe here, David."

"Really? How long do you want to hang around Niagara Falls? We only have about eighty, ninety dollars left, Sara."

"I have credit cards."

"Do you use one of those credit card protection services?"

She frowned. "Yes . . . through the credit union. What does that matter?"

"At Weeksbriar?"

"Yes."

"Then forget about the credit cards. They've probably already reported them stolen."

Sara gave him a bewildered look.

"They can track us down through those credit cards," David said.

"Well, what do *you* think we should do?"

David studied Hammond's ID card. "I have an idea." He glanced up at Sara. "It's probably very dumb."

FORTY-THREE

WEEKSBRIAR

WEEKSBRIAR SUPPORTED two fully equipped operating rooms on the third floor for animal surgery. Moravec was there, supervising the preparation of the operating theaters. He and Ellis had flown back from Niagara Falls as soon as it was known they wouldn't recover Townsend immediately. Something had gone wrong with the homing device—out of range, Turner said—but they'd find it again. Turner was positive of that. This time they'd take them as quickly as they found them. Time was too short now for anything else.

When Moravec spoke to Haldern, the director was less concerned about what Ellis had planned for Dr. Mills than that the BriefPac was missing. Yes, she was high on the Wintergreen list of candidates, but the fact that she was helping Townsend . . . Haldern now considered her an enemy, a threat, no longer an innocent bystander. Also the decision had been made to move Stuart Townsend to Weeksbriar. With David still loose they hadn't any choice. Moravec's job now was to make the necessary arrangements for surgery. "We haven't lost hope yet," was Haldern's departing statement.

Moravec wasn't so sure anymore. He was exhausted. He'd gotten a few hours sleep but not enough to keep him at his peak. Even so, he worked hard to prepare the third floor for transplantation surgery.

Moravec had both operating rooms rescrubbed. An adjoining lab was also sterilized that would serve as prep for both David and Stuart and, following the operation, recovery for Stuart. Halothane gas and oxygen tanks were ready in both operating rooms for the anesthesiologist and the proper sized tables wheeled in. AirMore would arrive with the rest of the equipment—bypass machine, EKG and blood pressure monitors, a defibulator and cardioplegic solution to cool down the donor heart after removal, actually stop it from beating, before it was inserted and restarted again. Stuart Townsend and Dr. McPhearson were scheduled to arrive in little more than eight hours. The operating progress would begin as soon as David Townsend was recovered. Ellis promised that would be soon. Moravec was beginning to wonder if it would happen at all. He was beginning to wonder if it should happen.

"Mr. Moravec, Dr. Ellis would like you to come to his office right away."

The security guard who delivered the message was out of breath.

Moravec rode the elevator to the first floor without speaking. He was in his shirtsleeves. He needed a shave and a bath. He desperately wanted to call Connie, to hear a voice unconnected with Weeksbriar, uninfected by Euromedic.

"They've been following a bus. A fucking *bus*!"

Ellis was at his desk. His face was red. Tiny lengths of hair stood out on his head, glistening in the morning sun from the window. He needed a shave too.

"Who's following a bus?"

"Turner," Ellis snapped. "She just called. They're in Cleveland, for chrissakes! Townsend must have found the homing device in Niagara Falls. He stuck it on a goddamn Trailways bus."

The news was at once tragic and comic. Moravec imagined half a dozen cars, all with their sophisticated tracking gear blinking, pulled up at a transit authority.

"It means Townsend is still in New York," Ellis said. "Somewhere."

Moravec shook his head. "I think it means your people

won't find him now." It was almost a relief. "Not in time, at least."

"The surgery team from Madrid is already on its way," Ellis said. He looked at his watch. "They'll be here in seven hours." For the first time, Moravec noticed, Ellis seemed lost, not in control. "What do we tell them?"

"It really isn't anyone's fault, you know."

"Do you think Haldern is going to accept that? He's going to blame me, Moravec. *Me*."

It was true. Moravec was too tired to feel sympathy. "I'd better call London."

"Wait!" Ellis came around his desk. "What if we go ahead with the surgery? What if we don't use Townsend's heart?"

"The whole point of this exercise was precisely to get David Townsend's heart. He is the perfect donor."

"Goddammit, Moravec, I don't have Townsend. Anyway, the point was to *save* Stuart Townsend. Maybe we can still do that."

"How? You don't have a donor."

"Oh, yes I do." Ellis pointed at the ceiling. "I have over fifty sequels in the psychiatric ward, twenty stored in ICPs, all of them tissue-typed with functioning vital organs. All we have to do is match one of them to Townsend."

"Without David, you double the risk. Besides, many of those people are suffering heart diseases as it is."

"*Some* of them," Ellis said. "It's a risk we're forced to accept. Townsend *is* going to die without the surgery. One chance in fifty is better than no chance at all." He went to the phone. "I'm going to set it up. It's all we can do now."

Moravec sat in one of the cockpit chairs, listening to Ellis give instructions. The realization struck him after Ellis hung up.

"What about David Townsend and Dr. Mills?" Moravec said. "What happens to them now?"

"We'll keep looking for them, naturally," Ellis said. "Eventually, we'll find them."

"And then?"

Ellis found another of his cigars. He was relaxed again. "You'd better call London. Explain the change in plans. Haldern will approve it. He hasn't got any choice."

"You realize, of course, that Stuart Townsend probably won't live more than several days. Your sequels are all suffering from diseases of advanced age."

"I don't think Haldern or the board cares how long he lives." He lit his cigar. "Even if he had a strong, healthy heart." The lighter snapped closed with a loud click. "All that matters is that he lives long enough to tell what he knows about the sequela. That's the important thing."

It was the all-important thing, Moravec realized. The people didn't count. Only the final objective mattered. "What will you do with David and Dr. Mills?" Moravec said. "I want to know."

"I promise you, Moravec, I'm not going to kill them. I know that's what you're thinking. But I won't do that. I'm not a barbarian. Anyway, I don't have to. I'll just find a place for them upstairs."

"For the rest of their lives?"

"It isn't so bad. We'll take care of them." Ellis exhaled a stream of blue smoke. "After all, we *are* doctors."

FORTY-FOUR

JAY COTTON'S RESORT MOTEL

IT WAS freezing in the phone booth outside the motel office. The doors closed but a full panel of glass was missing and David huddled in the opposite corner to avoid the draft. He knew it was more difficult to trace a call from a pay phone. He broke a ten-dollar roll of quarters and stacked them in two-dollar piles on the counter. The toll to New York was $1.40 for three minutes and he'd taken Sara's watch to keep track of the time. David decided to limit the call to a minute and a half. If someone was tracing the call he wasn't going to give them time to complete it.

"New York four-four-one-four, may I help you?"

"Hello . . ." He held the icy receiver close to his mouth. "I want to speak to Action Group Center." His breath was visible as he exhaled.

"Station code?"

"What?"

"What's your station code?"

David scanned the identification card. Two lines below Hammond's photograph was typed STA. V-1049.

"Ah . . . V dash one-zero-four-nine," the voice repeated promptly. "One moment, please." David watched twelve seconds tick by on Sara's watch. "Station verified. Are you calling from a secure line?"

David glanced nervously out the broken pane. "Telephone booth."

"Stand by, please."

"Look, I just want—" but the line clicked to hold. There was more clicking then a new voice came on the line.

"Group II control."

"Hello," David said, holding the receiver with both hands now. "This is Hammond, I—"

"ID?"

He read it from the card.

"You're AG-6, right?"

David wasn't sure how to answer. "What about it?"

"They're not too happy in London, you know . . . following a bus all the way to Cleveland. AirMore One has already left Madrid with the Hahnemann primary. It's a madhouse around here."

"Who's Hahnemann?"

"What?"

"Who's Hahnemann? What's he doing in Madrid? And what's an airmore?"

There was a long pause. "Who is this?"

"Townsend," David said calmly. "David M."

"*Townsend!* Oh, shit! How did *you* get this number?"

"I want answers. I've already had a peek inside your little computer. It's interesting, the racket you guys have going, but I don't care about that. I want to know what the hell you people want with me. Just what the hell are you trying to do?" David looked at his watch. "You have just over fifty seconds before I hang up."

"I'm not—"

"Who's coming from Madrid?"

"I don't know."

"Bye."

"No, wait! *Wait!* Don't hang up."

"So talk."

"Nobody wants to hurt you, Townsend. Tell me where you are. We'll send someone to pick you up. We'll explain it, but we have to get you back to the institute."

"I don't *have* to go anywhere. Sure as hell not a psycho ward."

"That was a mistake. You're not in any danger."

"Yeah, right. What about Sara?"

"Dr. Mills isn't important, *you* are. Tell—"

"She's important to me," David said angrily.

"Yes, of course she is. Look, if you'll—"

"Who's coming from Madrid? You have thirty seconds."

"Your brother."

"Yeah. Why?"

"I don't know. Just tell me where you—"

"I said why. You have twenty-five seconds."

"I can't explain anything in twenty-five seconds!"

"Talk faster. Stuart is hurt, isn't he? From the plane crash."

"I don't know. Really. I don't know."

"What's airmore mean?"

"AirMore is a hospital plane. Look, give me a phone number. I'll have someone call you who can explain better than I can. I'm just a MAG operator."

"What's Hahnemann mean? You said Hahnemann primary?" David looked at his watch. Then the phone line clicked suddenly and he heard a low, steady whir in the background. "This is telcom intercept," said a mechanical voice. "Confirmed trace-lock verification on this incoming. Interstate exchange. Coin operated. Niagara Falls, Ontario, Canada. Three-one-seven Victoria Highway." The line clicked again and the whir was gone.

David was stunned. He didn't know how they did it— he'd been on the phone only a minute and ten seconds—but they'd traced the call.

"Who are you people?"

But there wasn't any answer.

David slammed the receiver down, spewing quarters as he burst out of the freezing phone booth. He walked briskly along the path across the snowy courtyard toward the cabin, the rumble of the falls in his ears. They knew where he was. Exactly.

It was time to run again.

FORTY-FIVE

THE QUEEN ELIZABETH WAY

DAVID DROVE.

He told her what happened after they'd left the motel. For the last several minutes, neither of them spoke. He was driving north on the Canadian interstate, not because he knew where he was going, but because it was the nearest highway. He thought best on a highway, behind a wheel.

"Sara?"

She was leaning against him, not exactly snuggled, but she was there, close to him.

"Sara, you awake?"

She stirred against his shoulder. "Yes."

"I've been thinking."

"Me too."

"We can't keep running and we can't go to the police."

Sara nodded. In a small voice she said, "I know."

"You think they'd go for a trade? Their computer for . . . if they'd leave us alone?"

"I don't think so."

"Yeah." David sighed. "Neither do I."

"What about meeting the plane? I mean, confronting them and my brother at the airport."

She tilted her head up at him. She didn't say anything.

"Not so hot either, is it?"

She put her head back on his shoulder. "If they catch us, that's it. You know that?"

"Yeah."

"They can't let us go. If they want you for an organ

294

transplant for your brother, when it's over they can't let you go. They can't let either of us go. It doesn't matter anymore whether we submit voluntarily or not. It doesn't even matter if your brother lives or dies for your part of it. Euromedic won't stop looking until they find us because we have the proof—I mean, we know their secrets. If you survived the operation, assuming that's what they want you for, then they'd keep you locked away just in case they needed something else for your brother. I doubt that they'd resort to outright murder in your case, not, at least, until your brother was fully recovered. You're still a valuable resource for them for as long as your brother is alive. But the point is I don't think they'll ever let us go once they find us. And they will, eventually. They'll find both of us."

"Nobody's cutting into me. Not *this* Townsend. I have better things to do with my life than piss it away in some psycho ward, praying the brilliant Dr. Stuart Townsend doesn't have a relapse." David closed his arm around her. "We're not going to let the bastards win, Sara. You have to believe that."

She looked at him. "How?"

"Do you have any idea what that Hahnemann file is?"

"No."

"When I talked to them in New York they said the Hahnemann patient was coming from Madrid. They were talking about Stuart. You don't have any idea what that means?"

"None."

"What about Wintergreen?"

"It's a class file, but I don't know what it is. I've seen the name. It's in the restricted entry data section in the CC memory storage. Nobody I know has access to it. The director, of course, but—"

"But you've seen it? I mean, it's in the computer at Weeksbriar, right?"

"Yes, but—"

"I think it has something to do with Hahnemann. Those

files can explain it. We have to know what we're involved in. What have I got to do with Euromedic research projects?"

Sara merely shrugged.

"Hahnemann is the key to all of this," David said. "I'm sure of that. If we knew what it was we could do something. Or Wintergreen."

"I'd always assumed it was an administrative file. WRCRDS is a big system, David. There are thousands of files in it. I explained this to you before. Everyone works in his own section. I work in the hematology file section. That section alone has more than a hundred generic sub-files and I only have direct access to five or six. The rest are not of any professional interest to me. They're just there."

"Well, you have an interest now."

Sara was silent.

"There's only one thing left for us to do," David said. He smoothed her hair with his hand. "We're going back."

Sara sat up quickly. "What!"

"It's the one place they aren't looking for us . . . Weeksbriar."

"What!"

"We're going to see those files. Whatever this is about— the truth of it—is in those computer files. We'll take a look at Euromedic's secrets. It's about time someone did."

"We can't go back *there*!"

"Sure we can."

"My God! David, that's the last place we want to go."

"That's what they think too. It's an edge. They won't be expecting us."

"An edge? David, are you crazy?"

"What have we got to lose? A few days? That's about as long as we can keep ahead of them. They're bound to track down the car. I'm sure they're upset about having to go to Cleveland. Anyway, *I'm* willing to take the chance. If we find something, maybe we can make a deal. It's something, Sara. We have to *do* something. I'd leave you somewhere and go myself, but I don't know how to use the computer. You do."

"You *are* crazy! How would we get in? How would *you* get in? And even if we did, I don't have access to any files except my department's. They're all coded and I don't have entry authorization. It might be a good idea, David, but it just isn't possible."

"You'd better quit thinking about what's possible and start thinking about what's necessary," David said. "There's an army of Euromedics out there looking for us. I don't know what else to do and time is running out. Maybe it's a little insane, but slim odds are better than none at all."

"You don't understand. You're talking about breaking into a double-coded security system. WRCRDS is a very sophisticated data bank. You don't just ask it for information as if it were a reference librarian. It only responds to precoded authorization. We'd be shut off. The moment we made an illegal request—if we got the chance in the first place—the system would cut us off. It's programmed to block out any terminal that originates on a request for information from a restricted file without the proper log-on signature."

"But we have all the codes, remember?" He nodded at the BriefPac in the back seat. "Didn't you say the reason we couldn't get into the computer was because the terminal was locked out, not the codes? That the main computer was shutting off access because we were making a remote call? What if were *inside* Weeksbriar when we made the call? We wouldn't be remote anymore, would we? Wouldn't we be part of the system then? Tell me when I'm getting warm."

Sara was quiet. Finally she said, "I'll be damned. If we daisy-chained the BriefPac with a computer terminal . . . I'll be damned."

"Will it work?"

"Yes, dammit, it'll work. It would *have* to work. It would act just like a terminal in the system." She turned to look at him. "How did you figure that out?"

"You figured it out, not me. I don't know from computers."

"We *could* do it." Sara clapped her hands together. "David, we *really* could."

"Yeah, well, don't get too excited. I haven't figured out how we're going to get back into the place yet." He smiled, kissed her forehead. "But I'm thinking about it."

FORTY-SIX

WEEKSBRIAR

THE SEQUEL with the heart that best matched Stuart Townsend's belonged to a woman. Ellis had found her. Her name was Carla Jergenson and her natural age was twenty-eight though she looked fifty.

Moravec stood at the ICP and stared into the bubble. It was impossible to look at this woman and believe that she'd actually died of acute pyelonephritis—chronic renal insufficiency—in the sixth week of pregnancy. Her kidneys had failed suddenly and poisoned her system. Of course, the fetus had died too. Moravec wondered what effect METHYD-9 would have on newborn children. Would they come out of the womb as babies or five-year-olds?

"Excuse me, doctor, they're ready to transfer."

Moravec stepped aside as the nurse switched on the Intensive Care Pod's auxiliary power pack and disconnected the wall plug. Two orderlies wheeled it out of the room.

Carla Jergenson was dead—she had been for seven weeks—but her heart and other vital organs, except the kidneys and brain, were kept functioning mechanically. The blood that moved through her circulation system was artificial—perfluorocarbon, an oxygenated solution that together with a semi-cardioplegic chemical compound kept body cells alive at thirty degrees centigrade, which allowed the heart rate to slow substantially, easing the strain. It wasn't suspended animation and it wasn't coma. In a way, Moravec thought, it was worse than death. It was a medical trick. Carla Jergenson was dead but her body didn't know it.

Moravec approached the ICPs. The lids were cold to the touch. He read all the names. Ellis had brought him up here. He was proud of them. His "pod people," he'd called them. Victims in life, they were now victims in afterlife.

He heard the door open behind him.

"Doctor? The first AirMore jet from Madrid has just arrived."

Moravec didn't turn to see the nurse. "Yes, thank you. I'll be along soon."

"I'll leave the key in the door for you. Just drop it at the station when you leave."

Moravec nodded. The door closed. He stayed several more minutes. He thought of Connie and Christina. Before he left he unplugged all the ICPs from the wall outlets.

FORTY-SEVEN

NEW BROCKTON. 9:15 P.M.

DAVID STAYED on plowed roads but off the main streets when they reached New Brockton. Even though the snow had stopped, driving was hazardous, especially after dark. They stopped at a 7-11. David filled the tank while Sara went inside to buy coffee and doughnuts. They were both famished but they hadn't much money left. Still, the car came first. Without wheels they might as well give up. When he went in to pay for the gas, Sara was standing at the counter. A man in jeans and a heavy plaid jacket was standing beside her, holding a six-pack of beer.

" . . . so I'm standing next to Winslow, see. And he's closing this rabbit, four-oh silk all over the table because the guy's got seven thumbs. And he's telling me, 'Look, Gregory,' he says—you know how he talks—'Look, Gregory,' he says, 'I know we haven't set any records for speed, but the main thing here is not speed but concentration.' Then he raises his hands, see, like a calf roper calling for time, and says—you'll love this—he says, *'Voila!'* and rips his glove off because he's just stitched it to this eight-pound Canadian hare."

"What was that all about?" David said when they were in the car.

Sara was white. She held the sack of doughnuts in her fist. "Just get me away from here."

He drove to an elementary school parking lot. He shut off the lights but kept the car running.

"So, who was that guy?"

"Greg Tucker, he's a resident at Weeksbriar. We work in the same section." She put her hand to her neck. "God, he scared me to death when I saw him."

"I noticed. You left our coffee on the counter."

Sara glanced at the sack. "Oh . . . damn. I'm sorry, David. Seeing someone from Weeksbriar, it just rattled me. I didn't know what to do." She opened the sack, handed him a doughnut. "I thought everyone was looking for us, but Greg didn't even bat an eye."

"The *staff* isn't looking for us. Just the people from Action Group Center, whatever that is. I doubt if the regular staff even knows you've been missing for two days." David bit into his doughnut.

Sara stared through the windshield. "That's right. Ellis doesn't want to broadcast it, does he? He wouldn't want *anyone* to know. How would he explain it?" She turned to face him. "David, find a phone booth."

"What?"

"If Greg Tucker doesn't know that these people are searching for me, then I wonder if the security people know? C'mon, find a telephone. I think we've just had a break."

"Weeksbriar Research Institute. May I help you, please?"

Sara held the telephone between them so David could hear. They had found a pay phone inside a Piggly-Wiggly store. "Hello, operator, this is Dr. Mills. Have there been any calls for me? I haven't been able to get hold of my service."

"I'll check, Doctor Mills. No, ma'am. I don't see anything here in the message log. Sorry."

"That's all right. Oh, operator, can you connect me with the security desk? I think I left my office unlocked."

"Yes, ma'am."

David closed his eyes. "I hope you know what you're doing," he whispered.

"Ringing," said the operator.

"Security desk, Cooper."

"Hello, this is Dr. Mills. Sara Mills."

"Evening, Dr. Mills. Something I can do for you?"

"Yes, when I left Friday night, I think I forgot to lock my office. Would you see that someone checks it tonight?"

"Sure. What number?"

"Three fifteen."

"Three fifteen. Okay, we'll take care of it, Dr. Mills."

Sara paused a moment, looked at David. "Anything more about that patient who escaped?"

"No, ma'am. He's still loose last I heard. They'll find him sooner or later though. Some kind of special team out there beating the bushes for him now."

"That's comforting to know," Sara said.

"How do you know the guy wasn't bluffing?" David said. They were sitting in the car. Sara wanted to go into the institute alone.

"I know Cooper. He hasn't got the imagination to con an Eskimo out of a snowball."

"You're *not* going in that place alone. That's it. We both go or we don't go at all."

"David, be reasonable. The BriefPac will only work inside the institute. And *you* can't get in. There's only one entrance to Weeksbriar's research offices. The recognition system wouldn't even let you through the gate. If we're going to even try to get information from the computer, I have to do it." She crossed her arms. "It's very simple."

David watched a checker straighten the carts inside the store. "It's too damned risky, Sara."

"There's no other way."

"There's always another way. What's a recognition system?"

"It's part of the security. When someone walks in or out

of the building, a computerized scanning reads them. All our printers use a special ribbon that imbeds a substance on the paper that the scanner can pick up. If someone tried to leave the building carrying the research project printouts without permission it would trigger an alarm. I told you research labs were paranoid about people stealing their secrets."

"What else does it do?"

"It can detect metal in case any crazies decide to invade the place with weapons. They tell me it'll even describe what the object is to the security guards who man the computer monitors in the lobby. When you walk in you have to walk through two sets of thick glass doors—I guess they're bulletproof. The second set of doors only open if the scanner recognizes you. The guard has to make a visual confirmation of your face from the data on his monitor. It's a double-check system."

"What about visitors?"

"We don't have visitors unless they're approved by the chief of staff."

"Why don't you have ID cards like everybody else?"

"Plastic cards are too easy to forge, but don't ask me how. The choice was between BodyGuard and another system that used palm and fingerprints on lighted glass, but that one couldn't check for data printouts."

"BodyGuard?"

"That's what it's called. It scans the subject coming in using floor sensors and some kind of infrared or ultrasound system. It senses height, weight, skin tone, general body bone structure and the planes of the face. It looks up all those parameters in its directory until it finds a match, then sends a computer-generated photograph to the guard at the monitor with that person's name. The guard is there as a backup. If the photograph doesn't agree with the person standing at the gate, then that person doesn't get in until they find out why."

"How do you get your photograph in the directory?"

"David, forget it."

"C'mon. I'm interested."

Sara let out a deep sigh. "A Euromedic lab invented the system. All its facilities are equipped with BodyGuard so that everybody in Euromedic won't have to go through the hassle of security clearance checks every time they go to a lab. When you sign up with Euromedic you go through the identification process. It takes about two minutes. They take a color photograph and that's it. Now you know everything about the system that I know." She shook her head. "You can't get into Weeksbriar, David. Are you convinced now?"

David bit into a doughnut, staring at the line of checker stands in the grocery store.

"David?"

"Everybody in Euromedic? Not just Weeksbriar?"

"Every last one. If the cleaning lady from Saint Mary's came here she could just walk right in."

David chewed his doughnut.

"What are you thinking?"

"This high-class piece of sophisticated security equipment—it doesn't really care about people. It cares about paper. That's probably the real reason they developed it. Considering they're stealing everybody else's secrets, it makes sense that they'd be paranoid about losing their own. Anyway—" David looked at her "—I think I can walk in with you."

"*For chrissakes*—haven't you been listening?"

"I've been listening. And I think there's a definite flaw in the system. The security people think they're looking for a nut named Richard Kenneth Franklin. Ellis and his crowd are looking for David Townsend. But nobody's looking for Stuart."

Sara screwed up her face.

"Your BodyGuard has a blind spot," David said. He started the car. "I'm already *in* the directory."

"What are you talking about?"

"It can't distinguish between identical twins," he said. He gave her a wink. "I'm walking into Weeksbriar as Stuart Phillip Townsend."

FORTY-EIGHT

LITTLE MARY. 7:10 P.M.

MCPHEARSON WOKE sweating from a nightmare. His shirt was wet around the collar and under the arms and his chest was heaving. He had dreamed he was locked in a towering castle keep precariously situated on the Dover cliffs. He'd seen the pounding surf of a storm-wrenched sea below him, crashing against the rocks, and felt the sway of the ancient structure as it struggled from toppling over the edge. Someone had been calling him in a gentle voice that came like the wind: "Come down to me, Ian; come down from your place. You can't hide from us, Ian; you haven't a brace."

He rubbed his eyes, then focused them in the dim light on the intercom panel where a soft voice beckoned to him from the speaker.

"Dr. McPhearson, Dr. McPhearson? We're charging the patient's second bag. Will you want to come down, doctor? Dr. McPhearson?"

McPhearson switched on the cabin light and glanced at his watch. He had been asleep nearly two hours.

"Dr. McPhearson . . ."

"Yes, yes," he said, fumbling to find the correct panel button. "Hello? Hello! Damn!"

"Dr. McPhearson . . ."

"I'm here for godsakes!" he said pushing one button then another. "Hello!"

"Good afternoon, doctor," said a soothing voice finally. "We didn't want to disturb—"

"I'm coming," the surgeon said impatiently. He held the button with his thumb. "I'm coming straightaway. Is Graves there?" It was a foolish question—where else would he be?—but he'd just awakened and his head was full of cobwebs. "Hello?" He pushed the button several times. "Hello?"

"The intercom is automatic," and the voice. "You needn't depress the button except to ring up."

McPhearson stared at the panel a moment. Blasted machines.

"Would you like to come down, doctor?"

"Yes, of course—" he pushed the button again, then took his thumb away. "Yes, I'm coming now. Is he all right? Is Townsend all right?"

"The patient is fine, doctor."

McPhearson unbuckled the seat belt. "Right. I'm coming now."

The ICU compartment seemed smaller this time, McPhearson thought. Probably because the space was occupied by four people instead of two. Graves was there along with two of the nurses and everything was bathed in a green hue from the overhead lights. Like a submarine, McPhearson imagined, even if he'd never been in one. Everything was green from ceiling to floor including the digital readout displays of the monitoring machines that lined the walls. It was an atmosphere that made for cramped isolation, which didn't relieve McPhearson's anxiety. The heaviness in his chest had not gone away and he wished there were a window where he could get a breath of unrecirculated air.

"Refreshed, are you, doctor?" Graves smiled as if the expression were his only facial feature. The man personified triteness.

"I don't sleep well on airplanes," McPhearson said. He stepped sideways around a nurse to see Townsend in the capsule. "You've run electrolytes?"

308

"Twice, yes," Graves said. "On the hour, just as you requested."

"And?"

"Normal. The potassium level might be a bit higher, but it isn't serious. Just the same, we're charging the bag with forty meqs. instead of twenty-five."

"What rate?"

"Hundred twenty-five cc per hour."

McPhearson leaned down over the capsule. "How in blazes do you check his color with these lights?"

"Color?"

"Color, man, *color!*" McPhearson said. "He looks like some comic strip character in there."

"Doctor, I assure you—"

"Bring the lights up full and normal. I want to *see* the patient. If he were ashen you'd never guess it in this light. And increase the rate to two hundred."

Graves obeyed. He touched something on the wall and the lights changed to white.

"That's better," McPhearson said. He tugged at the latch that secured the transparent lid of the capsule to the main body, but it refused to disengage. "How do you open this bloody contraption?"

"Open it?"

McPhearson swung back to face his assistant. "Of course, open it! I want to see my patient, doctor. Do you mind?"

"But . . ." Graves's expression changed from cheerfulness to mild surprise. "But it isn't *necessary* to open the ICP, doctor. I mean, the system is self-containing. We don't even open it to switch bags. It's completely—"

"Don't you change the IV needle?"

"No."

McPhearson looked at him with amazement. "You *don't* change the IV needle!"

"Doctor, believe me, it isn't—"

The surgeon stepped back. "Open it!"

"But—"

"Open the bloody thing, I said! This is *my* patient and I won't have some damn—" McPhearson grabbed his chest. The heaviness suddenly changed to a bolt of pain. His eyes widened and he reached out desperately for something to hold him up as he gasped for air. Graves had stepped back, bumping into a nurse. Apparently, from the look on his face, he thought McPhearson was going to strike him.

The burning in his chest forced McPhearson to his knees. He tried to look up but hadn't the strength. It couldn't be possible! That was the only thought that came to him as he clutched his chest. It wasn't possible. This couldn't be happening to him. *He* was the doctor. *He* was the bloody surgeon.

It was an involuntary spasm that made him pitch over on his side. Then time stopped and everything that happened came in bursts of disordered sequences. He saw Graves's face, except it couldn't be Graves, because he wasn't smiling. He saw other faces, grotesque faces contorted in horror. He felt his arms being drawn away from him and someone was clawing at his shirt. He knew he was on his back because he could see light—a brilliant light—staring down at him from the ceiling. He didn't feel the fist as much as heard it, pounding his chest again and again, like a crop flaying a horse's flank. It was a curious image because he'd never in his life been near a horse. Then he saw the cardiac syringe with its long needle. He watched as the plunger was pulled back, drawing a tiny charge of his heart's blood into the syringe's epinephrine solution. He saw it injected and imagined the cold sensation as it drained straight into the heart cavity through the fourth rib interspace. There were more faces then, and voices that he couldn't match up. He saw lights and then he closed his eyes. It couldn't be happening, but he knew it was. It was the airplane. He knew it as sure as he knew himself. It was the airplane that was killing him. He didn't have to guess about that. When he felt himself being lifted he opened his eyes and expected to see a stormy surf impaling itself on the jagged rocks of the coast of Dover.

The surprise was that what he saw was a vision of peace and solitude. It was only a glimpse. There had been a moment when his brain and vision formed a picture that he understood. What he saw before they inserted him into a transparent pod was the man who had brought him here in the first place.

Stuart Townsend was asleep, but he seemed to be smiling.

FORTY-NINE

WEEKSBRIAR. 7:55 P.M.

ELLIS WAITED for the MAG satellite communication to go through in his office and ignored the wall-mounted security monitor as it scanned corridors and sidewalks on the eight-inch screen. The date-time display at the bottom of the monitor changed every ten seconds along with the picture.

```
SUN 01/02 1956:40 HRS . . .
SUN 01/02 1956:50 HRS . . .
SUN 01/02 1957:00 HRS . . .
SUN 01/02 1957:10 HRS . . .
```

Ellis wasn't worried about time; it wasn't his enemy anymore.

Moravec passed before him on the monitor. He'd appeared in a corridor, walking almost without expression before the screen switched to an empty lobby. Poor Moravec, Ellis thought, though he had no real sympathy for him. He was a man going nowhere.

The desk-top speaker phone beeped and Ellis touched the button below the glowing light. It occurred to him that it was after 2 A.M. in London.

"Yes?"

"This is MAGCOM, Dr. Ellis," said the strong voice of a satellite communicator. "We have a secure satlok to London whenever you're ready." There was an echoing twang to the connection.

"Adjust the audio," Ellis said.

312

"I'm sorry, Dr. Ellis, it's weather on London's end. There's nothing good coming from Britain tonight."

"Is Dr. Haldern ready?"

"Just a moment please."

More twanging. Ellis drummed his fingers on the desk. The monitor panned across the main parking lot as a few cars searched for spaces, the main lobby as a group of doctors left the building, a corridor with a row of doors, the nearest of which was marked LEDMED LAB—every ten seconds a new camera angle as the security monitor recorded the institute changing shifts. He gazed in bored wonder until he heard a series of clicks, then focused on the speaker.

"Twenty-one-oh-one MAGCOM," said the voice on the line. "Nine series on track. Syncing now. Go, London. You have eleven minutes forty-two seconds."

The operator signed off and Ellis was left with the noise of sound traveling through space.

"Hello? Luther? Are you there?"

"Dr. Haldern, this is Dr. Ellis. Jonathan Ellis, Weeksbriar COS? I put the call in to you, sir."

"What's happening there? Has AirMore arrived yet?" This wasn't the best connection, but the director's voice had a nasal twang that suggested chronic sinus infection. Ellis wondered if everyone in England sounded as if they had permanent colds.

"Not yet." He glanced at his watch. "We're expecting him later this evening, in just under ninety minutes. I wanted to tell you that everything here is going well. We have a new donor, the best possible match, under the circumstances and—"

"This entire business isn't going well, Dr. Ellis," said the voice from London. "We're very concerned."

"Yes, I appreciate that, but—"

"Someone is going to be held accountable for all this. You understand that. This entire recovery has been botched from the start." The line was silent a moment. "Stuart

Townsend is our first concern," Haldern finally said. "We must not let anything deter our primary objective here, Dr. Ellis. The patient's well-being is our only interest. This must be a team effort. For the good of the medical research community."

"Yes, I agree," Ellis said. He glanced at the monitor. An intern sat alone at a table in the cafeteria. "Hahnemann Sequela is Euromedic's first priority interest at present."

When Moravec entered the office, he walked deliberately to Ellis's desk and laid the second sheet of a green MAGCOM message in front of him.

"You should read this," he said.

"Moravec, for godsakes, can't you see I'm busy. I'm speaking to the director."

Moravec nodded calmly. "Tell Dr. Haldern that Ian McPhearson's just had a heart attack," he said.

Ellis's mouth dropped. "What!"

"What's that?" The director's voice came harshly from the speaker phone. "Who's there? Luther?"

Ellis turned the hardcopy tearsheet on the desk to read it.

MAGCOM MSG 192033 010681 2059:16 HRS
AIRMORE TX URGENT
ADRSE: WEEKSBRIAR CHIEF/STAFF

INFLIGHT TRAUMA
MCPHEARSON, I.
RECONFIRMING ID: MCPHEARSON, I.
CARDIAC FAILURE.

ONBOARD PATIENT TOWNSEND, S.
CONDITION UNCHANGED.
SCD = CRITICAL TEC: 123 + MAV
ALL OTHER = ROUT. NORM.

AIRMORE ETA NEWBROCK 2225 HRS
DO YOU WISH DIVERT JFK?
PLEASE ADVISE SOONEST.
GRAVES, A.

END TX

314

"It just came through," Moravec said. His eyes were tired.

"What is going on there?" Haldern's voice boomed from the speaker phone.

Moravec took the phone. Ellis didn't object. "Ian McPhearson had a heart attack on the plane," he said calmly.

"Heart attack? McPhearson? My God!"

Moravec looked at Ellis. "You'd better instruct AirMore not to divert to Kennedy. We want Townsend here."

The administrator went quickly to the house phone. "If McPhearson dies . . ." he glanced at Moravec ". . . Townsend doesn't have a surgeon."

"Dr. Graves is the backup. He will perform the operation, if there is one."

"If—?"

"Luther!" The director was nearly screaming.

"I'm still here."

"Are you sure it was McPhearson? It wasn't Townsend, was it? You're sure Townsend is alive?" His voice was strained.

"I'm sure."

Ellis glanced at the monitor screen. It had just changed to the main lobby. He stopped and stared at the monitor. It was three or four seconds before it changed again. He blinked. His eyes were playing tricks. He looked at Moravec. "Did you see that?"

"See what?"

"The monitor. It—" He reached for the disconnect button on the speaker phone. Without signing off he broke the line. He hadn't seen what he'd just seen, he told himself.

"What are you doing?" Moravec said.

Ellis dialed frantically. "I want the goddamn front desk," he said into the receiver. "What's the number?"

"What is the matter, doctor?"

"Nine hundred?" Ellis disconnected and dialed. "Watch

the monitor!" He misdialed the first time. He cursed, disconnected, then dialed again. The line was busy.

"Goddamn—"

"Ellis, what's the matter?"

He pointed desperately at the monitor screen. "Keep watching. Tell me when the front desk at the lobby rolls up."

Moravec frowned. He looked at the screen, baffled.

Ellis tried dialing again. "Unless I'm insane—"

"Oh, my . . . God!"

Ellis glanced at Moravec. His mouth was open as he stared dumbly at the monitor. Then Ellis saw it. His heart skipped. There were four people at the main desk. Two were security guards.

The other two were David Townsend and Dr. Sara Mills.

FIFTY

WEEKSBRIAR. 8:00 P.M.

IF SARA was nervous it wasn't apparent, David thought, except that her knuckles were white where she clutched the computer briefcase. They'd spent their last forty dollars at a TG&Y store on a raincoat, shaving cream and a razor for David. If he was going to impersonate a doctor he might as well look like one. David shaved in the bathroom of a Texaco station. He counted himself lucky that he hadn't sliced his neck. Don't be nervous, he'd told himself over and over in the mirror. Don't be nervous . . .

They stood together before the thick glass doors, waiting. There were half a dozen people on the other side ready to leave. It was Sara's idea to arrive during the nine o'clock shift change. Everyone was in a hurry.

"Evening, Dr. Mills," said a voice from a speaker above David's head. "Come to check up about your office door?" David saw one of the guards standing at the security desk in the lobby. He was smiling. Cooper.

"No, I just wanted to show Dr. Townsend around the place." She moved the BriefPac to the other hand.

The guard nodded, then glanced down at the monitor.

"What's in the briefcase?"

"Actually, it's a portable computer . . . and it's getting heavy."

"Sorry, doctor. Just a minute."

"Does it always take this long?" David said under his breath.

He heard her swallow. "No."

317

David expected to hear something. Some sort of whir, something to spot him when the scanner was on. But there wasn't anything. He wondered if they had time to change their minds. Just turn around and walk out. Were the doors locked behind them? If they reached the car, would they get past the gate? Weeksbriar security people carried real weapons, not electric guns. Would they use them if they ran? Would . . .

The glass doors opened soundlessly. David almost fainted with relief.

"You're a long way from home, aren't you, Dr. Townsend?" It was Cooper. He was staring at the monitor screen. David couldn't see what he was looking at.

"Long way?"

Cooper looked up. "Says here you're from a South African station."

"Oh, it's my vacation. It's just too hot down there right now. You know, below the equator." He didn't have the first clue about the weather in South Africa.

Sara took his arm and began to lead him toward a corridor marked BIOMET LABS. "This way, Stuart. I want to show you the lab then run by—"

"Excuse me, Dr. Mills, but I'll have to take a look at that." It was the other guard, the one who didn't smile.

Sara's fingers tightened on David's arm. "Pardon?"

"The computer, ma'am."

"Oh." She set it on the desk. "Is there something wrong?"

David watched as the guard unsnapped the clasps and opened it.

"No, ma'am, it's just that telecommunicating devices are not permitted inside the building."

"Really."

"Yes, ma'am. The company doesn't want anyone sending data out of the building or tapping into our computer. Not that you'd do that, but it's the regulation." He glanced up. "What were you going to do with this, doctor?"

Sara's fingers dug into David's arm.

"Actually, it belongs to me," David said. "I carry it with me everywhere. I just didn't feel comfortable leaving it in the car."

The guard nodded. "I'm sorry, Dr. Townsend. I'll have to keep it here. You can pick it up when you leave."

"Is it all right if I take some of my papers?"

"Sure." He turned the briefcase toward David. The telephone rang. "Excuse me."

David stuffed the cards with the codes into his pocket. He didn't know if they would do any good without the BriefPac, and he couldn't ask Sara. Her face was white. He closed the lid, took Sara's hand and started walking. Her fingers were ice cold.

"Dr. Mills?" It was the guard.

"Keep walking," David said.

"Dr. Mills?"

David turned with Sara to look back. The guard had his palm up, signaling halt, while he listened on the phone. "Yes, sir," he was saying into the receiver. "Yes, sir . . ." He shook his head. "No . . . yes . . . yes . . . what?" When he glanced up again his face had a peculiar look as though he didn't understand. He was staring at David. "Who . . . ?"

David took Sara's arm, increased his pace. "C'mon."

"David—"

"Don't look back. How do we get off this floor?"

"Left at the next corridor to the elevators."

A guard's voice filled the hallway. "Dr. Mills?"

They were fifteen feet from the corridor junction.

"Hey! Dr. Mills!"

David glanced over his shoulder. Cooper was following them. He wasn't running, he wasn't even hurrying, but he was calling after Sara. "Wait a minute, doctor. Someone on the phone wants—"

Then the first guard bellowed. "Hey, Harry—that's

Franklin! *That* guy—" he pointed at David "—the one who escaped!"

David pushed Sara ahead of him as they turned the corner. "Run!" he said. *"Run!"*

It was a long corridor. The elevators were at the far end. David's toe was throbbing by the time he'd run twenty steps. One of the two elevators stood open thirty feet away. Now it started to close.

"Don't let it close!" David yelled. Sara was ahead of him five or six steps. The doors were sliding toward each other. The two halves of the Euromedic logo painted on the doors were inches from union. Eight feet away, Sara lost a shoe but she kept running, hands up, reaching out. *"Don't let it close!"* Six feet away . . . four . . .

The doors bumped, the logo sliding together into a circle again. Sara slammed into it. David banged into her, knocking her down.

Behind him one of the guards yelled, "Hold it, Franklin!"

David turned. They were at the junction of the corridors, forty feet away, both of them in that stupid police crouch, arms extended, sighting down the barrels of ugly revolvers.

"Don't move, Franklin!"

Sara was on her hands and knees beside him, dazed from the collision. "David . . ."

David grabbed her. He swung her violently by the arm so that she was between him and the guards. They wouldn't dare shoot. Not at that range. They had to be sensible about it. It was too far. They wouldn't shoot for fear of hitting Sara. He closed his arm around her neck and held his fist against her throat.

"Get back or I'll slit her throat!"

An explosion filled the corridor. The bullet punctured an elevator door two feet over David's head. Sara screamed.

"Jesus, Miller!" Cooper yelled.

"It was an accident," Miller said.

Carefully, David raised Sara to her feet. He kept his fist

tight against her neck. "Put the guns down. I'll rip out her throat if you try that again."

"Just take it easy, Franklin . . ."

"Do it now!" David demanded.

Harry Cooper, the sensible one, lowered his gun. "Okay, okay. Just take it easy. No one's gonna hurt you." Miller didn't move. He held his position rigidly.

"Both of you!" Sweat rolled into David's eye. The raincoat was like an oven.

"I ain't movin', Harry," said Miller.

"Miller! Christ, you want him to cut her!"

"I ain't movin'."

David put his head close to Sara's. "*Do* something," he whispered.

Sara gulped for air. "Please . . . do what he says! *Please!*"

Miller relaxed his stance. The gun came down, but he continued to hold it in both hands.

David inched toward the second elevator. He could hear it. It had just stopped at the floor above. If he could stall these two long enough to get on it . . . but the elevator might bring more guards.

"Back up!"

Harry took a step backward. The other guard didn't budge.

Somewhere in the building an alarm went off.

"Move!" David yelled.

"SECURITY TWO AND SEVEN TO MAIN LOBBY," announced a female voice from a p.a. system. "SECURITY TWO AND SEVEN, MAIN LOBBY. CODE FIVE. GREEN CORRIDOR, SECTION 2-A."

"What the hell's that mean?" David said nervously in Sara's hair. He kept his eyes on the guards. He could hear the elevator again. It was moving.

"What the hell do you think it means?"

"You two turn around and start walking," David yelled.

"C'mon, Franklin, you can't get away with this."

David got a tighter grip on Sara. "You think I'm kidding!"

Harry held up his hands even higher. "Okay, okay!"

The sound of the elevator was louder. It was right behind him. "Get ready to run," David whispered. "Elevator."

"Harry . . ." Miller took a half step forward. "Harree . . ."

Cooper's eyes opened wide. "Miller, for chrissakes—"

Miller took another step. His revolver came up again. "Harry . . . he ain't *got* no knife."

"Oh, Jesus!" David said.

When the elevator doors opened, David shoved Sara toward them. "Go!"

A cleaning lady in a yellow jumpsuit with TIDY MAID, INC. embroidered across the back started to pull a mop-loaded cart out of the elevator. She didn't get past the threshold.

David stiffarmed Sara through the opening, knocking her against the cleaning woman. He jumped inside and pushed the first button his fingers touched on the panel. When he looked up, both guards were running.

David grabbed the cart handle and heaved it, sending it speeding into the corridor, rolling toward the guards. "Close, dammit! *Close!*"

The doors closed with a bump. Outside, David could hear the guards pounding on them. Then the elevator whined and began to move—down.

"We're going down," Sara said blankly. She glanced at the ceiling, then at David. "We're going *down* . . . to the basement! David, there's no way out from the sublevel!"

"Bitch, bitch, bitch!" David screamed at her. "You're not shot, are you!"

The elevator's ceiling speaker crackled. "ALL STAFF PERSONNEL STAY OUT OF THE CORRIDORS. THIS IS A CODE FIVE SECURITY ALERT. SECURITY TWENTY-SIX TO LEVEL TWO. SECURITY NINE AND TEN TO SECTION TWELVE-B, YELLOW CORRIDOR.

322

THIS IS AN EMERGENCY. STAFF PERSONNEL ARE INSTRUCTED TO LOCK THEIR DOORS. DO NOT ENTER THE CORRIDORS."

David slammed the palm of his hand over the emergency stop button. The elevator stopped. A red light flashed on the panel. He turned to Sara. "How do we get out of here?"

"We don't. There isn't any exit on the sublevel after five o'clock."

"After?"

"The kitchen is down there. There's a traffic ramp for deliveries and service vehicles to a loading platform. But the ramp door is closed and locked at five."

"Terrific. What else is down there?"

"The physical plant. A laundry. The employee credit union office, Zoolab, CC Section . . . and the kitchen. Everything but Zoolab is closed."

"Guards?"

"I don't know. Probably."

"What's Zoolab?"

"It's the livestock repository where experimental animals are kept." She looked at him defiantly. "It isn't a place you'd want to hide. It's full of caged animals."

"We sure as hell can't take this thing up again. Damn!" He noticed the cleaning lady. She was crouched in a corner, holding a broom in. front of her face. She gave David a nervous smile. Her right front tooth was gold.

He nodded.

Sara turned to her. "Hello, Inez."

Inez looked at them. She nodded at Sara. "Yes . . ." Her smile was still hesitant. "Good to see you." Her accent was heavily Spanish.

"Inez works the evening shift," Sara said, trying not to frighten the woman. "We can't stay here, David . . . stuck between floors."

David leaned against the railing. "CC? That's the computer room, right?"

Sara nodded.

"Closed?"

"Locked," she said. "A bank vault door. We couldn't—" Her eyes opened wide. She sucked in a sharp breath. "Dalton!" She pulled herself to her feet. *"Dalton!"*

"What?"

"Dalton's on duty." She reached for the emergency stop button. "The systems manager."

David grabbed her wrist. "Wait a minute. We're not going to get ourselves locked into a vault."

She shook his hand away. "It's the only safe place left in the basement." She pulled the button out. The flashing light stopped. She looked at David. "There isn't anywhere else." The elevator whirred to life. It started down.

David held out his hand to Inez. "Let me borrow your broom." He tried to smile. "Please?"

She hesitated, glancing at Sara, then handed it over.

A guard was waiting at the sublevel. When the elevator doors opened he was standing with one hand on his hip, smoking a cigarette. He was young, probably in his mid-twenties, anxious to find out what was happening.

"What's going on up there?" he said to David. He was holding a walkie-talkie. "I can't get anybody to answer me down here—" he nodded over his shoulder at the complex of overhead pipes and rows of uncovered light fixtures in the steel grid ceiling "—too much damn interference."

David flashed a look at Sara. "Somebody's broken into the biometrics lab on level two." He didn't even know if biometrics was a word.

"No shit!"

"You'd better hurry," David said. He stepped aside to let the guard in and nodded to Sara to get out. "Oh, and one other thing . . ."

The guard was impatiently pressing the main lobby button. "Yeah?"

He had half turned to look back when David hit him with the broom. The guard caught the force of it on the side of the head and slammed into the metal door, knocking his hat off. He fell backwards, trying to catch himself on the elevator's railing, and Inez screamed. David rushed to him and lifted his revolver, then jumped back before the elevator doors closed.

"My God, David! You didn't have—"

"Nobody's going to come after us when they find out an escaped psycho is down here with a gun." He stuffed the weapon into the raincoat.

"You . . . you wouldn't *use* it?"

David stared at her large green eyes a moment. "We'd better get moving."

She led him down a cement corridor past the laundry room, where several carts brimming with dirty smocks were crowded together. At the end of the passageway was a fire door stenciled:

CENTRAL COMPUTER SECTION
DALTON WILKIE: SYSTEM MGR.
CALL EXT. 510 IF NO ANSWER

———————————

AUTHORIZED STAFF ONLY

"If no answer?" David looked sharply at Sara. "Is anybody inside or not?"

Sara licked her lips. "I don't know."

"Can you get in if no one is—"

"No."

"Oh—"

"Let me handle this." Sara pressed a button on the console beside the door and David heard a bell ring inside. After a moment a tinny voice from the speaker beside the console said, "Yeah?"

"Dalton?" She held her breath.

"Who wants to know?"

"It's Dr. Mills. I . . . may I come in?"

"There's an alert on, you know," said the voice.

"I know. I . . ." She glanced at David. "I got trapped in the elevator. I figured this was as safe as anywhere."

For a moment there wasn't any response. Sara rubbed a sweaty palm on her coat and grasped the door handle. A few seconds later there was an electric buzz and the door unlatched with a mechanical click. "Come in, my little love bird."

"Love bird?" David whispered.

Sara pushed the heavy door and it swung open.

The computer room was brightly lit from a ceiling of flush-mounted fluorescent lights. The floor was covered with a dark blue carpet. Tall metal bookcases were bolted to the walls and filled with hundreds of three-ring binder notebooks of different colors and sizes, all of which were labeled with baffling titles: TEKMED SYSTEM COMMANDS, CONCOM MEMORY MAP FUNCTIONS, DBLTRK DEBUGGING PROTOCOLS, S&S HEX FILE OPERANDS, ASSEMBLY LANGUAGE MNEMONICS . . . The only other door in the room was simply marked COMPUTER. David saw a few library tables, but the room was visually dominated by a double row of computer terminals—five widely spaced CRT display screens per row, each position with its own entry keyboard and matrix printer.

"Good to see you, Sara," said a bearded man in jeans and a red plaid shirt. He was sitting at one of the terminal positions with his feet on the back of a chair, eating an apple. He looked about fifty, but it was hard to tell with the beard. "I'm just finishing supper. You want a peach?"

Sara shook her head and pushed the door until it clicked shut. "Thanks, no." She gestured toward David. "Dalton, I'd like you to meet David Townsend. David's a . . . a friend."

"Howdy," Wilkie said through a mouthful of apple.

"Dalton runs CC, David," Sara said. "He makes

326

everything work. He devours fruit like a monkey but he's the best systems manager around."

David nodded. The guy definitely belonged in a tree. Dalton Wilkie looked like he knew as much about computers as David knew about piloting the space shuttle. "Nice to meet you."

From a speaker on one of the consoles came: "SECURITY FIVE TO GREEN CORRIDOR, SECTION NINE." David put his hand in the parka. The feel of the gun was cool to the touch.

Wilkie dropped the core of the apple into a paper bag. "Do you know what on earth is going on up there? Sounds like world war three. People buzzing around, sending frantic messages all over the place . . . you'd think we had a maniac loose."

Sara glanced at David. She collapsed into the nearest chair. "Dalton, I . . . we need help. The security people up there . . . they're looking for us."

Wilkie frowned. "They are? What for?"

"Four days ago a patient escaped from the psychiatric ward," she said.

"Yeah?"

She nodded toward David. "Him."

Wilkie turned in his swivel chair for a better look at David. That was when David noticed the man had only one arm; his right shirt sleeve was folded and pinned back over itself where the stub ended just short of the elbow. "He don't look crazy," Wilkie said. "*Are* you crazy?"

David pulled the gun out of the parka. He didn't point it at anyone; he just held it out for Wilkie to see. "Sara, I don't know who this guy is. What makes you think you can trust him? He works for Euromedic like everyone else around here, doesn't he?"

Wilkie made a face. "Well, he *sounds* crazy." He glanced at Sara. "This fella's a friend of yours?"

Sara went over to David. "He's not crazy, he's just

327

stupid. Put that gun away. You silly bastard, we have few enough friends as it is. Dalton services the computer. He's my friend. Okay?"

David put the gun back in his pocket. "Look, I wasn't—"

"Oh, shut up." She turned back to Wilkie. "Dalton, I don't know if I can explain this to you. It's . . . it's just too incredible. But we need help. We're in a hell of a mess, David and I. And in a few minutes they're going to be at your door. Euromedic is . . . is—" she shook her head "—I don't even know where to start."

Wilkie scratched his beard. "Why don't you two take off your coats and sit down. I have some coffee. Just have a seat and you can tell me what it is that makes you so dangerous. I may not be the best-dressed programmer you ever saw, but beneath this flannel shirt beats the heart of a patient listener. You get that way, down here." He looked at David. "And if you don't mind, young fella, I'll have that gun." He held out his hand.

David didn't move. He shot a glance at Sara.

She nodded. "We have to start trusting somebody, David."

"If somebody comes busting in here—"

"If somebody does," Wilkie said, "it'll be King Kong's bigger brother. That's a four-inch reinforced steel grid fire door. It'll withstand three thousand degree heat for twelve hours or a phalanx of axe-toting firemen. An antiaircraft gun couldn't put a peephole through it. Nobody comes in here unless they're let in or use the key." He dug in his breast pocket and held up a slender piece of stainless steel that looked like a stubby fork. "*This* key." He put it back in his pocket, then motioned for David to hand him the gun. "C'mon. You're not going to shoot anybody anyway."

David took a step. He brought the gun out and handed it over.

"Hate guns," Wilkie said. He unloaded it, dropping the

328

bullets one by one into his shirt pocket. He slid the gun in a drawer. "It's how I come to be left-handed."

"ALL STAFF PERSONNEL ON LEVEL ONE AND SUBLEVEL PLEASE CALL THE SWITCHBOARD OPERATOR FOR SECURITY INSTRUCTIONS. ALL STAFF PERSONNEL ON LEVEL ONE AND SUBLEVEL PLEASE—"

Wilkie turned the speaker down. "Well, they've narrowed down the search. I expect they'll be calling me soon." He rose from the chair. "Anybody want coffee?"

Sara shook her head.

"I'm gonna pour me a cup." Wilkie walked to a counter with a hot plate and coffee maker. "You can start talking anytime—either one of you."

Sara sank into one of the console chairs. "I don't even know where to begin."

"I do," David said. He took off his brand new TG&Y raincoat and spread it across a chair, then walked to where Wilkie was making coffee. "I take mine black and you'd better put on another pot because this is going to take a little while."

"I'm not going anywhere."

"I'm from Oklahoma," David began. I drive a truck. My name's David Townsend." He held out his left hand.

Wilkie smiled. "Howdy." He shook his hand. "I'm not sure I'm glad to meet you." He turned and poured coffee into two mugs. "Leastways, not until I've heard you out." He held out one of the mugs to David. "So, what's got Weeksbriar's entire security force in such a frazzle over an Okie truck driver?"

David took the mug. He hadn't realized how dead tired he was until now. He sat down beside Sara. How *do* you tell a story like this? He sipped the coffee. His toe throbbed inside a shoe that didn't fit, his body ached from a dozen bruises. How explain the last forty-eight hours to a man who doesn't have any idea what it's like to steal a kid's sled and run for your life on a frozen pond from men in blue parkas with electric dart guns? David held the warm mug between his hands. He looked up at Wilkie. The one-armed man waited patiently. "Thursday my brother was in a plane crash in Spain," David began. "Friday morning they started killing me . . ."

FIFTY-ONE

SECURITY OFFICE. 8:45 P.M.

MORAVEC SAW Ellis through a glass partition in the security chief's office. He was standing before a bank of monitors, watching guards in pairs, checking offices and labs all over the facility. Before he entered, Moravec saw a young guard in a corner chair, out of the turmoil, holding an icepack over a lump on the side of his head.

"They're on the sublevel," Ellis said when Moravec had closed the door. "And Townsend has a gun."

"Luckily he didn't use it on its owner." Moravec glanced through the glass at the guard moaning under the icepack.

Ellis turned away from the monitors. "You don't sound very surprised."

Moravec sat down. "Nothing David Townsend does anymore surprises me."

"They had your BriefPac with them when they entered the building," Ellis said. "Why, do you think?"

"I haven't the slightest clue. My technical knowledge of those machines is limited to turning it on and turning it off. I am what is known as strictly an end-user. A computer illiterate. What I don't understand is why they came back here at all." Moravec felt the burning under his eyelids from lack of sleep. It was labor, forcing himself to think.

Ellis moved to a blueprint plan of the sublevel pinned to a bulletin board. "Security chased them into the elevator and they wound up in the basement. I've instructed our people to shut down all the elevators that access the sublevel and close off the fire escapes. There is a truck ramp, but it's closed and locked too." He looked at Moravec. "We've finally got the sonofabitch."

Moravec tried to read the white-on-blue drawing, but his eyes weren't up to it. "What's down there?"

"The physical plant mostly." Ellis pointed out the different areas as he talked. "This area. This is the kitchen, the laundry, CC section, Zoolab and the credit union office. But everything is closed or locked. Dr. Parker, one of our vet internists, is the only person still downstairs. He locked up as soon as he heard we had an escaped patient down there with a gun."

"Who told him that?"

"He called the operator to find out what was going on."

Moravec ran a hand through his hair. He studied the map. "How large an area are we talking about where they're hiding?"

"Big," Ellis said. "The physical plant alone is about four acres underground. Everything is down there except the air conditioning units."

"And you're sure they can't get out?"

"Absolutely positive."

"What about telephones? Are there telephones in the plant?"

"Of course there are phones. Extension lines of the in-house system. But they can't call outside the institute. All outside calls are routed through the switchboard. Anyway, who would they call?"

"I was thinking that we could call them," Moravec said. "If they're trapped down there sooner or later they'll want to talk."

Ellis considered it, nodded. "Yeah, maybe."

Moravec stared at the drawing. "I still don't understand what they're doing here." He sounded disappointed. "*Why* did they come back? And how did David Townsend get in? The equipment is programmed to accept Dr. Mills, but Townsend—"

"He just walked in. The scanner identified him as Stuart Townsend."

"Ah." Moravec smiled. "Of course, they're exactly the same."

"And they're going to be even closer," Ellis said. "You should be glad to hear that we're back to our original schedule."

"I'm sorry."

"Townsend is *here*," Ellis said impatiently. "Where he's supposed to be." He checked his watch. "And Dr. Townsend will be arriving on AirMore within forty minutes. If we can talk him out of there, we can have him prepped and ready for immediate surgery."

Moravec's smile was gone. "Tell him what?"

Ellis shrugged. "It doesn't matter, does it? Whatever will deliver him to me. That's all I care about."

Moravec believed it. He looked at the floor plan of the sublevel, studying the lines and symbols, and wondered what Townsend was thinking. It seemed an absolutely irrational move, coming back. For a man who'd come this far on sheer instinct and ingenuity, he'd made a significant mistake. If Ellis was successful it would prove to be a fatal mistake. Townsend must have known the risk. He wasn't crazy or stupid. He returned here for a reason. Now he was cornered. When he realized there was no way out, Townsend was going to be dangerous. He had a gun now. Threatened, he'd use it.

Moravec scanned the floor plan. Why had he come back? What did he think he could accomplish? What was he after?

FIFTY-TWO

COMPUTER CENTER. 9:30 P.M.

DALTON WILKIE contemplated his empty coffee mug. He was leaning backward in a metal swivel chair, his chin on the stump of his right arm.

Sara hadn't moved from the console. David had been the restless one—pacing back and forth between the other two, watching the time, going for coffee, testing the door, constantly moving—but he was the one telling the story and he felt more comfortable, less nervous, when he was doing something besides getting hoarse.

But now he'd stopped pacing, stopped talking. He'd told it all from the beginning, or at least from the beginning he knew and now he was—like Sara—watching Wilkie for some sign of acknowledgment.

Wilkie straightened in his chair. He set the coffee mug on a console stand and rubbed at the spot on his stump where his chin had rested. He stared at the floor. Finally, he shook his head. "Damn. That's the damndest thing I ever heard," Wilkie said. He glanced up at David. "Bar none."

"What else do you think?" David said.

"Well . . ." Wilkie scratched his beard. "You really think they killed that fella? What's his name, Franklin?"

"We think so." Sara's chair squeaked. "What do *you* think, Dalton?'"

Wilkie let out a long sigh. He scratched the top of his head. "You two took a hell of a chance coming here, didn't you? I mean, if what you say is true, this place isn't exactly

334

crawling with your friends and admirers. How did you know *I'd* be here?"

"I didn't," Sara said. "We were trapped in the elevator. I just came here."

"What were you going to do if no one was here? CC isn't manned twenty-four hours a day, you know. Someone's always on call, but . . . didn't you know that?"

"No." She glanced at David. He rolled his eyes at the ceiling. "Well, someone's always been here whenever I called down for something," she said defensively.

Wilkie got up from his chair. "Without the telecommunicator you can't get into the files, right?"

"Wrong," David said. He went to his raincoat and pulled out the computer code cards. "We still have these."

Wilkie looked at them, then handed them back. "Those are encoded for remote access. They won't work on this system."

"They won't?" Sara said.

"Nope. A remote has different data transfer requirements than a terminal online here, like speed of transmission. Those codes are designed specifically for remote entry into the system. If you tried to use them here the computer wouldn't understand what you wanted. You'd be shut off."

"Terrific," David said.

"You've got a HEMA classification, don't you?"

Sara nodded. "Yes, section fourteen."

"Are you a privileged user?"

"No."

"Do you know the world log-on code?"

"No."

"The intersystem log-on?"

Sara shook her head. She looked at the floor.

"Up the proverbial creek, aren't you?"

"There must be a master list of access codes *somewhere*," David said.

"There isn't any printed list," Wilkie said. "That would be a violation of computer security regulations. Everybody

335

is supposed to memorize their own access codes. They wouldn't be secret if everybody wrote them down." He waited a moment before he smiled. "Course, I don't need a list. I *run* the computer."

Sara's head shot up. "What?"

"You don't think all the people in this place can remember one code word plus a six digit file access reference, do you? Hell, half my time is spent looking up access codes for people who forgot them."

"You know *all* the access codes?"

"Know them? Damn, girl, I made 'em up. Anyway, I don't need access codes. The system manager has universal privilege."

"Then, you can get into—" It took a moment for it to register. "You can get into any file in CC!"

Wilkie's smile broadened. "That's right."

"Will you help us, Dalton?" Sara's expression was a plea. "What we've told you is the truth."

Dalton held up his hand. "My sainted mother used to tell me to watch out for people like you. People just naturally can't help being liars and cheats, she said. That's why we have religion. Fortunately, computers don't need religion because they don't know how to lie. The only way I'm going to know the truth is to take a peek at those files." He rolled his chair to the middle terminal position. "Just have a seat at the positions on either side of me. I'll link the terminals. You'll see everything that comes up on your own screens." Wilkie sat down and began typing. "I'm also the fastest one-armed, two-fingered hunt and peck typist you ever saw."

David watched his screen. A banner came up first.

WEEKSBRIAR RETRIEVAL:
CENTRAL RECORDS
AND
DOCUMENTATION STORAGE

Then the screen went blank and a second later printed:

```
WRCRDS/010681/WRM I/CC/2212 HRS
LOG-ON?
FILE REFERENCES? (LIMIT: 5)
```

Wilkie typed NOTLAD:A01000 in reply to the log-on request.

"That's CC's universal privilege code—'Notlad'?" Sara said. "Just 'Notlad'?"

"That's it. I made it up so I wouldn't forget it. It's Dalton backward." He smiled. "I know, I'm a clever devil. Now, what're the names of those files?"

"Hahnemann and Wintergreen," Sara said.

Wilkie's keyboard clicked and CRT cursors on all three terminals simultaneously danced in a straight line across each screen, leaving in their wakes green characters on black backgrounds. David watched in wonder. He couldn't even type. In another moment his screen went blank again. Then:

```
FILE NAME TO DIRECTORY NAME THIS SYSTEM:
HAHNEMANN = HANMAN
WINTERGREEN = WNTRGRN
READ HANMAN REQUEST: DENIED
PRIVILEGE VIOLATION
"NOTLAD" DOES NOT ACCESS THIS FILE
```

Wilkie squinted at his screen. "What the hell . . ."

"What does that mean?" David asked.

"A privilege violation means the user is requesting a file with an unauthorized entry code," Wilkie said. "Except it isn't unauthorized. Notlad is the universal entry code. CC is programmed to accept it." He stared at the screen then typed: GET WRCRDS LOG-ON LIST.

In a moment the computer came back with:

```
WRCRDS LOG-ON LIST
NAME?
```

Wilkie typed: ELLIS, J.

"Let's see if our brave leader had done something cute."

PRIVILEGE VIOLATION
ILLEGAL REQUEST
INQUIRER IS DENIED ACCESS TO THIS USER'S CODENAME

"Well, I'll be damned." Wilkie rubbed his hand through his beard.

"What is it, Dalton?"

"He's screwing around with *my* computer," Wilkie said. "That's not nice. I don't screw around with his doctor business." He leaned back in his chair. "The only other person at Weeksbriar who has universal privilege is the chief of staff, Dr. Ellis. He can call up any file or password, change the name, edit it, revise it, delete it . . . whatever he wants. That's what universal privilege means. He uses it so he doesn't have to keep a list of everyone's password to see what they're doing. I use it to fix programs when somebody screws up their input defaults."

Sara frowned. "So?"

"Ellis has *two* universal privilege access IDs. Notlad and something else. He's created another UP and protected it against Notlad access. He can do that. One UP can be programmed to deny another UP file entry—I'm locked out of any files with that new UP code. It isn't the way we do things around her, but it's possible." Wilkie let out a sigh. "Whatever is in those files, he doesn't want *anybody* to see them." He shrugged. "Course, that makes sense, you know. If those files are so secret they aren't going to want somebody like me to have access to them. Hell, I wouldn't have even known there was another privileged ID unless I tried to get into one of those files. And I don't have any reason to."

"We can't get into the files?" David said.

"*You* can't," Wilkie said. "I didn't say I couldn't. The good doctor's made it a lot more inconvenient for me, but nothing in this business is impossible."

"But if you don't know what the other log-on code is . . ." Sara stared at her terminal.

"A computer expert is a computer expert," Wilkie said with a wink. "Ellis, if you'll forgive me, is only a doctor." He pushed himself to the keyboard. "Now watch, my children, and see a genius at work." He began typing and the screen cleared itself, then displayed:

```
CC COMMAND MODE
WHAT?
```

David watched as Wilkie typed FUNCTION DIRECTORY and the screen flashed to five columns of words that were gibberish—STAT . . . XSUB . . . CONFIG . . . RAID . . . MAP . . . PIP . . . USERCUST.ASM. . . . WORM . . .

"There are several ways to circumvent a system's security," Wilkie said, "and most of them take a hell of a long time and lots of luck."

The cursor highlighted an entry in the third column, DUMP.HEX, then the computer asked WHAT? Wilkie typed LOAD. In a few seconds the computer responded: LOADED.

"One way to do it is called the 'brute method,' which is to tell a computer to define all combinations of letters from a single character to an eight-character string. Eight characters is the limit of most systems' password definition. Then one by one, try each combination until you come up with the right one. That's the primitive method and it could take months because there are two hundred trillion combinations. Course if you had a little time on your hands you could try and crack an alphanumeric password—combination of letters *and* numbers. That's twelve times more—two million billion combinations."

Wilkie tapped quickly over the keyboard: ENGLISH-ASCII CONVERSION. The computer responded: WHAT? Wilkie typed: ELLIS, J. to which the machine replied: CONVERTING.

"Another way is to know the person who knows the password in question but who isn't sharing it with you.

Passwords are kind of like telephone numbers—if you don't use it every day you forget it. That's why people choose passwords they can remember—like Notlad with me. A lot of times they're children's names, street names, colors, brands of cigarettes, anything as long as it's eight characters or less. If you know a fella well enough, you might get lucky and just guess what his password is. You'd be surprised how many people use Rosebud, for example. Anyhow, it's not exactly the most scientific approach to code breaking."

The screen blinked then rapidly printed:

ENGLISH-ASCII CONVERSION OF ELLIS, J. = 69 76 76 73 83 49 32 74 46

"But now we come to the more cerebral approach," Wilkie said. "It's something that's going to require a team effort, but at least we won't be at it for months."

Dalton typed in several more commands and the computer dutifully responded. David was fascinated. He didn't have the faintest idea what Wilkie was doing, but the allure was that he was sitting before a machine that was making decisions and providing answers in the time it took David to read the questions. Of course, he knew computers existed and what they could do—everybody knew that—but he'd never sat in front of one and stared at a terminal screen while data sped across it at the speed of light.

Then the screen blinked and within half a second was filled with numbers. David glanced up at Wilkie.

"What we have here, boys and girls, is that portion of CC's memory that contains the names and corresponding passwords of everyone in the Euromedic system who uses the WRCRDS files."

David looked at his screen again. It was still filled with numbers.

"Unfortunately for us, it's coded in ASCII."

"Ask who?"

"The American Standard Code for Information Exchange," Wilkie said, "A-S-C-I-I. It's what we use to make these little beauties understand us. Ellis has effectively locked us out of his designated UP files and without knowing what that means in terms of assembly language access he's confident that no one will ever get into them. Like I said, Ellis is only a doctor."

"And all these numbers are going to tell us what the password is?" David was bewildered.

"No, just one string in this record. That's all we're looking for. Ellis only denied access to certain selected files. I can still get into anything else in the system. If he knew what he was doing, he'd have protected this track of CC memory too. It's only a machine, you know. Somewhere it has to keep a record of all the codes and passwords and who belongs to them so it can figure out who has access to which files." Wilkie gestured toward his screen. "That's it."

"But . . . it's just a bunch of numbers."

Wilkie shook his head in disappointment. He looked at Sara. "You understand, surely?"

"Yes, of course, but—"

"Explain to the boy that he is in the presence of brilliance while I get another cup of coffee. Finding Ellis's string may take time."

David turned to Sara. "What the hell's—"

"I don't think you'll understand this, David," she said, "but listen anyway."

"Just keep it simple. You know me, crazy and stupid."

Sara flashed a patient smile. "Dalton called up the disc file that lists everyone's name and password and dumped it—that is, it's all displayed here, on our terminals."

"Yeah, I got that part . . . in asky-things."

"Computers don't keep data in words. It's all a binary system of data storage, and don't ask me what binary means."

"Zeros and ones."

"Very good. And ASCII text file is an alphanumeric file

341

that the computer can understand and translate to binary."
She pointed at his screen. "All those numbers correlate to
names and passwords."

"And we're supposed to change them back into English?"

Wilkie slid into his chair and set the coffee mug beside
the keyboard. "Not quite. I've already made the conversion
of Ellis's name into ASCII format. All we have to do is find
that same string of numbers in this file. The next string
following it will be his universal privilege code name."

David stared at the list of numbers. "How many strings
are there?"

"As many as there are people who have access to
WRCRDS in the Euromedic system," Wilkie said. "About
eleven thousand."

David shot an astonished look at him. "Eleven thousand!"

"And they are not stored alphabetically, just wherever the
computer has a place to put them. Which means we'd better
get started."

FIFTY-THREE

NEW BROCKTON AIRPORT.
10:05 P.M.

AIRMORE ONE touched down at New Brockton Regional Airport at exactly 9:50 P.M.

Dr. Ashley Graves was now physician-in-charge of Euromedic's most important patient. While he called Weeksbriar and spoke to the chief of staff, the MORE unit was unloaded from the nose of the plane.

"How is he doing?" Ellis said.

Graves was momentarily confused by the question. He had spent the past hour trying to keep alive the man who was supposed to be the primary surgeon on this mission. He was still wearing his surgical gown, ringed with perspiration.

"Which—you mean Townsend?"

"Goddammit, of course I mean Townsend."

"The patient is breathing normally, but the early signs of eventual ventricular fibrillation are already beginning," Graves said. "He's started throwing occasional PVCs on the electrocardiogram. His pulse is weakening and blood pressure is down five points in the last ninety minutes. I've moved the IPC unit to the operating compartment as a precaution against premature arrest. He isn't doing well at all, actually."

"How soon can you operate?" Ellis said.

"It would be rather pointless," Graves replied sadly, "without a donor."

"The donor is here. As a matter of fact, we have two donors."

"At the institute? Now? But I thought—"

"How soon can you operate?"

"Well, I'd have to see the donor, of course. He'd have to be examined, prepped—"

"If Stuart Townsend dies while you're poking around on a prelim of Townsend, doctor, I promise you the responsibility will rest solely with you."

"Now, look here—"

"The surgical staff that came ahead of you is ready and waiting. The operating rooms are ready. The equipment is in place. I have David Townsend or, if necessary, an alternative. But we won't need her. What I want from you is a straight answer—when can you operate?"

"Well, if the staff is prepared—"

"In one hour?"

"One hour?"

"It will take you twenty minutes to get here. Say another half an hour to get your patient into the OR and prepped. I'll have Townsend—my Townsend—on the third floor to you by, say, eleven-thirty. That gives you an hour and a half. Okay?"

Graves swallowed hard. "Yes, yes, all right then." He licked his lips. "You know, I've already had one trauma case tonight."

"McPhearson? How is he?"

"I'm afraid he didn't make it."

"Just don't make it two," Ellis said. "I'll see you when you get here."

Ellis set the phone down. He sat for a moment, tapping a pen on a pad. Stuart Townsend was alive, if only barely, and on his way. Graves would operate in place of McPhearson. Everyone would be here for the finale. He rose from his chair. It was time to bring out the guest of honor. David Townsend's turn at center stage would be spectacular. And brief.

FIFTY-FOUR

COMPUTER CENTER. 10:25 P.M.

AFTER TEN minutes David's headache started. After twenty-five minutes he was sure he'd go blind. With each passing line of numbers the fascination he'd had for CC wore off. The numbers just kept coming, row after row, sixteen sets to a line, a never-ending parade of them. He'd just press a key and a new line would appear, and another, and another . . .

```
73 70 32 89 79 85 32 67 65 78 32 82 69 65 68 32
84 72 73 83 32 84 7s 69 78 32 89 79 8g 39 82 69
32 84 79 79 32 68 65 77 78 32 67 76 69 83 69 33
72 49 32 75 46 32 48 53 47 48 49 47 49 57 56 49
```

Look for back-to-back seventy-sixes to start, Wilkie had instructed; they were the L's in Ellis. That was supposed to make it easy. Wilkie had divided the file into thirds and David had the middle section. If it was such a great computer, David had asked at one point, why didn't it do this? Why not tell it to find a pair of seventy-sixes? Why should they get cataracts?

Naturally, there was a reason. David didn't begin to understand it. He just went on searching. Another line. And another . . .

"Hey," Sara said suddenly. "Hey!"

David looked up. She was a little blurry.

"Sixty-nine, seventy-six, seventy-six, seventy-four . . ." She looked at her screen a little longer. "I found it!" She looked at Dalton. "I *found* it!"

345

Wilkie pushed his chair beside hers.

"There," she said. She pointed out one of the rows.

"The strings are separated by slashes," Wilkie said. "Forty-sevens are slashes." He put his finger on the screen. "Here. David, copy this string down."

"Go," David said. He tore a page from a pad next to his keyboard.

"Seventy-seven, sixty-five, eighty-two, seventy-one, sixty-five, eighty-two, sixty-nine—that's an E—and eighty-four. It's an eight-character password. Lucky we didn't try the brute method."

"I got it." David handed him the page.

Wilkie scooted his chair back to his position and with one key word cleared the screen and typed in: ASCII-ENGLISH CONVERSION. The computer asked WHAT? and Wilkie entered the string number.

The terminal screen blinked then replied: CONVERTING.

"Well, now," Wilkie said with a smile, "we'll see how clever he is."

The conversion took ten seconds.

ASCII-ENGLISH CONVERSION OF 77 65 82 71 65 82 69 84 = MARGARET

"Margaret? Who . . ."

"*Mrs*. Ellis," Wilkie said. "Well, it's simple. It's a name he's not going to forget."

"I guess he couldn't spell it backwards," David said.

"Now let's see if we can get those files." Wilkie started working at the keyboard again. The screen went blank, then the banner returned and after that the log-on, file reference request. Wilkie typed in MARGARET, then stopped. "Wait a minute. Let's not get too cocky here."

Sara turned from her screen. "What's the matter?"

"Ellis can still use the password. I don't know where he is or what he's doing, but if he finds out someone is accessing his secret files he can still get into the system and reassign file names or erase them altogether."

"We'll just have to take that chance," David said.

"Son, I don't take chances like that. Anyway, we don't have to." Wilkie smiled. "We'll rename his UP—erase Margaret and call it something else."

"You can do that?" Obviously it was a stupid question, David realized, by the look the computer wizard gave him.

"Watch."

REQUEST NEW LOG-ON SIGNATURE FOR ELLIS, J. appeared on David's screen.

The computer digested it then inquired: WHAT IS CURRENT SIGNATURE?

ELLIS, J. (UP) = MARGARET

The screen blinked acknowledgment.

ENTER NEW SIGNATURE
(8-CHARACTER LIMIT)

Wilkie typed: ELLIS, J. (UP)=

He glanced up from his screen. "Anybody got a favorite eight-letter word? Anything will do—just keep it clean. We don't want to expose CC to vulgar obscenities." He turned around. "Yes?"

Sara shrugged.

"Yeah, I know one," David said.

"Eight letters or less," Wilkie said.

"It's eight exactly."

Wilkie nodded at David's keyboard. "Good, type her in. Just so it's something we won't forget."

"I won't forget it." David pecked at the keys with one finger. He typed TOWNSEND.

FIFTY-FIVE

PSYCHIATRIC WARD. 10:55 P.M.

MORAVEC RAN to the first phone he could find, an extension in a lab on the surgical floor, and called Ellis.

"Yes?"

"Are you near a computer terminal?" Moravec was out of breath.

"Why?"

"Go—" he stopped to catch his breath "—go to your office. Erase all the files on Hahnemann and anything else you don't want anyone to read."

"What?"

"David Townsend and Dr. Mills are in the computer center in the basement," Moravec said breathlessly. "That's why he came back. That's why he was carrying the BriefPac. He doesn't know what's happening. He came here to find out—through Weeksbriar's computer. Go, quickly."

"Townsend can't get into CC," Ellis said. He sounded impatient. "It's an electronically locked vault door."

"I just spoke to the veterinarian from Zoolab," Moravec said angrily, "a Dr. Parker. He's been down there the whole time. He just ran upstairs to the security people. He was too frightened to be in the basement with a man who he believes is crazy and armed with a gun."

"So?"

"Dr. Parker is very worried about one of his colleagues. Someone else is still down there, he says. Dalton Wilkie."

"Wilkie? The computer systems manager?"

"Parker passed him in the corridor twenty minutes before

the security alarm sounded," Moravec said. "Wilkie was on his way to the computer center. We've been calling but no one answers."

"Then he isn't there. Wilkie would answer the phone."

"Wilkie hasn't left the institute, Ellis. His car is still in the parking lot. He hasn't signed out. I'm telling you, David Townsend is in the computer center. It's the only place in the world he can get to that has answers. I told you he wasn't stupid."

Ellis didn't respond immediately. "A smart man wouldn't let himself be trapped in a basement without exits. Anyway, Townsend couldn't get through the door. He doesn't have access. He couldn't"—Ellis stopped.

"Exactly," Moravec said. "Townsend can't get in, he isn't staff. But Dr. Mills is."

The pause was longer this time. "The only files Dr. Mills has computer authority to enter are those in the Hematology section," Ellis said. He wasn't so sure of himself, Moravec thought. "There's no way she can get into a restricted section. She doesn't have access to my data."

"*Our* data, Dr. Ellis. Listen to me. We can't take the chance. Erase those files. Townsend and Dr. Mills have eluded us and done things they shouldn't have been able to do for two days. Anyway, David Townsend has Mr. Wilkie. *And* he has a gun."

"Moravec, you don't know anything about computers. You said so yourself. Wilkie can't get into my documents. I have a special password that he doesn't know. He can't get to the Hahnemann information. Believe me it's safe. Where are you now?"

"Third floor. I'm with the surgical team prepping the sequel."

"We're *not* using the sequel! Goddammit, Moravec, you know that! We're using Townsend."

"You don't have him yet, doctor," Moravec said.

"Leave that to me. Even if Townsend is in CC and even *if* he got into those files, it doesn't matter. Who's he going to tell? In less than an hour there won't be a David Townsend. And nobody else in that vault is going to leave this building, Moravec. I promise you that. You just meet the MORE unit. It's on its way from the airport. Don't worry about anything else. The Hahnemann file is as safe as it would be in London."

Ellis hung up the phone, pleased with himself. He was in charge again. He knew exactly where Townsend and Dr. Mills were now, and if they thought they were out of his grasp then they were in for a shock.

Locked in the back of the bottom drawer of his desk was a clear plastic cylinder. Inside it was a red metal shaft that looked like an inflated tuning fork. The manufacturers who had installed the vault had made two stainless steel, electronic-coded keys—a silver one, which went to the systems manager, and a red master that normally was kept by the company from which duplicates could be cast. Euromedic had insisted that the master be held by the resident chief of staff. It guaranteed absolute security.

Ellis glanced at the row of monitors in the security office. Guards were walking the halls, locking doors in the corridors; routine procedure for an unauthorized person in the building. He pressed the intercom button to the dispatcher.

"Yes, sir?"

"Find the security chief. I'm evacuating all non-essential personnel from the research facility. I want it done quickly and orderly."

"Yes, sir."

Ellis wasn't worried about Townsend; he just didn't want anyone getting in the way. When he was ready for Townsend, he would go to the basement and get him.

FIFTY-SIX

COMPUTER CENTER. 11:10 P.M.

THEY ACCESSED the Hahnemann file first. Getting into it was a breeze.

WRCRDS/ 010281/WRMI/CC/2310 HRS
HAHNEMANN FILE

DO YOU WISH HARDCOPY TEXT?

"What's hardcopy text?" David asked.

"A printout version of the file," Sara said, eyes fastened on her terminal. She glanced over at Wilkie. "We'd better make at least one copy of everything we access."

"Yeah." Wilkie entered the request.

HAHNEMANN FILE HARDCOPY CODE
FILE IS 23495 BLOCKS IN LENGTH
BEGINS BLK # 102000 ENDS BLK # 125495

TO COPY ENTIRE FILE ENTER "ALLFILE",
OTHERWISE ENTER CASE NUMBER, BLOCK
REFERENCE OR NAME (LAST NAME FIRST).

ENTER REQUEST:

"We can't print the whole thing," Wilkie said. "It'll take hours to print twenty-three thousand blocks of text. I don't think we've got that much time."

"Then concentrate on David's file. That's what we're here for."

Wilkie nodded. "David M.?"

"Yes."

Wilkie entered it, spelling Townsend with two n's, entered it again and tapped the return key. He glanced at David. "Nervous?"

"I passed nervous days ago."

The information appeared in the time it took David to look at Wilkie and glance back.

```
TOWNSEND, DAVID M(ICHAEL) IS AN
ADDENDUM FILE TO CASE NO. 2-1450.
SEE TOWNSEND, STUART P(HILLIP).
FILE IS 29 BLOCKS IN LENGTH
BEGINS BLK # 12403 ENDS BLK # 12432.
```

"It's not a big file," Wilkie said. "Shouldn't take long to print."

"What're blocks?" David wanted to know.

"Computerese," Wilkie said. "A block is a little more than twelve hundred bytes of data."

"Bites again," David said wearily.

Wilkie laughed. "Typewriter character strokes to you. About thirty pages in this file, give or take." He typed something at the keyboard. "Here goes."

The monitor went blank as the computer began a new run.

```
RETRIEVING "TOWNSEND, DAVID M(ICHAEL)."
STAND BY FOR PRINTER OUTPUT
```

The laser printer beside David shattered suddenly, spit out an empty page of green computer paper, then began printing. Lines of words banged across the page as fast as the tractor feed mechanism could pull the perforated pages through the machine. The machine was on the second page before he got his breath back.

"We'll have the whole file in a couple of minutes," Wilkie said over the noise. "In the meantime I'll get on another terminal and start a run on these other files."

David nodded. Sara was reading the data from the screen as the printer slammed it out on the paper. David sat down. He'd had enough of staring at a screen. He separated the fifth page along the perforation as it rolled out of the machine, folded the paper in his lap and started reading from page one.

```
FILE NO. 2-1450
STUART PHILLIP TOWNSEND
OPENED 09/09/78

ADDENDUM/A
DAVID MICHAEL TOWNSEND
OPENED 04/03/79

INCLUDES:
MEDICAL HISTORY
PSYCHOLOGICAL PROFILE
CURRENT MED-MAG UPDATES
SPECIAL NOTES

WARNING:
HAHNEMANN PROJECT FILE MATERIAL IS
CLASSIFIED "MOST SENSITIVE." IT IS
FORBIDDEN THAT ANY PORTION OF THIS
DOCUMENT BE DUPLICATED.

END PAGE 1 . . .

ADDENDUM-A/2-1450 PAGE 2
MEDICAL BRIEF
GENERALLY UNREMARKABLE SUBJECT IS IN GENERAL GOOD HEALTH. HE IS
NON-SMOKER AND A MODERATE DRINKER. NO ALLERGIES. NO EVIDENCE
OF SEVERE PSYCHIATRIC STRESS. SUBJECT WAS TREATED FOR BROKEN
RIGHT INDEX FINGER 6/14/61 (AGE 11) AFTER FALL FROM GARAGE ROOF.
NO OTHER SIGNIFICANT INJURIES. FOR SPECIFIC BIOMEDICAL REFERENCES
SEE SECTION 6 THIS FILE.

THE CIRCUMSTANCES OF THIS SUBJECT'S CASE ARE NOT TYPICAL OF
HAHNEMANN PROJECT PERSONNEL. DUE TO THE EXTRAORDINARY SITUA-
TION WITH REGARD TO THE HAHNEMANN SUBJECT S.P. TOWNSEND,
EXPEDIENT MEASURES WERE DEEMED URGENTLY NECESSARY. ON AUTHORITY
OF THE EUROMEDIC BOARD, SUBJECT WAS COVERTLY TRANSFERRED.
```

TO WMRI UNDER THE IDENTITY OF R. K. FRANKLIN (SEE 32-392 THIS
FILE). SUBJECT SUBSEQUENTLY TO BE TRANSFERRED TO MADRID, SPAIN,
FOR EMERGENCY CARDIAC SURGERY.

END PAGE 2 . . .

There were twenty-seven more pages.

David read every page of the file, then read it again. It was more than a bad dream. When he finished he dropped the last page into the paper tray. He was aware that Sara was standing beside him but he was too shocked to do more than shake his head.

She touched his shoulder. "David."

He stared ahead. "I don't know whether to laugh or cry. It's so insane I feel like I've fallen down a rabbit hole." He looked up at her. "They want my *heart*!"

"I know . . ."

"I'm just a piece of meat to them . . . and not even a special cut. 'Generally unremarkable,' it said." He picked up the file. "Did you read it? Did you see what they're trying to do?"

"That's not the half of it." Her face was pale. "Look at this." She offered him another printout.

He pushed it away. "No, thanks. I've seen enough."

"No you haven't. You haven't seen anything."

"What?"

"Do you know what your brother was doing? The research project he was working on?"

"Stuart was a microbiologist. I'm not even sure I know what that means."

"He was doing progeria research," Sara said. "Do you know what that is, progeria?"

"No."

"It's a children's disease . . . an extremely accelerated aging process. It occurs once in eight million births. Kids who have it rarely live through their teens. The disease is always fatal. There isn't any cure."

354

"Sara, I don't mean to be cruel, but what has that got to do with anything? What Stuart did doesn't make any diff—"

"It's important you understand this, David," she interrupted. "I'm going to tell you why all this has happened . . . what it's really about."

"I *know* why." David pointed at the file. "My brother's a big shot microbiologist with Euromedic and he needs a new heart—mine. You were right about the transplant, Sara, just slightly off on the part number. No wonder they didn't ask me."

"Will you please just shut up for once and listen to me!" Sara's face was suddenly red with anger or fright, he wasn't sure which. She was trembling, but she stared directly into David's eyes. She held up the printout pages. "This is a synopsis of the Hahnemann project, David. It explains everything."

Sara was close to hysteria. He glanced at Wilkie. The computer expert was standing silently on the other side of the console. "I'd listen," he said.

"You have to understand what they've done," she began, "from the beginning. Don't interrupt, just listen." Sara pulled a chair beside David and sat down. "This is all about enzymes and genetic research. About ten years ago, a geneticist named Dr. Julius Hahnemann experimented with laboratory mice, studying premature aging. He and a microbiologist named Rennit combined altered DNA cells with a tissue culture to produce a special enzyme-producing tumor. The tumor was injected into the mice near the pituitary gland in the brain. The chemical reaction of the enzymes in concert with the hormones of the pituitary gland arrested the disease. It wasn't a cure—that is, the disease was still there—but they'd slowed the aging process to almost normal. You follow me so far?"

"I don't know what a pituitary gland is, but I get the picture. The rats stopped getting old too fast."

"Mice."

"Rodents, then."

"But there was a side effect. The mice became peppier, more active. They had more energy, more vitality and they—they got smarter."

"Smarter? Mice!"

They ran mazes quicker, solved laboratory problems faster. It was astounding, according to the report."

"Just what we need—smarter mice."

"The results were the same with other laboratory animals. Even the primates. In every case, the control group showed more energy and intelligence. They couldn't explain it . . . it just happened."

"That's what Stuart was working on?"

"Your brother came along later. This was in the early seventies, and it was an enormous breakthrough, arresting the disease. But the experiment was still in its primary stages. There would be years of testing ahead. And all of this was in secret. They weren't ready to let it out that what they'd done was, in effect, to develop a new strain of enzyme. Remember the oil-degrading microorganism? Well, this was something like that. They weren't sure how it would be revised, especially since it produced an unexplainable side effect."

"Good old medical science."

"The enzyme was named METHYD-9 because it acted on methylaminotetralin hydroxylase. Euromedic called it the Hahnemann project."

David made a face. "Where do I come in?"

"I'm not finished. Euromedic got very interested in the research, but not because it neutralized the children's disease. Because of the side effect. They thought they'd discovered gold. If they could inhibit aging in humans *and* increase intelligence and productivity, it would be an unparalleled achievement. A discovery like that could make them millions. The trouble was that the enzyme only produced that side effect in the treatment of progeria— animals with the disease. It didn't have any effect on animals that didn't have the disease. The next step was to try it on a human subject. They found a five-year-old boy in Kenya, a terminal case, and implanted the tumor. It worked. In a year, he was growing like a normal child."

"Was he smarter too?"

Sara nodded.

"How come I never heard about it?" David said. "If this is such a breakthrough, how come these guys have never been on the Donahue Show or in *Newsweek*? I thought doctors went in for that kind of stuff. You know, look what I did?"

"First of all, David, this kind of experimentation with humans is taboo. In England and the United States it's illegal. That's why they went to Africa. Besides, it wasn't perfected yet."

"So it could make money for them, you mean."

"Medical research is expensive, David. I'm not trying to defend what's going on here, but it's normal to investigate the profitability of certain aspects of new techniques. If it's marketable then it can pay for the research that's gone on before. Theoretically, there's nothing wrong with that approach."

"You believe that?"

"It doesn't matter what I believe. That's how it is."

"Stuart was involved in this . . . perfection?"

"Yes. He was a member of the team. That's what makes him so important, David. Euromedic sponsored everything. They got them hundreds of subjects to work with, from all over the world. Hahnemann insisted on being the first test case. Well, actually the second, after the Kenyan boy. For two years they tested it on people. They were so confident that the rest of the team eventually underwent the surgery too."

"Stuart?"

"Yes."

"That makes sense. He always was a sheep."

"Everything was going fine until last year—Hahnemann

died. He didn't just die. He aged to death. Somehow the enzyme broke down. It has some sort of built-in cycle. After sixty months it just quits working.''

"Quits?"

"All those people who had the surgery started getting sick. Without the enzyme to protect them they were exposed to the progerian degenerative effect. They started dying and nobody could do anything to stop it.''

"Stuart—"

"No, the South Africa team had more than two years left in their cycle. They went immediately back to work to solve the problem. They called the test cases sequelas—it means the aftereffect of a disease. Hahnemann Sequelas. And apparently they discovered a cure or procedure or something to make it work right. Euromedic put them all on a plane to bring them back to London. This was a very big deal, David. Euromedic didn't want to take any chance that any of this might leak out. They put all their eggs in one basket, you could say, and shipped them to London.''

David thought he understood now. "Then the plane crashed.''

"Yes, and your brother was the only survivor on that plane.''

"They want my heart to keep him alive.''

"Yes.'' Sara nodded. "He's the only one who knows what they discovered.''

"Christ!''

"Somewhere along the way they came up with another idea . . . to produce income.'' She handed him several pages from the printout. "This.''

"What is it?''

"Look at pages fifty-three and fifty-four.''

He searched through the folded sheets. Page fifty-three was headed: HAHNEMANN SUBJECTS. Below it was a numbered list of names in alphabetical order followed by a date, case number and citizenship. There were one hundred and fifty-two names on the first page, two hundred and eleven on the next. He scanned the pages. Several of the names he recognized—heads of state, politicians, actors, fashion designers, monarchs, attorneys, sheiks, college presidents, athletes, businessmen, journalists. They were from everywhere—England, United States, Russia, Japan, Australia, Brazil, China, Israel . . .

David looked up at Sara anxiously. "What *is* this?"

"A very select group of people," she said. "They're sequelas too. A very elite, very secret club of rich guinea pigs. They're people who have paid a great deal of money to be included in this project."

He looked at the list again. "These people have had a tumor implanted in their brains?"

"You're getting smarter all the time."

"Holy—Why?"

"Why? Staying young. What do you think we've been talking about, David? This Hahnemann procedure cuts the aging process in half. It makes them more productive. A lot of people find that important. So far over three hundred and fifty."

"They're nuts."

"They consider it worth whatever risk is involved. What would *you* give to be thirty when you're sixty. Imagine what that might mean to a senator or a prime minister? Just believing that they'd be more productive is reason enough for some of these people. Vanity doesn't know national boundaries."

David studied the pages again. He found his brother's name.

TOWNSEND, STUART P. MAR 1981—NO. 2-1450—AMERICAN.

"If your brother dies then Euromedic's most prized secret goes with him."

"All those people are dying?"

"No, not yet. But it's why they're in a panic. They didn't make this available to the elite group until about three years ago. If Euromedic doesn't save your brother then they *will* start dying and all hell's going to break loose. In the meantime, psychiatric wards like Weeksbriar are going to be taking in new patients."

"Psychiatric wards?"

"Oh, I forgot—" Sara tapped the printout. "That's in there too. Euromedic is hiding all its mistakes in psychiatric facilities. When a Hahnemann turns up sick, they just stick him in a place like Weeksbriar."

"That's who those old men were!"

"The people getting ill now are the early test cases." She nodded at the file. "Franklin was one of them. That's how they had such quick access to a body. He died at Brentwood the night before they kidnapped you."

"He was already dead?"

"They didn't have to kill him. Why should they kill anybody—they already had bodies of these sequela cases stacking up. Franklin died of aortic valve incompetence brought on by acute spastic cerebrospinal paraplegia."

"Cerebro—?"

"Syphilis. His heart failed from a supplementary action of the disease. I don't know if he really had syphilis but it explains why he'd be admitted to a neuropsychiatric hospital like Brentwood. Syphilis attacks the brain." Sara leaned back in her chair. She rubbed her neck. "Anyway, that's what this has all been about. I don't know what we can do about it, but at least you know why you're here." Sara stood up. "I think I'll have that coffee now, Dalton."

"You left something out," Wilkie said. "I think David deserves to know everything."

Sara shrugged it off. "You tell him." She walked to the coffee maker. "I'm tired of talking. Anyway, what difference does it make?"

David turned toward Wilkie. "What?"

"Part of the grand plan, before it all turned to shit." Wilkie moved to one of the console chairs. He massaged his stump. "Euromedic ranked everyone who works for them as candidates for this operation of theirs. It was supposed to be an honor." He nodded at the file before David. "It's in there somewhere, toward the back . . . ranked by priority."

David stiffened. "And?"

"Sara's one of them," Wilkie said. "She was number twelve."

"God . . . damn!"

"Watch your language," Sara said. "You're in the presence of a high-ranking lady."

"What about the kid in Kenya?" David said. "The first guinea pig? What happened to him? I mean, he must have died before Hahnemann. How come that didn't alert them?"

Sara stirred a spoonful of sugar into her coffee. "I guess if there's any justice in all this, it's that boy." She gave him a grim smile. "Nothing happened to him. He didn't get sick. He's fine. He's the only person who was ever treated with METHYD-9 who actually had congenital progeria. Everyone else had the disease artificially induced." She looked up at David. "How about that?"

"Crazy," David said. He shook his head. "We're going to have to do something about these crazy doctors."

"Like what?"

David turned the pages of the printout. He stared at the words, thinking not reading. He had never killed anything in his life. He looked at Sara. "Like make sure my brother dies."

FIFTY-SEVEN

AMBULANCE STATION.
11:15 P.M.

MORAVEC SHADED his eyes from the headlights of the bus as it hissed to a stop at the emergency entrance. He'd been waiting fifteen minutes in this whipping wind and he was freezing. Weeksbriar's hospital facility was located behind the research institute, facing west—where the wind and snow and cold were coming from. His coattails flapped in a swirl of wind as he crunched over hardened snow to the bus's side door. It opened and a male nurse helped him inside.

"You're late," Moravec said, stamping his feet. "You should have been here ten minutes ago. Where's Dr. Graves?" He took off his hat and beat the snow off against his coat.

"We had to wait behind a snowplow on the highway. It delayed—"

"Never mind. Where's Dr. Graves?"

"Dr. Graves is in the surgery compartment."

"Surgery . . ." Moravec looked up sharply. "Townsend isn't—"

"Oh, no sir. The patient is still alive, but—"

"Show me where."

Moravec followed him through a door to a compartment filled with monitoring equipment. Two nurses were seated at a console that displayed vital signs on a CRT screen. They were dressed in green surgical suits; one wore a microphone and spoke into it, reading data from the screen.

Graves and a nurse were in the compartment at the rear of the bus. Moravec could see him through the glass partition. He was bent over an open ICP. He moved to the partition and motioned for Graves to come out. He could see the face of the man on the cart. He'd never seen Stuart Townsend before, but he'd seen that face. It was David Townsend to a T—twenty years from now.

"What's he doing?" Moravec asked the male nurse.

"Verapamil injection," the nurse said. "The heartbeat was too fast. He was throwing PVCs all over the place. Verapamil will settle him down."

"How bad is he?"

The nurse shrugged. "Pretty bad, I think."

I should have expected that, Moravec thought. He looked at Graves again, who nodded to him. Moravec paced in what little room there was in the compartment, pulling at the brim of his hat. One of the nurses stood to adjust the light intensity on the EEG monitor and Moravec stepped back to give her room, leaning against one of the two remaining pods. He glanced down through the plastic lid into the gray face of Dr. Ian McPhearson. He was covered with a green sheet to his chin. A pair of shoes and a tie had been placed at the foot of the capsule.

Graves came out of the compartment, patting a cloth to his forehead. He looked grim. "Dr. Moravec?"

"Yes." Moravec nodded anxiously toward the partition. "The patient?"

"Atrial flutter . . . arrhythmia." The surgeon shook his head. "It's starting, I'm afraid. He's been too long on epinephrine. The basal metabolism is out of balance." Graves patted the cloth on his large neck. The sweat ring around his collar extended to the middle of his chest.

"And?"

"He'll be dead inside thirty minutes unless we begin now. Where's the donor patient?"

"Now?"

"He could arrest any moment," Graves said. "He's

gotten progressively worse since we left AirMore. There's been a sudden drop in his pulse and respiration is bad. There isn't much time."

Moravec nodded. "Yes, of course. As soon as you're set up in the OR."

"Where is it?"

"Level three. It's been ready since this morning. The surgical team is there now, waiting. Have your driver pull into the emergency bay. The attendants will help your people make the move. The freight elevator is being held for you. All you have to do is get Townsend prepped and into the OR."

"He is prepped."

"What about transferring him onto the surgical table?"

"That *is* a surgical table," Graves said, trying to be patient. "Dr. Townsend is completely ready for surgery. We will move him and the monitoring equipment at the same time. The unit was built for emergencies like this." He glanced back through the partition at Townsend's enclosed body. "When the patient is in the OR we will remove the shield and the operation can begin immediately. The only thing I need, sir, is the donor."

Moravec glanced at his watch. "Then you'd better get moving. The donor has been prepped. She's waiting for you now."

FIFTY-EIGHT

COMPUTER CENTER. 11:20 P.M.

TOWNSEND SAT staring at a computer screen. "I don't know what," David said. He'd been mesmerized by the blinking cursor. "But we have to do something. Somebody has to. It might as well be us. We have to tell the people who will end this nightmare, the people who *can* end it."

"Tell who?" Sara said. "Who's going to believe it? Nobody's going to believe a story like this. I wouldn't believe it."

"Somebody will."

"You still don't have the slightest idea what Euromedic is, do you? Or who belongs to it? My God, there are a half-dozen Nobel laureates on staff from biophysics to microbiology. You think you can challenge that kind of power? Who do you want to tell? The police? Your congressman? The AMA? Why, they'd laugh in our faces. Then *they'd* put us away."

"I don't think so. Who do you think they're afraid of?"

"Afraid of? Euromedic? Don't kid yourself."

"They're scared, all right, down to their socks they're scared. But it's not the cops or the government or the AMA or you and me. Why do you think they've got all those people in psychiatric hospitals? Just to give them a nice warm place to die? Hell, Euromedic can't kill them and they can't let them go. They're too valuable as guinea pigs." Townsend held up the Hahnemann file. "This medical razzle-dazzle castle of cards would collapse on itself if anyone found out what they're really doing here." He gave her a wicked smile. "And I know how to do it."

"*You* do?"

"All we have to do is introduce these Hahnemanns—" he tapped his finger on the folder—"to *those* Hahnemanns." He nodded at the ceiling.

"The sequelas?" It took a moment for it to register, then she looked at him with delight. "My God, of course!"

"They may not believe *us*, but they can't argue with living, breathing proof. Those people in the psycho ward are their own proof." Townsend turned to Wilkie. "Can you send this data someplace? I mean, call up some data bank and send it to them on the telephone?"

Wilkie nodded. "Could, I guess."

"Do you have to have permission to go through Weeksbriar's switchboard?"

"Hell, no. CC has its own telecommunication line— dedicated to computer use only. Can't make a regular phone call, but I can communicate with a data base as long as it's in the United States."

"Could you send a copy of those files out? Someplace safe? Someplace Euromedic doesn't own or have access to?"

"I don't think a place like that exists."

"C'mon, Wilkie. There has to be someplace."

Wilkie scratched his beard. "Well, there's Infodata in Virginia. It's a subscriber-access data base. Mostly people with personal computers use it to store data files that their systems are too small to handle. I used it to play computer adventure games on my Apple at home." He looked sheepishly at Sara. "They won't let me play games on CC."

"Will it be safe there?"

"Safe from Euromedic?" Wilkie shrugged. "Good question."

"Send it," Townsend insisted. "We'll just have to take the chance."

"Now?"

366

"You got something else to do?"

Wilkie pulled himself up to the terminal. "I can do it. But it may take a while. We're talking about some very long files."

"You're the resident computer genius. Just send them to a place where we can get at them later. Those computer records are part of the proof. We can still beat them, Sara."

Wilkie turned in his chair. "There's just one thing."

"Yeah?"

"The only time we send data out of here is when we're communicating with the MAG network. It's always been at the direction of the Weeksbriar chief of staff."

"So?"

"So this is technically an unapproved transmission."

"Nobody can cut us off, can they?"

"No, but my guess is that somebody's going to know it."

"So, let them know," David said. "They can't shut us off and they can't get in here to stop us. We'll drive 'em crazy."

Wilkie turned back to the terminals. "I wish my mother could see this." Then he began sending orders to the computer.

FIFTY-NINE

OPERATING ROOM 1.
11:45 P.M.

MORAVEC WATCHED the scrub nurses wheel Townsend out of the prep room into OR-1. They had removed the shield and transferred him to a table. Graves had changed his mind about using the ICP to operate. He was not a tall man and with all the monitoring equipment on the pod it couldn't be lowered to a comfortable level for him to operate.

In OR-2 the removal team was ready. Carla Jergenson lay under the bright surgery light still encased in the life-support pod.

Moravec waited for Graves. The rotund doctor, dressed in greens, seemed like a different man under the surgical mask. He was not at all nervous. He checked the equipment, motioned to the anesthesiologist, then moved to the patient, his gloved hands held up. His glance touched Moravec and he nodded. As Moravec left the room he heard Dr. Graves say, "Shall we begin, ladies and gentlemen? Scalpel, please."

Moravec brushed past the attendants in the hall and found a house phone. The operation had finally begun. Saving Stuart Townsend was the job he'd been appointed to, and he was seeing to that the best way he knew. Haldern was wrong about sacrifices for the good of all. What he'd seen in the last two days was evidence that Haldern was wrong. Five minutes in Ellis's pod room proved it. Stuart Townsend didn't need to be saved; he needed to be helped. And David Townsend needed to be saved.

Moravec jiggled the phone connection. He waited another moment before he realized the phone wasn't working. He searched the corridors until he found another phone. It didn't work either. He took the stairs to the first floor and hurried to the admitting office.

"I need to use your phone," he said to the duty nurse. When he picked up the receiver there was no dial tone. "What's the matter with these phones?"

The nurse listened, dialed, shrugged. "I don't know. It was working half an hour ago."

"How can I get the security office?"

She reached under the counter and brought up a red telephone. "Straight line."

Moravec picked it up.

"Security."

"This is Dr. Moravec. Let me speak to Dr. Ellis, please."

"He just left, sir. He's gone to get the key."

"Key?"

"Yes, sir. To the computer center. He said it was time to get the patient."

"Dr. Ellis has a key?"

"Yes, sir—"

"Call his office. Tell him to call me as quickly as—"

"I'm sorry, sir, with the switchboard closed I can't make any calls, just receive them."

"The switchboard is closed?"

"Yes, sir. On account of the evacuation. With that crazy guy in the building, Dr. Ellis didn't want to take any chances."

"My God! Look, when he comes back tell him to call—" Moravec stopped. Ellis couldn't call him. "Just tell him not to go after Townsend," he urged. "Tell him the surgery is already started. We don't need Townsend."

"Who's Townsend?"

Nobody knew who Townsend was, Moravec realized. It was Franklin who had escaped.

"Just tell him not to go into the computer center. All

right? Find him, tell him that. Tell him Dr. Moravec said the surgery is already under way. Can you do that?'' Moravec glanced at his watch. Graves had been operating for five minutes.

"Yes, sir. If I see him I can, but I'm not supposed to leave my—"

Moravec dropped the phone. He hurried into the nearest corridor. Ellis was a fool to bash his way into the computer center. Townsend had a gun. The corridor ended in a junction with another hallway. He turned right, reaching for the elevator button. The button wasn't there. Neither was the elevator.

"Bloody maze!"

He had gone down the wrong corridor and now he was lost. He started back. At the next junction he ran into a black woman pushing a laundry cart.

"Which way to the research side?"

"The what?"

"The research institute! How do I get to it?"

"Ah, which floor?"

"Any bloody floor!"

She pointed the way he'd come. "All the way to the end, I think. Then right."

He started down the corridor at a brisk pace. Halfway he began jogging. He shouldn't have waited until the operation started to call Ellis. Five minutes earlier wouldn't have mattered. Ellis wouldn't have been able to stop the operation then. When he reached the end of the corridor he was out of breath. He turned right and stopped dead. There wasn't a corridor. There was a ladies room. Moravec swung around. The other side of the hall was a men's room.

"Damn!"

He started back. The corridor seemed to stretch out a mile. He started running.

SIXTY

ELLIS'S OFFICE. 11:50 P.M.

THE PRINTER was typing and shifting at sixty characters per second when Dr. Jonathan Ellis entered his office. The supply of paper from the box beneath the printer stand had been pulled through the tractor feed and lay in a pile of continuous pages on the floor. The plastic daisywheel spun in a whirling blur, slapping out letters on the paperless platen.

"What the hell!"

Ellis moved quickly to the machine. The printer in his office was his own idea. He'd had it installed as a check on information that went to MAG Central. Whenever CC transmitted anything out of Weeksbriar, he wanted to have a hard copy of it. Then, if there ever was any question, he had proof of exactly what was sent. The procedure required a lot of paper, but in the long run it was worth the space required to store the printouts. The trouble was, nothing was supposed to be going to MAG tonight.

Ellis switched off the printer. His breath caught when he read the screen on his desk-top computer.

```
***NOTICE***
TELECOMMUNICATION DATA PORT
OPENED WITHOUT COS AUTHORIZATION.
TIME/DAY 23 HRS 27 MIN 20 SEC/SUNDAY
PLEASE REPORT THIS VIOLATION TO THE WKSBR COS OR SYS MGR
```

```
ILLEGAL TRANSMISSION:  23:27:33  SOURCE:  RM 6  ACCESSED:  HAHNMAN
ILLEGAL TRANSMISSION:  23:29:12  SOURCE:  RM 6  ACCESSED:  HAHNMAN
ILLEGAL TRANSMISSION:  23:30:04  SOURCE:  RM 6  ACCESSED:  HAHNMAN
ILLEGAL TRANSMISSION:  23:32:47  SOURCE:  RM 6  ACCESSED:  HAHNMAN
ILLEGAL TRANSMISSION:  23:34:25  SOURCE:  RM 6  ACCESSED:  HAHNMAN
ILLEGAL TRANSMISSION:  23:37:15  SOURCE:  RM 6  ACCESSED:  HAHNMAN
ILLEGAL TRANSMISSION:  23:39:28  SOURCE:  RM 6  ACCESSED:  HAHNMAN
ILLEGAL TRANSMISSION:  23:41:00  SOURCE:  RM 6  ACCESSED:  HAHNMAN
ILLEGAL TRANSMISSION:  23:42:52  SOURCE:  RM 6  ACCESSED:  HAHNMAN
ILLEGAL TRANSMISSION:  23:44:31  SOURCE:  RM 6  ACCESSED:  HAHNMAN
ILLEGAL TRANSMISSION:  23:46:22  SOURCE:  RM 6  ACCESSED:  HAHNMAN
ILLEGAL TRANSMISSION:  23:47:19  SOURCE:  RM 6  ACCESSED:  HAHNMAN
ILLEGAL TRANSMISSION:  23:49:43  SOURCE:  RM 6  ACCESSED:  HAHNMAN
```

Someone was sending data out of Weeksbriar. The accessed file was Hahnemann. The computer recorded another transmission before Ellis realized that room six was the computer center.

"Jesus Christ!"

Townsend was in his files. Ellis punched the clear key and the screen went blank. He had to erase everything before any more went out. He entered his password in answer to the log-on prompt and grabbed a handful of pages from the floor while he waited for the computer to acknowledge. The heading at the top of all the pages was the same.

```
HAHNEMANN PROJECT -RESTRICTED ACCES-
```

He couldn't believe his eyes. When he looked at the monitor the situation wasn't any better. The screen cursor was blinking in the top left corner. Below it was the error message.

```
UNRECOGNIZED LOG-ON SIGNATURE
FIRST OFFENSE
CHECK YOUR SPELLING, PLEASE
```

How many times had he ever misspelled Margaret? He started again, typing deliberately with one finger. M-A-R-

372

G-A-R-E-T. The terminal screen acknowledged the entry then flashed another error message.

UNRECOGNIZED LOG-ON SIGNATURE
SECOND OFFENSE
THE ENTRY CODE "MARGARET" IS NOT A RECOGNIZED SIGNATURE IN THIS SYSTEM. USER PLEASE NOTE THAT THIRD OFFENSE ERRORS ARE LOGGED AND TIME-DATED AND THE TERMINAL POSITION REPORTED TO THE SYSTEM MANAGER. IF YOU REQUIRE ASSISTANCE PLEASE CALL CC SECTION AT EXT. 302 OR 303.

Ellis sat up straight in his chair. He hadn't misspelled it this time. What the hell did it mean—Margaret wasn't a recognized signature? What was wrong with the goddamn machine! He addressed the computer once more.

REQUEST VERIFICATION OF LOG-ON SIGNATURE "MARGARET" FOR SYSTEM USER ELLIS, J.

The response came in seconds.

SRCRDS VERIFICATION:
THE SIGNATURE "MARGARET" DOES NOT EXIST IN THIS SYSTEM. ELLIS, J. IS A PRIVILEGED SYSTEM WITH UNIVERSAL CLASSIFICATION. FURTHER ATTEMPTS TO REQUEST INFORMATION CONCERNING THIS USER ARE ILLEGAL AND WILL RESULT IN STATION TERMINAL SHUTDOWN. THIS VERIFICATION EXCHANGE HAS BEEN LOGGED AND NOTED. TIME/DAY 23:52:02/SUNDAY LOG ENTRY NO. 016

Ellis could only stare at the words. DOES NOT EXIST burned into his brain. An icy sensation at the back of his neck stiffened his hairs. The computer was telling him—*him*—Jonathan Ellis, chief of staff of the Weeksbriar Research Institute, that he didn't have access. It had denied his universal log-on. Then he realized that nothing was wrong with the computer. It was only doing what it was instructed to do.

It meant the Hahnemann file wasn't safe.

He slammed his fist into the keyboard, killing the display

monitor. *"I'm* Ellis!" The chief of staff screamed at the machine. "I'm goddamn Johathan Ellis!"

Ellis fumbled with the key in the lock of his bottom drawer and jerked it open. He found the plastic cylinder with the red electronic key and stuffed it in his pocket, knocking over his chair as he scrambled out of his office.

It meant nothing was safe.

SIXTY-ONE

11:55 P.M.

MORAVEC'S CHEST was heaving when he pushed open the door to Ellis's office. His coat and tie were somewhere in one of the corridors where he'd thrown them off. He'd expected an argument from Ellis, who would be in a rage, but the operation was by now committed. One doesn't stop heart transplantation surgery to change donors, he wanted to tell Ellis. He'd been thinking exactly how to word it while he ran through the corridors. But Ellis wasn't in his office.

Moravec tried the phone, hoping for a miracle. When he set it back down he noticed the printout pages on the floor. He held up a string of pages, scanning through them. They were all from the Hahnemann file.

"Ellis!" He tossed his head back, eyes closed. "I told you, you bloody fool!" Moravec wanted to cry out his anger, but there wasn't time. He didn't know who was more dangerous now—Townsend or Ellis.

He pushed himself to the hall. The security office was the next floor down.

"Hello? Hello?"

The security office was empty, not a single guard on duty. Moravec looked at the bank of monitor screens. All the halls were quiet and empty.

He stood in the middle of the corridor. "Guard! Is anybody here? *Anybody?*" The only answer was the echo of his voice. He went back to the monitors. They had all changed together. More empty halls. None panned the sublevel. There were no cameras in the basement. Then Moravec realized Ellis had gone to get Townsend and had taken an army with him. Cameras would not record the massacre.

He had to stop it.

Moravec turned too quickly toward the door. He banged his knee hard against a corner of the console. He winced, stooping down to grab his leg. He saw the chart when his eyes cleared. It was taped to the corner of the dispatcher's desk. He almost didn't recognize it for what it was.

Weeksbriar Circuit Breaker Schematic
Maintenance Room S-112

It was a diagram of the entire institution's electrical plant with floor and lab designations coded breaker by breaker. At the bottom of the chart was the section for the sublevel. CC was breaker number eighty-seven.

Moravec ripped the chart off the desk. He hobbled to the legend on the wall that identified the location of every room in the building. S-112 was on the sublevel, beside the elevators. He careened into the hall. The stairway that led to the basement was around the corner.

Perpiration saturated Ellis's smock despite the cold of the basement. He was standing before the large gray vault door. Not a sound penetrated Central Computer's several inches of steel.

Ellis held his hand up, indicating quiet to the guards behind him, with their guns unholstered. Ellis wiped his hands on his smock and took a gun from his pocket. The weapon was officially registered to the chief of security, who kept it in a desk drawer. The hand grip was cold to his touch. From his breast pocket he withdrew the red stainless steel key and inserted the prongs into the panel lock.

"Easy as pie," he said to himself.

His watch showed ten seconds to midnight. Ellis counted off the seconds in his head.

Ten, nine . . .
He twisted the key slowly clockwise.
—six, five . . .
There was a click as the electronic lock disengaged.
—three, two . . .
He gave the door a push and it swung open.
—one . . .
Easy as pie.

MONDAY
JANUARY 3

SIXTY-TWO

MIDNIGHT

DAVID AND SARA were standing behind Wilkie's chair,
watching him type commands. As each file buffer at the
Virginia data base filled to capacity with Hahnemann
evidence, he closed the file, gave it a name and opened a
new file. The process took about two minutes per file. He
was naming them sequentially—NOTLAD 1, NOTLAD 2,
NOTLAD 3 . . .

The computer was up to NOTLAD 14 when the bell rang.

David wheeled around as the door opened. He saw Ellis
and behind him a dozen guards. All of them had guns.

"Hold it right there, cowboy." Ellis had a wild look in
his eyes.

Sara gasped when she saw him.

Ellis made a movement with the gun. "Move over there,
doctor."

"Dr. Ellis—"

"Move!"

Sara took a step to her right.

"You think you're so clever, don't you?" Ellis was
talking to David. The gun was pointed at his chest. "Well,
you're not so fucking clever, Townsend."

"Just take it easy now," David said. Ellis was six or
seven feet away.

"Where's the gun you took from the guard?"

David nodded at the file drawer. "In there. We didn't
want to—"

"Where are you sending my documents?" Ellis was

sweating profusely. A bead of perspiration dripped off his nose. "Where?"

David realized he was standing directly in front of Wilkie's chair, shielding the system manager from Ellis's view. He wasn't sure if that was good or bad for Wilkie. Not that it mattered. The gun was aimed at him.

"Documents?"

"Don't screw with me!" Ellis screamed. Something seemed to snap in him. "How did you change Margaret!" He looked at the terminals. His face contorted when he saw the printouts stacked on the console. His fingers tightened on the gun. The hammer cock was a distinct click.

At the sound, one of the guards said, "Dr. Ellis . . . ?"

"Where are my files?"

Nobody had a chance to answer. The overhead lights flickered. Then the alternate fluorescent ceiling panels went dark. An amber light at each computer console started flashing. A deafening bell went off nearby.

Ellis's head jerked up, startled. "What is—"

Then the rest of the lights went out. The computer consoles died with a diminishing hum, the screens fading to black in a pinprick of light.

Wilkie kicked back in his chair, ramming into David, who was propelled into the darkness. The weapon, when it went off, looked like an explosion, a brilliant shooting star. It was a flash from four or five feet away and he couldn't get out of the way. He was already moving, stumbling sideways, but he wasn't as fast as the bullet. The jolt knocked him reeling into and over a printer stand. He fell on his face, on the bony part of his right cheekbone. He heard another gunshot. Sara screamed. Then there were three shots close together. With each shot there were brilliant bursts of light, then darkness. Flash-dark, flash-dark, flash-dark. Fast. Somewhere in it he saw Wilkie. And the bell, loud, insistent. Then the ringing stopped, and he heard animals howling. He was on his back when the emergency lights came on, wall-mounted battery lights that bathed the room in a yellowish hue. He rolled to his side. The pain in his chest nearly blacked him out. He touched himself and has hand came away wet and sticky. The front of his shirt was squishy.

"David!"

David didn't see where she came from. All of a sudden she was beside him, on her knees. Everything was hazy.

"He . . . shot me." He tried not to take deep breaths. He could feel the blood going out. "Damn . . ." Pain squashed his chest when she pushed him on his back. "What's . . . that . . . yelping?"

"Zoo Lab . . . the bell fright—oh, God!" She sucked in her breath, staring at his chest. "Dalton!" The bearded man's face came into view over her shoulder. David bent down, looking where Sara was opening the shirt. He made a face.

"Oh, God—Dalton!"

David started to look, then changed his mind. He was breathing in grunts. He was very warm. He could feel himself sweating.

"We've got to get him to a hospital!"

He felt her hand on his head. Somewhere animals were going crazy.

"Where's . . ." It was a monumental effort to get the words out. " . . . Ellis?" He had to open his eyes wide to keep her in focus. The fire in his chest was spreading.

"Don't talk, David. Please."

She said something else, but he didn't hear it. Then the lights came back on, and hurt his eyes because he was looking straight up at the ceiling. He tried to keep his concentration on Sara. Her face swam in and out of his vision. She was talking fast, and crying, but he couldn't hear a word. Probably just as well. She talked too much anyway. Then he started losing pieces of time. Blank spots. He didn't hurt so much in the blank spots, then he'd have a stab of pain and see things. Not much of it made sense.

He saw people in blue uniforms. They all had frightened

faces. He didn't know what they had to be frightened of, he was the one shot. He saw Wilkie's face. It was angry. He was shouting, but David couldn't hear anything because of the damned dogs.

He saw another familiar face. It took a minute to place it. He finally remembered. The guy in the herringbone coat. They guy from Niagara. Moravec. He didn't look very happy either.

Then there were more faces. People in white coats. He didn't recognize any of them.

David felt himself floating and that hurt most of all. He was up in the air and it hurt like hell. He opened his eyes and saw someone below him sitting against the wall, feet and arms splayed out. He sort of looked like Ellis except there was something wrong with his neck. He was wearing a red tie. It was the longest tie David had ever seen. And he just sat there against the wall, staring straight ahead. How did he do that, David wondered, not blink?

Then David felt himself moving. Really moving. He passed in and out of pools of light from overhead fixtures. It must have been a tunnel. A long tunnel. The lights were coming closer and closer and he was getting dizzy. When it started getting darker, he didn't mind at all. The darkness seemed to be closing in around him. The pain was ebbing. That was good. He felt cooler too. He had the sense that he'd been here before. It wasn't so bad, the darkness. And it was getting more comfortable. He didn't even mind the cold so much.

SIXTY-THREE

OPERATING ROOM 1.
12:20 A.M.

A NURSE dropped a stainless steel tray of instruments when Sara burst into the operating room. Her hands and clothes were splattered with Townsend's blood. She took a moment to catch her breath and look around. There was cardiac equipment all over the place and a large operating room staff. She recognized Euromedic's OR hierarchy—two scrub nurses in yellow gowns, two circulating nurses in pink, an orderly in yellow and the anesthesiologist in white. There were three men in surgical greens. Everyone was masked at the operating table except the nurse who had dropped the tray.

"Replace those instruments quickly," someone said.

One of the figures moved from the operating table and Sara saw the patient. His eyelids were taped closed. He had been intubated, the trachea tube extending from his mouth to the ventilator. A heart bypass machine was already taking blood, oxygenating it and sending it back to the patient through clear, narrow tubes. She could see into the chest cavity, actually see the heart beating.

"Clamp that."

Blood spurted across the blue coverlet on Stuart Townsend's chest.

"Higher, please. Good."

"Suction?"

"Here."

Rubber fingers worked between clamps and tubes,

poking, prodding the heart up on its side. Sara recognized the aorta, thick as a hose, at the top. The major arteries had been severed.

"You've already started!"

One of the surgeons, the fat one, glanced up over his mask. "What's that woman doing in here? Ger her out."

Before the orderly could reach her, the door to the adjoining OR pushed open and a nurse appeared. "Donor's ready."

The fat surgeon nodded. He didn't look up. "Two minutes."

Sara stared bewildered at the surgeons. "*What* donor?"

"Get that woman out of here! This is an operating room."

There was a rumbling in the corridor. Something on wheels was coming at a hundred miles an hour. People were running, panting.

"You'd better get her out of here," said the orderly.

Sara stepped into the hall as the ICP sped past her. It crashed through the double doors of the room next door, wheeled by two sweating attendants. Lagging behind came Moravec.

"I told you the *prep* room," he said, panting.

"I—"

"C'mon." He pulled her by the arm into the room where they had just delivered David. The compress bandages she had applied to his wound were soaked with blood.

"He's losing blood fast," Moravec said. "I told you to get blood." He pointed to a portable supply bin that was marked AIRMORE. "In there. Start an IV. Quickly."

Sara obeyed. Moravec was slapping David's arm and pinching it when she had the IV ready. "I can't find the vein," Moravec said. He made several insertions with a needle. "Blood loss has collapsed the vein."

"What do you want me to do?" Blood was rolling down David's side, saturating the sheet.

"Turn his head and hold it. I'll have to go into the jugular."

Sara held David's head. His skin was clammy. He was bleeding from the nose. When he exhaled, blood trickled from a nostril. She looked at his chest. The blood streaming out had bubbles in it.

"Oh, Jesus! His lung is punctured."

Moravec inserted the IV needle in David's neck. "I know. Tape his head down."

"Why are you doing this?" Sara said. "Why are you helping us?"

Moravec held the IV bag high. "Tape his head down or he'll rip out the needle."

Sara wound tape over David's forehead and around the edge of the cart. In the next room she heard someone call for lidocaine.

"What's going on in there?"

"Exactly what you think, Dr. Mills," Moravec said. "Have you ever assisted in emergency surgery?"

"No."

"You're going to assist in one now. Get a stand for this bag, then scrub up." He nodded at a stainless steel sink. "Over there. There are gloves in that cabinet."

"What are you going to do?"

"Townsend is hemorrhaging. I'm going to open him, stop the bleeding until help arrives."

"Help?"

"Yes. I called the police from the switchboard."

"You—"

"Hurry, doctor, this man is bleeding to death. And sterilize a surgical kit, you'll find them with the gloves."

Sara found a green surgical gown and tied it around her dress. She washed her hands and arms up to her elbows. Moravec had sponged off David's chest around the wound and painted it with antiseptic. He was laying coverlets when Sara returned with the gloves and instruments.

"Are you a surgeon?"

Moravec looked at her. "I used to be." He handed her a light. "Hold this high."

He made incisions laterally from the bullet's entrance wound, on each side. Sara heard in the operating room, high-pitched beeps.

"What's that?"

"Cardiac alarm," Moravec said. "He's arresting. Hold the light up, please."

A nurse rushed through the swinging door, searching through the cabinet for the plane, then disappeared back into the OR. As the door swung back and forth Sara heard the chief surgeon issuing orders.

"Fibrillating . . ."

"Epinephrine . . . bicarbonate amp . . . quickly . . ."

"Defib, four hundred joules . . ."

"Stand back . . . again . . . stand back . . ."

Moravec glanced up. "Change that IV, doctor." He looked back at Townsend, wiped his forehead with his sleeve.

"How is he?" Sara said.

Moravec blinked back sweat from his eyes. David's lips were blue. "They're doing their best."

"I mean David!"

"I'm trying," Moravec said. "I'm doing the best I can."

Police and firemen arrived. There were six squad cars, a pumper and hook and ladder at the emergency entrance. Then two ambulances with a surgeon and trauma team. Some sheriff's deputies showed up, but the place was already crowded.

Sara let the team of paramedics in.

"What have we got here?" the police surgeon said. He was tying on a mask.

"Gunshot trauma," Sara said. "Chest."

"Are you a surgeon?"

388

Sara shook her head, nodded to Moravec. "No, but he is."

The police surgeon went to Moravec's side. "Holy shit!" To his partner he said, "Whole blood, stat. Got a heavy bleeder here . . and ruptured lung."

"Can you keep him alive?" Sara said.

He snapped on a pair of rubber gloves. "It's what we do, lady, if we can."

When the room crammed up Sara moved away. Moravec was still in charge—he was the surgeon—but she had done everything she could do. Before she left she glanced at the medic for some sign. He shrugged.

A policeman took her to an empty examining room and gave her a cigarette. She was there a long time. Nobody knew exactly what to do with her. She sat down and smoked the cigarette. Her first in three days. She was tired beyond herself. She tried not to think. Just concentrate on the cigarette. Then her fingers began to shake and she couldn't stop them. She ground out the cigarette. Then she cried.

The detective who came to see her was named Guillo. He was about forty-five and wore bifocal glasses that constantly slid down his nose, so that he was always peering over them. It was four in the morning by the clock on the wall and he didn't look like a man who usually was up that late. She asked if the surgery was over, but he didn't answer.

"Would you like some coffee, doctor?"

"What happened?" Sara asked.

Guillo frowned.

"In the OR?"

"Oh." He shrugged. "I don't know."

"It should be over by now."

The detective sat down. "I need some answers, doctor." He wasn't friendly or unfriendly.

"Please, tell me what's happened. Do you know anything? I have to know what's happened to Townsend!"

Guillo ran his hand through his hair. "Look, doctor, I'm just a cop, okay? I need some answers. Crazy things been going on around here."

Sara nodded. "No kidding."

"You work at this place, right?"

"I used to, yes."

"You want a lawyer?"

She hadn't thought about that. She shook her head. "It doesn't make any difference." She looked at the clock.

"It *makes* a difference," he said. "Do you want a lawyer?"

Sara shook her head.

"Yes or no, doctor."

"No."

"Okay. Now . . . what's been going on here?"

"I couldn't explain it to you in a thousand years."

Guillo gave her an easy smile. "Sure you can, doctor. You want a cigarette?"

"No."

"I guess you know this fella named—" he checked a scrap of paper "—Mor-a-vec?"

"I know who he is, yes."

"Works for an outfit called Euromedic."

Sara smiled wearily. "Yeah. We *all* work for Euromedic." She leaned forward on the table.

"And Ellis? You knew him too, right?"

"One of the guards shot him . . . in the dark," Sara said. "Doctor Ellis shot Townsend."

"Yeah, I already talked to the guards. Accidental, they said. Shooting Ellis, I mean."

"I don't know. It was dark."

Guillo pushed his glasses back. He blew his nose on a wrinkled handkerchief. "I've been talking to a fella named—" he checked his paper again "—Wilkie. I guess you know him too? Wilkie?"

"Yes, of course."

"He was telling me about some file. Handa-man?"

390

"Hahnemann."

Sara looked into his face. "Dalton told you about it?" She didn't know why she was so surprised.

"What is it?"

"It's a computer file."

"What computer?"

"This one . . . here at Weeksbriar. Did he tell you what it was?"

The detective moved his glasses again. "Kept babbling about Virginia. Transmitting to some computer place. It didn't mean much to me. I thought you could—"

"Will you stop about that now! I want to know about Townsend. I want to know if he's all right. I have to know!"

Guillo took off his glasses and rubbed his eyes. He blinked at Sara, then sighed and rapped on the door. "I'll be back in a minute." He told someone to bring her coffee but she was too nervous to drink it. Her stomach was in knots. If David was dead . . . she pushed it out of her mind. He wasn't dead. He *wasn't!*

In a few minutes, Guillo returned. Sara shot up from her chair. She was exhausted and the movement made her dizzy. She held onto the chair for support.

"They're all finished in there," he said. He didn't look her in the eye.

"What happened?" All she could get out was a whisper.

"The guy in the operating room—" Guillo looked at her. "He died."

"Which one?" Sara's fingers tightened on the back of the chair.

The detective looked at his slip of paper. He licked his lips. "Townsend," he said.

"Christ—which Townsend? There were *two* operations! *Which Townsend died?*"

Guillo glanced up at her with a quizzical expression. "Which?" he said. He frowned and pushed his glasses back. He stared at her *"Which?"*

SIXTY-FOUR

TOWNSEND'S ROOM. 6:30 A.M.

"HE'S COMING out, I think."

"Is he?"

"Yes. Look."

Townsend came awake slowly. The first thing he saw was a concerned female face. Then he saw the IV stand and the plastic bag of clear liquid connecting a tube to his arm. There was a dull pain in his chest. He knew not to move. His vision went in and out of focus. Someone bent over him.

"I don't think he's quite awake yet."

"He's been under anesthesia for a long time."

He couldn't place himself. He didn't know where he was and that frightened him. The light in the room was very bright and he squinted against it.

"He's light sensitive."

"That's normal. It'll pass in a little while."

"Does he know where he is?"

"Give him a minute."

He tried to remember back to the last time he was awake. When he remembered, the confusion, the screaming, he was even more frightened. He felt a hand on his head. It was cool. He closed his eyes again.

"He's dropping off."

"No, it's the light. Give him a minute."

The hand felt good. After a minute he opened his eyes again. His vision was much clearer despite the brightness.

He saw the face of the woman over him. She didn't look familiar.

"Now he's all right," she said. She took her hand away and moved from the bed. For a moment all he could see was the white ceiling.

Then he saw Sara.

She looked terrible, David thought. Her face was splotchy and her green gown was covered with dried blood and her eyes were red and glistening. Then she gave him a smile and tears rolled down her cheeks and she suddenly looked wonderful.

"I love you," she said.

He couldn't move his head. He tried to look around. "Where . . . ?"

"County General," she said. "Don't try to move, David. You've had a major operation . . . but you're going to be fine. Really."

David closed his eyes. When he opened them again he said, "Stuart . . . ?"

She shook her head. "I'm sorry."

"What about . . . files?"

"You should be asleep, David. I shouldn't even be here." She wiped her eyes with a tissue. "I just wanted to see you for a minute. I'll come back again in the morning."

David made his expression into an urgent plea. "Tell me . . . about files."

"Euromedic got them back," she said quietly. "I don't know how. Dalton understands it. It means we don't have any proof." She swallowed; her shoulders moved when she sighed. "They won, but I don't care. I just care about you."

David didn't care either. If the world was ready for Euromedic and its plan for a perfected order of human beings, there was nothing he could do to stop it. He looked into Sara's eyes. He tried to smile. "Meant to ask you . . . before." He had to force the words out. "You ever been . . . to Oklahoma?"

Her eyes squeezed shut and she shook her head. When she looked at him again she was smiling, and crying. He found her hand beside his on the bed and squeezed. Then she cried.

LONDON, EIGHTEEN
MONTHS LATER

IT WAS raining at Gatwick Airport when David and Sara arrived. They had received round trip tickets to London with a brief note:

> The Hahnemann Project is dead. The victory is yours.
> Please come to the wake. Moravec.

A uniformed chauffeur escorted them to a limousine with darkened windows and a green Euromedic logo on the door. Rain danced in sheets as the driver held an umbrella over Sara and helped her inside the long black car. David climbed in after her. Luther Moravec was waiting.

"I wasn't sure that I'd see you again," Moravec said. He held out his hand to David. "Thank you for coming."

"It wasn't my idea to be here," David said. "And we bought our own tickets." He ignored Moravec's proffered hand. Sara had insisted that they come. She said they owed Moravec at least that; he had saved David's life, after all. That was true, of course; but then it wouldn't have needed saving if not for Moravec. "We read about your appointment as director of Euromedic. You're the big boss now. So what do you want with us?"

"Congratulations first, I think," Moravec said. He turned to Sara. "It is still doctor, I hope."

Sara smiled. David wished she hadn't.

"Yes, Dr. Sara Townsend. Research staff, Memorial Hospital, University of Oklahoma College of Medicine."

"I'm happy you haven't given it up . . . your work. You are a very bright young doctor, if you don't mind my saying."

"And alive," David said. He wasn't smiling. "Don't forget alive."

"I don't want to be your enemy, David," Moravec said. "Euromedic is not something evil, please believe that. What happened to you won't happen to anyone again. The Hahnemann experiment is over."

"We're tickled to death to hear that," David said.

Moravec nodded as if he had expected David's cynicism. "I asked you to come because I wanted you to know that Euromedic is prepared to face whatever consequences may be in store as a result of the Hahnemann experiment. Particularly and especially you and—" he nodded to Sara— "Mrs. Townsend."

"Why are *we* so lucky?"

"I think that's obvious," Moravec said. "At least it will be shortly." He tapped his knuckles against the glass partition that separated them from the driver's compartment. The limousine moved away from the curb into the rain.

"I have something for you," Moravec continued. He lifted a briefcase and handed it over.

David opened it. Inside were six thick notebooks in blue plastic folders. "What's this?"

"The history of the Hahnemann project," Moravec said. "Everything is there. Names, dates, objectives . . . everything."

David handed one of the notebooks to Sara and thumbed through another. The table of contents listed the activities of the Johannesburg research team month by month. He saw Stuart's name several times. When he looked at Moravec he was confused. "I don't get it. You're *giving* this to us?"

"I'd like you to read it first. Afterwards, if you still feel the same, you're welcome to do anything with it you like."

Sara looked up from a notebook. "David is in here . . . Weeksbriar . . . the kidnapping . . . ?"

"Especially that, yes."

"This could ruin Euromedic," she said.

"Perhaps, perhaps not. That's the chance I'm taking."

"Why?" David said. "Why now? Why us?"

"I'm giving it to you now because I can . . . now. You, more than anyone else, have the right to be the person to expose it—if that's what you want to do. Euromedic owes you that. So do I. The only way I know to prove to you that Euromedic doesn't do business that way any longer is to give you these files. If you can believe that we've changed then maybe it will convince others. Several hundred very important people are going to begin dying soon. We can't stop that. In the last year and a half we've tried to unravel the enigma of METHYD-9C. We failed. Maybe it's for the best."

"Do you think I *won't* take this to the authorities . . . or a newspaper?" David said. "If you do then you're damned mistaken."

"I just hope you will read it first, David. Maybe you'll see that these were not dangerous people. They were overanxious, even foolish, but not dangerous. They just tried to reach too far, to expedite. It isn't a crime to want to improve the lot of civilization."

"Improve?" David shook his head. "Selective improvement is what they wanted. Euromedic didn't tell the world what they had, did they? They only wanted to improve an elite fraction. We've heard that before, haven't we? A different generation, but the same message. You're wrong, Moravec. Hahnemann, Rennit, my brother, they *were* dangerous. And if you don't see that then you're dangerous too."

"You may be the judge of that. Euromedic is doing things differently now. The Hahnemann project had been terminated. The Johannesburg lab is closed. I've ended some of the information gathering practices. We're truly a medical research establishment now. If we survive we'll continue on that course."

"And what about the next director? And the one after that? Do you speak for them too?"

Moravec didn't answer but glanced up as the limousine stopped. Through the rain-blurred window he saw Grosvenor House. "Your hotel," he said. "You may stay as long or as briefly as you like. You are my guests in London. You needn't contact me again if you don't wish to. Whatever you decide—"

"We don't need any help in making decisions," David said. He reached for the door. "And we'll pay our own way."

"Please—" Moravec reached across Sara to touch David's arm. "I have just one question before you go. It's very important to me how you answer it." He looked at Sara. "Both of you."

"What is it?" Sara said.

"If there were someone to whom you'd dedicated your life, and you discovered that person were permanently damaged by some illness over which you had no control— would you permit, if it were in your power, to allow that person to participate in an experiment that would temporarily restore her to full health even if it shortened her life?"

"Euromedic isn't a person," Sara said. "You can't compare the life of a corporation and a person on the same scale."

"Life and death are real in either case," Moravec said. "What would you do?"

David helped Sara out of the limousine. At the desk he saw a copy of the London *Times*. A front page story announced:

EUROPEAN MINISTER SUCCUMBS
TO MYSTERIOUS ILLNESS

David folded the newspaper and tucked it under his arm as they walked to the elevator. "It's started," he said.

"I saw." Sara took his arm. "What are we going to do?"

David stared at the light on the elevator indicator as it moved across the row of floor numbers. The weight of Moravec's briefcase was heavy in his left hand.

"David?"

"I don't know." He switched the briefcase to his other hand as the elevator doors opened. "I don't know."

The rain had stopped when Moravec arrived home. There was an aroma of pastry in the house. From the den came the *plink-plink* of piano keys. He glanced in. Christina was seated before the baby grand with Michael at her side, his diaper sagging around his knees.

"Hi, daddy. I'm teaching Michael his do-re-me's."

"Where's mum?"

"Baking."

The radio was playing in the kitchen. Connie was stirring dough with a wooden spoon but set it aside when she saw Moravec. She came to him, kissed him. She was as lovely as ever.

"They came, didn't they—David and Sara Townsend?"

Moravec nodded.

"You gave them the project notes too?"

"Yes."

"Did you ask them?"

"Yes."

"What did they say?"

Moravec held her close, then pulled back slightly.

"It wasn't a question they knew how to answer," he said.

Then he touched the skin around her eyes. The bruise was gone, the discoloration fading almost to yellow on her cheekbone. Tomorrow it wouldn't even show.

BLOCKBUSTER FICTION FROM PINNACLE BOOKS!

THE FINAL VOYAGE OF
THE S.S.N. SKATE   (17-157, $3.95)
by Stephen Cassell
The "leper" of the U.S. Pacific Fleet, SSN 578 nuclear attack sub SKATE, has one final mission to perform — an impossible act of piracy that will pit the underwater deathtrap and its inexperienced crew against the combined might of the Soviet Navy's finest!

QUEENS GATE RECKONING   (17-164, $3.95)
by Lewis Purdue
Only a wounded CIA operative and a defecting Soviet ballerina stand in the way of a vast consortium of treason that speeds toward the hour of mankind's ultimate reckoning! From the best-selling author of THE LINZ TESTAMENT.

FAREWELL TO RUSSIA   (17-165, $4.50)
by Richard Hugo
A KGB agent must race against time to infiltrate the confines of U.S. nuclear technology after a terrifying accident threatens to unleash unmitigated devastation!

THE NICODEMUS CODE   (17-133, $3.95)
by Graham N. Smith and Donna Smith
A two-thousand-year-old parchment has been unearthed, unleashing a terrifying conspiracy unlike any the world has previously known, one that threatens the life of the Pope himself, and the ultimate destruction of Christianity!

Available wherever paperbacks are sold, or order direct from the Publisher. Send cover price plus 50¢ per copy for mailing and handling to Pinnacle Books, Dept. 17-184, 475 Park Avenue South, New York, N.Y. 10016. Residents of New York, New Jersey and Pennsylvania must include sales tax. DO NOT SEND CASH.

THE TOP NAMES IN HARD-HITTING ACTION:
MACK BOLAN, DON PENDLETON,
AND PINNACLE BOOKS!

THE EXECUTIONER: #1:
WAR AGAINST THE MAFIA   (17-024-3, $3.50)
by Don Pendleton
The Mafia destroyed his family. Now the underworld will have to face the brutally devastating fury of THE EXECUTIONER!

THE EXECUTIONER #2: DEATH SQUAD   (17-025-1, $3.50)
by Don Pendleton
Mack Bolan recruits a private army of deadly Vietnam vets to help him in his bloody war against the gangland terror merchants!

THE EXECUTIONER #3: BATTLE MASK   (17-026-X, $3.50)
by Don Pendleton
Aided by a surgical face-change and a powerful don's beautiful daughter, Bolan prepares to rip the Mafia apart from the inside!

THE EXECUTIONER #4:
MIAMI MASSACRE   (17-027-8, $3.50)
by Don Pendleton
The underworld's top overlords meet in Florida to plan Bolan's destruction. The Executioner has only one chance for survival: to strike hard, fast . . . and first!

THE EXECUTIONER #5:
CONTINENTAL CONTRACT   (17-028-6, $3.50)
by Don Pendleton
The largest private gun squad in history chases the Executioner to France in order to fulfill a bloody Mafia contract. But the killers are no match for the deadly Bolan blitz!

THE EXECUTIONER #6:
ASSAULT ON SOHO   (17-029-4, $3.50)
by Don Pendleton
Bolan vows to rid the British Isles of the fiendish scourge of the Black Hand. An explosive new Battle of Britain has begun . . . and the Executioner is taking no prisoners!

Available wherever paperbacks are sold, or order direct from the Publisher. Send cover price plus 50¢ per copy for mailing and handling to Pinnacle Books, Dept. 17-184, 475 Park Avenue South, New York, N.Y. 10016. Residents of New York, New Jersey and Pennsylvania must include sales tax. DO NOT SEND CASH.

THE DESTROYER
By Warren Murphy and Richard Sapir